By Caite Dolan-Leach

Dead Letters

We Went to the Woods

Dark Circles

DARK CIRCLES

Ballantine Books

New York

DARK CIRCLES

A Novel

Caite Dolan-Leach

Published in the United States by Ballantine Books, an imprint of Random House, a division of Penguin Random House LLC, New York.

BALLANTINE and the HOUSE colophon are registered trademarks of Penguin Random House LLC.

LIBRARY OF CONGRESS CATALOGING-IN-PUBLICATION DATA
Names: Dolan-Leach, Caite, author.
Title: Dark circles : a novel / Caite Dolan-Leach.
Description: New York: Ballantine Group, 2022. |
Identifiers: LCCN 2021028821 (print) | LCCN 2021028822 (ebook) |
ISBN 9780593356043 (hardcover) | ISBN 9780593356050 (ebook)
Subjects: GSAFD: Mystery fiction. | LCGFT: Novels. |
Detective and mystery fiction.
Classification: LCC PS3604.O429 D37 2022 (print) |
LCC PS3604.O429 (ebook) | DDC 813/.6—dc23
LC record available at https://lccn.loc.gov/2021028821
LC ebook record available at https://lccn.loc.gov/2021028822

Printed in Canada on acid-free paper

randomhousebooks.com

2 4 6 8 9 7 5 3 1

FIRST EDITION

Title-page spread and page 2 images: © iStockphoto.com

Book design by Dana Leigh Blanchette

It is one thing to be part of the audience at the court-room Roman circus, and quite another matter to be in the ring. The audience is there to distract or justify itself with questions of right or wrong. The gladiators know only that one of them must win. They are not suspending judgment. They are *creating* judgment: ours.

—JAMES BALDWIN,
The Evidence of Things Not Seen

Not to be born is, beyond all estimation, best; but when a man has seen the light of day, this is next best by far, that with utmost speed he should go back from where he came. For when he has seen youth go by, with its easy merry-making, what hard affliction is foreign to him, what suffering does he not know? Envy, factions, strife, battles, and murders.

—SOPHOCLES,
Oedipus at Colonus, trans. R. C. Jebb

DARK CIRCLES

*H*ello listeners! I'm your host, Olivia Reed. Some of you may know me from binge-watching classic TV on Netflix, but what you maybe don't know about me is that I am a Total. True crime. Addict. Like all of you! I'd like to welcome you to the series premiere of my new podcast. It's going to be a wild ride, I promise.

But. What I can't promise is an ending. That's because we'll be getting to the bottom of this mystery in real time, as the case unfolds. I've been living in the small Finger Lakes community where these strange events have been happening, and as I record this first episode, out here in the middle of nowhere, I honestly have no idea where the story is going to take us.

But here are a couple of things I can tell you. I can tell you that young women living here on Seneca Lake have been dying, and they've been dying in pretty bizarre and untimely ways. I can tell you that these deaths take place on specific dates that link them together. I can tell you that the deaths seem to be connected to a small community of spiritual practitioners who work here on the shores of the lake, in the heart of New York wine country.

And I can tell you that I, through a series of strange coincidences, have found myself in the middle of this odd community. I'll be telling you what happens as it happens, or as close to that as I can, given my circumstances. Which I will also explain.

I want to be clear: I'm not a journalist (even though I did play one, briefly—true fans will remember). Occasionally, I'll be speculating about what's going on, and sometimes I'm just straight up spitballing. But I think there's value in releasing episodes of this *podcast even before we know the full details of what's going on. And here's why:*

Because I think that without outsiders looking in on this secretive organization, people are going to keep dying.

Because I think that people who hear this podcast may come forward with more information, as has happened with other true crime podcasts.

And because I think that you, all you listeners, can solve a crime that up until now, no one even thought was a crime.

Here's what we know so far:

Four young women are dead. The first died in March of 2015, and the most recent died just last week. All of these deaths have taken place within twenty miles of each other, and three have occurred near the same short stretch of highway that runs along the east coast of Seneca Lake. Two of these deaths have been labeled as suicides, and two as accidental deaths. All four have taken place on the date of a seasonal solstice or equinox. And all of them seem to have been connected through the same small constellation of people.

I'll be walking you through the details of these cases, and trying to get to the bottom of what happened with each of these young women. And, ultimately, I'll be trying to make sure that we find justice for all of them. Hopefully, along the way we'll also talk a little about why this story is important, and its place in the larger context of stories about violence, particularly violence against women. I'll need your help, but I know you're ready to give it.

Once again, I'm Liv Reed, and this is Vultures.

CHAPTER 1

The thing my goddamn manager doesn't understand is that I don't need to go on a retreat. Exhaustion, she keeps saying to me, whining on the phone like I'm a three-year-old who needs to go down for a nap. I'm not a stubborn toddler, I'm a grown-ass human who knows what she needs.

The problem, as everyone keeps informing me, is my IMAGE. Apparently, it's acceptable to be a fragile starveling with dark circles under her eyes—but it's *not* okay to lie down in the middle of Mercer Street after a friend's vernissage and later have a well-documented meltdown in front of your ex's apartment. A thin line, apparently, between glamorous self-destruction and mental illness. The latter, I am told, is what currently plagues me. Not that I'm necessarily sick, Jessica is quick to say, but my *image*, how people *see* me, is of someone who's not entirely well. I've gone from being cutely disastrous to acutely unhinged. Not a good look, everyone says. I find it hard to care. But then, that's what the Team is for.

It takes them forty-eight hours to convince me to go on the retreat. I spend the entirety of these two days and nights in my SoHo loft, trying (unsuccessfully) to wean myself off the medications that have been part of the daily fabric of my psyche for nearly five years. The drugs are a symptom, not the problem, Jessica keeps saying, in measured tones, when she calls me every six to eight hours. We just have to focus on getting you well—then everything will fall into place. Everything. The Movie isn't totally off the table. It's still a possibility—IF you get well.

———

The retreat they want to send me to sounds ridiculous. I mean, every spiritual retreat does. Center yourself, rid yourself of toxins (what even are toxins?), find your secret self buried under all that ego dirt, center your intentions, center your body, heal your spindly, malnourished spirit. FIND PEACE. Who the fuck wants peace???

I am told that exhaustion is a common affliction for people like me, people with a Team, and there are great programs to help Us through these dark days. Lena Dunham's manager sent me a DM on Instagram to say just that. I'm sure Jessica called in a favor there.

But here I am, packing a small suitcase, Jessica standing nearby, not quite supervising but not *not* supervising, either. She's explained about what I can bring to the retreat and what I can't— her vigilance is an extension of her desire to control me, control my whole life, to feel my entire soggy, tender self at her mercy. It's why she takes good care of me, and why I am utterly under her thumb. We are each other's lives. I've gone beyond resenting her here, in my apartment (the apartment she found for me, secured for me, rents for me), and I float about, thinking of her almost as a piece of the furniture. This is not something I like about myself. She clicks her well-groomed peach-colored claws on my mahogany coffee table, no doubt remembering all the times she has had to Do What's Best for me. And done it well. Done it the way I never seem to manage. My own sweet little succubus.

The retreat is not one of the famous ones. It's not in Malibu, or Hawaii, or even in Thailand, which is where I frankly hoped I was going to end up. (Southeast Asia bucket list, amirite?) The price tag for treatment at this one is cheaper, and it's lower-profile, which suits my needs perfectly, I'm told. But I guess there are other reasons for choosing the House of Light. For starters, it is NOT, technically, rehab. It is a well-respected Spiritual Center, a site for those seeking realignment and personal growth. It is a place of yoga and morning meditation and soft bamboo-blend fabrics where we all will hold hands and snuggle our crystals and . . . I guess wake up with the sun?

Because it is not rehab, the focus is not on substance abuse. I think this is why Jessica likes it best, since I will be spending time there for rest and relaxation, not to dry out. I'm there for sun salutations and quinoa! She has even called the director who passed on a project I pitched, who will say, if the press asks, that I'm working on a film with him, a story about a clean-living hippie out in the sticks working on her daily asanas as she finds her way toward harmony after the tragic death of her daughter.

I'm not entirely sure what to pack for a spiritual retreat, but it's while looking at my closet that I decide I might actually go through with this. Who could I be, in loose palazzo pants as I wake at dawn? Some glowing healthy goddess in a robe, hair tousled and skin flushed? No longer the girl in tight sequined gowns or carefully androgynous pantsuits that cost eight thousand dollars, sloshing out of limos and beckoning for bottle service. Healthy, aware, wholesome, the poster girl for Goop. And what would Ryan think of her, that glowing creature? Maybe he would want her?

Jessica is there the whole time, my observant shadow self. She fingers the kimono I pack and restlessly refolds it, undoing my clumsy work. I balk when she removes an elegant, fluttery dress from the bag and clucks at me, pointing out my frivolity.

"This is stupid," I counter petulantly. "Why can't I just get centered here, in my own house?"

"Go," she says. "Don't you think you need to break the cycle? That there's more for you out there?"

"But what if I'm totally isolated?" I whine.

"Then you're totally isolated. And cut off, and alone, in a

brand-new place where you have no choice but to find another piece of yourself. Do you want to just keep doing *this,* forever?"

"No, of course not," I say, meaning it. But also, meaning the opposite. Meaning that maybe I do, that maybe this exact thing that I have done for more than a decade is the thing that I do best, the thing I'm meant to do. Maybe I don't have a higher plane, or a better self, or a more sophisticated artist inside me. Maybe I am just the ingénue, the young star of a successful but ultimately un-important TV show, the pretty, damaged creature whose face you might recognize in a magazine, but maybe not in a restaurant. Maybe that's it for me.

"Maybe I am exhausted," I admit to Jessica.

"Maybe you are. And maybe you just need some time away from yourself."

I've made a career out of this pursuit, getting away from my-self. But when she says it, luggage waiting itchily at her side, I think, God. Yes. What a thought. And maybe time away from you.

I've texted Ryan a few times since the disaster of last week, but he never responds. I've deleted our conversation thread, so I have no record of what I might have said before, and this worries me im-mensely, like a hot, throbbing zit waiting to erupt that I stroke compulsively every time I think things will be okay. But if I get help, we can mend our fences. Hadn't he said that, at some point? That I need help?

Jess takes away my phone but lets me take Richard in the car, though I know that he can't come with me to the House of Light. Already I am abbreviating it, HOL, the hole where I will go to disappear. She knows better than to try to separate me from my dog now, when I still have a foot in my own house, in my life. She has spent years managing me, in all senses of the word. She knows when to push and when to let me collapse, willingly, into leather seats while someone else drives me, taking me somewhere I'm not sure I want to go. She thinks she knows me. So does everyone, I guess; they've seen my dappled thighs and the puff of a vacation paunch and my unmade face after a long night as I trudge into daylight for my coconut water. Celebrity.

My anti-anxiety meds wear off somewhere on Route 17, and I become, frankly, unmanageable. Maybe Jess does know me better than I know myself. She knows, even, that I have kept my iPad, and that I have been secretly texting Ryan, everyone I can think of, from a diner off the highway, panicked and already regretting my complacence.

No one will respond.

I try to muster rage at this silence, and it is my inability to do so that makes me suspect that I have been out of control, that maybe all of them are right to treat me to this radio silence. Have I done something unforgivable? I don't remember exactly what I've done and said in the last week, and what I do recall is worrying. I vaguely remember the press circling, waiting for me to go down like a wounded wildebeest. Jessica had spoken in hushed whispers about a photo in *Us Weekly* that she thinks I haven't seen. I've seen it, though.

"I think a little time away from everyone will clear everything up," Jess says. "He'll forgive you. Everyone will. Maybe you should even call your dad, when you're done? He did call from London, and I know he's worried."

I can't believe she's bringing him up right now. She knows she's got me, vicious little spider. She reaches over and squeezes my hand, and I lie down on the leather seat, snuggling my face into her thigh. Her fingers work through my hair and rub arcane circles across my scalp, stroke the tense muscles of my neck. Her thumb finds that spot at the back of my skull, and she breathes with me. I am soothed.

I settle into Jess's lap, and into the next few weeks at this god-forsaken retreat in the middle of nowhere. I mean, who doesn't need to be more centered?

. . .

It's dark when the driver pulls onto the gravel that leads us down toward the retreat. Jessica has told me that there is a lake, some-where in the swampy darkness below, but there isn't a single light, there are scarcely any stars, and the "lake" is just an empty maw of black beyond the outline of some trees. I'm not sure I have ever been anywhere so *without* light—it is the opposite of New York, and it honestly gives me the heebie-jeebies. (This phrase is some-thing my character on the show, Mina, said often, and the thought of her temporarily bolsters my courage. I miss her. I miss feeling like I could saunter into any situation—meth dealers, sinister grandfathers, cemeteries where the dead are raised—without a second thought.)

Even the building we park in front of is completely dark.

"Liv, this is it," Jessica says softly, touching my shoulder. I napped for an emotionally wiped-out thirty minutes after my meltdown, and I have been feigning sleep ever since, unable to face conversation.

"I'm awake," I say. "Mmph." Richard stirs in my arms, and I clutch him closer. The thought of walking into that building without him makes my pulse spike, and I press my mouth close to the top of his little French bulldog head, with his own Richardy smells. I kiss him there, clasping him fiercely. "Oh, my baby," I say, my throat thick.

"I know this is hard, but it's just for a few weeks. I'll take such good care of him, you know I will."

"You won't foist him off on the fucking dog walker? Like you did that time I had to film in Spain?" I have never forgiven Jessica for this betrayal, and it comes up whenever I need the higher ground, in any argument. The long list of personal grudges we share—mine spoken, Jessica's silent but ever-cataloged. He had gotten kennel cough, and it was one of the few times I've seen Jess genuinely remorseful.

"Of course not. He's going to stay with me, I'm going to walk him every day, he'll sleep in my bed—"

"And Ryan? You'll get Ryan to come and take him to the park? He hates going to the groomer without him, and I know how much Richard misses him—don't you, baby?" I nuzzle the top of his head again, and Richard sleepily licks my cheek.

"Yep, I will be in touch with Ryan, and I'll let him know how you're doing. I know he'll want to know."

This seems optimistic to me, given his deafening silence, but whatever.

"Bye, buddy," I say, and deposit Richard in his snuggly travel bag on the seat beside me. I scoot out of the car before I can change my mind.

The driver has brought my bag to the front door, and I pick my way very carefully up a stony path that is sort of illuminated by the vague glitter of solar-powered lights. The wattage is probably about ten percent of my iPhone and really isn't getting the job done. But hooray for alternative fuel sources.

Jessica taps at her phone, a frown between her eyebrows. "I don't understand—they were expecting us. Why is it so dark?"

"And why is the door locked?" I ask, jiggling the handle. I peer through the glass, trying to get a sense of what lies beyond it. Seeing a flash of movement, I squint closer. I jump back when a pale face looms in front of my own.

"Jesus," I say involuntarily. A hand unlocks the door and pulls it open.

"Namaste," a voice half-whispers. Oh boy. "Jessica? Yes, of course. We expected you earlier. Please come in."

I give Jess some unsubtle side-eye and follow her through the door. Our greeter has got on some kind of flaxen robe of indeterminate shape and color.

"Pretty dark," I say flatly.

"Yes, we have an electricity curfew here at the House of Light. The lights go off about an hour after sunset, and come back on at dawn. It encourages everyone to live with their natural rhythms."

"Hmm," I say. "Neat."

"Your room is ready, and I think we've already completed all the intake forms. The payment was, I believe, verified this afternoon?" the woman says. Jessica coughs delicately. We have not discussed how much this little mental health vacation will be costing me.

"Yes, everything was confirmed earlier. Is there anything else you need from me?"

"What, you don't want to stick around for morning yoga, Jess? A nice cup of matcha?" I ask.

"We don't allow outside visitors for the first fourteen days of the retreat," the woman intones. Not familiar with sarcasm, I guess.

"I've got to get Richard back home," Jessica says swiftly. "Liv, you're sure you're okay? You're ready for this?"

"Little late for that. But I'm good. Take care of Richard. I guess I'll talk to you tomorrow?"

"Um," Jessica says. She's still holding my phone. The robed woman holds her hand out for it, and Jessica gives it over, not looking at me.

"You will have phone privileges after a few days of practice," the woman explains. "We'll go over all of this during your first morning intention session."

I raise my eyebrows.

"That didn't come up during the hard sell, did it, Jess?" I ask. She shrugs, meeting my eyes with a smidge of sauciness. "Right."

"If you're ready, I will show you to your private space," Humorless Acolyte prompts.

I shrug. "Okay, no time like the present."

"We really like that sort of positivity. Presence is our goal, after all," the woman says. I imagine she is now smiling. This is not something I'm excited to witness in broad daylight.

"Good luck, Olivia. I'm rooting for you. And I've got everything covered," Jess says.

"You'll try to line up the movie?" I needle one last time.

"Of course. Love you, babe. I'll be thinking of you." With a squeeze of the hand, she leans in toward me. I snap my teeth near her ear as though I'm about to bite her, and she swats me playfully away. "You'll be fine."

"Hrmph," I mumble as I'm led off.

The woman in the flowing garments heads off down a narrow hallway. I start to follow her without my bag, and she pauses pointedly to look at it before I realize she wants me to fetch it. I haven't carried my own suitcase in a while, and I'm startled into feeling a vague sense of embarrassment at her unspoken calling out of my privilege. I do so love a silent holier-than-thou. I shoulder my bag and follow her, clumsily, through the dark.

"Flashlights are forbidden, too?" I attempt feebly the second time I trip over a slight step.

"We find the dark heightens some of the sense work we do. The first time you have a session in the Chamber, you'll understand." I can hear another smile in her voice.

"Um, Chamber?"

"Don't worry. It's very relaxing."

Yeah, sounds like it. "Mhmm."

Finally, she pauses in front of a door and unlocks it with a key she has produced, silently, from one of the pockets of her rough-hewn garb.

"This is you. We've put you here, in Chiron. Your assistant insisted on lake views, even though I told her all but two rooms look out on the water."

"My manager."

"What's that?"

"She's my manager. Not my assistant."

"Oh. Well. I think you'll really appreciate our non-hierarchical structure here. It will feel like a relief." Oh God. "I'll leave you to settle yourself in. I just need to collect your other devices."

"I thought . . . this wasn't, like, rehab."

She chuckles. "It isn't. But we still require something like a 'detox' at the beginning. Your mind needs time to get quiet, expand on its own. We stick to traditional media for the first week. No technology."

I sigh. Fuck you, Jessica.

"It's not connected to the internet," I lie. "I just use it to read. You know, in the dark? When I can't sleep?" I assume that my eloquent glance around the pitch-black room is lost on her.

"We feel the nighttime hours are for reflection, for going inside yourself rather than looking for answers outside. You'll have plenty of time in the day to read whatever you like. I'll just grab your iPad and leave you to settle in."

I grit my teeth and fish it from my bag, not very graciously.

"It's late now—you should get to bed. We start very early." She backs out of the room and closes the door. I hear a lock being flicked. When I reach out for the handle, I confirm that I am, indeed, locked in.

"This place better not fucking burn down in the night," I mumble bitterly to myself. I strip naked, flinging my clothes across this room whose dimensions I can only guess at. It's too much work to go hunting for my La Perla slip, so I fumble through the dark until I smack my shin into what feels like a bed. I crawl in, tugging the blankets over my torso, tucking them under my armpits so that I feel cocooned. The thread count seems to be surprisingly high. Lying in the dark, my mind racing, I think:

Who the fuck are these people?

CHAPTER 2

An otherworldly procession of chimes jolts me out of the sleep I have just settled into. Having spent the night thrashing, I'd managed to doze off just before dawn. Which, upon cracking my crusty eyelids, I perceive that it now is. The sun is barely up, and in the pauses between the clatter of the chimes (and was that a gong?) I hear birdsong.

And the sight from my bed is spectacular. I sit up, too startled and impressed by what I see to feel bitter about the early wake-up. The western wall of my room is floor-to-ceiling glass, and it looks out on a glistening stretch of lake. A small balcony offers a perch on which to gaze out at this scene, and a cliff drops off just beyond its lip, plunging all the way to the shoreline. My first thought is about how I can get down to the beach.

Shit. Maybe this won't be so bad.

I'm tired, and yearn vaguely for an Adderall, but a cup of coffee will probably be enough to get me upright and functional. I slide out of bed, naked, and crouch down to where I tossed my suitcase last night. If I were in the city, I would be worried about someone seeing my stripped self—a stalker across the street from my loft, paparazzi angling for a shot of my nipples to sell to the glossies, breasts pixelated to suggest but not display the color of my areolae. But it's pretty evident that none of that is a risk here.

Digging through my things, I reflect on how unlike my mornings in the city any of this is. I hear birds instead of sirens, see water instead of brick, mist off the lake instead of fumes from the subway manhole. Nothing honks. And best of all: not one human in sight.

I select a silk tunic that I sometimes wear when I have a messy house party at my apartment—it's the sort of item in which you can greet other people but also comfortably pass out after too many martinis and not enough canapés. Perfect for that rehab life. Or retreat life. Or whatever.

My door is still locked. I quickly put on my face. Rehab casual is what I'm shooting for, dewy-faced and clean, just a swipe of mascara, some highlighter on my cheeks, spot cover-up for hyper-pigmentation on my chin, a lip that is somewhere between nude and berry. I look around, but there are no mirrors anywhere, so I complete the whole operation in the slender rectangle of my Guerlain compact. Bastards can't take that away from me! I slide open the screen door onto my balcony.

It is exquisite. The birds are louder, and I smell pine and dirt. And maybe woodsmoke? I realize that I haven't been out in the country for years. *Iroquois Falls* was supposedly set in the country, but almost all of it was filmed on set, except for the occasional shoot in some godforsaken corner of Northern California where they could get some shots of us against real trees. The waterfall scene at the end of the first season (after Mina has sleuthed and scrapped and figured out the show's first big reveal) was done against a green screen.

Holy shit, are we going to, like, make s'mores and learn to light a fire? Maybe that's more wilderness camp than retreat, but fuck, how many group circles can you cram into a day? I should have brought hiking boots. I can get Jessica to send me some, maybe those adorable Italian ones I bought but never wore. I've never needed them before. We picked them up during the summer trip after season three wrapped; she had made me leave L.A., get away from my dad and my work. Ryan and I had decided to take a break, and I was sulking, bored. It'll be fun, she said. She wasn't wrong—she almost never is. We had cavorted up and down the

Italian coast, just the two of us, eating more pasta than I could justify, Jess getting a wicked sunburn she blamed me for. I'd come home nut-brown, four pounds heavier—and in a better mood than I'd been in for a while. Years of Jess getting things right, of knowing me just so: that's the reason I'm here, of course.

I breathe in the air for a couple minutes, taking in the nature. I find, though, that this provides limited entertainment. I'm tempted to try to hop off my balcony to walk along the edge of the drop-off, but this seems a bit reckless. At least for the first day. I'll save my rebellions for when I really need them. One of the first things an actor learns.

At a loss for how I'm meant to spend my time, I do a half-hearted sun salutation, then another. I feel very wholesome. Basically cured. Starting to notice the preliminary flutterings of anxiety, I check my door again.

This time, it opens.

Padding in my socked feet down the pine hallway, I almost give in to the temptation to tiptoe. I feel like I've snuck out, like I'm creeping through the building. I don't hear any other voices or see any other people—just a stretch of other doors, all on my right. I pause in front of one and consider trying to open it, but what if someone is on the other side? I listen for human stirrings within, but I hear nothing.

When I run out of hallway, I'm forced to choose between two doors. I think I can hear voices on my right, so I try that door first. It doesn't open. I go left.

The office I find myself in is painted white, like everything else I've seen here at the retreat. A rough wood table serves as a desk, and it is almost criminally clean. Plants are tastefully scattered throughout the room. Overall, the impression is one of order, extreme tidiness. Jess would love it.

I want to snoop, but there are no crannies in which to poke about, no drawers to rifle through. Everything is on display, subject to scrutiny; if anything's hidden, it's hidden in plain sight. I walk over to the window and look out.

I can see the southern tip of the lake from the office, but the real view is centered on the grapevines stretching out across the field. It's quite lovely, really, even without the sprawl of water visible from my room. Not bad real estate they've got here.

"Olivia, you're late," someone says behind me, and I turn around, startled.

"Um . . ." I say. "Is there some kind of plan I'm not aware of?"

"Of course there is. I assume that's why you're here, after all." The woman speaking to me isn't the same as the one who let me in last night. This new woman is tall, rail-thin, of indeterminate age. Also, she has no hair, or practically none—her head is monastically close-cropped. A bold look, to be sure—not everyone has the bone structure for the Soviet prison 'do. God knows I wouldn't let anyone write it into a contract for me. She smiles at me, as though amused by my confusion.

"And you are?" I ask as haughtily as I can manage, given that I'm wearing pajamas and don't have any real idea where the fuck I am or what I'm supposed to be doing.

"I'm Rain. I'm your link with the Light while you're here, making sure you get all the support you need to help you with your Process." She sidles over to her desk, and I notice that she isn't wearing any shoes. With each step, I can see the soles of her feet, so dirty they're almost black. Pedicure, babe. Her gait is springy, younger than her face.

"You're my camp counselor."

She grins at me and shrugs. "I like to think I'm more of a . . . guide. Someone who can help you find the resources to begin your journey."

"Oh, I'm definitely ready to manifest some positive intentions. Really lean into my intuition," I say. I lived in L.A. for more than five years, so this is not exactly my first New Age rodeo.

Rain looks at me, cocks her head. There's a long pause before she speaks.

"I'm glad you see it that way. Still, I expect there will be . . . aspects of your practice that are more challenging than others, and my task is to make sure you have everything you need to succeed. How are you finding the space so far?" Rain asks. "Are you comfortable?"

"Slept like the dead. I noticed, though, that there aren't any mirrors in my room?"

"Did that make you uncomfortable?"

"It's just a bit odd, really. I'm sure my hair is a complete wreck."

"Do you want me to disagree with you? Tell you that you look beautiful?"

Ah, I see what we're doing.

"Sort of an obvious place to start, don't you think? Suggesting to an actor that they're maybe hung up on looks?" I ask pointedly.

"I didn't start there. *You* did."

I sigh. "Right. My bad. Yes, the rooms are lovely, the view is great, I can't wait to spend all my free time doing yoga on the deck."

Another long pause.

"You're already familiar with yoga, I take it?" Rain asks.

"Is there anyone left in the Western world who isn't?"

"Or Eastern, for that matter," she points out, with a coy smile. She has dark, intense brown eyes, and her skin has the ageless quality of someone in their fifties or sixties who has worn a lot of sunscreen. Her cheekbones are pretty stellar, in fact. She continues: "In any case, I'm happy to hear that. We've found that people who are already grounded in bodywork have an easier time developing a holistic strategy for their own individual practice. Given your unique . . . background, I thought we might want to start our work with the physical self in order to reach the spiritual."

"Work? Practice? I thought this was a retreat."

Rain laughs. "Many people come here with the wrong impression, that this place is merely a holiday, a time to escape the demands of a modern life that has grown toxic and soulless and full of pain. They *want* to retreat. But the House of Light isn't that. It isn't that at all."

"You might want to change the name of the program then," I suggest. "Given the connotation of 'retreat.'"

"Let's do just that," Rain suggests heartily. "Why don't we call it instead a . . . return."

"Return? To what?"

"To the knowledge that you already possess. To a sustainable way of life that you have either forgotten or moved away from. A return to the self you have lost."

"I have a lot of selves. Professional hazard," I point out.

"No. You don't," Rain corrects me. Gone is the humor, the warm grin she had on her face. She is serious now. "You have just one, and you've forgotten it. Here, we'll help you move closer to it, understand it, and rebuild your life so that you never risk losing it again. There are more than enough selves in the world without you feeling entitled to multiply your own."

Right, it's good to know the party line. This is one of those groups that's about "finding self" rather than "locating compassion" or "emptying the ego." Though those things will probably come up, too. I find that the terminology of these kinds of places gets a bit repetitive—they're all using the same self-help thesaurus.

"Well, that all sounds just great," I say. And I'm not even lying. Fuck it—who doesn't want to go find some glimmer, some version of themselves they don't actively loathe and want to escape? I've made a career of trying to lose (or conceal) my authentic self. And if I put on a convincing enough performance here, I'll get a nice certificate in Spiritual Achievement. And I may just get that role in the movie about the Manson family I've been trying to land for the past three months, the carrot Jess has dangled before me. Also, I find that I do frequently lose weight on these things—a diet of brown rice and hot lemon water plus five hours of yoga and nature hikes turns out to be great for the figure, especially after a lot of late, gin-soaked evenings. "I'm beyond ready to get started. Really. This is overdue," I say enthusiastically. Rain's smile is back. I will take my Oscar now.

"That's really great to hear. A lot of seekers come in quite unwilling to do the work, and we can squander weeks just breaking down their resistances. I hope we don't have that problem with you, Liv."

I nod sincerely, with just a touch of pious acknowledgment: *I understand how difficult that must be, Rain. Though I am unworthy, I come here willing.*

"I find it . . . very draining to be around inauthentic people," she continues. "Their energy depletes me, because I'm so sensitive to it. You'll only ever get depth from me. And I have a good feeling about you."

"I'll do my best not to be a disappointment."

"I know you'll try." She takes another long look at me, stretching out the silence. It's uncomfortable to be so minutely examined, even for someone who is used to it. "So, I'll just sketch out some of the broad strokes of how the days are organized here, and then we'll talk about your individual needs and goals, what you'd like to achieve."

I nod again, eager-beaver acolyte.

"The first day or two we find it beneficial to socially and physically detoxify, spend some time in silence with ourselves. You'll be in your room for most of today, and you can do what you like with that time. I find it invaluable to disconnect from others for periods throughout the work, and be really present in what arises from that solitude."

"Wait, I'm in solitary? For how long?"

"Just a day or two, depending how it goes for you. I'll check in on you later, and again tomorrow, and we'll monitor your feelings, see if you'd benefit from more time."

"Okay. I assume I'm fasting, too?"

Rain smiles, amused. "I see you have some preconceptions of how this works. But yes, water and an herbal supplement will be available in your room until tomorrow. We want to clear you of toxins, and the adaptogens can help stabilize your energy. Then, if it seems like you're ready to be integrated, we'll introduce you to the group. We do Group Work every morning and most afternoons. Everyone is assembled next door right now, in fact."

"How many people are here?"

"We like to always have twelve seekers in the House."

"All genders?" I ask.

Rain smiles and nods. "Group Work is more challenging for some than others, and we try to . . . accommodate for that here. Still, it is essential for our compassion work to sit together and hold the experiences of others."

There it is. I feel the impulse to look at a watch, in a pantomime that is built for the stage—I've never worn a watch. Five minutes before "compassion" got dragged into it. There should be a self-help drinking game.

"Of course. For me, for my work—my professional work, that is—group time has been essential for me to practice empathy, understand how others think, what they've gone through," I explain.

"I don't want to bullshit you, Liv. I think your profession will be both boon and liability, here at the Light," Rain replies, serious again. "Something we'll need to keep an eye out for is artificiality. We want to locate your authentic, genuine self—not encourage you to perform it," she says, her voice turning cool and stern.

Busted. I'll need to be less of a ham for Rain, I guess. A carefully timed tearful confession? A tough exterior that cracks at crucial moments? I don't think she'll be an impossible audience—

I find that the self-help zealots are usually too busy thinking about how they come across to notice whether they're actually getting through to you. Ironic. I am at home with my fellow performers here.

"That's very perceptive," I say, blushing and dropping my eyes as though I've been caught and feel a delicate smidge of shame.

"We'll get to know each other very well over the next few weeks."

"Did my manager . . . specify the exact length of time?" I ask.

"We tentatively discussed a full lunar cycle," Rain says. "At the new moon, we'll reconsider. See if you need to extend."

"I'm here for whatever it takes," I say, with just a note of desperation underneath my complete commitment to get this done.

"We're really looking forward to working with you, Liv. But I feel like I should offer up a warning. The Process of Return isn't necessarily a pleasant one. This is not a weekend in Cabo. You're going to spend time with awake beings, and that can be uncomfortable. Waking up is painful, and you will feel that. It's my job to be Shiva to you, the destroyer of your world. Don't expect it to feel good."

"Sort of like your first SoulCycle class after a long break," I say. "It hurts, but you have to break it down to build it up."

"We're a somewhat different tribe than SoulCycle." Rain giggles, as though laughing at an inside joke. "But sure. It's not unlike exercise. Discomfort that leads to progress."

"Climb that mountain," I agree.

"This will be really transformative for you, I can tell. Not everyone's energy is suited for the Light, but what I get from your energy is that you're ready to change. To advance. I'm excited for you."

And so am I. As weird as it is, I can't wait to get my barefoot, bare-faced, quinoa-munching cult vibe on.

. . .

STAR, MAY 12, 2008
The Ghost of Rumors Haunts Young Lovers

Iroquois Falls costars Olivia Reed and Ryan Lockhart have been spotted smooching while filming in Canada. The pair, who play opposite each other in the major hit currently airing on the CW, were caught on camera getting cozy outside a bar while they apparently took a little R&R time from filming the intense (and often quite dark) romance they portray on-screen.

Reed has recently made headlines for her bohemian lifestyle: hitting the clubs in New York and being seen with a number of older gentlemen in quick succession. Though many have speculated about these relationships, her manager and longtime friend, Jessica Meisner, has said that "Liv has a less conventional idea of what constitutes a relationship than maybe some other people. When it comes down to it, she just wants to live life and experience as much of it as she can."

But her hard-partying lifestyle may have come at a cost: rumors are that Olivia recently lost out on a role in an upcoming superhero franchise. Though the official press release stated that it was due to "scheduling conflicts," others have speculated whether the real reason is due to her weight and mood fluctuations. Both issues have been mentioned as making her "difficult" to work with. Another source close to Reed said: "Yes, she's had something of a troubled past, and she can come across as something of a diva. But ultimately, it's her talent and her drive that gets her over the finish line."

Regardless of her personal ups and downs, we know that fans can't get enough of watching the new pair together: either in real life or their electric, on-screen chemistry. We know we'll be tuning in for our favorite guilty pleasure next Thursday night, no matter what!

CHAPTER 3

My feeling of virtuous well-being lasts about ninety minutes into my solitary-confinement regime. I meditate, chant a mantra or two, and do some more yoga, and that pretty much wipes out my inner resources. There is nothing to do in this room—someone has even been in to make the bed and, I suspect, have a peek through my things. I sit on my raised deck, looking out at the lake, and try to glean some spiritual meaning from the light changing on the surface of the water, but, I mean, come on. It's late summer, the light is beautiful, whatever. A thriller it is not.

I try to peer around the edges of the deck, to maybe catch a glimpse of my fellow inmates, but the architecture of the building is sneakily efficient at this quarantine, and I can only just make out the edges of a railing. Private suite, indeed.

As promised, there is an electric teakettle in my room, and someone delivers sliced lemon every few hours. The first time this happened I was genuinely spooked, because it took place while I was out on the balcony, and I poked my head back inside to find a tray of lemon slices and a glass bottle of water sitting on the small desk, as though they had been summoned out of thin air. The staff at certain five-star hotels could take note of the discretion in this place.

In the early afternoon I start to get the disembodied, light-headed experience that I associate with a cleanse; I feel woozy and low-key, which is actually a relief. As my appetite increases, my desire to go exploring dissipates, and I spend a good hour on my slender bed, fingering the expensive sheets and planning out the roles I will line up when I get out of here, leaf fully turned over.

It has been years since I went a full day without speaking to Jess, and her absence hovers in the corner where she should be, busy and self-effacing. I keep expecting her to prompt me to get changed for an audition, or to run lines with her. She has played every scene partner I've ever worked with, inhabiting their lines in trailers and in the backseats of cars, a stand-in for made-up people. She knows every item of my wardrobe, every role I've lusted after, every set I've worked on. If I were to disappear, I think she could slide into my skin and play me, indefinitely.

I met Jess while I was a bit at sea. The school semester had ended and I had scraped through my exams distractedly; I knew I was being given a pass because of everything that had happened and I was in too much of a muddle to be appreciative. Fed up with my melancholy (and sometimes suspicious) lurking around all day, my father had proposed that I get out of the house and mingle with my peers. So, four days a week I gritted my teeth through Leadership Seminar, a youth group with somewhat confused messaging and an overall lack of coherence; I had the strong impression that its main function was to provide a line on a CV for college applications. We worked with at-risk youth, homeless shelters, Habitat for Humanity—we were essentially a free, underage workforce for organizations that had low labor standards.

Most of the people in Leadership were try-hards and Christians, the types of kids who played trombone and whose parents had invested a lot of money in orthodontia. We wore hideous yellow T-shirts and engaged in appalling group chants tailored for each occasion and I hated it. I considered myself to be the only sane member of the group. Until Jess.

Jess didn't try too hard and she never suggested a group prayer and when I saw her sneak out the back of a soup kitchen to smoke a cigarette, I followed her. She nodded at me and offered me a smoke, my first.

"I didn't take you for a rule breaker," I said.

"Back at you," she smirked. I wasn't sure what else to say, but the silence between us felt comfortable rather than awkward.

"Are you from around here?" I finally asked. She didn't go to my school.

"Just moved. From Cooperstown. New York."

"Your parents get a new job or something?"

"My parents are still in Cooperstown," Jess said, tossing the butt of her cigarette and stubbing it out with her motorcycle boot. She didn't elaborate, and her frosty coolness prevented me from getting more details. Even in the years that followed, she didn't really speak about her parents, or what had caused her, at seventeen, to leave home. I always got the impression it wasn't a happy story and left it at that.

"I'm doing this shit as community service," she finally added. That story I would eventually learn more about: driving without a license, unregistered vehicle. She'd been given the choice of a fine or two hundred hours of Leadership Seminar.

All that summer we whittled away the time at what was essentially camp, and at four P.M. sharp every day, we would take off, roaming the streets of Great Barrington and wasting a season together. Jess was shorter and rounder than me, but in possession of a supercilious confidence that made her commanding. She called the shots, and in those untethered months after my loss, I loved that. Bart had narrowed his eyes the first time I brought her home, seeing her sitting on the porch with her scuffed boots up on the railing. He had recognized in her the same self-determination he had, and her possession of a good piece of me. And, sensibly, decided not to fight her for it.

Even after I went back to school, we were tied at the hip. She would wait for me in the coffee shop after school most days, and we would walk aimlessly around, then sometimes go to her apartment to spend all evening watching movies. Jess demanded little of me, and I liked the brisk unneediness of her presence, her self-command.

When she said we were moving to New York, I didn't really think too hard about it. I threw together an application and a very moving essay about my mother's disappearance, and off we went. Jess said she'd find work, maybe in a bar, maybe selling something. I told her about the summer my mom had spent trying to hawk beauty products door-to-door in one of her sporadic periods of employment. Sure, Jess had said with an amused smile. Maybe I'll do that.

In the city, she lost a smidge of her impervious chill; getting a job was harder than she'd expected, and she ended up as a receptionist at a New Age medicinal practice. Having to do such trivial work fell short of her idea of herself as scrappy, untouchable. But she paid half the rent on our grubby studio and began to hustle in earnest, dreaming up the career that she more or less dragged forth from me.

"Any idiot can see you've got something, Liv," she said. "Let's make that work for us. We don't have to be receptionists or teachers or bartenders. Let's make a life out of it."

Dad was as enthusiastic as Jess about the plan. He'd been spending more and more time in the city and had taken to dropping in on us. Ostensibly, he was there to support me in Mom's absence, to hold my hand and to bolster my thespian ambitions. In reality, he was there to sip cognac on my couch, recounting the slushy stories of his own "uni days": long-winded and toe-curling in their desperate yearning for a lost youth, a mis-imagined future.

The only person who didn't make me feel embarrassed by Dad's presence was Jess. She would even sit and listen to his brandy-soaked ruminations when I was too worn-out to pretend I cared; sometimes it felt like she was filing away all the little trivia he spewed for her own private use. If my art was to produce

human emotion, Jess's was to soak it in, then deploy it in the service of practicality, efficiency.

They both pushed me to go do pilot season; they were equally
insistent, though they used distinctly different tactics to nudge me
toward L.A., getting an agent, the whole horrible, hungry clamor
of it all. The audition felt like such a long shot that I barely
thought about it until I got a callback, then another, and then
miraculously, got cast across Ryan. I barely remember filming
that first bananas episode that people still reference; it felt so improbable that things had worked out. But as Jess kept saying: I
was born for it.

We had no idea if *Iroquois Falls* would be picked up, but when
it was, Jess and I headed west. I don't remember there being any
question of her coming, too, though. I don't know that I would
have gone without her. I needed her quiet approval when I dressed
every morning, the tug of her small, quick fingers plaiting my
hair before I went for a run.

I lie on my bed now, remembering that first year out west, the
glittery magic of realizing that I'd made it. Which is what I believed, of course: that I was set, that this was my break, and that
for the rest of my life, I would be An Actor. Jess there, holding my
hand, or my cigarette, or my costume change, on the phone, always in reach. How scrappy she must have been to not have been
nudged out, to cling to her meal ticket so ferociously. Even nip-
ping at my dad every time he wanted to share the crumbs of my
success. She was my fierce little mongrel, tenacious and sharp.

I try to identify the birds from their trilling outside. The screech
of a raptor? The *who-hoop* of a dove? I know fucking nothing
about nature.

By early evening I am crawling out of my skin and completely
over this mandatory self-reflection. I am sick of the inside of my
own head, of the same tedious loops I have to inhabit when I am

myself. I yearn for my Peloton. I run lines for *Play*, the Beckett production that had, among other things, landed me in this mess. Imagining the spotlight that would queue up my lines is distracting enough, but anxiety starts to creep back as I get deeper and deeper into Woman 2, and so I abandon my rehearsal. The show will open without me, after all. I think they got Lili Reinhart to headline in my stead.

I consider more yoga, but instead I find myself outside on the balcony, inspecting the railings and determining whether or not I can get down, away, out. The balconies are reasonably high off the ground, since the building is situated on this steep slope, and the drop-off is worryingly close—one misstep and I might go careening over the cliff into the water and rocks below. But if I climb over the side of the deck, I'll have to drop only six feet or so. I briefly consider making a harness out of a sheet, but this seems a little too "escape from the mental hospital." A bit early in the program for that—Mina didn't have to pull that particular stunt until season three.

I do a quick costume change out of my rich-housewife leisure wear into leggings and sneakers, and take a last look around my room. I'm not intending to leave forever, of course. I just need to take a run, see a slight change of scenery from the one I've been staring at all day. Find out where I am, explore. The architecture of the building restricts my view of the world to my own balcony and its vista out on the lake; from what I can glean, the exterior of the Light curves and bulges, like a rustic Gaudí. Clever dividing walls on the decks separate me from my fellow inmates; privacy is enforced.

I've swung both my legs over the railing and am preparing to lower myself down when I'm interrupted.

"I wouldn't stage a jailbreak if I were you."

I freeze at the woman's voice, unable to turn my head far enough to see her.

"It's not worth the headache."

"What's the worst they can do to me?" I ask. "I'm here voluntarily."

"Ha. They can make you regret volunteering," she says.

I awkwardly flip my body around so that I am at least facing her, hanging off my deck like it's the *Titanic*.

She's standing in the corner of her deck, craning her head around so that she can see me. She's not far away, but the angle of the building means that I can see only her upper body.

"Right. So you think I should . . . clamber back in?" I ask.

"I think it's entirely up to you. But I do know that if you manage to jump down without breaking an ankle, there is absolutely no way to get back up. Then you have to walk through the front door. Which means having to deal with Devotion. Which, as I think I alluded to, is not entirely worth the hour or two of freedom. You don't want to be on her bad side."

I consider my new neighbor's words. On the one hand, sure, rocking the boat is never fully advisable. On the other hand, these people have no power over me. So what if I piss off the creepy orderly?

"Up to you," the woman says with a shrug. From what I can tell, she's petite, with dark hair. Pretty, but pinched, in a way. She's wearing a very colorful caftan and silver bangles that clink when she moves. "Just thought I'd be neighborly."

"I don't think I'm supposed to interact with the neighbors, either," I point out. "I'm doing my time in solitary."

"Yes, your Intake. That's what I mean, though. Some Intakes are longer than others. If you just grit your teeth and get through it, you'll probably be allowed into group tomorrow. Unless your vanity and worldliness are especially pronounced, that is." She grins, and though the humor is genuine, there's a ghoulish quality to her smile.

"Oh," I respond. "I didn't . . ."

"Of course you didn't. They start slow with the messaging. But hey, at least the food is good. Hope you're gobbling up those adaptogens."

My arms are aching from being stretched out like wings behind me. I have to either get down or go back. With a resigned sigh, I turn and fling my legs back over the edge of the balcony.

"I see you're a good little girl," the woman says. "Rain will approve."

"I just know it's easier to get your way if you're not . . . openly hostile right out of the gate."

She chuckles darkly. "A lesson I would do well to learn, no doubt. I'm sure you'll be full of insight and wisdom."

"I'm sure that's what it will look like to the babysitters," I say sweetly. "I'm just taking a break from my life, getting my healthy complexion back. I'm happy to play along."

"Doesn't look like there's anything wrong with your complexion. What are you, a model?"

"An actress."

"Ah, how nice. We seem to get more musicians and writer types here. The House of Light isn't typically flashy enough to attract the glitterati, but they *do* like to cultivate the well-to-do and the moderately famous."

"You seem to know a bit about it. How long have you been here?" I ask, not without trepidation. It's possible there are lifers here—most centers have one or two benighted souls who just can't figure out where else to go.

"Two weeks. But I'm a local. The Light is a bit notorious, this side of the lake."

"I thought the whole point was that it was low-profile."

"Sure, they don't have a website or Instagram. But there's not really any such thing as low-profile in a rural community. We're all up in each other's business out here, I'm afraid. The reason I got a bed in this plush little paradise is because my father-in-law is tight with one of the official members here. He's been selling them weed since the eighties. Even though substances are supposedly frowned on."

"I should think so," I say. "Normally rehab has a fairly strict policy about that sort of thing."

The woman laughs again. She is sad, though ready to see a kind of dark humor everywhere. Like she understands the absurdity of her condition and finds it deeply distressing but also pretty damn amusing. Her attitude is fascinating, and I file it away as potentially useful for a role, someday.

"Well, I think you'll come to understand that the House of Light isn't your typical rehab. Rain says it's not rehab at all. It is so, so much more."

"Why do I find that the opposite of comforting?"

"And well you should. This is not a comforting place. But again, as Rain likes to point out, being too comfortable stands in the way of growth, expansion. This place is for Jupiter, for enlarging your conscious self." Her tone is unreadable. Is she really a true believer, or is she still mocking them?

"As long as it doesn't expand my physical dimensions," I say lightly.

"Hear hear! We're not supposed to worry about such superficial concerns. But you're quite safe. The chia seeds and alfalfa sprouts are very low-cal."

"They usually are." I scuffle my feet on the deck. It's just starting to grow dark, and I can see the lights of a boat cruising up the lake. The woman on the other deck watches, too.

"God, I'd love a cigarette," I say after a while. Not because I especially want one but because this is the sort of situation that really warrants one: companionable silence with a stranger, shared complicity, a sunset on the water.

"I'd fucking kill for a drink," she says after a minute.

"Cheers to that." We stand around, both staring out at the lake. There's the boat, and we watch its lights cruising north. I occasionally glance at her profile, trying to get a better sense of her. But she has withdrawn, and even though I'd like to stay and talk, grill her about this place, this program, I suspect she'd shut me down. The sunset has made her sad, faraway.

"I'm going to head back to my uninterrupted self-interrogation," I finally say. "You know, work on my interiority." The woman nods her head in acknowledgment. Just as I slide open the door and prepare to disappear inside, she stops me.

"What's your name, by the way? You never said."

"Olivia. Liv."

"Oh, I like that. Your name is an imperative all on its own. 'Live.' And not a bad one, at that."

"I . . . strangely never thought of it that way." This isn't true. Jess said this to me, and it did, at the time, frankly blow my mind. But people like to feel like they have insight into you, feel like they are clever and perceptive for pointing such things out, so I let her think she's the first to have said it.

"What's your name?" I ask, one foot already inside.

"Ava. My name's Ava."

. . .

I'm going to go in reverse order with these deaths. That might seem like an odd way to organize things, but I think you'll understand why. Because to explain these deaths, I need to explain how I ended up involved in them.

There's been some gossip about my recent behavior. I get that, and whatever, I'm not here to dispute rumors or justify myself. I'd been working a little too hard these last few months, and I haven't been sleeping a lot. A few dramatic things happened in my personal life, and, unsurprisingly, given our celebrity culture, those things ended up being quite public. I'm sure you've all seen the tabloids and read the tweets, and I won't give them any extra time here. If that's what you're interested in hearing about, go spend five ninety-nine on the gossip rags or go fuck around on TMZ.

This isn't about how I ended up here at the House of Light. It's about what happened after I arrived.

The spiritual retreat I ended up going to isn't rehab. I want to be clear about that. It's a place where people take some time away from the pressures of their daily life and just work on fostering healthy habits. There's a group of people out here who help you do that, and they're called the House of Light. What they do here wasn't really made clear to me at first, and, frankly, I can't say for sure that even now I totally get it. You sort of need to see it to understand it.

While I was staying at the Center, I met the person who introduced me to these cases.

I'm not going to lie: at first I thought she was totally fucking nuts. She was reasonably put together, but the reality is that we were both at a pretty wacky wellness retreat, and by definition not fully on top of our shit. And there was something about her: an intensity, maybe even a desperation that seemed a little off. So I definitely dismissed her at first.

But, as I would learn, she had a reason to care. And in spite of my reservations, I found myself intrigued. And it wasn't long before I was too deeply involved to stop investigating the deaths. Because before too long, they directly impacted me.

. . .

In the morning, I dress in my jersey knit tunic and sit, cross-legged, on my bed. I can hold this position for a while, and this is how I want to be when this Devotion person comes to knock on my door.

She doesn't make me wait long. About forty minutes after dawn, my door opens, and I crack my eyelids with a pleasant and peacefully awakened smile. I am ready for the day, and for whatever these people want from me. Devotion seems unmoved, even when I give her my very best "Namaste." God, I hate the enlightened. She is silent and dour-faced, and bears what I think is a pretty serious burn along most of the right side of her face. I try not to stare; and given the frosty chill that goes beyond the surface level of her eyes, it's actually very easy to break my gaze.

She says nothing to me, just beckons, and I follow her down the same hall as yesterday. I glance at the same doors, especially the one next to my own room. Is this Ava's door? Is she still behind it? But Devotion moves on at a smooth, crisp pace, and I follow her, imitating her posture and her poised but diffident air. When she turns her head at a sound, I subtly imitate her, trying to catch her exact gesture, the considered but confident way she moves through space.

Today, instead of going left into Rain's executive office, we go right, through the door I tried to open yesterday. There is a group of people already gathered, sitting in low-slung, opulent lounge chairs. A quick head count tells me there are eleven people here, in addition to Rain.

Devotion bobs her head and gestures me toward the vacant chair on the end. I settle in, assessing who watches me take my seat. There are several men present, and I am used to male eyes following me, keeping track of each movement, judging what kind of woman I am based on how I hold myself. I want them to notice me but not, necessarily, to want me. I need everyone intrigued by and aware of me, but sexual desire will only get in the way here. Until I need it to work for me. Until then, I need to be striking, damaged, and mid-profile. Not flashy, not under the radar, just simply visible.

Further glances around the room clarify that I am not the only striking person here. In fact, everyone is arresting in their own way. Not exactly beautiful but strange, noticeable. I spend my time in casting calls and theaters, so I'm used to this, but it's unexpected here in rehab. There should be a dumpy middle-aged mom who is overly fond of chardonnay, a worn fifty-something guy who has been abusing his son's Ritalin, a washed-out teen who can barely prop herself up from disaffected ennui and the, like, total grimness of existence. These people are all remarkable. They're young, and none of them has that bruised, used-up quality that rehab folk normally do. And none of them seems to take special notice of me.

I sit back, perplexed.

"Olivia, welcome to group. I'm so happy to introduce you to everyone, and invite you into the work we do together." Rain stands while everyone sits, almost in first position. I half-expect her to start doing pliés.

"Hi," I say. "I'm . . . happy to be here." I could swear I hear Ava snicker. A sharp glance from Rain suggests that I'm not imagining this.

"Everyone, I'd like you to meet Olivia. She's an actor, from New York, and she's here to get centered, like everyone else. I also suspect she thinks she might get some insight for a role out of this," Rain adds casually.

I flinch. Hey there, Rain. An aggressive gambit. She's telling me she calls the shots and isn't impressed by me. Duly noted, girl.

"I love the space, so far," I say. "I'm really interested in hearing what you all have been working on." Devotion hands me a cup of tea and skulks away.

"Well, Olivia, today I think it's good if you just listen and hear what we usually do here in Group Work. Once you've done a session or two, I'm sure you'll feel comfortable participating."

If you've ever had to listen to someone else's dreams for two hours, you'll have an idea of what the rest of the group session was like.

"I'd like to conclude today with our usual moment of being-in-now," Rain says as the session winds down. It's been grueling, but Rain has nothing on certain tyrannical directors. "I invite everyone to fully inhabit their bodies and breath and take in this here and now, this presence. This presentness requires space, and this world is an overcrowded one, so carve out a circle of light. Invite the gratitude of this presence into yourself, and exhale with fully present beingness. With that exhale, let go of the pain demons that reside in you, of the negativity that poisons your body." We have been asked to lie on the floor in Savasana, and Rain is walking amid us. When I briefly open my eyes, I see the hardened soles of her feet as she pads away from me.

"This work, of confronting your shadow and moving toward light, can be very difficult. Painful. For some people, it can even be dangerous. You may touch things that are too dark, too powerful for you to combat, and your psychic energy might get siphoned off by the wrong things, further weakening you. This is the oldest struggle there is, the fight between dark and light.

"Get used to feeling unsure—unsafe, even. That's normal. It's not just normal, it's necessary. You aren't safe, not while you remain in darkness.

"Everything you think you know is wrong. Dismantle your Self. Break down your Self. Kill that Self, if necessary. Because that is what you need to do to exist in Light. Each of you has come here for a reason, and you are all in this workshop together for a reason. Use that. Use me. We are all just instruments of Light."

I can't help cracking an eyelid during this exhortation to see if I can catch Ava's eye, but her face is obediently closed, and I can detect only the faintest hint of a smile on her lips.

"Open your eyes and be filled with Light," Rain chants softly, and all of us in this demon-ridden group of stragglers open our eyes. The sunlight is indeed blinding as it reflects off the lake. Devotion opens the door of the meeting room, and everyone begins to stand up.

"Let's all move up to the observation deck for our morning yoga," Rain says.

I sigh. I'd hoped for a wheatgrass smoothie breakfast or some such thing, but I guess that's not included in the programming yet. The probiotics are still something to look forward to, I suppose.

Devotion leads the way outside and up a flight of stairs to the roof, part of which is a balcony overlooking the water. The view is even more spectacular from up here. Yoga mats are lined up in a row, and I glimpse another acolyte setting a jug of cucumber-mint water on a small pedestal. I wonder how many people work here. I wonder how many of them are sworn to silence.

I had assumed Rain would be leading us in our yoga practice, but she doesn't make an appearance on the deck. Instead, an impossibly tiny woman in a sports bra and leggings stands in front of the class and, in a voice so soft I can barely hear it, guides us into our sun salutations.

We start off slow, and with each cycle increase our pace. The sun salutation that is ingrained in my kinetic memory, the one I learned in London, has an extra step in it, and I have to resist each time, forcing my body into this version. There's a mindless pleasure to it—indeed, this is what Rain had spent much of our session rattling on about, distancing ourselves from the mind. I am relaxing, happy to be just in my body.

A commotion from below interrupts our sixth salutation. I am on the forward lunge, my heart thumping briskly and a light sheen of sweat greasing my forehead, when the young man next to me abruptly stands upright and rushes to the railing at the edge of the deck. We are all close on his heels.

Down near the waterline, partly obscured by trees, a cluster of police officers are gathering. There are also people wearing volunteer firefighter uniforms.

"Maybe they're fishing someone's cat out of the lake?" a girl next to me suggests nervously. I think her name is Robin; she cried during the group session and seems like a full-on convert to whatever HOL is selling.

"I don't think they typically use crime-scene tape for cat rescues," Ava says drily, appearing at my shoulder. She points, and I see the yellow plastic fluttering, a cold signifier of something that's gone badly wrong. Two people wearing police jackets are unfurling the distinct ribbons all along the shoreline.

We all see Rain hurrying across the lawn, Devotion at her side. They have clearly heard, or been alerted to, the ruckus below. As they proceed briskly down the steep incline toward the water, Devotion skitters along behind Rain as she makes her self-assured way to the rocky shore. We watch as she approaches someone who looks like they're in charge, but she's too far away for us to hear her.

"What on earth?" the young man named Jon says. "What could have happened?"

"Boating accident?" Robin proposes. She's clearly the optimistic sort.

Because while the cops are pulling something from the water that is vaguely canoe-shaped, it doesn't really look like a boat. And if it were just a boat, they probably wouldn't need the body bag that someone is spreading out on the shore.

. . .

Our yoga instructor tries her best to usher everyone inside, but we are resolute, and Robin is the only person who allows herself to be shepherded away from the railing. The rest of us are transfixed by the scene below.

I had an appearance on a crime show before *Iroquois Falls* aired, and I'm reminded of what it felt like when I was playing Girl Corpse #2. I remember having to lie perfectly still while two men lifted me into a bag and then waiting, as the camera panned over my heavily made-up, blue face, before a pair of hands did up the zipper. I was in the dark for only seconds, but it was a distinctly rotten feeling.

An ambulance arrives, splitting off from the House of Light driveway to veer down toward the shore. The driver can't get all the way to the scene, and parks on a small bluff just shy of the action. Trees and foliage obscure a lot of what's happening below us, but we all gape as a very human form is removed from what looks like a small raft and is placed in the black bag waiting on the shore. It's hard to tell from this distance whether the person is male or female. Statistics, of course, suggest it's a she.

Overhead, birds circle, their dark wings unflapped.

Rain, meanwhile, has been deep in conversation with a capable-looking woman who seems to be barking orders. Rain turns around and heads back up the hill toward the House of Light. The body has already been loaded into the ambulance at this stage, so we all scamper back down the deck stairs to intercept Rain and see if she will dish.

"I understand you all have questions," she says before we can swarm her. She holds up her hands in the slightly choreographed way she has of moving, as though she is conscious of every small gesture. "I'll answer as many of them as I can, but right now I need to go to the station and speak to the investigators. All I can say so far is what you no doubt already know: that a body has just been pulled from Seneca Lake. We don't yet know if the person is connected to the House of Light, we don't know if there's been a crime. I will tell you anything I find out. Meanwhile, I don't want the day to be completely overtaken by this . . . drama. This is an excellent opportunity to practice mindfulness and stillness in the face of chaos. Devotion will handle lunch harvest and preparation, and I hope to be back by our afternoon session."

A few voices clamor to ask questions, but Rain is already resolutely striding off toward the parking lot. Devotion steers us back toward the kitchen in her wordless but forceful way, and we turn, like good cattle, and fall in line.

"What the actual fuck," I say to no one in particular. Devotion shoots me a dirty look.

"Do you think Rain is a suspect?" a person whose gender I don't want to make any assumptions about asks with dark curiosity. "I mean, why else would she be going to the station?"

"Who was the body, do you think?" some dude speculates. "Could it be someone from here?" Everyone peels off into small groups and pairs, some to the kitchen, others to the garden, accustomed to the routine of meal prep in this place. I fall in next to Ava, who has hung back, silent and thoughtful. She pulls a bowl of salad greens and a smaller bowl of purple-and-yellow flowers from the fridge.

"What do you think?" I ask her. She plucks out a violet from the bowl and pops it into her mouth.

"I think it was just a matter of time before it happened again," she says breezily.

. . .

I'm not sure what exactly brought me to the House of Light on this particular date. Dumb luck? The practitioners here would probably suggest that it was something more forceful, more intended. Maybe fate, maybe something like destiny, written into my future since the moment of my birth. Or possibly that my intentions had manifested themselves in this unusual way.

All I know is that I was there when they found her, on the day that summer became fall. And from that moment on, I knew that fate or not, whatever had conspired to bring me here, I was now involved. And the mystery would only draw me deeper.

And, of course, almost immediately after that first body was found, I learned from my quirky, possibly crazy source that it wasn't the only one. What at first seemed like a tragic accident started to seem like something much stranger, much darker. And I knew I needed to learn more. And the woman who gave me this information seemed to know it, and to draw me further and further in.

CHAPTER 4

"Um, what?" I ask, thinking I've misheard her. "What do you mean, *again?*" I drop my voice, though I'm not sure why. I have the sense, as I often do, that I'm improvising a scene, and with someone who is totally fucking nuts.

"I had a feeling there would be another body soon. And it's right on schedule. Guess I timed my check-in right." Ava shrugs, and starts shaving a cabbage into meticulous slivers.

"You're going to have to be more specific," I say. Ava says nothing, just focuses on her cabbage. "Another body?" I prompt. She stops her knife work and looks up at me. I can't read her face—rare, for me.

"You really are very tall," she says after a long pause. "Statuesque, really." I'm nearly bouncing in anticipation, but I stay quiet, waiting for her. Another trick from improvisation exercises with difficult partners.

"We can't really talk here," she finally says. "Devotion has big ears."

"Where then?"

"I'll come to your balcony after lights-out." I nod, and resume my own task of rinsing collard greens. We are, apparently, on a macrobiotic diet here at the House of Light. There is no plastic in this kitchen, no copper or nonstick dishware. We eat only what is in season, and consume no animal products. When I ask about the diet, a petite girl educates me.

"When you eat a dead animal, you ingest all the negativity they experienced. You're basically eating pain and fear and death and exploitation. Obviously, we try to avoid that."

As we all amble about the kitchen, preparing lunch, the gossip clearly centers on the body that came out of the lake. Whenever Devotion leaves the kitchen, speculation runs wild.

"What if it's someone who's involved with the House of Light?" Robin repeats. She has raised this question nearly every three minutes since we left the observation deck. She seems very much to want it to be the case, the little ghoul.

"Probably just some dumb tourist that fell off their paddleboard because they drank too many White Claws," Jon says dismissively.

"Then why would Rain need to go to the station?" she counters.

"Because she's in charge of the beach down there. Like, legally."

"Oh my God, do you think we'll get sued?" someone asks. She is one of the three people dressed in an oatmeal-hued kimono. We?

"I'm sure it's just a paperwork thing," another resident responds, dumping a pot of cooked beans into a colander. Devotion reappears in the kitchen doorway to summon us all to the long table outside for lunch. From her expression, she seems to have guessed what we've been nattering about.

We sit at the long wooden table and heap giant portions of vegan salad onto our wooden plates. Jon eats the most. I avoid the brown rice but eat a hefty helping of the cabbage salad (I think it's meant to be coleslaw, but I find that it tastes better if I don't think of it that way). Devotion's stern presence silences us.

I fidget almost constantly for the rest of the day. Rain does not, as she promised, reappear for our second group meeting in the afternoon, and instead Devotion leads us on a silent "contemplative walk" through the woods. It's a beautiful day, finally cooling down from the heat of the summer, and the light seeps through the trees like we're the ones now in an inverted colander. I focus on my posture, switching to different kinds of gaits, depending on the feeling of each moment. I alter my breath accordingly. I manage to entertain myself for the entire two-hour hike by silently goofing off with this bodywork, and by the time we get back to the House of Light, I'm in a very good mood. I don't miss any of the pills I've been taking, and this suggests to me that I didn't have a problem with them in the first place. Suck it, Jess.

No. I am practicing gratitude. I am grateful for this opportunity to find a center in myself. I am #blessed.

Devotion seems to want to limit the chatter, and moving us from the contemplative walk to expressive therapy (watercolors, light dancing off the lake, so tranquil, we are so very tranquil) to sunset meditation is an effective way of keeping the gossip at bay. I know this should feel like a prison, but I'm actually very content to drift from one peaceful exercise to the next. I'm still desperate for the dark, and for Ava to come visit me. And explain.

While most of the time feels like a spa day, the lights-out process does smack ever so slightly of a medium-security mental ward. (I'm guessing, at least, from my three-episode stint in a similar institution during season two of playing Mina, when she is temporarily committed to an asylum because her family learns that she is speaking to the dead.) We are escorted to our rooms and the doors are left open until it's time for the power to go out, at what I'm guessing is about eight or eight-thirty P.M., roughly an hour after sunset. Apparently we're serious about living with the sun's motions here. I'd hate to return in the winter.

When the lights go out, someone comes to check that we're in our beds. It's vaguely redolent of childhood, when a parent would come and make sure you've brushed your teeth and changed into your jammies, maybe read a story or two. I think of my dad, picking out the books he loved when he was a child, reading me musty hardcovers with notched pages and adoring the sound of his own voice. I would wait until he left before opening *Harry Potter*.

After ensuring that we're all snuggled in, they close the doors behind us. I listen for the click of a lock but don't hear it tonight. After maybe fifteen minutes of lying silently, listening for Ava, I creep out of bed and to the door.

The handle turns with just a tiny click. I step through the doorway with a shallow breath, trying to adjust to the darkness of the hall. Reluctant to let my door shut behind me, I pause in the hall, getting my bearings. Both the front door and Ava's are to my right. I let my own door close slowly, shutting it just short of latching into place. I take three cat-burglar steps down the hall.

A flashlight appears, and Devotion rounds on me before I have time to spin and disappear back into my room. She shines the light directly into my face, and I'm confronted with her one single expression, that of irritated disappointment. She shakes her head and points back to my room, and, feeling like I have no choice, I retreat back into my private cell. There must be sensors on the doors or in the hall. My estimation of the operating budget of this place ratchets up a notch.

I sit on the edge of my bed, my pulse elevated even though I'm in no particular danger. A mild transgression that leads to no punishment, and yet, here I am, a quick surge of adrenaline reminding me to behave. What funny creatures we are socialized to be.

• • •

LIV: So, let's start off with some basics. How about you introduce yourself.

AVA: My name is Ava Antipova, and I'm a client here at the House of Light.

LIV: (I've caught up with Ava in between sessions here at the Light. While socializing is generally discouraged, we've managed to find some time to record a conversation in our downtime. This turns out to be very lucky, timing-wise, but I didn't realize that while I was interviewing her. That only became apparent later, as you'll see.) So, Ava: This isn't the first time you've been here, is it?

AVA: (laughs) No, it isn't. I've been coming here periodically for about two or three years, as a sort of mental health retreat. My father-in-law was a member of this community way back, when it was a bit, shall we say, chiller. So I'm privileged enough to be able to pull some strings when I need to take a break.

LIV: But that's not the only reason you're here, is it?

AVA: (chuckles) No, I guess you could say that I've had an abiding interest in the House of Light for the past couple of years. I've been, well, keeping an eye out. Checking in to retreats on specific dates and all. My mental health time-outs have all been, uh, conveniently timed.

LIV: And what is it, exactly, that you've been looking for?

AVA: You mean, aside from lasting inner peace? (LIV laughs.) Well, I noticed about two, two and a half years ago that there was a worrying trend. Over a relatively short time span, I read about the deaths of three women, all in the same twenty-mile radius. They all took place on the date of a solstice or an equinox. They were all young, eighteen to twenty-five; they were all vulnerable and described as lost by friends and family. Their deaths were all ruled as accidents or suicides, even though they were mostly strange ways to die. The deaths all happened pretty close to where we're sitting right now. And, from what I've been able to discern, they all seem to be connected to the House of Light in some way.

LIV: Okay, can you walk me through that? Forgive me, but it does sound a little . . . tenuous.

AVA: Oh, believe me, I know! Look, I know this all has a bit of a conspiracy-theory vibe—I'll be the first to admit that it feels far-fetched. But I've been really looking at these deaths for a while, and I definitely think there are some connections. Could it all be coincidence? Sure, I suppose, technically. The world is a strange and mysterious place. But it feels fishy to me, at least. And there is, of course, the fact that if it is all coincidence, I just accurately predicted a fourth coincidence.

LIV: You mean the body of the young woman that was just recently discovered here at the Light.

AVA: That's the one. If it's just a weird fluke, how would I be able to guess that this would happen? The reality is that I was pretty sure it would, and I was pretty sure when, and that's why I'm here.

LIV: I mean, I was there with you when the body was recovered, and I can verify that you weren't surprised. At all.

AVA: Nope.

LIV: If this is the case, how come no one has looked into this yet? Surely law enforcement would be paying attention if . . . there was some suggestion of foul play.

AVA: I know, you were just about to say the word "murder" and the totally bananas quality of this kind of hit you, right? Surely law enforcement would care if someone *murdered* four women.

LIV: Right.

AVA: I mean, that I can't tell you. I don't want to lean too hard on the conspiracy-theory angle. But I'm sort of hoping that by talking about this, bringing this to light, these women might get the justice they deserve.

. . .

Ava hangs off her balcony in the dark.

"I didn't think you were coming," I whisper.

"I wanted to wait for Devotion to go to bed. It normally takes her about an hour."

"How do you know?"

"She meditates or prays or whatever in the common room with a single candle. When it dies out, she goes to bed. Or, at least, to her quarters."

"Where are her quarters?" I ask. I realize how little I know of this weird place.

"There are cabins on the other side of the vegetable garden. For staff. And for some of the older members who come out here to do personal retreats."

"I didn't know that was an option."

"It's not—for the general public, at least. You have to be Light to use the grounds. Part of the inner circle."

"I see," I say, though I don't. "Can we talk here? Or should we . . ." I gesture off toward the woods, the trees.

"We'll talk here, and make it quick. I don't know when Rain will be back, if she isn't already. I don't want to bump into her wandering the grounds."

"Not to mention that's a crime scene down there. There could be cops still."

"Good point." Ava stares out at the lake, lips pursed. She's an odd girl, with her snarl of dark hair, her guarded eyes. She seems, frankly, haunted.

"What were you talking about earlier? With the other bodies?"

"Look, I can't be sure of anything," she says. "There's not exactly . . . I may be introducing some conjecture into everything."

"Meaning?"

"We'll know more tomorrow, I think. But I'm guessing that the person they pulled out of the water today is a young woman, in her twenties. Probably pretty, probably damaged. Emotionally, I mean. The cause of death might not immediately be obvious, but they're going to rule it a suicide."

"You think she did it herself?"

"Oh no, not necessarily. But that's definitely what they're going to decide."

"So you're suggesting . . . murder?" I ask.

"Oh, don't look at me like that," Ava snaps. "I know this sounds crazy. But the date is exactly right. Just like I figured."

"The date? The end of September? I think you might need to back up here."

"For Christ's sake. There have been three other young women in a twenty-mile radius of this place who have turned up dead of an apparent suicide on an equinox or solstice in the last five years. That I know of."

"Okay . . . what does that have to do with the House of Light?"

"Well, that's what I was hoping to find out. There seem to be some links, but they're not all totally obvious. There are some . . . I guess you could call them 'factions' at play in the history of this place. Makes it complicated. But I was hoping to put the pieces together. Before the next one." Her mouth is set in a grim line as she looks down at the water.

"You think that there have been four—murders? And that the House of Light is somehow involved?" I'm trying not to sound too dismissive, but homegirl is coming off as pretty unhinged. I remind myself that I am at a spiritual retreat space. People who are totally squared away don't typically find themselves opting for a very expensive month of semi-silent meditation and sauerkraut.

"Look, if you don't believe me, that's totally fine. I've been piecing this together on my own for this long, I'll be fine getting it the rest of the way."

"Okay," I say with what I hope is a supremely chilled-out shrug. After a longer moment of consideration, I ask, "Why did you tell me, then?"

"Why do you think?" she says with a snort. "Because of who you are."

"So you did recognize me," I say, after another pause.

"I'm sure I'm not the only one, either," Ava answers. "But Rain feels it's counterproductive to highlight 'worldly success,' so no one is allowed to mention it in group. Our celebrity alum come here at least in part for the anonymity."

"I see."

"The House of Light explicitly courts mid-level celebs—no offense—by promising them quiet, no special treatment."

"I see."

"They've been hoping for converts all along, though. They need their Travolta, their Tom Cruise. I think Mila Kunis was on the hook for a while, but I haven't heard anything about her in a bit. Would have been quite the coup. You'll do just fine, though."

"I see."

Ava smirks at my impassive expression, my repetition. "Look, I get how it sounds. But I'm not some wacko conspiracy theorist. At least, I'm not *just* that. There is something very odd going on out here."

Living in L.A., I was cornered at more than one party by people eager to explain to me that the government was trying to irradiate our bodies with long-range waves and that was proof that turmeric was an alien technology sent here to help us protect ourselves. And even that was not as bizarre as, like, run-of-the-mill Scientology stuff. I'm used to some logical leapfrogging. Okay, I muse. Maybe.

I'm about to ask more questions, but I hear a door close inside the building, somewhere nearby. Ava freezes.

"Fuck, that's probably Devotion," she says. "I'm pretty sure if I get caught out of my room one more time I'll end up having to do something really unpleasant. Like fertilizing the orchard."

"Won't they just kick you out?" Normally that's how rehab works—either you play the game, or they send you onward.

"Not here. They don't really send seekers away around here. Bad business practice. Get back in your bed!" Ava hisses to me as she disappears. I slink back inside and have just flung the blankets over my face when I hear the door click open. I consciously slow my breathing, glad that my face is concealed. The door closes just a moment later.

I toss the blankets back and stare up at the ceiling far above me. I'm not sure how seriously I can take this new character in my life. Her story smacks of complicated justifications. Honestly, it feels baroque. It's hard not to think that she's stretching the facts to suit her narrative. That her own vision of whatever happened to these three—or four—women is obscuring the reality. I sympathize, I do. I know what it's like to get so lost in a fiction that you lose sight of what's real.

But should I really buy into this conspiracy yarn, spun by a complete stranger? She could be anyone, with virtually any motive. She could just be entirely crazy.

And as I'm nodding off, letting my mind drift, it occurs to me that even though she explained that she was telling me all of this because of who I was, she never said why that mattered.

CHAPTER 5

In the morning I am again awakened by the gong-chime thing. Though it's not in my room, it's extraordinarily loud, and I realize it's coming from outside. Blearily wrapping a rough-spun silk kimono around my shoulders, I stumble out onto my balcony, searching for the source of the sound.

Outside, it's not actually morning. There are still stars in the sky, which is transitioning from ink to gray, and over the roof of the building, I can detect some shadowy hints of pink where the sun will make its appearance. Not terribly soon, in any case.

Devotion is standing with another person, the first non-client man I have seen since I arrived here. At least, I assume he's not a client; he's wearing baggy flaxen robes that are similar to Devotion's, though these are an incongruous peach color. I can see the jut of Ava's balcony to my left, though she's not out there yet. The gong rings again, then a third time. I suspect that I have awakened faster than the other kids on retreat; I'm used to weird call times and early starts. I'm also used to staying up all night and hitting the day with a shuddery bump.

"Good morning, seekers," the man says in a soft-spoken voice. Not ideal for public address. I know a few voice coaches who would take him firmly in hand. "I'd like to ask you to put on trainers and join me at the front of the House for a morning meditation." He sounds British, like Dad. "We'll be leaving in five minutes, so as to catch the sunrise. Please move through your morning toilette with reflection and efficiency."

I shuck off my pajamas inside, feeling out of place without the ability to complete part of my morning routine: there's no mirror where I can look at myself naked, inspect how my body has changed in the night. To see if I am still the same person. I can catch a glimmer of my frame in the window, and I turn a few times. Satisfied, I tug a few things from my dresser: light sports bra, leggings, a zippered hoodie. I haven't curled or blow-dried my hair since I got here (naturally), and the texture is unfamiliar as I tug it into a messy top bun. My "trainers" are the last thing I pull on as I leave my room.

I linger in the hall, hoping to catch Ava, but the sound of the gong informs me that I've dallied too long, and I trot along the length of the hall. In front of Rain's office, I pause. I don't have time for snooping, but I'm very curious, and seemingly alone.

Bizarrely, the door isn't locked. If Rain were the mastermind of a murderous cult, you'd think she'd have some basic security. In the cold almost-light of day, I'm beginning to feel certain that Ava was pretty wildly off base.

I shut the door softly behind myself and zip across the room. Rain's desk is immaculate, and I don't have time to go through it anyway. I'm looking for only one thing.

I'm about to sprint back through the door when I see a door-frame with a curtain in the corner of the office.

Behind it, a tiny nook juts out of the side of the office: a small, private room with a cushion on the floor and something like a shrine in front of it. One of the walls is glass, affording a view of the lake. And, I note, a span of balconies. I don't have time to count them, but I'm betting you can see all of them. Something to bear in mind, at least in daylight. Or under a full moon.

On the other wall is a large frame draped with velvet. Feeling something akin to trepidation, I reach over and tug aside the fabric, even though it seems like a minor sacrilege.

The picture is quite large and of very good quality. It is of a very thin man with long hair; he is wrapped in a shawl that exposes his spindly arms. He sits in classic yogi pose, with his hair in a topknot, a thin beard tapering downward. His eyes are almost troublingly blue.

The gong sounds again, communicating a fresh urgency, and I drop the velvet and back out of the small meditation chamber. I can vividly imagine Devotion churning through the door and upbraiding me silently with her simmering glare, but I reach the door and squeak through it unseen. As far as I know.

I am, of course, the last one to join the group assembled outside.

"Shit, I'm sorry, I'm a heavy—" I start to say, but the man holds up a finger to his lips and smiles at me warmly. I arrange my face to express that I got it. I bob in a half-bow, half-curtsy, and someone, I think it's Devotion, makes the most unexpected giggling sound. The man starts to chuckle, too, and before I realize what's happening we're all laughing, goofily, clustered on the lawn in front of this odd architectural fantasia, which curves and conceals as though deliberately keeping its secrets. I can't help joining in the silliness, and on the side of the group, even Ava looks amused. Still smiling wildly, the man cocks his head over his shoulder and begins to march up the long drive. He's now carrying a long walking stick, and I'm envious of it as the incline steepens. From my side, I hear one of the young women whispering to a friend. I really should learn everyone's names, but there's a wacky combination of Beckys and Jubilations that is hard to keep track of.

"They're saying Rain got arrested," she hisses.

"What? You mean she's been in jail this whole time?"

"Apparently! No one knows what really happened, but . . ." I can't catch the end of her sentence as she edges away from me, clearly not wanting to be overheard.

The sky is fully gray when we get to the top of the hill and the ground levels out to a flat field. On one side is a vineyard, looking unexpectedly Tuscan and stretching on into the distance. On the other is a field of wildflowers, gold and purple and white.

The silly man lets us catch our breath—I'm guessing we've hiked at least an uphill mile in under twenty minutes, so we're all winded—then points with his stick behind us. We all turn, and the view of the lake is breathtaking. It's glassy and still and nearly blends in with the tree line that conceals the House of Light.

The man sits down in the field, not in the traditional om position but, rather, on his knees, his feet supporting his buttocks. Two or three of the other clients follow suit, and I'm guessing they've done this before. I drop biddably to my haunches.

Devotion crouches next to him and produces the gong. She smacks it lightly with a felted stick and rubs the metal in a circle, extending the sound into a sort of hum. She makes no sound, but the man next to her chimes in with a throaty drone, almost but not quite matching the pitch of the instrument. Others join in, and I do, too. Again, this is no weirder than things I've done in rehearsal.

We moan and chant in unison for what is probably about twenty minutes. I expect to get bored, or tired, or fed up, but almost the opposite happens. Everything but the vibration of my vocal cords fades away, and my eyelids fall half-closed, so that all I can see is the change of light as the sun comes up. Even the knee I sprained badly during a dance sequence years ago doesn't bother me in this crouched position.

When the sound stops, I open my eyes, content and calm. We sit, silently, until the birds are fully chattering and the sky is light. The day has begun. I wonder if I could begin every day this way, whether maybe things would be better, easier.

"Thank you for beginning the day with me," the English man says in his soft voice. "I am grateful for your presence." He settles back into a cross-legged position. "Today, I'd like to talk about our shadow selves. This morning, we arose in the dark, and walked upward, toward daylight. I won't belabor the metaphor, but I'd like to explore what that might mean in the metaphorical language of light—"

"Where's Rain?" Jon interrupts. "Normally she does the sunrise vocalization with us."

"Rain had other obligations this morning. I was very grateful for the opportunity to be with you for the sunrise. I hope you found my substitution . . . satisfactory." He breaks into that infectious grin again. Though his words sound like so much yoga-babble, the look on his face is genuine, as is his pleasure.

"Is something going on?" Jon insists.

"There's always something going on," the man responds. The curve of his eyebrow suggests that he knows this is infuriating. Relenting, he answers: "But yes, there are some things happening at the Center that have required Rain's . . . attention. It's not my place, however, to talk about them. She will be back, and she will explain everything you need to know. You should, of course, understand that this won't affect anyone's Process. At all. Those of you who were scheduled for personal readings or time in the Chamber will still receive that attention, and any and all of the day's usual contemplations will take place as scheduled."

Only two or three people look relieved; everyone else seems frustrated. I glance at Ava, waiting for her to speak out. Surely this is her area of paranoid expertise? But she says nothing.

"When will Rain be back?" a blond girl who has said nothing since I've been here asks. I had almost assumed she was on a vow of silence, too.

"I don't know when anything on this earth will take place," the man answers serenely. "Anyone who claims to is . . . let's say, a false prophet." He winks, and I could swear it is directed at me. "But, if I had to speculate, I'd say sometime just after lunch. Now. Let's continue with the discourse."

. . .

I try to catch Ava's attention as we walk down the hill toward the House of Light, but she studiously avoids me, weaving among the other clients and refusing to catch my eye. I notice someone watching me as we stroll, and I suspect that she recognizes me, even in my decidedly unglamorous state.

The morning is spent in the garden, weeding. I wrestle with a stubborn stalk of what I'm told is burdock for what feels like an hour. By the time I manage to tug out most of the plant, I am covered in tiny stickers and have lost whatever Zen the sunrise meditation afforded me. When we break for lunch, I'm relieved. It's grown hot in the September sun, and I'm ready for my low-calorie vegan snack.

I approach the English man, who has been working on a trellis for some climbing flower and clear my throat.

"Hi. I'm Olivia." I extend my hand, as though we're meeting at a cocktail party, and not crouching in the dirt.

"I'm Dawn," he answers. His smile is dazzling. If I'm not careful, I'll end up with a little crush on this man. Given my penchant for inappropriate dalliances, this would be entirely typical of my fool self. A brief image of Ryan, the first time I met him, crosses my mind, and I resolutely refuse to think about him. He'll forgive me; everything will be fine once I'm out of here.

"Hi, Dawn. I know we're supposed to head straight to the kitchen, but do you think I could maybe take a quick shower?" I gesture down at my body. He smiles in amusement at my sweaty shirt, my dirt-streaked wrists, the pink rash on my upper arm where I brushed against a nettle.

"I'll do you one better," he says.

"Something better than a hot shower?" I ask skeptically. "Unless you've got a hot tub and a bottle of wine squirreled away somewhere, I doubt it."

He laughs, loud and throaty. His mirth seems irrepressible—really, I've said nothing witty enough to merit that response. Though I do probably look bedraggled and absurd. "I was thinking a swim, actually."

"Hell yes. That sounds marvelous."

"I'll take you down to the boathouse. It's locked," Dawn says.

"I'll just go grab my suit."

"If you think you need it . . ." he says, his mouth curling up. I smile mischievously in return. Tempting, tempting.

"The paparazzi are everywhere," I finally say with a shrug. "Now, if it were dark . . ."

He smiles and shrugs back. "See you at the door in five, then."

I scamper toward my room, zigzagging in front of a pair heading for the kitchen. I really should learn everyone's name. But then, all the activities seem designed to keep us separated, or at least silent. Ava watches me go from the garden.

I had the forethought to bring two swimsuits, though Jess couldn't tell me whether there was a pool. I had a feeling. One is a fairly skimpy white bikini, the other a red one-piece. I'm tempted to don the white one—see what Dawn makes of that—but I should play it safe. The red one it is. Yet again I yearn for a mirror. A towel from the bathroom and I'm out the door, racing in flats for the front.

Dawn is still wearing his linen . . . garment, and I feel a little silly in my suit. I wrap the towel around my waist and try to look composed. Though it's warm in the sun, I can feel fall in the shade.

"Lead the way, master," I say and Dawn laughs again. He heads down the hill, and I follow, though I can feel my bad knee now. I suspect I was overtraining to slim down for the play, and it twinges after this morning's abuses.

"I'm actually glad to have a minute to welcome you," Dawn says as we enter a copse of pines. "Normally Rain is the only person to do counseling and readings for the first week, but your case interested me."

"Oh, really? Why's that?" My case?

"I saw in your file that you're an actor," he explains.

Sure, from my *file*, I think. Maybe he honestly doesn't recognize me, though. How refreshing.

"That's true. Or at least, it's often true. I guess I'm . . . between gigs at the moment," I say.

"I'd like to talk about that, eventually. Once, in a different life, I was an actor, too."

"Oh, were you. I guess that makes sense," I say.

"It does?" he asks.

Excellent, he's fishing. "Oh, you know. The way you carry yourself. And of course . . . well, there's your face."

I get the smile I've been working for. I sure have missed male companionship the last couple days.

"Nothing ever really came from it," Dawn explains with a modest shrug. "I didn't have your talent. Or drive. What I did have was a decent-sized trust fund and an even larger appetite for cocaine." We pick our way carefully down a steepening incline.

"Is that how you ended up here?" I ask.

"Circuitously. Had to try a few rehabs out west first, blow a few grand on blow. But I met some people in a group out there, and they told me I should spend some time here. Take a class or two."

"I guess it worked."

"More than you know," Dawn says with a grin. "I know this can be weird, at first. I've been to my fair share of rehabs, self-help retreats. Hell, even churches."

"They can . . . blur together a bit," I concede playfully.

"At first that's how I felt about this place. But it's . . . just different. The people here are different. Rain? Did you know her parents took her to India when she was just ten years old because they thought she could read people's minds? She spent a good chunk of her childhood at an ashram because she was so gifted."

"So . . . Rain is psychic?"

Dawn laughs. "No. At least, she says she's not. Not exactly.

Sometimes I'm not so sure. But she has an affinity for knowing what people are feeling, that's definitely true. Is that all that different from clairvoyance?"

I nod my head noncommittally.

"Everyone here is different," he goes on, "extraordinary in their way. Devotion trained in a Zen monastery and studied martial arts for decades."

"Is that why she's . . . silent?" I ask.

"Rain says she speaks only when necessary. Apparently, language is somewhat overused in our busy, ego-driven world. Rain says so much speech is about the self and its importance. Devotion is moving away from that."

"And what about you?"

"Me?"

"What part of the Eastern world did you go explore? What's your gift?" I nudge him gently with my elbow.

Dawn chuckles. "Rain . . . says I have a buoyancy to me. That no matter what happens, no matter what I lose, I always . . . float. She calls it 'the bluebird of luck.'"

"Well, that sounds very useful," I say.

We stumble the last few yards toward a rocky beach. I look up and down the shore. There's a small rustic structure to our left.

"I don't see it," I say.

"See what?"

"The pool."

Dawn laughs uproariously.

"What?" I counter.

"There's no pool, Olivia."

I survey the lake with some suspicion. There's a skein of seaweed curling visibly at the surface. The beach is not sand. But I don't want to look like a prissy noodle. I can work with this.

"Right."

"I'll unlock the boathouse for you. There are extra towels

there. And a shower, if you still want one." He beckons me toward the small building and opens the door for me. I peer inside. Nothing fancy, but it's cute.

"I sort of thought this would be, um, roped off still," I throw out tentatively, wondering if he'll tell me anything.

"Ah. Well, the crime scene is a bit up the beach. Near the boat launch." He points north, up the lake. A curve of the waterfront and a stand of trees obscures the view.

"Oh," I say, disappointed. I'd hoped to catch a glimpse.

"How competent a swimmer are you?" he asks.

"Just fine," I answer, falsely modest. I used to swim a hundred laps a day when I lived in L.A. "I reckon my buoyancy isn't too bad, either. I think I'll float."

"Then I recommend going straight off the dock," he says, grinning. He points to the spindly little pier that stretches out into the water. "You'll miss the worst of the seaweed that way."

"Okeydoke," I say gamely. I drop the towel on the boards and kick off my flats, stride out onto the dock. Splinters are a real risk. I turn back to make sure he's watching me, and sure enough, he's standing on the shore, eyes glued. I square my hips like a gymnast and head toward the lip of the dock, picking up my pace as I near it. I race the last few steps and launch myself into the water in what I suspect is a fairly elegant dive.

The water is cold, but not as cold as I was expecting. At the surface it's tolerable, but it gets colder in sharp layers as I descend. A few feet deep and I brush against seaweed, so I kick my way to the surface. When my head reappears, Dawn is applauding.

"Very impressive," he says. I say nothing, but breaststroke easily through the water, doing a lap or two parallel to the shoreline. I'm waiting to see if Dawn will join me. He seems to be deciding, too. When he shakes his head (resisting the urge?), I smile, my lips just below the water.

"Coming in?" I call.

"I'm afraid I've got to go help with lunch," he answers, full of regret. "Will you be okay down here?"

"You bet," I call back, surprised. I didn't think he'd be allowed to leave me unsupervised.

"Lunch is in thirty. Don't be late or Devotion will make sure we both suffer for it."

I laugh, though I inhale a bit of water as I do.

"And don't drown," he adds over his shoulder as he leaves.

Somewhat tasteless, I reflect, given yesterday's body.

I paddle happily, refreshed and relaxed even as the chill sinks in. From just this far out in the lake I can see the boat launch and its beach, with the cordon of yellow tape. I swim in that direction.

I draw closer to the beach, but there isn't that much to see, as far as I can tell. Just rocks and tape and a few small flags. Although as I get nearer, what looked to be just beach detritus takes shape.

It almost looks like a boat. It's made of driftwood and is fashioned in the shape of a rowboat, with an angled bow and a wide tail end, though there is no stern, and the sides taper down to the water. It's lined with leaves and branches: pine boughs and what I think are oak branches, with some wildflowers scattered in. I can make out something spiky. I swim a little closer, though I'm entering a swatch of seaweed.

At the prow of the boat, there's a large crown made from wood and plants; it reminds me of the crown I wore to the Heavenly Bodies Met Gala. A halo of thorns radiates out in long skewers, and something that might be grapevines is woven throughout. I tread water, suddenly reluctant to get closer.

"Hey, this is a crime scene!" a voice calls from the beach, and I snort water. "You can't come over here!" A woman dressed in uniform emerges from the trees, holding a camera. "What are you doing here?" I duck my head under the water and kick furiously back in the direction I came, surfacing only when I can't hold my breath any longer.

I turn ninety degrees when I see the dock and the boathouse, and stroke my way toward shore. I can't haul myself out of the water onto the dock, so I'm forced to kick my way through the warm, slimy fronds of seaweed. When I can touch, I lower my feet to the bottom, but the rocks are sharp, and I can barely pick my way out of the water. I'm glad Dawn isn't here to see me stumbling clumsily up to the bank and back to my towel. As I step onto the deck, I leave half a bloody footprint on the wood. I'm bleeding from the callus below my big toe where I've sliced my foot open.

Hopping inelegantly into the boathouse, I find a Band-Aid and wrap myself up as best as I can. The cut doesn't really hurt, though it looks quite deep. I feel foolish, first for having been spotted and then for hurting myself. Cursing, I head up the hill, for lunch and Devotion's recriminations.

Wondering, the whole time, what the hell I saw on the beach.

. . .

I expect to be scolded when I make it back up the hill to the Center: I'm dripping wet, late, and I haven't helped prepare lunch. I scuttle past the entrance to the kitchen so that I can slip into my room for some dry clothes, and hurriedly pull on a caftan and run a hairbrush through my snarled hair.

When I reach the kitchen, though, they're all bustling around, and my presence (or lack of it) goes unremarked. Everyone is chattering and abuzz as they take bowls of cabbage and carrots outside to the picnic tables. I grab a pot of grains while I glance around, hoping to find Ava somewhere. Instead, I meet Devotion's eyes, and she gives me a stern look that suggests she knows where I've been. I hurry to take my dish outside.

There, I see why everyone is agitated: Rain has returned, and is standing at the head of the table, wearing the same clothes she had on yesterday. We're all whispering as we set the table, rushing in the hopes that she'll explain everything. Rain stands there, poised and unflustered, while we all scamper about. She is almost motionless, but I notice that she curls the toes of her still-bare feet into the grass, as though she's looking for purchase in the soft dirt.

Finally, everything is on the table and we all sit down. Rain waits, letting the silence stretch on.

"Hello, everyone," she eventually says, her voice clear and sturdy. "As you all no doubt realize, there has been a tragedy. I have been speaking to the police in the hopes that we can learn exactly what happened here." I look down the long table at Ava; she's seated about four people down, across the table from me. "Dawn tells me that many of you were on the observation deck yesterday and saw the police down at the beachfront. He also says you were all there, watching, when a body was removed from the scene." She conveys a sense of disapproval with this sentence, as though our rubbernecking was disgraceful. I suppose it was.

"I've been asked not to release the name of the person involved, but I can tell you that the body of a young woman was found on the beach just below the House of Light early yesterday morning. A pair of kayaking tourists apparently noticed an unmoored rowboat bobbing just offshore from our beach, and when they approached it, they saw what seemed to be a body. They returned to their cabin and phoned the police, who came to investigate, as you know, not long after sunrise."

Rowboat, eh? The thing I saw on the beach was most certainly not a rowboat.

"I'd also like to share with you something else, lest gossip start to circulate unchecked. The woman who was found was, unfortunately, a former client of the House of Light. She spent several months with us last year, and her death comes as a shock to all of us. We will hold a ceremony for her this evening, just after sunset." Rain pauses, and though she seems perfectly at ease and in control, her face is lined, her eyes puffy from lack of sleep. I glance at Ava, who meets my eye. "Okay. Now, are there any questions?"

"Was it Hannah?" Jon blurts out. He looks stricken.

"As I said, the police have asked me not to release any names. They'd like to make sure that her family is informed before people start speculating."

Now Jon looks chastised.

"Were you at the station all night?" a girl named Tia asks. "Did they hold you for questioning?"

"I was in Watkins Glen last night, voluntarily. I was answering questions at the station, and then later, at the hotel with an attorney, providing information to the investigation. Again, this was entirely voluntary. I want only to help learn what happened to—to her."

"Was it murder?" someone asks morbidly.

Rain's mouth clenches. "There hasn't been a ruling by the medical examiner yet. The police are exploring all options."

"Are you a suspect?"

"What did I just say?" Rain snaps, her voice uncharacteristically heated.

We fall silent. Rain composes herself.

"Not as far as I know," she answers, trying to lighten her tone. "Now, if that's all, I'd like for this event to not overshadow the work that we're trying to do here. I'd like for us all to reflect on the fact that death is as much a part of life as anything else, and that we must be present and open to it, even when it happens like this, unexpectedly and early. I'd like for the rest of the day to be spent not in macabre speculation about what has taken place"— she makes eye contact with at least three people at the table, as though to single them out—"but, rather, in being thankful for the lives we have been given. And for us to recognize that—this person is now in a better place, beyond pain and shadow. If you would please all take one another's hands, let's have a moment of reflection and gratitude."

Everyone obediently links fingers. Those lentils will be stone-cold by the time we eat them. Yum.

Rain tilts her head back, and though she has kept a strictly neutral expression this whole time, I think I can see the glimmer of a tear, something like suffering on her face. When she angles her head back down, she nods to the other end of the table, where Devotion is standing. Devotion opens her mouth.

The sounds that come out of her aren't words; nor is she precisely singing. I guess it is, technically, music, though it resembles a pitched wailing. She throatily keens for nearly two minutes, and whatever her song is, it's eerie. I look down the table to see Ava staring at me. Her face is expressionless.

When we all finally sit to eat, no one feels much like talking.

• • •

Well, folks. I have a confession. The idea of doing a podcast wasn't exactly mine. I had to sort of be . . . nudged into the whole idea. I love a good podcast, but the idea of doing one had never crossed my mind.

When Ava suggested that I make a podcast about the Seneca Girls, I admit, I was skeptical. I didn't have the expertise, the background. But Ava pointed out that I had something more important. A platform. She thought more people needed to know about what was going on, and wide publicity might be the best way to get to the bottom of what was happening. The most important thing, she said, was to find out the truth.

Not long after I started seriously considering her proposal, I began to have reasons to doubt her sincerity, and her motivations. Even her willingness to let go of the project and hand it over to someone else was uncharacteristic of her; Ava cares about control, a lot. And her personal connection to the story made it even more unlikely that she would relinquish the reins to a stranger, even if that stranger was famous. But I didn't know that yet. And even if I had, I doubt it would have mattered.

• • •

"A podcast," I say slowly, when she proposes it the first time. I've caught up to Ava in the afternoon, after an especially heinous group session. Though I narrowly avoided having to speak, the price of that silence was listening to Tia sob intermittently about what sounded like a breakup but turned out to be the sale of her pony as a teenager. Horse girls.

"I know it sounds like a weird idea," Ava says, quick to explain. "But. It's kind of, like, the trend in true crime these days. People are actually solving cold cases. If *you* did a podcast, it would automatically be a big deal. People would listen just because it's you. And then people would start asking questions, looking at the details of all the different cases. It would be like enlisting a few hundred strangers to help us." Her eyes glitter with an enthusiasm I'm not at all comfortable with.

"You don't think it would work if you just did it on your own?" I suggest hopefully. Like, your crazy, your problem?

"If I could even get it off the ground. Which is doubtful. And like I said, I'm not entirely credible."

"Why don't you go ahead and explain what you mean by that," I prompt.

Ava sighs. "Well, I'm a fairly prominent drunk around here," she says neutrally. "From a long line of distinguished and prominent drunks. My family is . . . well, they were sort of high-visibility lushes. We own a vineyard just up the lake, and we had a . . . family tragedy a few years ago that was somewhat high-profile."

"Oh yeah?"

"My sister died. And the whole thing looked a bit fishy."

"Sort of like these deaths you're looking into now," I suggest.

"Right. At the time, I *might* have been running around all over the lake asking questions and generally implicating other people in her death. And I might have been half in the bag the whole while. Or wholly in the bag, at least half the time." Ava winces. "Then, after her death, which coincided with my mother's, I may have gone on a flamboyant display of self-destruction that included . . ." She takes a deep breath. "That included at least one scene of very public disorderliness. And some nudity. And a DWI. This is a small town. People are not inclined to take me seriously. And now that I have a baby, there's considerably less leeway. Nothing gets people wagging their fingers quite like a bad mother."

"You have a kid?" I ask, flabbergasted. She does not strike me as the maternal type.

"A daughter. And a very patient, put-upon husband. He tolerated my shenanigans for a bit but eventually told me I needed to dry out and sort my shit out. Or, you know. Else. Hence my first stay here, about two years ago."

"Did it work? Did you get clean?"

"For a little while. Now I'm what you'd call a pretty high-functioning alcoholic. I only drink once the baby is in bed, and only when there's someone else around to look after her. It's not a secret, Wyatt knows. And it's why he approves of me coming here from time to time. Keeps me centered." She smiles bitterly. "His dad, as I mentioned, is an original House of Light member. He can usually pull some strings with Rain to get me a bed here when I need one. Needless to say, I haven't told them about my . . . research."

"I'm not surprised," I say.

"I know it sounds nuts. And you're probably even more convinced that I'm batshit now. But something's going on. I can feel it. And I've got the documents to prove a lot of it. Social media accounts, items in the paper. But I know that if it's just me, nothing will ever come of it."

There's a note of melancholy pleading in her voice. I feel bad for her, I really do. She was clearly unhinged by the death of her sister, and then had a nasty bout of postpartum depression. Now she's looking for something to fill the void her addiction has left, and so she's constructed this elaborate fantasy.

"I know you think I'm crazy," Ava adds. "I get that. I've gotten enough looks like that to recognize it. But will you do me a favor? Will you just think about it?"

I consider this. "Okay," I say finally. "I'll think about what you said."

I've never wanted internet access so badly in my life.

CHAPTER 6

That evening, before dinner, I have my first reading.

While everyone attends Group Work, I am summoned to Rain's office. Inside, the lights are dim, and she is burning incense. I half-expect her to tell me to get undressed and lie on the table. Instead she gestures for me to sit on a cushion on the ground, and she joins me so that we both sit lotused and facing each other. She is quiet for longer than is strictly comfortable, and I resist the urge to babble. Finally she smiles, as though I have passed a test.

"Olivia. I'm glad that we're finally doing this."

"I guess I'm not sure exactly what we're doing," I say. "I've never had a 'reading.'"

"Of course not. You've never spent time at the House of Light before. Let me explain. Part of the Process involves personalized readings with advanced members of the Light. We've all been through the same treatment, and we've been training for years to be able to give readings for others. It's basically a therapy session that uses a number of techniques, both Western and non-Western. I've studied your astrological chart and your case notes, as provided by your manager. We'll also be doing some energy work. It resembles Reiki, but there is also a specific type of monitoring we are trained to do that will help us assess past traumas and sensitive areas. We will likely incorporate other bodywork at some point, identifying your unconscious resistances. How does all of this sound?" She pauses to assess how I'm taking this.

"I'm game. I've done a lot of those things before, so I don't think I'm too unfamiliar with anything," I respond.

"I should be clear, though. The work we do is not like any other treatment you've received before. This is not tarot. This is not a psychic reading. That stuff is for charlatans and hucksters and has no place here."

"Noted," I say. They all say that.

"Our Process is distinct. Unique. We think of it as a new technology, almost. It might bring up things you haven't addressed before, or don't want to. Your shadows. You need to be prepared for that."

"Sure," I say.

"Great. I'd like to start with you lying on your back in a relaxed position. Open your hips, and let your breath come evenly. I'm going to start at your third eye and work down, letting the energy flow between the two of us. I want you to give up any resistance and just feel my energy as we work."

Rain's hands hover lightly over me, moving along my chakras. It's not unpleasant. She pauses over my belly.

"I can feel something here. Some sort of blockage. Do you use an IUD, by any chance?"

"Yeah," I say, surprised. "For a few years now. Other birth control—"

"Don't try to explain too much. I just needed to know what foreign body I was sensing here. I have a way of intuiting flow, how the body is functioning. Or not functioning, when I'm asked to consult on medical cases. But that's good, very good. I'm happy to hear that you're keeping track of your womb. It can easily become a place for shadows to sort of hide out." She continues, inching her way along my body and occasionally making little noises. She grunts when she nears my bad knee. I'm impressed, and quite relaxed.

Finally, she returns to my head and sits behind me, her palms on my temples. We breathe together for a minute or two, and I feel calm, serene.

"Liv, we're going to go deep here, so I need to ask you if you're ready," Rain says. Her fingers have moved to the sides of my neck, along the lines that always tense when I'm stressed. I can smell her clean linen clothes, the spice of someone who wears only natural deodorant beneath them. I open my eyes and tilt back my head to look at her, and she smiles down at me, calm. "Go ahead and keep your eyes closed. It's easier if you're fully in yourself while we talk. Just think of me as . . . a conduit. As someone who can help you in dialogue with yourself."

"Do I need someone to help with that?"

"Everyone does. The work we do here is, at its heart, very simple. We all seek to speak to our own souls. But what I can help with is getting the conversation going."

"Okay," I say, trying to relax my shoulders.

"You always start with your body," Rain observes. "Any challenge that's asked of you. You take a deep breath, or change your posture, or resettle your feet. You are your body first."

"Isn't everyone?"

Rain gives an amused huff. "No. The things that seem most natural to us are often what make each of us so distinct. In my first reading, my teacher made me aware that I start everything with my head, from a place of intellectual . . . distance. I had never thought anything of it, but of course he was right."

"This is . . . your guru?"

"I prefer 'teacher.' 'Guru' sounds rather . . . too New Age," Rain says, and it's my turn to laugh. "Yes, I know, I know. The House of Light is . . . fairly New Age. But I don't love all the connotations associated with the term. I don't like to lump us in with every crystal-carrying, chakra-centering juice cleanse in the Western world. The House of Light is a philosophical and spiritual practice."

"That's what they all say," I point out.

"Let's get back to the reading, instead of deflecting," Rain chides. "Your defenses are up pretty high for someone whose profession involves a certain . . . degree of vulnerability. But then, I guess that endless vulnerability can be quite . . . uncomfortable from time to time. It can't be easy, to always be giving yourself up so that you can let something new in."

"It's not so bad." I half-shrug when I say this, and the twinge in my neck intensifies. Rain, feeling it, rubs her fingers in soft circular motions where it hurts. She lifts my head slightly, so that it's gently cradled in her hands.

"To be so vulnerable requires trust. I want you to trust us, to trust me. But I know that sometimes your trust in others has been . . . misplaced."

"It happens," I say, trying to be light.

"Please don't do that. Don't just brush off your pain as though it was inevitable. Or worse, deserved. You have trusted the wrong people, and it has hurt you."

"Who hasn't, though?"

"I mean recently," Rain gently corrects me. "You're here because someone betrayed your trust."

"Did you get that from the tabloid photos? Or from the fact that I'm in an inpatient retreat?"

I can hear the smile in her voice as she continues: "I don't imagine there's a lot of trust between you and the people who profit from exploiting your image. You don't trust the paparazzi responsible for your recent PR mishap. But I get the sense that someone's betrayal is what caused you to be where you were when you were photographed. What happened, Liv? Do you want to tell me?"

"I don't know if I do," I say. My voice is small, and I want to crawl back inside my body. Rain puts a hand on my chest, and one on my forehead—she isn't restraining me, but it's like she's using her hands as a sort of human lie detector.

"I can feel your energy trying to withdraw here. Take a deep breath, and don't try to run away from it. Your body needs to understand there's nowhere to go."

These words cause a sudden burst of panic, and my entire body tenses up.

"See, you're trying to escape it," Rain says, her voice deep and calm. She moves one of her hands back to my neck, and she holds it there. "Breathe. There's nowhere to go."

I take a few breaths. Steady on, Liv. "I had taken a few pills too many and I wanted to speak to my boyfriend. He had . . . well, he wouldn't speak to me, and I needed to know why. I needed him to talk to me. So I went to his house."

"And he still didn't want to speak to you."

"He wouldn't let me up. But I knew he was up there. He'd just posted, and I could see his lights. So I started calling up to him. I tried to climb the fire escape, but I . . . wasn't exactly in the best shape to do it. Which is when this photographer showed up. His name is Vorchek. This guy is *always* there. He follows me *everywhere*. And I was just . . . I was so angry. I wanted to deal with this incredibly personal thing, but here he was, trying to get a picture up my dress while I tried to climb a fire escape, and I sort of just . . . snapped. I basically landed on him, and I would have kicked the shit out of him, but someone pulled me off him and, I guess, called the cops. Photos of that followed, and . . . it was all around a humiliating night. 'Starlet Cracks Under Pressure,' and all that."

"You felt exposed in your pain. Yet you've given so many performances that expose your pain. Your breakout role as Mina, in fact, relied on your ability to show people that vulnerable, hurt side of yourself. I don't see why this pain was different."

"It was just . . . mortifying . . ."

"No, Liv. You're missing something. Or, rather, you're trying to mislead. Where was the betrayal here? Who betrayed you?" Rain's fingers sink into something meaty and deep on the back of my neck, and something inside me lets go.

"I did. *I* betrayed me." Unbidden, tears pool on the surface of my eyes, spilling over to slip straight across my concealed crow's-feet, toward my ears.

"Say more."

"I . . . I was the one who had hurt him. Hurt Ryan. I . . . Oh God. I was cheating on him. With the director of my play. It had been going on a little while, and several people found out and I knew it was only a matter of time before Ryan found out. I needed to know if he already knew and . . . when he wouldn't let me in . . ."

"You punished yourself. By exposing your pain and shame."

"I thought if I showed him that I was sorry—"

"No, you performed that you were sorry," Rain interrupts. "You made a show of remorse that benefited you, not him."

"I needed him to know," I say softly.

"No, you needed him to *see*. Him and everyone else." Rain's fingers work outward from the tender spot she has located, and waves of nausea radiate through me, alternated with troughs of relief.

"Yes," I finally say. "I knew everyone would know soon enough. I wanted them to see that I . . . regretted it. I knew they would hate me—we're the golden couple, everyone loves to see us together. And I went and slept with this controlling older man—my director, for fuck's sake!—and everyone would know about it and judge me and hate me."

"They would feed off your pain and shame," Rain says, her fingers digging lower, finding another spot. I gasp, but she holds the pressure. "And you. You would feed off your guilt and their hatred. Because to hate you, they have to look at you. And as long as they're looking, you have the fuel you need. Why? Why do you need them to look at you? Why mustn't they ever turn away?"

"Then how will I know they're there? That I matter to them?"

"You don't trust them to go on caring if you're out of sight?" Rain presses on. "Is that because someone important lost sight of you?"

"She didn't lose sight," I say, finally crying in earnest.

"Who didn't? Your mother?"

I nod, sobbing. "She looked away. And she never looked back."

Rain's fingers release their pressure and just linger, massaging soft circles at the nape of my neck.

"There it is. There's the whole story," she finally says, after I've cried for a long minute. "Oh, Liv. I'm so glad you're here. You have so much to give. So very much potential." Her hands pat me, releasing me.

I sniffle. "Oh yeah?" I say, sitting up to face her. "I feel like I'm something of a damaged basket case, actually."

She smiles softly, and I can see that though her skin is luminous, she has gentle wrinkles nearly everywhere. I still can't tell how old she is, in spite of years of training to assess a woman's vintage, her defects. She reaches out and pats my cheek.

"You have immense talent. And immense spiritual potential. But if you let those gifts go undeveloped, you risk tragedy, for yourself and those around you. You have not used your gifts to their full extent; nor have you explored the darkness you're capable of.

"I believe you have the possibility to change lives. But left unchecked . . . you have the ability to destroy them. Let's work on that, in future sessions." After a long pause, she asks, "What do you think?"

Dazed, I look away. "Um, yeah, okay," I say.

I really have no idea what just happened.

• • •

At the beach that night, I am still befuddled and hazy. I'm even wondering if there was something in the tea Rain gave me before we started. I've done both Reiki and astrology readings before, but they never left me feeling quite so damn loopy. I stagger around in a long dress, one of the few things I brought that has a zipper, bobbing my head whenever someone speaks to me. I'm not my sparkly self, though, that's for sure. A Lana Del Rey song loops in my head: "Tearing around in my fucking nightgown, 24/7 Sylvia Plath . . ."

After the sun has set, everyone is clustered near the water, which laps delicately at our big toes. We are lighting paper lanterns in honor of the dead girl, loosing them over the lake where she died. There will be poetry, I have been warned. I'm in too much of a muddle to really care.

Jon does indeed recite something that is spoken word–adjacent, and pretty painful to witness. He seems sincere about it, though. His act is followed by an interpretative dance performed by Tia and the small quiet girl. They dance on the dock, and in the gloaming, we can barely make out their shapes as they move. It's actually quite pretty, like silent shadow puppets.

We light the lanterns, which lift off from the shore.

"Let her soul go with light," I hear Dawn say, as though to himself. He bows his head.

"Did you know her?" I ask. In the dark, it takes him a moment to suss out who I am. When he does, he smiles warmly.

"You know, that is what we do here. Learning to know the self, to come to know the other. I thought maybe I could know her. God knows I tried."

I say nothing.

"But with something like this, I start to wonder. Whether you can ever really know an other at all. There is such a huge gap between what someone shows you of themself and what really takes place in those dark crannies of the soul. What they want. What someone is truly capable of. Maybe that little piece of private darkness belongs to the self alone and is never truly illuminated. It's the one thing we can call our own, I guess. That darkness that evades light. We want to protect it. And maybe, sometimes, to pass it on."

He smiles, although sadly this time, and strides off into the dark before I can say anything. I didn't know it at the time, but what Dawn just said to me was one of the closest things to blasphemy I would ever hear a true member of the Light say.

———

As we walk back up to the Center, I feel someone hovering at my elbow, and I can guess who it is.

"Have your first reading, then?" Ava asks.

"Yep."

"Quite something, aren't they? I had my first after my sister died. I wanted to find out how it works, you know, with a twin chart. Geminis, no less," she says, and an incisor flashes as she grins. "Still, it's pretty impressive stuff. I don't think it can be all fortune-teller mumbo jumbo. Not unless they are all extremely gifted at the cold read."

"They all do readings?"

"I've had four, with three different people. They're all a bit different, but the gist is the same. You are very strange, and you are very powerful. Learn our ways so that you don't slip into darkness. And all that."

"Right," I say. "So it wasn't just me."

"Don't get me wrong—they will have figured out some particular way that you are a very special snowflake. And it will probably be the exact way that you desperately *want* to be a snowflake. And who knows, they might not be wrong." Ava laughs. "I think they had to dig deep for me, at first. There wasn't much that mattered to me, back then. They thought they'd get me with motherhood, then with partnership. Then with what they were calling 'cultivation,' if you can believe that." She snorts.

I think for a minute. "Because of your family's vineyard?" I guess.

"One supposes."

We slow our steps as we approach the front door, knowing we'll be separated momentarily.

"It's the carrot to their stick," she continues. "They offer you the thing you want. Then, when they sense you pulling away, they can threaten to take it from you. Or, more accurately, they can threaten that you will take it from yourself, by resisting. Effective." We walk down the hall, everyone peeling off into their rooms. "It's like they tell you you're Harry Potter, and they say, Choose us, choose Hogwarts. Or stay in the dark, as a Muggle. Who doesn't fucking choose Hogwarts? Who doesn't choose their own secret gift?"

"Well?" I ask, as we both pause in front of our doors. "What did they figure out motivates you, in the end? The thing that you're most interested in?"

"It was the obvious choice, all along," Ava says, grinning impishly. "The only thing that really matters. Death."

"Um . . . what does that mean?"

"Oh, it's pretty straightforward. They told me if I found my true self, I could speak to the dead."

Later, as I lie in bed, staring at the high ceiling of my room, I hear a rustle at the door. Thinking it's Devotion come to check on her somnolent patients, I prepare to fake sleep. Instead, I see a piece of paper scoot across the pine floor.

Crouching, I read it.

I think it's time we busted out of this joint. Fancy a field trip?
—A

CHAPTER 7

I'm dressed and waiting when the *tap-tap-tap* comes knocking on my window, twenty minutes later. Costume-wise, I've gone for a secret agent palette, hues of black, all quite snug.

Ava hoists herself over the edge of my balcony without a word, and I balk.

"How will we get back in? Where are we even going, for that matter?" I whisper.

"Hush. I'll explain on the way."

I pause, considering the advisability of following the crazy lady who speaks to the dead off into the darkened woods. But I'm terribly bored. So over go my lengthy legs, and I drop onto a cushion of pine needles and grass.

Ava trots ahead, her small feet confident in the dark. She makes good time for someone so tiny. When we've gotten a few hundred yards from the Center, she explains.

"We're going to my house," she says. "It's about two and a half miles down the road. I'll show you the research I've collected. Then you can decide for yourself whether I'm a conspiracy theorist or whether I'm onto something."

"Won't your family know you're home?"

"Wyatt . . . well, he'll probably just make us a cup of coffee. He can hardly order me to go back, after all."

"Okay . . . and how do we get back in?" I ask again.

"It's all about timing. We'll stroll in when everyone is heading in for morning session. Devotion unlocks the front door when she comes to get the rooms ready for group. If we scoot in when everyone else is leaving their rooms, no one will know."

While not exactly fail-proof, this plan is good enough for me. I'm itching to check my email, and I intend to borrow a device from Ava in short order.

We hike up the road that runs parallel to the lake. Two cars pass us, but it's quiet, past the witching hour. We don't speak much, and I find myself relaxing into the sounds of crickets, the blink of fireflies. If this place is anything like the one where I grew up, a few hours to the east, in the Berkshires, we'll have the first frost in a few weeks, and the insects will be hushed.

After nearly an hour of walking, Ava turns right down a steep drive. Though it's dark, I can see the shape of a house perched on the hill. Ava heads straight toward it, across the lawn, which is damp with dew. She mounts the stairs that lead to the front door boldly, and grins when the door opens.

"Good. He never has gotten in the habit of locking a door," she says. Her assurance that her husband won't freak out when he sees her here seems overly confident, in my opinion. No matter who your spouse is, they're going to be alarmed if you show up in the middle of the night when you're supposed to be in rehab. I wonder what sort of marriage this girl has.

Ava flicks on the light in her kitchen and goes straight to the fridge. She pulls out a bottle of white wine and dexterously proceeds to pop the cork out. She pours a few substantial glugs into a wineglass and raises her eyebrow at me.

"Want one?" she asks.

"Sure," I say. I'm not sure that I do, but I'm feeling all kinds of strange suddenly. I don't know this woman, yet here I am, breaking into her house and standing in her kitchen. Like wandering into a scene you weren't scripted to be in.

"Right. So, come on to the guest room. That's where I keep my 'project,' as Wyatt likes to call it."

"Does he know . . . your suspicions? What you've been working on?" I ask.

"Not exactly. Someone with a little more gumption would likely go snooping, but I'm not sure he really cares. He lacks the imagination to worry about it, I think. He thinks I'm interested in local back-to-the-land movements. He's also under the impression that I'm on a self-help binge. An obsession that he's fully willing to support, I might add." She laughs bitterly, and takes a deep sip from her glass. I follow her down the hall.

The guest room probably has a beautiful view in the daytime, but at night it just reflects your own image back to you in shadowy echoes. A large desk is strewn with books, sheets of paper, printouts, a scrap of newspaper here and there. In the middle sits a laptop.

"I hope it's not too pushy of me, but do you think I could just log in to my email really quick?" I ask, my fingers itching to tap in the keystrokes that will put me back in touch with my life.

"Ha. Yes, I'm sure you must be jonesing. Go for it—it's already connected to Wi-Fi. I'll be right back." She sets the glass of wine down on the desk and vanishes from the room. I eagerly plonk down in front of the laptop and pull up my Gmail.

I'm expecting a million messages, hopefully from Ryan, but there's just a random collection of spam and work things. Jessica has forwarded a few things on, but she clearly doesn't want me thinking about work. And as far as she knows, I won't be checking this for days. My dad has sent a cloying message expressing his support, trying to weasel his way back into the Olivia Industry in my moment of weakness, no doubt.

Frustrated, I log in to Instagram through the browser. Random DMs from fans (which I don't read), a couple hundred likes for the last photo I posted, which I don't fully remember ever taking. But nothing from the person I was hoping to hear from.

"There's a sleepy girl," Ava says behind me, and I momentarily think she's talking to me. When I whirl around, she's holding a toddler with a head of black curls.

"Hey there, beauty," she coos, and the little girl in her arms sleepily burrows into her shoulder. "Olivia, this is my daughter, Zora."

"Wasn't that your sister's name?" I ask.

"My sister was Zelda. I wanted their names to be similar but . . . I wanted her to have the chance to be her own person. Growing up a twin, I didn't always have that. And we have a thing with the letters in a name, in my family. She would have to be a *Z* or an *A*. Hence: Zora."

"Well, she's adorable."

"She's a little hellion. But she's my little hellion. I just wanted to hold her, for a bit. It's hard to leave her." Ava's voice softens, and she plants a kiss on the little girl's forehead. Her expression is fierce with some emotion, the only time I've seen her anything other than amusedly ironic. "Anyway. While you're on that laptop, you can pull up a few files. I put together a chronology of everything I've found so far and referenced which supporting documents will back it up."

"That sounds quite organized."

"I used to be an academic," she says, shrugging. "The file is called 'Seneca Girls.'"

I find it on her desktop, and begin scrolling.

• • •

Welcome to the second installment of Vultures! *We've had some really amazing responses to last week's episode, and I'll be going into that in a little bit. But first, just a little recap of everything we covered last week. And then we'll talk about all the questions we still have.*

Ava finally convinced me of her story when she showed me her research. I'd seen the body pulled from the water at the House of

Light, but the other deaths were all so strange, and the connections between them so peculiar, that I felt sure they were connected.

The first girl to die was named Allison Giordino. She died on the spring equinox, March twentieth of 2015. Witnesses saw her jump off of Ithaca Falls into the icy whirlpool below. She was dead by the time first responders arrived on scene, and her death was ruled a suicide. Traces of psilocybin—also known as magic mushrooms—were found in her system during the autopsy.

Shortly before her death, Allison had begun working at a non-profit organization that is directly affiliated with the House of Light, the Oikos Phaos Institute of Research. Allison was very young, just eighteen, and had started work at the Institute following some legal difficulties. I'll get into her past more deeply later, because, as you'll see, it's relevant.

The second woman to die was named Theia Nunez. Theia died in a fire that took place on September twenty-second, 2017, in the national forest just a few miles from the House of Light. Local officials at first claimed that a campfire got out of hand because of that summer's drought, and several acres of the forest burned in the space of just twenty minutes, while firefighters responded to the sudden outbreak. Theia was reported missing by her roommate when she didn't return home from a hike. Responders later located her remains in the forest, close to the heart of the fire. Investigators said there were signs of arson. Her death was ruled accidental.

Her roommate said that Theia had been acting strangely in the months before her death and had apparently "joined a cult" that was consuming all her time, causing her to leave her job in food service and disappear for weeks at a time. Though the roommate couldn't offer details about this alleged cult, she said Theia had shaved her head and had stopped taking her prescribed medication.

The third woman whose death appears linked to these other tragic fatalities was named Amy McNealy. Amy died on December twenty-first of 2018, the winter solstice. Anonymous hikers discovered the body of the twenty-eight-year-old woman in a sweat lodge. Because of the cold weather, it wasn't immediately clear how long she had been dead. She was, however, wearing some sort of horned headgear, and her body had been decorated in paint that was described as "ritualistic." An autopsy revealed that she had been dead for two days, having died of smoke inhalation after becoming unconscious due to dehydration. Her death was ruled accidental.

This sweat lodge is less than a mile away from the House of Light residences. A trail through the woods connects these cabins with the sweat lodge, suggesting that members knew of the lodge's existence and used it regularly.

She, too, had recently ingested psilocybin, as well as a significant amount of benzodiazepines.

I am, of course, waiting to hear details about the fourth woman. All I know right now is that she died on the autumn equinox and that her body was found in something like a Viking funeral boat on the shores of the Center where I have come for spiritual realignment. And I only know that much because I was there when they pulled her out of the water and I saw it myself.

At first glance, these deaths could be read as a tragic coincidence. There is a phenomenon that is often referred to as the Werther effect: people sometimes carry out copycat suicides after a highly visible (or closely personal) suicide. But there is obviously something suspicious about these similar circumstances. Is it just a simple ripple effect? Or is it possible that all these young women met someone at or through the House of Light? Someone who may have participated in their deaths?

. . .

I'm about to start opening the further documents when the baby gives a squawk behind me, and I jump.

"Jesus, Ava. What are you doing here?" a male voice drawls sleepily from the doorway. "And why did you wake Zo?"

"Sorry, darling," Ava says, in a tone of voice I haven't heard from her before. Conciliatory and not totally insincere but also not . . . fully believable. Like a talented actor who isn't bothering to give a good performance. "I made a friend at camp and she desperately needed to use the internet. You know how they are about cellphones and Web use at the Light."

I stand up and hasten to hold out a hand to shake, hoping to come across as rattled but grateful.

"I'm so sorry for barging in. Ava said it would be okay. . . . I'm having something of a family emergency, and not being able to get in touch with everyone, well, it's driven me a bit mad. I hope we didn't . . ." I trail off, since it's obvious that we did disturb him.

"Family emergency, hey? Well, Ava does have a bit of experience with those," he says, shooting her a cloudy glance. "Of course you're welcome to the internet. But I did think sneaking off-site was usually frowned on."

"Oh, come, you know how utterly ridiculous they are. Liv is just there for a bit of a break, like me. She's not there for Rain's brainwashing or spiritual hocus-pocus. I doubt she'll buy into the whole MLM kit and caboodle."

"Just needed to get away from my life, for a minute," I agree, with a helpless shrug.

"Right," he says. The baby, who has been calmly nestled into Ava's shoulder, squirms a bit.

"Where you go, Mama?" she says plaintively, getting fussy. Ava smooths her dark hair.

"Nowhere fun, baby. But it's important. Mama's head is funny."

"Please don't say stuff like that to her," Wyatt says gruffly. "She repeats those things, you know. To her teachers."

"Her teachers already know Mommy's a bit 'troubled.' Besides, no point in lying. My mother certainly tried to pretend everything was fine with her, and look how that went," Ava responds bitingly. "Let's go get a sippy cup from the kitchen," she continues. She picks up her own wineglass as she leaves the room. Wyatt stays in the doorway for a moment longer, looking at me.

"I am sorry for intruding," I say. For some reason, the character I've selected to play for this circumstance has a vaguely mid-Atlantic accent, Hepburn posture. Katharine, that is. Wyatt softens, as I hoped.

"It's not your fault she roped you in. I'll bet she didn't even tell you that she had a family?" There's a desperate quality in this last, bitter question.

"No, she did. She talks about you all the time. Especially . . . Zora."

"Well, I'm sure you've heard more about Zelda than about Zora. Or me. But I suppose that's just . . . how she was made."

I say nothing, but I do reach out and put my hand on his forearm. He looks startled, as though no one has touched him affectionately in a long time.

"I'll just go and see what they're up to in the kitchen. Take your time in here," he says, and ducks away.

I sit back down in front of the laptop and skim the document I was reading when Wyatt came downstairs, unsure of what to do with this slender suggestion of something fishy. It's not exactly conclusive, but I will admit that it's a bit odd. The combination of dates and the links with the House of Light do suggest something of a story. And that's all we really need, I muse. Get the podcast off the ground, get a decent batch of subscribers invested, some buzz, and if it's even moderately successful there could be a movie adaptation to follow. I'll be in a position to produce, if not necessarily guaranteed to star in it. It does have a sort of pretty logic to it. I wonder.

I flip through the documents that are stacked on the table, then shuffle them into a heap. Casting about for something to hold

them, I locate a tote bag from the public library and slip everything inside. I'll be able to sort through them at the House of
Light, I'm sure, and figure out if Ava's theory has teeth. I'm excited at the thought, like when I've read a script that I know I
want to take on.

Before I head to the kitchen, I poke around the room quickly.
It's impersonal, clearly just a guest room when Ava isn't using it
as her office. But hanging on the wall is a picture of two girls,
about twelve, identical and intense-looking. I'm not one hundred
percent sure, but I think the one on the left is Ava. The other, presumably, is Zelda.

I stroll down the hall, swishing the tote bag over my shoulder,
then pause before emerging into the light.

"I just don't know what you're getting out of these stays over
there," Wyatt is saying, irritably. "I mean, Dad gets you in the
door, which is already pretty tricky, but it's still not exactly cheap."

"I thought you couldn't put a price on my mental health."

"Well, the idea is to help you stay sober."

There is a meaningful pause. I think I hear the glug of more
wine being poured.

"The idea is to help me maintain some sort of chemical and
emotional balance while dealing with my grief. Which, in turn,
helps me manage my drinking."

"And how's that going?"

"Come now, Wyatt, you never used to be nasty. What's
changed?"

"I think you can answer that better than anyone," he snaps
back.

Ava clucks her tongue. "Someone's cranky."

"Someone was up most of the last few nights with the baby.
Who is now awake."

"I'm sorry I woke her up," Ava says, sounding like she wants to
make peace. "I just wanted to hold her for a minute. I don't know

if I'll be able to come back before my twenty-eight days are up, and I just, you know . . . wanted to smell the top of her head." The last words are muffled as she, presumably, nuzzles into the kid's firmed-up fontanelle. "I miss her. I miss you." There is another pregnant pause, and I strain, trying to hear what's going on.

"Well, we want you to come home. Squared away and happy."

"You know I always do. And I'm usually much better."

"Why do you think I put up with it?" he asks, seemingly assuaged. "Maybe next year don't disappear right in the middle of harvest, though, yeah? It's been insane around here."

I decide to emerge.

In the kitchen, the three of them are giving a good impression of a cozy family. Wyatt sits on a stool, and Ava stands between his knees. Their sleeping child is propped between them. Happy domesticity, a three-headed critter.

"Did you get what you needed?" Ava asks, taking another sip of wine.

"I did, thanks. Things are . . . okay at home. Not perfect, but they'll keep for another few days. Until I have my phone back."

"I'm really glad to hear it. There's nothing like family illness to really disrupt your life. I can't imagine trying to do the retreat when you're thinking about it," Ava says briskly. "Let's all go sit in the living room for a bit. Wyatt, do you think it's too early in the year for a fire?"

"It's not very cold," Wyatt says, frowning. "But I did already clean the chimney, and there are a few logs on the ring outside. Getting ready for the frost, and all. Do you want me to light one?"

"Yes, let's. We have an hour or two to kill before we head back, and I love the idea of sitting by the fire, even if it is too warm. Liv, come plonk down next to me on the couch."

I follow her into the living room, and she points to a couch facing a floor-to-ceiling window. I again assume that the lake is there, in the dark, somewhere beyond the deck. As I nestle into the cushions, she hands me the kid. Zora comes to me willingly enough, and, surprised, I let her settle into my arms.

"Hold her for a sec, will you? I want to open another bottle to breathe," Ava says, whisking back to the kitchen. I hear her rustling around, then the slippery *thonk* of a cork being pulled out. "I want to see how last year's cab sauv is coming along, and it will pair well with the fire."

"You said this is a vineyard. Did you make the wine yourself?" I ask.

"Yes, our little plantation is limping along. It's been in a bit of a decline for years, so turning it around has been something of a project. But I think the wine's improving. We've hired a fairly talented winemaker, which helps a lot. And at least there's someone moderately sober kicking around. Which has not always been the case."

"Running a vineyard seems like a risky choice for an alcoholic," I say.

Wyatt comes inside with the wood as I'm finishing this thought, and I immediately regret voicing it. He snorts. So does Ava.

"That, or a considerable advantage. And a cost-saving measure." She grins, sitting in a chair next to me to watch her husband light the fire. His shoulders are very broad. She seems entranced by the flame, and I think uncomfortably of the girl who burned alive. "In any case, we're very happy, aren't we, Wyatt?"

We sit in the living room, chatting, for more than an hour. I sip the wine, which is okay, I guess. Ava wrinkles her nose at it but pronounces it an improvement on last year's vintage. Wyatt asks polite questions of me, and I can see that he likes me, is interested in me. I make a point to soften myself out, in contrast to his pointy wife. Zora falls fast asleep in my lap, which is utterly endearing, and I fall quite in love with her after thirty minutes of this.

"She's very easy to enjoy when she's like this," Ava says, chuckling. "Less so when she's having a meltdown at the grocery store. Not that we go to town that often. I'm a bit of a shut-in." The wine is finally drunk, and we're all quite sleepy. Wyatt announces that he's headed back to bed to get a couple hours of sleep before he has to be up and out in the fields, and I hand Ava her daughter, who curls familiarly on her chest, as though she wants to burrow inside her mother's rib cage. We watch the fire burning down.

"Your research is pretty interesting," I say when I'm certain Wyatt is upstairs and out of earshot.

"I think so. I do have a tendency to spin a yarn when there's not much there to substantiate it," she admits, "but I do think there's something there. It's just too odd when you look at how they're all connected, in some way. The House of Light connection . . ."

"And the dates, I guess? The fact that they all take place on the solstice? Or, I guess, equinox?"

"Basically, yeah. It could be a coincidence, but it's a fucking weird one," Ava says with an overly casual shrug. She needs me to believe her. Though she's been downplaying all these details, tossing them out offhandedly, I know she's taut with desire for me to buy in.

"Especially with all the focus on nature at the House of Light. And astrology. And the rhythms of the sun and all," I say.

"And you haven't even been at the House of Light for magic mushroom day," Ava replies with a grin.

. . .

Do you worry about getting enough probiotics and vitamins in your daily diet? Worried that your holistic well-being isn't being totally supported by the food you eat? As someone whose work depends on clear skin and a balanced appetite, I'm always looking for ways to regulate my pH and my gut health. That's why Glow supplements have become completely essential to my daily routine: they make sure that I roll out of bed camera-ready. Make sure you're doing everything you can to promote balance and that healthy glow that only comes from inside with Glow, the supplement that lights up your life. Get the first month free with promo code "vultures" at www.glowfrominside.com.

· · ·

We watch the sun coming up as we trudge back to the Center. I'm getting used to this whole sunrise jazz. I'm sleepy, and the wine has made me slushy, but we sober up as we walk, and I rather enjoy the alert but dreamy state. Ava isn't super chatty, but I don't mind that, either.

We lurk in the ditch once we've arrived back at the Center, waiting for Devotion to come around the path and unlock the door. The timing is tight, but at Ava's signal, we both dash for the door, and we bump into Tia and the petite girl in the hall. We walk with them to group, and I feel very pleased with our subterfuge.

Group Work is hard to sit through this morning. My fatigue hits me the minute everyone starts talking, and somehow the green tea just isn't doing it, caffeine-wise. Stifling yawns, I manage to keep my eyelids propped open, but I am not especially present, a fact Rain calls me out on about halfway through.

"Olivia, you seem like maybe you're not fully here for Janelle right now," she says sternly. "Is there something else you're focusing on?"

"No, I think I'm just finding some of what Janelle's saying triggering, and it's hard for me to hear," I answer. This typically is a good strategy for Group Work, and though Rain doesn't look convinced, she lets me be and I manage to make it through the session.

Floating down the hall afterward, all I can think of is sleep, but Ava elbows me in the ribs.

"We'll need to make a plan for how to move forward," she

murmurs. "Try to be next to me when we do Earth Work later today?"

I yawn in response and nod. I need a nap before I can contemplate further skullduggery.

I hit my pillow hard and sleep for a couple hours.

Before lunch, I spread out the documents I've brought from Ava's house on my floor. Then, nervous about someone walking in, I prop a chair in front of the door. She has a folder for each of the three women she's been looking at and, on top of everything, a list of the documents in each file.

Ava has clearly compiled a fair bit of documentation to back up these claims, and what I'm able to flip through in these files supports her theory so far.

As I'm shuffling through the pages, something bold stands out.

. . .

Soon after we began researching these deaths, we noticed another pattern, however. One that was in some ways even more basic than the weird dates and the affiliations with this organization. Something that should have been more apparent, maybe.

I wonder if anyone out there has guessed what we missed at first? Tweet @oliviascreed, or comment on the Reddit thread.

. . .

Flushed with my fresh insight, I spring through the door to head to Earth Work. We've been promised an afternoon of digging irrigation trenches, and while this doesn't excite me, I do want to bounce my ideas off Ava. I rush down the steps to the garden.

Everyone is already congregated there, a hush settled over the group. Apparently, I'm late and I've missed something. Ava shoots me a glance before looking back at Rain, who stands before us, barefoot and downcast.

"I am very sorry to have to be the one to tell you all such devastating news," Rain is saying. "We all knew that Hannah was troubled while she was here. But we need to accept that her suffering has ended, and that she died with dignity and bravery. We will grieve her passing, but we must also admire her conviction. Her desire to always keep working to be better."

I sidle close to Ava, who mumbles, sotto voce: "It's official. Her name is Hannah, and she was here at the Light for a good chunk of last year. And surprise, surprise. Her death has been ruled a suicide."

"I see," I whisper back.

"We will be observing an afternoon meditation in her honor, on the sundeck, instead of Earth Work today. If any of those who practiced with her need to speak with any of us, please seek us out. We are all looking for ways to remember and mourn her with grace." Rain bows her head, and I can read real heaviness in her shoulders. Whatever her pious mumbo jumbo, she feels the weight of this girl's death. "Please join me on the sundeck when you feel able, and we'll reflect on the transience of life as we watch the afternoon fade."

Robin, the fragile girl, breaks down sobbing, and one of the oatmeal-clad acolytes holds her, stroking the line between her shoulder blades.

"But she was always so strong!" Robin wails.

Ava peels away from the group.

"Did you know her?" I ask.

"We overlapped for a few days during my second retreat," she answers. "But no, I wouldn't say I actually knew her. She was on her way out, supposedly cured. Honestly, she seemed pretty stable. But who knows what her life was like on the outside." Ava shrugs, callous.

"Or who she might have been in touch with after she left," I say.

Ava glances at me, trying to get a read on my tone. "Interesting. Does that mean you've been considering that my theory . . .

might hold water?" she asks. I can tell she's anxious but trying to hide it.

"That's an interesting way of phrasing it," I say coyly. "Water. Did anyone say what the cause of death was?"

"It's a little macabre, actually," Ava says. "She, er, strangled."

"Wait, what? How?"

"I guess she rigged a sort of noose to the prow of the boat and sort of . . . tightened it until she passed out. Then I guess she eventually, well, died."

"Jesus. How long does that take?"

"Unsurprisingly, no one has really gone into those details with us," Ava says.

"But surely that's not exactly a common way to commit suicide?"

"Oh, people do it. Bedsheets, prison. That sort of thing. But no, I imagine it's not the easiest way to go."

"Couldn't someone else have done it to her?" I ask.

"One imagines. But that's not what they're saying. Again, unsurprisingly."

"Fuck me." I pause to reflect. I can't even begin to imagine how someone would go about such a venture. It's not something I've really explored, even in the misery of my teens.

"Listen, something occurred to me while I was looking through your notes," I say. "Another thing that links all the deaths together."

"Oh?" Ava looks immediately intrigued.

"Haven't you noticed something else that seems a little weird about all the deaths? Aside from the pagan importance of their dates?" I needle.

"And their affiliations with the House of Light, I presume?"

"Yes, something else that's rather pagan," I tease.

• • •

Good work, fellow sleuths! Clearly some of you are a bit sharper than we were, at least immediately. Yes, the circumstances of each of the four deaths all do share something that, when paired with the dates, starts to take on a rather strange significance.

Allison died by drowning. Theia died in a fire. Amy died of smoke inhalation. And Hannah strangled while out on a lake.

Each death shares something . . . well, you might say "elemental." Fire, water, and air.

Which made us wonder: How would you die from the fourth element? How on earth?

CHAPTER 8

I can't say I was exactly meditating during our memorial meditation for Hannah. Caught up in the flush of hypothesizing, I was too busy thinking about how these four women were connected, how they could have met such strange ends. The phrase "ritual killings" kept flashing through my mind, like some earworm picked up from a bad late-night crime show. But how else to explain it? All four women find themselves connected to a back-to-the-earth cult-adjacent group, and then all four die, ostensibly by their own hand, on a significant date and with natural elements as a cause of death. Surely coincidence is out of the question?

I'll admit: any thoughts I had of Hannah were not, I'm afraid, about her as a human being. I didn't think of the torment she must have been going through as the end of her life neared. I didn't think about her parents, her friends, her cats waiting for her in an apartment. I wondered only if she would be found to have ingested psilocybin, whether she had been seen with any members of the Light in the days before her death, whether there was any evidence of a struggle that had been concealed.

I went to bed with these thoughts, and fixated on one thing: tomorrow I would get my phone back.

• • •

I leap out of bed the following morning ready to fucking eat the day. It's a feeling I recognize from certain months working on *Iroquois Falls:* entire weeks when I would pass every waking moment in a detached state of fixation, days on end when I, Olivia Reed, almost ceased to exist. Where I was just Mina, hurtling around and trying to root out the evil that seeped into the ground around her, to discover her best friend's killer, ever the precocious teenage gumshoe. The self-annihilation of obsession fuels me. I'm giddy with anticipation at the idea of getting my phone back, of being able to google things. Of being able to ring Jess and talk through my plan, my idea for the investigation and the podcast. She'll be essential, after all.

When the doors open, shortly after sunrise, I bound down the hall toward Rain's office. The door is locked, but after several taps, I'm permitted entry to the holy sanctum of this gloriously weird joint. I can't help glancing at the door to Rain's secret shrine when I enter. She grins at me with that toothy look of hers, the lines around her eyes cracking. She is genuinely happy to see me.

"Good morning, Olivia. I see you're good and ready to start the day. Would you like to schedule time in the Chamber?"

"The what?" I balk, thrown. Rain's smile widens, as though she knows how strange it sounds and thinks it's hilarious.

"The sensory deprivation chamber. We like everyone to spend some time in it during their first week here. It's a bit intense, so we wait a couple of days after Intake. But it can be very . . . clarifying."

"Er . . ." I mumble. I don't especially relish the idea of being trapped in a sightless, soundless tank by the people I suspect are involved in four murders. But I hadn't particularly wanted to film in the freezing cold water tank at the end of the last season, especially as things grew tense with my director. Nevertheless, I'd done it. And been nominated for a People's Choice Award. "Sure," I say with a shrug.

"Super-duper! Let me just see when we have an opening . . . tomorrow, after lunch?"

"I think I've probably got a gap in my schedule," I answer.

Rain gives me that wild grin again. She must know it's unsettling; her whole demeanor is calculated to disrupt, to unnerve. I've got to say, it's a disarming management style. If I ever get to direct something, I'll try to remember it.

"I think Community Work is just starting," she prompts, all business again. "Devotion won't like if you're late."

"Actually, there was the one other thing . . ."

"Yes?"

"It's been five days. I was hoping to get my phone back?" I suggest gently.

"Ah," says Rain. She leans back in her chair, her sense of humor entirely gone, her expression icy. Beneath the desk I can see her bare feet. "Well, I'm interested that you brought that up. Since, of course, it hasn't even been two days without contact to the outer world. For you, I mean."

"I'm pretty sure it has been. I got here five nights ago so . . ."

"Yes, but you checked your social accounts about twenty-four hours ago."

"What," I enunciate slowly, "are you talking about?" Sure . . . but how would she know?

"I understand the need for a little rebellion. This . . . environment isn't natural at first, and I know it takes some adjustment. Still, we do have the detoxifying period in place for a reason. You'll have to trust me on that."

I don't say anything. However Rain knows it, she knows that I left.

"Was that all you wanted to talk about?" she asks.

"Look," I say. "I understand the policy, but you have to understand. I'm something of a public figure, and it's next to impossible for me to just disconnect completely. I need to be able to stay on top of my responsibilities—"

"Your manager assured us that she would deal with all of that while you completed your Intake. Don't you trust her?"

"You don't know anything about me and Jessica," I bristle, surprising myself. "That's beside the point, in any case."

"Ah. I see. You must have a complicated relationship, sharing, as you do, one career."

"That's not how I would put it."

"How would you put it?"

"Jessica . . . orbits my career," I say, unintentionally lofty.

"She also helps make your career, though. Would it be fair to say that you wouldn't have the career you do without her work, her labor?"

"Well, shit, then you may as well give credit to my clinging father for nudging me into this business. And my mother for the shit she pulled. And every director who's given me a part, and every goddamn intern who's brought me a coffee in my trailer—"

"And? Do you give them credit?"

"This is so entirely not the point!" I cry, frustrated. "Why are we divvying up my achievements?"

"Perhaps to lessen them. Perhaps so that you don't feel as burdened by your successes—and failures—and can find a way to see yourself without them, to see the world without the lens of your fame and ambition, your flaws and your thirst. You can't locate your soul when your ego is clamoring so loudly. Let me help you break it down, dismantle it. Let your inner child speak, rather than your underself."

"Thanks, that is utterly meaningless," I snap, and turn on my heel.

"I'll see you tomorrow for your appointment in the Chamber," Rain calls, unruffled, as I leave.

Only after I've shut the door do I realize that I still don't have my phone, and that I didn't even extract a promise for when it might be returned to me. I begin to reflect that I'm not here to address my exhaustion, or my reliance on pills; maybe this whole process is about how I cede control, let others call the shots.

After Community Work, Ava commiserates.

"They don't ever give your phone back after a few days," she says, patting my shoulder in consolation. "At best, they use it as incentive for the first two weeks you're here. 'If you speak more in group' or 'If you find a quiet space for yourself during Body Work, you can have it back.' That's always how it goes."

"But I need to use it! We need to look into Hannah, see if she has any social connections with the other three," I hiss, glancing around for Devotion.

"Well, it wouldn't even matter if you had your phone for that. There's no Wi-Fi or cell signal here. You have to get all the way up to the road before you can even check email."

"How are we supposed to do research?"

"The old-fashioned way, I guess. Ask questions, look around."

"And how did Rain even know that I'd checked my email and Insta?" I ask.

Ava pauses, then shrugs. "Honestly, my guess is that she was bluffing. She assumes that everyone tries to sneak a little internet."

"You don't think she maybe knows about our nocturnal field trip?"

"How would she?" Ava counters.

"Surveillance? Cameras?" I suggest.

Ava frowns. "Possible, I suppose. I'd be a little surprised, though." We'd reached the end of the corridor, and we were meant to be headed to our rooms to change for a kayak session on the lake. Devotion was out of sight, but I could sense her wordless presence lurking around the corner, ready to silently prod us along the cattle route of our day. I was beginning to chafe at the structure and repetition of these days.

"What's the next step, then? How do we find out more about Hannah?"

"Like I said," Ava answers breezily. "Ears to the ground, Sparky."

. . .

I shuffle down to the boathouse, exasperated by the morning's shortcomings. Hard to get excited about another wholesome group activity and yet another phatic drone about the serenity of nature. I crave an Adderall. And, for that matter, French fries and a good roll in the hay. All this clean living is fucking exhausting.

My mood brightens when I see Dawn at the boathouse. He's wearing drawstring shorts and a light sweatshirt, unzipped, with nothing underneath, exposing the concave tip of his belly. Mmmm. I saunter over to flirt, but the whole mass of Lightlings descend down the rocky beach at the same time, and we're immediately caught up in donning life jackets and locating oars for the plastic hulls we're about to set out in.

It's a warm day, and the musty smell of the jackets mixes with sweat as we clamber into the kayaks. There are only seven, so just half the contingent loads up; the other half stays behind, making cairns out of the flat shale rocks that line the shallow beach. Ava, crouched, is stacking stones into precarious pylons just at the water's edge as we wobblingly push off and paddle toward the center of the lake.

I pick up my pace to keep up with Dawn, who, as a confident oarsman, is easing out in front of us, leading his little crew of rehab patients like a mommy duck with her clumsy ducklings just behind. Disappointingly, he turns us away from the crime scene, tacking vaguely south as we seek the center of the lake. I have no doubt we'll be subjected to some tortuous metaphors about depth and centers and profundity and stillness when we get there, so I resolve to speak to Dawn before we do.

He seems to sense my attempts to keep up with him and playfully jerks ahead of me every time I get near. I'm sweaty and my shoulders are aching when he finally lets me catch him, the others several kayak lengths behind.

"Good morning, Miss Liv," he says, not in the least winded.

"Oh, hi," I respond.

"Feeling competitive today?"

"Every day," I answer, and he laughs. I like his laugh immensely.

"I like that about you." We ease into a comfortable pace, just a few feet apart as our oars dip into the blue-green water.

"Well?" he says after a few moments. "What's on your mind?"

"Probably the same thing that's on everyone's," I say, realizing that it's likely true. Ava and I are probably not the only people consumed with the morbid goings-on of the past few days.

"Hannah, you mean," Dawn confirms.

"It just seems . . . well, not altogether encouraging," I say. "We're all here to . . . get better. Find ourselves. And either Hannah didn't manage to, or she succeeded all too well. And didn't like what she found."

"Ah." Dawn takes a deep breath. "Do you think that's what happened to her? That she went soul-seeking and couldn't face her shadow self?"

"Well, no one likes their shadow self. It's what we spend our whole lives avoiding, right?"

"But also confronting."

"And trying to vanquish?" I ask.

"No, I don't think one can," Dawn responds. "We're not meant to vanquish it, just learn to let it . . . be. To exist. To not consume us."

"Doesn't seem to have worked for her."

"Don't make the mistake of thinking you know everything about Hannah," Dawn says sharply, in a tone of voice I haven't yet heard from him. "The picture you see isn't necessarily whole, Liv."

"Okay, what am I missing?"

Dawn looks at me quickly, assessing my interest. I adopt a fretful, self-concerned expression. I want him to think that I am worried only about myself, what will happen to me at the end of this quack journey. Shouldn't be too hard to convince him; I'm an actress, after all, the most self-obsessed of all creatures.

"Her path isn't yours, Liv. Hannah achieved something extraordinary while she was here. She found a true calling, and pursued it, with her whole spirit."

"What the fuck are you talking about?"

"Though I abhor that it ended in her death, I can only admire the single-mindedness with which she sought the truth. She was brave, and unflinching. In the end, I think maybe she did even have a measure of peace."

"I say again, what the fuck? She committed suicide. She strangled herself, Dawn." He flinches when I say his name.

"That may be. But not because of her inner journey."

"Um . . . what else would cause her to take her own life?" I ask, flummoxed. "Are you saying . . . there were other people involved? Were you there?"

"I'm saying, sweet Liv, that everyone's path is different. I doubt that you will be called to venture into the dark places that Hannah explored. I don't think that's where your gift will take you. You are a creature of light—you are meant to bring art and joy and beauty to this world." Dawn stops his kayak and turns toward me. "Look at your face—you can tell just by looking at you. Don't dwell on the darkness that Hannah found. I don't think it will come looking for you." He reaches out and cups my cheek, looking into my eyes for a moment with a beseeching intensity so forceful I almost want to obey. Then he breaks his gaze and swings his kayak around to face the others, who have just caught up to us.

"Well, my fellow seekers. This is the deepest point of Seneca Lake. At six hundred and eighteen feet, it's one of the deepest bodies of fresh water anywhere. I'd like to sit and be in this spot for a few moments—as long as the sun allows it—for us to contemplate the stillness beneath us . . ."

After dinner, I find myself sneaking from the kitchen, where we all did the dishes, to prowl the halls. An uneasiness has settled over everyone; I can feel it in the pauses of Tia and Jon's conversation, and I think I can even read it in the cast of Devotion's shoulders. Everyone is tight, disrupted.

Ava spent dinner with her big eyes following everyone, spookily silent. The girl does not seem to have an instinct to blend in, to go unnoticed; she doesn't seem to mind if she chafes against everyone, rubs them the wrong way. In compensation, I find myself super-engaging, active-listening with my whole body whenever anyone speaks.

Robin mentioned Hannah's name once, and Tia, who also seems terrifically fragile, burst into tears and fled the dining room before we'd even lapped up all our macrobiotic gruel.

I'd like to pretend that it's some gumshoe desire to get answers that has me skulking down the hallway, listening intently for the pitter-patter of Devotion's feet or the rasp of Rain's hardened soles against the pine floors. But, fittingly for rehab, it is pure addiction that has me panting through the dimming light.

I need my fucking phone.

There's only one place that it can feasibly be: Rain's office. Every other corner of this place is open-plan, all transparency and tidy corners. (Of course, when you have a constant crop of manual laborers depending on menial chores for their own personal salvation, griminess would be strange, if not inexcusable.)

After dinner is one of the unstructured moments of the day, a brief window of free time before we do our Savasanas together in the group room. Then lockdown. My absence might be noted in the kitchen, but I'm sure I can concoct some plausible excuse for my absence now. Like: all this fucking green juice is wreaking havoc on my colon.

Rain's door is unlocked—indeed, a quick inspection of the door makes it evident that her door can't lock. How odd. Why lock up the inpatients and not lock any of the other doors? Just to show us they can, I suppose.

The office is spotless, as usual. Nothing sits on Rain's desk, which is little more than a slab of wood. Aside from a few chairs, and some plants by the window, there is basically no furniture in the whole room. Like Rain herself, the aesthetic principle seems to be one of overwhelming austerity.

I stalk immediately to the hidden meditation nook I discovered earlier and gingerly poke my head inside. Thankfully, it's empty. Again I pull up the velvet curtain that hides the face of the guru and look at his strange eyes, feeling, in spite of myself, entranced. Why doesn't anyone ever talk about him, even mention him? You'd think if they'd found their savior, the House of Light might want to go and spread the good word. Why the secrecy?

The nook is as empty as the rest of the office, though: clearly no cubbyhole for confiscated electronics. I back out and creep over to Rain's desk, where I peer under and around the edges, looking for drawers, boxes, anything. There's a peg on one side of the desk, and from it dangles a leather thong with a key. But there's nothing to open with it.

I find what I'm looking for after running my hands against the walls for a few moments. Behind Rain's desk is a small cutout. After I've given it a gentle push, a segment of the wall pops open with a click. I flinch at the noise, but glory at my sleuth work. A custom-made safe. The key opens the door and voilà!

The safe is divided into twelve different cubbies, all big enough to fit an iPad and a phone and not much more. The cubbies are labeled according to room, and I find mine swiftly enough. Though I'm tempted to take my iPad, too, I realize there's no point. All I need is my phone. For now.

Before relocking the safe, I pause, wanting to look in Ava's cubby. I don't know the name of her room, though. I could pull out the contents of each of these slots to inspect the gadgets of my fellow inmates, but what would these chilly slabs of aluminum and plastic tell me?

I lock up, replace the key, and move toward the door. Ava said there was no reception here, but I power up my phone (not dead, thank God) and confirm the total lack of bars, just in case. No surprises, however. Dead zone.

A door creaks, and I freeze in place. I'm incredibly exposed: Rain's desk won't conceal me even if I hide under it. My breath becomes shallow and nervous. I could just lie and say I was looking for Rain. Would anyone believe me? And, of course, there's my phone. I slide it into the elastic of my underwear and lunge for the meditation nook, tugging the velvet curtains shut just as I hear the door click open.

From beneath the curtains, which hover just a few inches off the ground, I can see Rain's bare, cracked feet crossing the floor of her office to her desk. As soundlessly as I can, I sit upright, my back against the wall, not wanting her to see a sliver of my face glued to the ground. She moves so motionlessly I can't tell where she is in the room, and all I can do is strain to hear the shuffle of papers. Or the sound that the curtains will make when they are abruptly pulled back.

The side of one foot becomes visible, pausing just outside the nook. I wait for her long fingers to snag the velvet, but instead I can see her toes curl and then flex as she cracks her big toe. I hear her deep breath, and then her toes are gone, a flash of dirty sole. The door closes.

I wait thirty seconds, plucking up my courage to vacate the safety of the meditation nook before swiftly crossing the office floor. I check the hall before slipping out into it.

I make it to the Community Room just in time for our evening poses and settle into the guided meditation with the rest of my cohort. There's an alarming moment during down dog when the instructor uses her flattened palms to change the angle of my spine and the dip of my pelvis; I'm sure she'll brush against the contraband in my skivvies, but she doesn't, and I biddably tilt my womb toward the sky. Afterward, when the sun is set, we all stroll back to our rooms for our evening confinement. Ava catches my eye, looking curious, as though she can sense, catlike, the aura of mischief wafting off me. But I just smile blankly and head to my room, eager for lights-out and the deep silence of dark to settle over the House of Light.

Around moonrise-ish, I crawl from my bed and poke my head out onto the deck. I don't hear Ava out there, and from what I can see, her terrace is empty, so I proceed with my plan. I've nicked some yoga straps from the Community Room, and I slipknot them to the banister. Lowering myself down, I pray that I'll have enough upper-body strength to hoist myself back the way I came. If not, I'll have to stay out all night.

On the ground, I feel the exhilaration of the late-night trouble-maker. I dash as quickly as I dare along the rear of the building, watching my steps carefully so I don't tumble over the cliff just to my right. The whole building is dark, but, to my alarm, the light at the farthest corner of the building flips on just as I'm about to curve around the side. It's at least eight feet above me, and I'm protected by almost complete darkness, but I still freeze, panting.

It's Rain's nook, and I can see her above me, wearing her color-less, flaxen garb. She flings back the curtain on the portrait in her office and kneels in front of it. I wait, expecting her to take up a more comfortable meditation pose, but she remains crouched, her knees on the hard wooden floor. She reaches out to stroke the portrait, and her shoulders begin to shake. Is she crying? She is saying something and shaking her head and I can't really tell from here but is it, maybe, "I'm sorry"?

Leaving her to her . . . whatever, I break into a comfortable speed walk to climb the hill to the road. I keep to the edge of the dirt driveway, knowing I'll be less visible near the tree line. Finally, I arrive up by the road. Daring to illuminate my screen, I open my phone. And lo: three bars.

With something of the relief of a smoker preparing to light up after a long flight, I collapse into the tall grass off the shoulder of the road and sink into my phone.

. . .

Thank God for Instagram. How on earth did people look into things before the glitzy cobweb of social media? In just thirty minutes with my phone, I know more about the last two years of Hannah's life than I'd be able to glean from days of conversation with her friends and family. At least, I know more about how she wanted her life to look.

Her handle is easy to find. Though there are lots of Hannahs kicking around out there, the algorithm that suggests her to me is ruthlessly efficient, and when the third profile I click on has a photo of the Light on the grid, I know I've found my girl.

For the first time, I see her face. She's young and white and pretty (of course), and as you move backward through her grid, she grows a bit plumper; clearly she's been losing weight. She's posted only one thing in the last two months: a trail through a pine forest, filtered to look otherworldly. At the very bottom of the frame a boot is visible—hers? It's captioned: "Our path is un-known but will reveal itself when we're ready." As I scroll back through her photos, most of the images are of trees, water, snow-covered fields. All pretty generic, but she does have an eye. In her earlier posts, there are more selfies, as well as a handful of photos of her with friends, or at least other people. I zero in on these pictures, scanning them for faces I know.

In particular, I look for Allison, Theia, or Amy. I pull up Google images of their faces to reference. Finally, I think I've found some-thing.

. . .

It's a strange idea that the pieces of a case all hinge on a handful of photos and a few attenuated digital threads, right? Look at how many crimes are being solved by people with free time and some decent broadband. Whether it's distinctive traffic lights in Montreal or missing cuff links tracked through eBay, the whole world is now legible—and solvable—through a screen.

Hannah, as it turned out, was the first I was able to do a deep dive on. And it was only because she documented her whole life, prodigiously, on social media, at least until the last couple of months of her life, when she seemed to slowly fade off-line.

One of Hannah's older photos was of her here, at the House of Light. In the picture, she stands smiling on the lawn where we eat dinners when the weather is decent. Behind her is the picnic table, set with dishes and a colorful tablecloth. There are just six people in the photograph, which suggests that this photo wasn't taken while Hannah was a client at the Light; this is a more intimate setting, possibly between friends. I recognize two of the people in the photo from my time here at the Light: Rain and Devotion. With them is Allison, just a few weeks before her death. There's a woman I don't recognize, but she's tagged in the photo, and this is one of the first threads I'm able to pull on. To speak to someone who knew Hannah and Allison both. And the last person in the photo, a man with very blue eyes, is someone I think connects these dead girls. In fact, I'm still looking for him.

. . .

A car drives by the shoulder where I'm sitting, and I'm jolted out of my single-minded contemplation of the screen in front of me. My battery is running low, and there are a few other things I want to get started on first.

I open up Voice Memos and drone into the microphone for a few minutes. When I've recorded what I think will be the first episode of a podcast, I save it. Then, impulsively, I send it to Jessica with the subject line COMEBACK. WHAT DO YOU THINK?

It's time to creep back to my room so I can sleep for a couple of hours before sunrise. I'm blinded from my screen time, and I pick my way back down the driveway carefully, not wanting to go ass over teakettle into the gravel.

As I approach the building, a movement to my left catches my eye. I quickly bolt behind a tree, heart hammering. After a long breath, I peer out, and look into a clearing in the trees. We walked through it with Dawn the other day, when it was light and filled with the last of the summer's wildflowers, all goldenrod and milkweed. Here, in the dark, the vibe is very different.

In the center of the clearing is a circle of maybe ten people, seated on the ground. They all wear light colors, and I imagine these are the same rough-spun costumes worn by most everyone who works here. It is so quiet that I'm surprised no one heard the crunch of gravel as I walked by.

A loud retching sound interrupts the stillness, and I squint, trying to figure out its source. In the middle of the circle, I can make out a small figure, crouched over on her hands and knees. She (and I'm reasonably sure it's a she) has her back curved violently and seems to be vomiting. This goes on for a painfully long time, at least two minutes, her whole body convulsing, racked with the process of emptying itself out. No one in the circle flinches or goes over to comfort her. Her throat sounds raw, her breathing in between each convulsion desperate.

Finally, the retching subsides, and the small figure shivers, collapsing prone on the ground. After a long pause, she stands; even in the dark, I'm fairly sure it's Robin. She is shaking a little, but she tilts her head up to the sky, arms outstretched.

Four people get up from the circle and approach her, and I assume they're going to help her, give her water, carry her to a warm room. Instead, they crouch down at her feet and appear to be scratching at the dirt. Simultaneously, they stand, hands cupped, and walk in four opposite directions, away from one another. They stop in unison, bend down, and begin to dig in the dirt. They're burying Robin's vomit. I shiver.

One of the buriers has walked in my direction and is now maybe just thirty feet away. It's Devotion, and I'm suddenly not feeling mischievous and brave anymore. I don't want to be out here. After she has covered her grim little offering with dirt, she scans the trees where I stand, and I am afraid to move at all. Does she see me?

But she turns to walk back to the circle, and though part of me wants to see the rest of this strange ritual, I want to be safe in my bed even more. I creep slowly backward, and only once I'm several yards away do I turn around and race back to my room, my heart a-skitter. In my amped-up state, the yoga bands prove no difficulty, and I haul myself up onto my balcony with surprising ease, if no particular grace. In my bed, I reassure myself that what I saw was no stranger than most of the activities I participated in at an all-female wellness retreat in Sedona. But something has me spooked.

And, sometime before I finally fall asleep, I remember that I still have my phone, and that my cubby in Rain's office will be short half its contents should anyone happen to look inside. I settle into sleep uneasily, feeling as though the walls around me are watching.

CHAPTER 9

I'm disoriented when I wake up, not remembering where I am in the light just before dawn. I roll over and reach for Jess, half-expecting her to be there in the bed with me, waiting for me to get up. Sometimes, I'll roll over and find her still asleep, a hank of my hair in her mouth, like a dozing toddler—one of those moments when she lets her guard down, and I see that she needs me, too. Long discussions of our futures, of our grand designs, would keep us whispering late into the night, and eventually we would slide into sleep together. We have awakened to find our fingers looped, as though we were afraid to lose each other in the night. I could look at her mouth, pursed in worried dreams, and know that she wouldn't leave me, ever.

But Jess is not here, and I flop over in my lonely bed before the clench of anxiety seizes me, remembering where I am and what I saw last night. I flail around for my phone, checking it out of habit, knowing there will be no reception but needing the consolation of its synthetic light nonetheless.

I crawl from bed and dress with none of the whimsy of the earlier days. I don't want a frolicsome kimono or a fluttering caftan with leggings beneath, in a concession to the chill of the day. I need a costume of strength and flexibility. The sort of thing I can run in.

I feel better with the snug of my yoga pants hitched up around my midriff, the hang of an oversized sweatshirt shielding my angles from view. Sneakers on, I wait for the doors to open. Unsure of what to do with my phone, I slide it into my waistband, hoping to opportunistically slip it back.

The first order of business today is to find Ava and tell her about Hannah's circle of overlapping friends, ask her if she recognizes any of the people in the photos I've saved to my phone. With any luck, she'll be able to connect some missing pieces.

I wait in front of her door so that we can walk to the Community Room together. She startles at the sight of me lurking in her doorway.

"Eager beaver this morning, are we, Liv?" she asks. She looks like she hasn't slept well. Surely she wasn't up into the small hours for a late-night cabal?

"Did something keep you up last night?" I ask innocently.

Her face gives nothing away, but I am, suddenly, reluctant to trust her. "Just bad dreams. And the constant, low-grade anxiety that comes from drying out," she says with a shrug. "Jesus, the sweats alone are enough to keep one clammily thrashing about all night. I hate this shit."

"And yet you come here voluntarily."

"What is going on with you today? You seem like you're in a weird mood."

"Guess I had bad dreams, too," I say. "Probably just part of the fun of detox."

"Look, I talked to Robin about Hannah," Ava says. "She was—"

"When? When did you talk to her?" I interrupt.

"Umm, last night? After dinner? Why?"

"No reason, just . . . Anyway, did she say anything interesting?"

"Only that Hannah didn't seem all that unhappy or unstable. She was a pretty committed believer in the Light and called everyone here her 'family.' Robin said it didn't make sense that she would just fall out of touch with everyone and go off on a downward spiral," Ava explains.

"Well, true believers are necessarily not the most balanced of individuals," I point out. "And I'm not sure Robin's analysis is necessarily . . . the most reliable."

"Why would you say that?" We've reached the Community Room, even in spite of our dawdling.

"She just doesn't seem . . . well. She seems sort of caught up in the whole 'Light narrative.' If you know what I mean," I say. I'm not sure I want to tell Ava about what I saw. The window for doing so will close almost immediately. And here in the morning, it feels less sinister, more silly. Dawn and Devotion come into the room, trailed by a slight young man with a shaved head.

"Good morning, everyone, let's get going on Community Work. I'd like you to welcome Andrew to our group today. He's on his way to complete his Intake. Okay, let's—"

"Where's Robin?" I interrupt. Andrew has seated himself in her place. Dawn glances at Devotion.

"Robin has completed her course of treatment, actually," he answers.

"What, just like that? Overnight?"

"When the time is right, we don't like to question it. She was ready to move on."

I have nothing to say to that. I swallow the snarl in my throat. We sit through a tense Group Work session. I volunteer little; I'm too busy wondering about Robin, whether something happened to her after I saw her. I'm also crushingly aware of the phone wedged under my waistband. What if someone knows, what if someone saw me, what if someone has looked in the safe.

After Community Work, I corner Ava and tell her I've got my phone; we creep out the side door again, and I quickly record some of her thoughts and theories on the case, to make sure I have a few minutes' worth of her voice on record. I want to start drawing up a script, and I need some audio to flesh out the first episode with. I still don't tell her about the night before, and she volunteers nothing.

"You're sure you're okay?" she asks before heading back for her own session with Rain. I nod and wave her off, eager to do yoga on the roof by myself for a few minutes before lunch.

I've barely begun my warm-up when Dawn appears.

"Well, hey there," I say, wiping some hair from my face. "Going to join me?"

Dawn frowns. "Actually, Liv, Rain asked me to send you to her. I believe you're scheduled for a session in the Chamber?"

"I thought it was for later?"

"Please, just go check in with her," Dawn says. I'm taken aback by his brusqueness.

"Is everything okay?" I ask.

"I never know how to answer that question," Dawn says with a sigh. "I think you should go start your session."

Glancing back at him and rattled by the coolness in his voice, I head back inside.

I drag my feet crossing the hallway, very reluctant to confront Rain. Surely she can't know what I saw? But, of course, there's every possibility that she did. I'm starting to think there might actually be cameras here.

"Liv," she greets me when I enter. No smile today.

"Morning," I respond.

"My apologies for pulling you away. I know we said that we'd do your Chamber session this afternoon, but I've been called away from the Center—"

"More police business?" I ask.

Rain frowns. "Not exactly. In any case, I won't be around later, and I like to be with clients during their first session. It can be a bit intense."

"What exactly is the Chamber, by the way?"

"Oh! Well, as I said, it's a sensory deprivation chamber. It's meant to help assist in your detox. To help you get centered in your breath and in your body. Ideally, we like everyone to spend a couple sessions a week in the Chamber."

"Right . . ." I say uneasily, not feeling great about this.

Rain leads me outside, across the lawn, and toward a small pavilion that lurks at the edge of the lawn. From Ava's descriptions, I suspect the staff housing is just beyond, along a path that cuts through a small copse of trees that provides privacy from the Center. She ushers me inside and gestures toward a small changing room.

"Please take everything off."

I shrug and begin shucking off my clothes with the door open, unfazed. Rain arches an eyebrow and tactfully looks away, but she doesn't change her posture or lose her poise. Which is good, because I have to slip my phone into the leg of my pants very carefully.

There are two further rooms in the pavilion; at a glance through the doorway, one looks like a massage room, with a table and a slab of hot stones. Rain points me in the direction of the other room, which I enter. It contains a white pod, a bit larger than a human, spaceship-like.

"The Chamber," Rain explains. "You'll enter the Chamber and spend some time just reflecting, listening to the sounds of your breath. It will help recenter you for your next reading."

"Seems . . . simple enough," I respond. I'm nervous but feel like I need to be relaxed, nonchalant. I've spent entire days filming in water tanks, shivering my ass off while my mascara drips and my hair draggles. I don't expect this to be any less comfortable than the day we shot the boating accident scene for *Iroquois Falls,* after Mina has escaped her grandfather and stolen the boat, the evidence she has smuggled out tucked in her jacket. I stand there, naked and expectant. Rain opens the hatch on the futuristic white pod and wordlessly gestures for me to insert myself into it.

"So, is this meant to, like, symbolize a return to the womb?" I joke, sliding into the warm liquid.

"Is that what you'd like it to be? A return to a time before birth?" Rain asks, not really asking. She shuts me in. I take a deep breath, and lean in.

The first few minutes are strange, but not unpleasant. I'm all for intense experiences, and this one is just mildly discombobulating. I paddle my fingers and toes in the water, I listen for any ambient sounds, I mumble a few things to myself. I don't hate it, but after a while, I grow fidgety. Even if Rain can hear me, it's not like we have a safe word. I hum tunelessly to keep myself company. I'm left alone long enough that I imagine the beginnings of panic, force myself not to think about what happens if I'm locked in here indefinitely. My fingers reach for the borders, tentatively shoving at the ceiling of the pod. When it doesn't budge, I can actually hear the sound of my heartbeat growing louder. I feel like I'm being tested, so I don't cry out, but I practice Teflon Mind and deep breathing and every other trick I've learned at retreats over the years.

Finally, I hear a crackle, followed by a voice. After the uterine hush of the session, it's jarring, and I resist the urge to sit bolt-upright. It's a relief.

"Can you describe any of the things that have been happening for you, Liv?" Rain's voice asks fluidly. The distortion of whatever audio system they've rigged makes her sound very distant.

"I thought I'd stick with the womb metaphor," I say, for the sake of making conversation. Mom shit always works with therapists, and Rain seemed to like it last time.

"And? What sort of feelings did that bring up for you?"

"Oh, I guess nothing too surprising. A return to comfort, safety, a feeling of being held."

"Well, with your moon in Cancer, it doesn't surprise me that feelings of motherhood are complicated for you."

"I don't think I said it was complicated," I correct.

"You were lying, though. From which I can only conclude that you feel more than one way about it."

I say nothing.

"Is that all you were considering?" Rain presses. "Or was there maybe something else going through your mind without the . . . mediation of all your senses?"

"Honestly, I think I was enjoying the lack of interference. No sounds, nothing to look at . . ."

"And no one looking at you?"

"There could be a camera in here," I point out.

"Do you think there is?"

"Well, there's a microphone," I say.

Rain snorts. "Indeed. There's really nowhere in the world you feel unobserved, Liv?"

"We live in the panopticon," I reply with an invisible shrug.

"Is that why you're so watchful, always observing everyone?"

"It could be. Or maybe I just feed off their emotions, their moods."

"You seem to be interested in . . . very particular emotions and moods, since you got here, to the Light."

Again, I say nothing.

"Your interest in Ava has . . . well, it drew my attention."

"Oh yeah? She's an odd girl."

"She's a very troubled individual. She spends a lot of time at the Light, hoping for some . . . relief, I suppose. From her obsessions, her fixation on death and darkness. I think she comes here for a pause in her quest for complete self-annihilation."

"Pretty sure she comes here for just a little R&R. Have you ever lived with a two-year-old?"

Rain says nothing for a long moment. "Yes, I have," she finally answers. There's another long silence. "Can I ask you . . . has Ava told you about her sister?"

"Yeah, her twin, right? She died, I think."

"I take it Ava . . . hasn't shared any details of that death with you."

"Just that it was a few years ago."

"Yes. It was actually June twentieth of 2016. The summer solstice," Rain says casually. Too casually. I have two simultaneous thoughts: *She knows* and *Holy shit, Ava has been playing me.* "I wonder if that date has any significance. To you, or to her."

"How did she die?" I ask slowly.

"She died in a barn fire. There was some discussion of drugs, an overdose. Ava was sure it was a murder and ruffled quite a few feathers. Rather dramatic, the whole thing. I don't think Ava has ever quite gotten over it."

No shit. "Hmm, weird," I say. "Quite the thing to get over, I suppose."

"I thought that might be one of the things that interested you about her. Her tragic story. It seemed like it might resonate with . . . well, your work and your personal history, both."

"Guess not. I just thought she was sort of interesting."

"She clearly found you interesting, too. She's come to me several times to speak about you. I thought at first it was because of your celebrity, but she seems much more interested in your comings and goings, your treatment. It's maybe the most engaged I've ever seen her."

"That happens sometimes. When people know your work, they think they know you."

"Indeed. But it's clear that she has a much more personal fixation on you. She's been keeping track of you, and wanted me to know about some of the things you've been focused on . . . outside of session."

I'm fairly sure I know what's happening here, but there's no point in confessing until I'm genuinely busted.

"Any idea what she might have been so fixated on?" Rain asks.

"I can't even begin to guess. It sounds like she has a lot of work to do on her own."

"No guesses at all? That's too bad. I was hoping that there was something . . . in the dynamic between you two that would help you advance, to access a higher self. If I thought the obsession was shared, or productive, I'd help foster it, let you two explore. But if it's just Ava, spiraling into another one of her manias . . ."

I say nothing.

Rain lets out a long sigh. "I see. Well, you may as well climb out, Liv. I think that's enough."

The latch of the pod pops open, and I squint at the sudden introduction of light to my corneas. It's clear that I've failed some sort of test, but I'll be damned if I know which one, or what I should have done differently. I am unbalanced, as much from the deprivation of my senses as Rain's questioning.

"Go ahead and get dressed and meet me in my office, please," Rain orders over the speaker. Reaching for my robe, I bustle to do as she says.

I walk back outside and head toward the main building. The Chamber has at least instilled in me a gratitude for the sight of sunlight, the sound of the breeze. It's a perfect autumn day, and I want to run in the opposite direction, to disappear into the vineyards and hike through the trees.

But I force myself to rejoin Rain, and sit back in the seat in front of her desk. Her face is impassive, although her index finger drums on the desk several times before she speaks.

"I feel like that was a very productive session," Rain begins.

"Really?" I ask, surprised.

"I had some questions I needed . . . resolved. I feel like we addressed them."

"Okay," I say, somewhat baffled. Unlike our first session, the Chamber seemed like a rather ham-fisted attempt to get information from me. Insight did not abound; inspiration did not spring forth. "I suppose it was fairly interesting."

Rain lets a long, pregnant pause linger. "The Light isn't for everyone," she says finally. "Our methods can be . . . too challenging for some people. Particularly those who don't want to confront their own artifice, their darkness." I bristle, even though I know that she's baiting me. "It's understandable if you don't think you'll be able to see through the whole cycle here at the Center." She pauses again, waiting for me to rush in. I manage not to interject. "I understand you've had a lot of questions about our methodology here. How and why we do things the way we do."

"Well, I am interested in the people here. And what becomes of them," I say. Rain's face changes swiftly, transitioning from imperturbable to irritated, even angry.

"Since you arrived, you've done nothing but seek out negativity, others' suffering. First Ava, then Hannah. Hannah's—death— has merely given you something to fixate on instead of your own damage. You'd much prefer to obsess over conspiracy and pain than your own shortcomings. Which are significant, as far as I can tell."

"Ouch, Rain."

"I'm sorry if that feels harsh, but I suspect people have not been harsh *enough* to you, in your life. You're used to everyone being taken in, tolerating your whims and foibles. I'd be doing your soul a disservice if I played along."

"Well, I feel very seen," I respond.

"Stop trying to manipulate me," Rain says with complete authority, and I flinch. We sit in a tense silence for several achingly long beats. I'm intrigued as much as I am desperate to end this conversation. I'm also taken aback by the change in Rain. She's gone from unruffled—unrufflable, even—to downright pissed. She looks genuinely disgusted with me. After a lengthy and piercing stare, Rain stands. With a sinking feeling, I see that she's unlocking the safe behind her desk. She pops it open and turns to look at me, her face neutral.

"Okay, yes. I took my phone back," I admit swiftly.

"I'm aware. Even though we agreed that you needed more time away from it."

"*We* didn't agree. I don't feel like I have any agency in my own Process here."

"If you were able to fully guide your own Process, you wouldn't be here! If you could trust your own instincts, why do you think—" Rain stops herself from saying whatever was on the tip of her tongue.

"Right, I'm such a disaster that I can't be trusted to check my email."

"And is that really all you did, Olivia?" Rain's voice has cooled. She has shown more emotion in this one short conversation than the whole of the time I've known her. I don't answer her question, for once not trusting myself to lie.

"I wish I could explain to you how disappointed I am, Liv," she finally says softly, menacingly. "If you only knew how much— how much I hoped that you would find the Light."

I'm alarmed—now Rain looks truly distressed. Gone is any attempt at impartiality. For whatever reason, I seem to have really upset her.

"My intuition is critical to the Process, to the work we all do here. So I trust it, implicitly. I have to. It's very rare for me to be wrong. And quite disturbing. But it happens, of course. Sometimes my own shadow conceals what I should have seen. It just took me far too long to discern it." Rain holds her fingers up to her eyes and takes a long beat, breathing deeply. "I really thought I saw so much potential in you." She drops her hands, and her disarming smile is suddenly back.

"Please don't worry about your things. Devotion will have them packed and ready at the door. A car is waiting for you. I'm sorry we couldn't do more to help." Rain stands up and turns to face the windows.

"Wait, what?" I cry. "You can't . . . you can't kick me out! I didn't sneak in drugs—and this isn't even rehab!"

"You violated our trust, Olivia." She shrugs, not turning

around. "I can't allow you to stand in the way of others' treatment. I don't take this decision lightly, believe me. But with everything going on here, at the Light, right now, I can't have someone who . . . dissembles with so little compunction. Who so recklessly shrouds herself in darkness. As much as it breaks my heart, after everything . . . this Process isn't for you. The Light isn't for you. Please take care of yourself." Rain has turned fully away from me, and I know she won't turn back. Rain is lots of things, but indecisive isn't one of them.

"I'm sorry, Rain," I whisper. I'm not, exactly, but I am very sorry to be kicked out. "I hope maybe someday . . ." I don't finish the thought. Instead, I square my shoulders and walk out of the House of Light.

VANITY FAIR, APRIL 2011
By Sally Ann Miles

Liv Reed joins me for our interview twenty minutes late, dressed casually in a pencil skirt, cropped T-shirt, and sneakers. Given her reputation for being a little wild, I'm surprised that she's this close to on time. We're meeting at the Langham in London, where she has spent the summer in between seasons of her hit show, *Iroquois Falls*.

"London is one of my home bases," she explains. "My dad is English, and I'm spending the summer with him. Plus, it's nice to have a change of scene while I clear my head from all the drama before I go back to it."

The "drama" she's referring to could be almost anything. It could be the painful adolescence that Reed rarely speaks about it. Or it could be the tempestuous relationship she's been having with her co-star, Ryan Lockhart; the young pair have been very

much in the public eye since they announced
relationship not long after season one of the *127*
took off. But it seems more likely that Reed is re-
ring to the on-screen drama of her show.

"*Iroquois Falls* is such a dark, complex story,"
Reed explains, sipping from the Perrier (with lime)
she has ordered. "On the one hand, sure, it's just a
somewhat soapy teen drama. But really what it's
dealing with is death, our inability to say goodbye to
those we love. My character, Mina, is driven by that
simple reality: that the person she's always loved
most is gone, but he isn't actually truly gone, for her.
He's still there, still speaking with her, quite literally, and every decision she makes is in service to her
one driving motivation: to find out how he died. You
get to see the really dark corners of loss in the show,
not just with Mina but with *all* the characters who
are missing Elliott. His parents, his family, his other
friends. It's painful. And sometimes senseless."

Those who have watched the show are familiar
with its heavy themes and porous genre boundaries:
the *Twin Peaks*/noir vibe that is layered over with
teen melodrama and set to a soundtrack of moody,
indie rock (usually with a banjo or two, to reflect the
Appalachian setting). It has been described as "*True
Detective* meets *The O.C.*" *Iroquois Falls* appeals in
part because of its refusal to be classified, and its
mash-up aesthetic has been a hit with audiences, particularly the coveted youth segment who are flocking
in droves to streaming services. As the glamorous
heart of the show, Reed is poised to be the emblem-
atic star of the millennial media consumer, and she
seems to know it.

"Look, I thought I was going into theater," she

th a bubbly, self-deprecating laugh. "I
ced snobbily at Hollywood. I doubt that I
be here if my friend and manager, Jess,
d of nudged me into it. And then when I
cript for *Falls,* I realized that this work was
what I wanted to be doing. She's always
eed adds.

n I catch up with her manager, Jess Meisner,
phone, Meisner acknowledges that Reed hadn't
had silver screen aspirations.

iv . . . well, she lives in the moment. She's right
e, and chasing the next moment, not looking at
two, three years down the line. Her ability to just be
there, and to crave what's coming next, is what makes
her so electric to watch, I think. She's not calculating
or plotting, she's just following instinct." I ask Meisner if this is why she thinks they've had such a fruit-
ful partnership.

"Sure, I think that's part of it. I'm more of an
organizer, you know. I have five-year plans, I'm
thinking about the dry cleaning and whether there's
a car coming to get us and all that. All friendships
have balances like that; you have to even each other
out."

Whatever their dynamic, Reed's star is on the rise;
Iroquois Falls has been renewed for another season,
and Reed hints at an upcoming film project that has
her excited.

"It's not a done deal, and I know crossing over
from TV to film can be rocky, but I feel good about
it. I'm young, I've got a lot of time to do the work I
want to do. For now, I just want to be Mina and figure out what happened to Elliott." Will we finally

find out who (or what) killed her love interest and ghostly sidekick this season?

"You know, I can't say for sure. But like with every season, we'll get a few more pieces of the puzzle and a little closer to the truth."

CHAPTER 10

I don't recognize the driver of the car parked in the gravel outside the House of Light; he's certainly not the person who conveyed me here. I say nothing until I'm inside the town car, door heartily slammed.

"To Manhattan, then, miss?" the driver asks after a tactful pause.

"Fine. Yes. Whatever," I grumble ungraciously, slouching down in my seat. I pull out my phone, which flickers into usefulness as we crest the top of the drive. We head down the lake, and I glance out at the water in the afternoon sun.

I've already pulled up Instagram and learned that Lili Reinhart is both (a) filming a new project (☺) and (b) having drinks with her beautiful man (♥) when we drive past Ava's house. The ads on my feed are almost exclusively beauty products, and I want them all; send me your serums, your oils, your blemish patches! I glance outside just as we're about to pass the driveway.

"Wait, stop!" I shout. The driver pulls over to the shoulder and glances questioningly in the rearview mirror. "I need—hang on just a minute, would you?" I'm already half out of the car.

"Need to be sick, miss?" he asks, commiserating. Probably not an uncommon problem on the rehab run.

I sprint down the hill toward the house, not fully conscious of what I'm contemplating. But the idea of going back to New York right now feels impossible, and not just because of what I've learned at the Light. I need to stick around. It seems evident that

Ava's motives for investigating this story are shady as hell. I can't trust her. But I need to know.

I'm momentarily worried that no one is home; the door remains unopened after I've pounded repeatedly on it. But then I hear footsteps in the hall, followed by the click of a latch.

"Good morning?" Ava's absurdly wholesome husband says. He's holding their little girl in his arms, and she looks sleepy.

"Hi," I say breathlessly. "I'm so sorry to just show up like this but I'm—"

"Oh God, has something happened to Ava?"

"No, it's not that. At least—look, I have a really crazy favor to ask."

"She hasn't . . . nothing happened with her?"

"Like what?" I ask. He says nothing, just glances outside, as though to be sure his wife isn't with me. "No, she was fine the last time I saw her. But . . . the thing is, I had to leave the Light unexpectedly and, well, Ava said I could regroup here. That I should come and ask you if I could stay for a night or two, that is."

"Oh, really," he drawls. Evidently this is the sort of thing Ava might actually do, because he sighs in resignation. "Of course, if Ava invited you, you're welcome. The guest room is open."

"Oh, fantastic, it would just be for a night, two at most. Things are a bit topsy-turvy right now." My Hepburn-in-a-screwball-comedy accent seems to have returned. Haha, whimsical mayhem, isn't it droll. "I'll just . . . grab my bag." I bolt back up the driveway to where the driver and car await me, and demand access to the trunk.

"Miss, I was told you'd be heading straight back to Manhattan. The full fare was paid up front . . ." the driver reminds me.

"Don't worry about it. Consider it a bonus. Or a day off. Don't worry about telling anyone you didn't take me all the way there. I have a few things I need to take care of here."

"As long as you don't get me in trouble, I won't tattle on you," he says, and winks. "My name is Fred, and here's my card. Call me if you ever need a driver around the Finger Lakes."

"Thank you!" I call, and slam the door. I manhandle my belongings down the hill while—Will?—Wyatt, that's his name, watches me with just a glimmer of amusement. I get the feeling he's seen his fair share of wild antics.

The driver may already be on the phone to his boss, who will notify either Rain or Jess, whoever was responsible for the car being booked. It won't take long for everyone to figure out that I haven't even made it three miles from the Light. But there's little they can do about it, after all.

"Thank you, I really appreciate this," I say sincerely, as Wyatt effortlessly lifts my small suitcase up over the lip of the doorway. Lord, look at his triceps. Positively indecent. His other arm supports the weight of the black-haired baby, whose big eyes regard me drowsily from over his shoulder as I follow him into the living room.

"Like I said, it's not a problem. Though I should warn you, I'll be gone most of the day and into the evening. Harvest season and all."

"Don't worry, I don't need a babysitter," I reassure him. He gives me a doubtful glance as he plunks my bag down. "No, seriously. I didn't get kicked out for . . . relapsing, or anything like that. I'm not even . . . I'm not an addict."

"Look, it's none of my business."

"Well, it sort of is," I say. "You're inviting me into your home, where your little girl lives."

Wyatt snorts. "Girl, you should see some of the company Ava keeps. I'm sure you're perfectly squared away, in comparison. Besides, we sort of have a policy . . . of not turning anyone away from our house. Particularly anyone who's . . . well . . ." He trails off.

"Struggling?" I finish with a twist of my brow.

"Yeah, basically."

"Because of Ava's sister?" I ask.

"In a manner of speaking. We believe in hospitality."

"Well, again, I truly do appreciate it. You're a lifesaver."

Wyatt seems to like those words, and he smiles back at me. "Let's just get you settled in," he says.

After he's shown me to my room and bustled out of his own house (and after politely declining my vague offers to watch the kid), I flop down on my new bed, wondering what the fuck I'm doing. I've acted on impulse and trusted my instincts, something I've learned to do in scenes over and over again. But my instincts aren't as reliable when it comes to real-world decisions, and this does feel like a pretty strange thing to do when I pause to think on it. Or fully reflect in the extant moment of now, as Rain might suggest.

Why have I been forced out of the Light? Is it because of my cellphone infraction? Or, more alarming: Is there any way someone could have seen me witnessing the ceremony by the lake last night? There's no way they could possibly know about my and Ava's suppositions regarding the dead girls and HOL. Unless. Unless Ava told them.

But then, what would she have to gain from revealing the suspicions that she herself had tried to keep secret? Surely getting me ousted from the program would undermine her whole project of roping me in and deploying my celebrity for exposure. Unless that was a ruse all along. Perhaps by betraying me she has earned credibility with the Light, and will therefore be allowed to get closer, learn more? I remember uneasily that she met with Rain just before my session in the Chamber, and that Rain kept mentioning her, discussing her.

Well, whatever. Whatever Ava's motivations, her past, however she was planning to use me, she has succeeded only too well. Because now I need answers, and I have no intention of stopping just because I've been booted to the curb or betrayed by my kooky sidekick. Now I'm out here, on the loose, free to figure out what the fuck is going on with those people.

And free, of course, to involve the public. My adoring fans, the true crime junkies, the bored lonely masses seeking to ascribe order to a disordered world by answering simple questions: Who did it? Why? Free to reorder my own world, and get myself back where I belong.

. . .

I've been tapping away at a script for my first full episode when my phone starts ringing. Jess, of course.

"Hello, Jessamine, my love. Haven't heard your dulcet tones for days!"

"Liv, what the fuck?" Jess snarls.

"Hey now, tone of voice, young lady," I respond. "I thought you'd be happy to speak to me."

"I just got off the phone with Rain, and apparently, you couldn't last a week in rehab?"

"I thought it wasn't rehab."

"On retreat, whatever the fuck. What happened?!"

"I guess the demands of such structured living didn't suit my artistic temperament," I say with a shrug. "I would have called earlier, but I figured you'd be hearing about it soon enough."

"Jesus, Liv," Jess says with disgust. "How are we going to publicly explain this? I already tweeted that you were going to be taking a social media break for mental health, people were all about it! Not to mention the cost of a full month at the Light, *which* we paid up front. You don't think you could have hung in there just a bit longer?"

"Those people are nuts, Jess. Didn't you vet them, like, at all?"

"Yes, thank you very much, I did. They seemed just fine, even a notch or two down on the crazy scale compared to one of the places I found in California. Wait, you're not still talking about that serial-killer dead-girl shit you sent me, right?"

"What did you think of it?" I ask.

"Seriously, Liv? I thought you must still be high. It sounded like incoherent, paranoid ravings. Or, if we're being generous, a desperate attempt to try and focus on anything other than sorting your own shit out. Though this is elaborate, even for you."

"Well, aside from the details of the story—which I'm still working out—what did you think of the concept? I mean, of the idea of making a big-deal podcast."

Jess is silent for a long moment. "Look. If the timing were different, and you had the right story, I would, in principle, be behind it. I think it would be on-brand, and it would be a nice way to boost visibility, particularly if you were attached to a true crime project."

"Sort of in line with the Manson film we want," I prompt.

"Yeah, Liv, except the whole plan was for you do your stint in rehab, demonstrate your overall level of stability, and then try to rebrand a bit. Not announce to the public that you're going to rehab, only to reemerge a few days later with disjointed—what? Accusations that the very rehab program you attended was . . . systematically murdering young women in ritual killings?"

"Well, about that—"

"Liv. Stop." I can hear her take a deep, frustrated breath on the other end. "Is this . . . is this about your mom?"

"Wow, Jess. Can't really believe you're going there," I say, surprised.

"It's just . . . well, I can understand why all of that might be coming up for you now. Given the whole environment at the Light, and given what happened to her . . ."

"I really don't see how they're connected." I sniff.

"Really? Your mom disappears when you're sixteen, somewhere into the Pacific Northwest. And now you . . . are investigating the deaths of a handful of lost young women whose deaths seem to be, what, not fully explained?"

I'm silent. Though it is the height of blindness, I honestly had not really seen any connection until just this minute. Leave it to Jess.

"I get how painful it was, Liv," Jess says softly. "You remember, I met you right afterward, and I know how much you struggled. You and your dad both. It's why he's always been so protective of you, so involved in your life—"

" 'Involved' is one word for it," I say.

"And I know you never really . . . dealt with all of that, at least not entirely. And within a few years, look at you, you're the star of a TV show with, what else, a maternal figure who is mentally unwell and largely absent. Playing a character obsessed with a mysterious death. I don't need the degree in psychology I never got to connect some of these dots, babe."

"Okay, Jess, I hear what you're saying," I concede. "My mom's disappearance fucked me up, and I might still be working through it in some weird, less than healthy ways. But that doesn't change the fact there are, well, real facts on my side here."

"What facts?" Jess cries. "You sent me some mumblings about fragile girls and pagan rituals and, what, the elements?"

"Okay, okay, I grant you, my thinking wasn't as organized as it maybe could have been. But I have facts, and several points of connection between all four cases. Not to mention that really fucking weird place I just left, Jess. I mean, even if they're not murdering girls in the woods, there is something seriously fucked-up going on there."

"Liv," Jess says sadly.

"Let me just get my facts together. I'm writing out a script right now, laying out all the information and making it a bit more cohesive. Let me send you that, and then we'll talk about me coming back to New York in a few days—"

"What do you mean, 'a few days'?" Jess interrupts, in the tone of voice she reserves for caterers who have badly fucked up.

"Ah, right. I'm taking just a little time here on the lake to organize my data," I explain.

"Olivia, I don't know what to say to you right now," she finally says. "But you should know that I think this is really unhealthy and is a truly terrible idea."

I know from the silence after this proclamation that she has hung up the phone. Whatever—at least I'll have a few more hours of peace and quiet to figure some of this shit out.

• • •

I putter in socked feet through Ava's house, wondering about its inhabitants. I mimic Ava's walk and her gestures, a slope-stepped gait, exaggerated facial expressions. I wonder what it would be like to live in her house, her skin. To pick up that baby each morning with the hint of a hangover, to look out on these grapevines and know that you are responsible for them. To shuffle into bed late some night, after a few hours of obsessing over dead bodies and sipping vinegary red wine, and shuck off your clothes and slink in with that tall-drink-of-water husband. I linger on those thoughts, and lie on her bed before I head to her office.

It's not that I'm not thinking about what Jess said. She knows me well enough to get fully under my skin, and she clearly wanted me to reflect on my motivations. And I suppose really, she's not entirely wrong.

• • •

I'm going to share with you all something that you may not know about me. It's personal, and it's not always the right idea to let the personal intersect with the larger story you're telling. But my history feels relevant to this larger story. People love to reflect on why we fucking love true crime so much, right? We learn how to be safe from listening to these stories, we revel in the darkness of certain kinds of circular thinking. And, goes one theory, we relive our past traumas.

My mother disappeared when I was sixteen. She was a strange woman, always, but when I was a kid, she was a pretty attentive mother. Really attentive, actually. She was super quiet and re-served, but she was the sort of parent who was there when the school bus dropped you off, and there were always snacks made when you got there. Like, the good snacks. Homemade cookies and shit, not celery sticks. But even when she was present, she wasn't entirely present, you know? She liked to play make-believe, and disappear into a world of fairies and pirates. We would spend whole days inside made-up worlds. She loved the movies.

So imagine my surprise when, at the age of sixteen, I got off the bus and found . . . just an empty house. Mom had been there in the morning, had sent me off to school with a cucumber sand-wich (I was in a vegetarian phase), but by the time I got home, she had simply disappeared. Most of her things were there, tidy and unimposing as ever. She'd taken just a small bag and a handful of clothes, leaving the rest undisturbed. There was no note, no ex-planation, no hint of where or why she'd gone. No sign of a dis-turbance or struggle, no trace of another person.

My father was unbothered for two full days, saying he figured she had gone to the gym or to stay with a friend. Never mind that my mother had no friends that I knew of, and going to the gym for forty-eight hours would be a somewhat remarkable feat. When he reported her missing on the third day, he still seemed uncon-cerned, as though she might just turn up in time to cook dinner. As you can maybe imagine, their marriage was not exactly rock-solid. My dad is English, and he was stiff-upper-lipping his way through life: Mom's disappearance was treated with no drama— keep calm and carry on.

The cops took things a little more seriously, and were able to determine that the last charge to her (shared) credit card had been to purchase a flight on the morning of her disappearance. She had, apparently, flown to Seattle.

And that, folks, is the last definitive information I've ever heard about my mother. An APB went out, a handful of tips were phoned in, but nothing ever came of it. We never got a ransom note. I don't receive cryptic postcards on my birthday, no phone calls of soft but audible breath. After a life of remarkable invisibility, my mother disappeared without a trace.

Make of that whatever you will.

CHAPTER 11

Ava's office is a nice place to sit and work. After I've spread out all her documents, it's quite pleasurable to sit in her chair and flip through all the macabre pages. I have taken her on as a role, and it feels like an easy fit.

But like most afternoons of research, I find myself on the internet pretty quickly, scrolling through feeds and cross-checking lists of names to see who might be following whom, what locations might be tagged by the same people. I have spent many of my less productive hours methodically researching reality-TV stars, so this mode of inquiry feels both intuitive and satisfying. Of the four women, Hannah is by far the most prolific poster. She is also the only one of the four with a Twitter feed. I recognize at least two of her tweets as House of Light snippets of wisdom ("Whatever is not light is dark" and "I walk with my shadow self").

I do screen grabs of the photos that snagged my attention earlier, and pore back through Hannah's other pictures. Even with careful perusal, I don't find any other pictures of the Light. And aside from the one photo with her and Allison, no other images of my other three dead girls appear on her feed. But I stare at this photo of Hannah and Allison at the House of Light, standing there with Rain, Devotion, and two mystery people, one man and one woman. One of them is tagged @flxtreehugger, the woman. I send her a quick DM, asking if she'd be willing to tell me a little about herself. There's no way to make this sound anything other than totally weird, but hey, I'm famous.

@oliviascreed: I'm working on a movie and I got your name from someone who said you'd be a great resource to interview about spiritual practices in the area? Do you think maybe you'd be willing to talk to me and help me prep for this role? I'd be eternally grateful ☺

As the day winds down, I begin to wonder (again) what in the hell I think I'm doing. Jess is probably right. This is a weird way to work through my childhood trauma, and do I really think that I can solve this? Am I really on the hunt for . . . a serial killer? It seems so laughable that I almost walk straight out of the house, ready to return to my life. But the reality of what my life actually looks like these days, with its tenuous career plans and my personal shambles, gives me enough pause to turn back, to open one of Ava's bottles of wine, and to sit on the couch researching how to publish a podcast.

Two hours and two glasses of wine later, I am fully aware that I lack the technical ability and patience to do all this myself. I'd normally call Jess and ask her to set it up, but she's evidently washed her hands of me for the moment. Instead I send an email to a friend who runs a decent-sized media company. I rattle out a quick pitch, and make promises I have no idea whether I will be able to deliver on. Such is the biz.

Pleased with my day's work, I decide to take a walk down to the lake. I flip through Ava's closet, but everything there is made for someone quite a bit shorter. I can't even get her hiking boots fully on my feet. Oh well, I don't need her costumes at the moment.

Yet another glorious sunset. (This beauty almost gets boring. It's been as reliably attractive as L.A. evenings, and I'd welcome a storm, lashing rain, something more gothic and appropriate to my sleuthing.) As I walk, I consider what my father will have to say if this podcast succeeds, goes even moderately viral. He will try to insinuate himself into it, will discover some way to get involved, get the spotlight on him, I muse. Maybe we can play up my mother's disappearance, paint him as a possible suspect, and then bring him on the show for some heart-wrenching reunion with his estranged daughter. I don't know if I want to throw him this bone, but if it will get buzz going, I'll consider it. Everyone loves to see a starlet deal with their shitty parents, God knows why. I've maybe aged out of the starlet bracket, though. Former starlet—ouch.

. . .

The reality, of course, is that Dad was a suspect, obviously. When your self-effacing wife of nearly two decades up and vanishes, any half-competent law enforcement will look at the husband. It's the one thing we know about crime: The husband did it, right? The sloppy purchase of an airline ticket on the morning of her disappearance, the lack of a note, the abandoned teenage daughter—I mean, come on. And though I don't genuinely think my dad has murder in his heart, I spent a grim week pacing the property of my childhood home, looking for disturbed earth, signs of a struggle, an earring in the grass. I found the pieces of a vase I had buried in a shallow grave under a tree after breaking it as a child while trying to do a bottle dance with it on my head, but that was the only cover-up I located. I didn't know what to think, or how to feel: my whole life had been upended in a single afternoon.

The specter of his possible guilt hung over him for years, and it tormented him. Yes, he liked the attention, the handful of interviews, the chance to play the heartbroken left-behind. The now-single father, just trying to do right by his little girl. I think he even enjoyed the dark glamor the suspicion afforded him; it lent him an air of danger, made of his toothy grin something sinister, or double-sided at least. But I heard him sob for her one night when

*he thought I was at a friend's, and once, I found a pillow wearing
her nightgown. This spoke of a tenderness between them that I
had rarely seen, but in his weary moments making macaroni or
beans and toast for our dinner, I noticed that grief and loneliness
were pulling his craggy jawline downward. My mother's disappearance gave my father jowls.*

. . .

I swim for so long that I get a crick in my neck, then dry off on the
rocks of the beach. There are the remnants of what might have
been a dock jutting out into the lake, but it is just the nibbled-on
skeleton of a structure now. Whenever the breeze picks up I'm
reminded that it is in fact autumn, despite the unseasonable
warmth. The cold and darkness are coming, though; you can feel
it in the shadows or whenever a cloud skates by overhead. I twist
and turn my neck, remembering the first time I felt this particular
twinge.

It was during season three of *Iroquois Falls*. It had been an
incredible time professionally, but pretty shitty personally. I wonder if this is my fate, to do my best work when I'm miserable.

Mina had been stomping around all over the county, going toe-
to-toe with threatening meth dealers and suspicious family members for two years. She was beginning to understand that her own
biology was implicated in what was happening and why she was
able to speak to Elliott beyond the grave, and was drawing ever
nearer to the grand finale of the season, when she learns the truth
about her grandfather. And, of course, throws herself off the waterfall. I can't help but think of Allison.

Ryan and I had gone public, only to have a pretty public
breakup—the first of several. My partying was blamed; I had
been hitting the clubs, staying up late. I wasn't shimmering with
the glow of health and good decision-making; I was too thin, and
the bags under my eyes were telltale. Jess tagged grimly along on
each raucous evening, clutching up my phone and the credit cards

I left behind in my careless wake. From the outside, I'm sure I looked like just another self-destructive starlet, and my bad behavior masked the real grief I felt: the loss of a friend, an equal, someone who was yoked together with me in the whole maddening circus of celebrity. Ryan and I were comrades, even if we were a dysfunctional romantic pair.

One morning, I insisted Jess and I stop at the beach on the way home, and we found ourselves shivering and barefoot in the sand, Jess picking up my scarf every time I let it trail in the surf. I collapsed, giggly, onto a dune, swilling champagne from the bottle. When I handed it to Jess, she grabbed it, took a swig, and put it down on the other side of her body.

"Hey," I protested. "Share."

"Liv," she said. "Look at me." I did, though a false eyelash was coming unstuck. "If this is what you want to do, that's okay. Lots of people just do a season or two of a show and call it quits. If you want to just . . . spend the next decade stumbling around Hollywood calling for bottle service, then, you know, that's your prerogative. I'm not going to try to stop you."

"Okay, buzzkill much," I mumbled, petulant and sobering up quickly.

"You have to do you, Liv. But I have to do me, too. And this is not what I want. I do not want to follow you around picking up your shit. I believe in you, and I believe in your work. But this isn't you, and this isn't your work." She shrugged and looked around at the ocean, as though wondering what she was doing all the way out here.

"What are you saying?" I asked, frightened.

"I want to find out what happens with Mina. Will she confront her grandfather and find out what he's been up to all along? What about the long-lost half sister that keeps getting hinted at? And what does this have to do with her mother's nervous breakdown? *That's* what I care about. I don't care about your drama with Ryan, I don't care about scoring from Ryan's friend's dealer. I don't even care that much about the tabloids, you know? I want to see you work, and I want to see your work take off."

"I want that, too," I sniffled.

"Okay. Then let's get the fuck out of the sandbox and call a trainer. If you're going to be in any condition to film in four weeks, you'll need one."

"A shower first," I said, and Jess laughed. As we walked back to the car, she chucked me gently on the shoulder and then looped her arm in mine. In the car on the way home, I fell asleep with my head on her lap as she combed the tangles and sand out of my hair.

I make my way back up the hill and let myself inside. I want to call Jess, want to yammer out my theories to her. We've been together so long that it feels strange not to depend on her now, not to externalize every thought and want and notion to her. I imagine, though, that she feels my absence as persistently. Does she wake up and look at her phone, expecting my texts? Does she make two salads at lunch like always, one for me and one for her?

There's some daylight left, and I sit on Ava and Wyatt's deck, wrapped in a blanket from the couch, my iPad propped on my knees. I take this opportunity to catch up on everything I've missed: scrolling through various accounts, checking to see who is trending. There was a minor blip from Jess's press release last week, but frustratingly few mentions after that. I grit my teeth. I will not be a has-been at thirty. Well, thirtyish.

At least Deuxmoi has a tip about me. I'm not completely out of the scene.

Anon Pls. Liv Reed is supposedly at a rehab in upstate New York? Heard it from a friend who is actually in a position to know. Can't say more but apparently she's gotta dry out after all her recent antics ;)

When I hear the door open, I close all the social media tabs and open up Kindle. The sun has just set behind the hill across the lake, and it's getting dark. Time for the farmer to pack it in for the day?

Wyatt bustles about the kitchen, making a bottle for Zora, but when he's finished he comes out onto the deck to politely ask me about my day.

"One of the best I've had in a while," I answer with a shy grin. "It's so beautiful and peaceful here. I don't think I would ever get sick of it."

"Well, come February you might," he answers, but I can tell he's pleased.

"How's the harvest coming?"

"Oh, hard work, as usual. It will be pretty much wrapped in a week or two. We're not doing much late-harvest at the moment. Ava thinks the sweet wines are 'cloying,' and mostly there's not too much of a market for them. There's cheaper sweet gewürtz, if that's what you're after."

"And the kiddo? Who looks after her, while you're out tilling the fields?"

"Sometimes my parents. Sometimes daycare. And I've brought her with me a couple of times, believe it or not. She loves it if we're just sitting on the tractor, all snuggled up in her BabyBjörn."

"I bet she does," I laugh. "I can think of worse ways to spend the day." The innuendo that I wouldn't mind being snuggled up against him for the day is intentional, but I should be a little careful about flirting here. "Do you, um, want to go get cleaned up? I can finish her bottle. I mean, not finish it myself, but I can hold it while she does," I clarify, sounding flustered.

Wyatt glances down at himself and chuckles when he sees that he is in fact quite grubby. "Yeah, a shower is in order, I guess. You sure you don't mind?"

"Not at all. I love babies."

Wyatt shifts the toddler into my arms, and I lean back in the chair with a contented sigh, tugging the blanket around both of us. Zora barely acknowledges me, just continues to fixate on her bottle. Isn't she a bit old for a bottle, though?

As Wyatt ducks inside, he turns back.

"Actually, I was going to ask if you wanted to come for dinner."

"Oh, I hadn't even thought that far. . . . Yeah, of course."

"We're going to my parents' house, just up the lake a bit. I barely have time to grocery shop, let alone cook during this season, and, well, without—" He stops himself.

"Without Ava here, I'm sure you're more than usually short on time," I finish.

He tilts his head: *Yeah, basically.*

"I'd love to join you, if you're sure it's okay," I say.

"Of course, can't leave a guest to starve! Let me just get cleaned up." He disappears into the house, and I rock the kid a bit. She finishes her bottle and looks up at me, just noticing that I'm a stranger. I wait for tears, but she's unruffled.

"Pretty hair," she finally says, grabbing a fistful of mine, putting some of it in her mouth, and then resting her head on my clavicle again. I think I like her.

Wyatt returns and relieves me (not, I'm sure, before he's had a chance to notice what a pretty tableau we make here, just past the gloaming), and I throw on a pair of leggings and a sweater for dinner. I want to look relatable, approachable. As we walk out the door, I note that Wyatt is a few inches taller than me, but not too many.

He chats comfortably as we drive the few miles to his parents' place, telling me about his high school romance with Ava, his degree, his vineyard, his daughter. He seems to have gotten everything he wanted; his desires were not outsized, but nor were they entirely modest, and he appears pleased with himself, in spite of his obviously complicated relationship with his wife. In fact, a complicated wife seems to be the one hiccup in his story. But without the wife, you don't get the perfect daughter. Or the vineyard.

Wyatt's parents live in the woods, in a funky house set back in the trees. I carry the wine and Wyatt carries his daughter as we go inside.

"There's my perfect button!" a man with a gray ponytail and a red nose coos the minute we've taken off our shoes. On the ground and suddenly energized, Zora races toward him and is immediately tossed into the air and swooped around a corner.

"I'm less popular with my parents these days," Wyatt says with uncharacteristic dryness. I giggle.

"Well, you have stiff competition," a matronly woman says, popping her head out from the kitchen.

"Don't I know it," he replies with a laugh. His mother has noticed me instantly and is waiting for an explanation. "I hope it's okay I invited someone along," Wyatt rushes to say, as though just realizing that showing up with another woman might look a bit peculiar to his folks.

"Hi, I'm Olivia. Thank you so much for having me," I say, moving forward with the wine bottles. We do all the pleasantries, introductions, issuance of gratitude and of hospitality required of socialized women, regardless of the century. I offer to help in the kitchen as Wyatt meanders toward the woodstove and his father. Dora (for that is her name) lets me open the wine and chop a few cloves of garlic, but I am then dispatched to the living room. No one asks where Ava is.

Dinner, once it's on the table, is pork chops and homemade applesauce and salad and is the most home-cooked, country meal I can remember having since childhood. It is delicious, and I say so. I am, tactfully, asked very few questions about my presence, but I don't feel unwelcome or resented. I entertain myself by pretending I am their future daughter-in-law, the perfect, frictionless addition to this ambition-free life in the woods. I am careful not to let any anglicisms pollute my speech, lest I be asked about my upbringing.

After dinner, I excuse myself and pop to the loo, ready to go home, unexcited about facing the ordeal of apple pie and ice cream.

Heading back to the fire and the family, I almost miss it. There are several other photos on the wall: a young boy who has to be Wyatt, this house in various stages of construction, Dora and Steve in front of a temple in India.

But the photo I find myself frozen in front of is, unlike many of the others, in color. I can see the distinctive outlines of the House of Light behind the people in the photo, and there are Dora and Steve, huddled in with the others. There, too, is Rain: a bit younger, and with a couple more inches of hair, but still barefoot, thin, erect. And in the middle of the photo is the man whose photo hangs in Rain's office, with his white wrap and his walking stick and his guru beard. His arm is slung around a young man I recognize from my entire day scouring through social media, though he's barely more than a kid here. The guru and the young man share the same striking blue eyes.

I pull my phone from my pocket and take a few photos, though there is glare from the frames. I check out the other photos on the wall, too, looking for any other pictures of the Light. There is one of a strange mandala out in the woods, made of rocks and framed by pine boughs, that looks like it could be related to the Light, and there's one that I'm fairly sure is from the beach at the Light: this one is in black-and-white, and it's just a blur of unclad bodies in the lake, no identifiable faces.

Back in the living room, I curl up on the couch, now watching Dora and Steve with much more interest. I wait for my opening.

"So, Wyatt tells me that you guys used to be members of the

House of Light?" I interject in a conversational lull. From Wyatt's quick glance at me, I know he's aware that he said no such thing. Dora and Steve look at each other, some unreadable marital conversation taking place in that one second of eye contact.

"Used to be," Steve says with a shrug. "It was a different place back in the eighties, even the nineties. Before they got . . ." He shrugs again.

"Dogmatic," finishes Dora after a pause. "Things got a bit rigid after . . . Well, organizations change, I guess. With any shift in leadership there's bound to be some stuff that's different. We just weren't as crazy about the vows of silence and the tithing—"

"I don't know if it's fair to call it tithing, Dodo," Steve says. "That's kind of Catholic."

"Well, it did get sort of 'organized religion' after he passed. It was all official texts and silent retreats and mandated maintenance donations. Not to mention all that jargon!"

"Yeah, I guess we were more involved when it was just a place to go and be with nature, to commune with your neighbors."

"You mean take hallucinogens with your neighbors," Wyatt says with a snort. Steve laughs and shrugs: *Yes, and why not?*

"Do you have any contact with them now?" I ask.

"Well, I'm not sure there's ever really any leaving the Light, not entirely. But I guess we decided not to become ordained members, and that means we're definitely not real involved anymore. There's a weekend, usually in spring, where the old guard heads out there together, but it's very relaxed, compared to the formality of what they do now."

"Olivia actually just spent some time at the Center," Wyatt says. He's outed me as punishment for bringing this up.

"Oh, really," Dora says, and her mood shifts as she gives Steve another glance. "I've heard a lot of good things . . ."

"Actually, I think I agree with you," I say. "It was all a bit regimented, a little too jargony, as you said. I just wanted a bit of a cleanse, some yoga and meditation. They seemed sort of . . . doc-trinal. So I left early."

"Good for you, think for yourself," Steve says, getting up to put another log in the fire.

"And of course, the woman in charge," I say. "Rain. She's kind of a lot."

"Well, I wouldn't say she's in charge," Dora says. "Maybe for the day-to-day stuff. The Light was there for her after a really dark time in her life. I mean, what happened to her daughter made her . . . Well, I think she maybe wouldn't have survived without the Light."

"Her daughter?" I ask.

"Oh, she had a little girl. She died suddenly, but I don't have the whole story. Rain found the Light after she'd . . . had some mental health issues. All completely understandable, poor thing."

"I'd go nuts myself," Steve says, planting a kiss on Zora's head. She has been flipping silently through a book while we sit, the self-contented only child. Like I was.

"We all have a lot of compassion for Rain. But she's not the one who changed the Light. It's different now because of Luke."

"Well, sons have a tendency to want to be different from their fathers," Steve grumbles, with a loving but irritated look at his son. Wyatt rolls his eyes.

"So Luke is . . . the guru's son?" I ask. "I couldn't help noticing the picture in the hallway. Are they the two in the middle, with the really distinctive eyes?"

Dora squirms in her seat. "The Light has just gotten, well, less-inclusive over the years. Luke doesn't much like outsiders, and, well, I think we're outsiders at this point."

"Strange policy for people who invite the public to come stay with them," I point out.

"Can't turn away paying customers and possible recruits," Wyatt says resentfully.

"Let's not talk any more about the Light," Dora interjects.

"They were a big part of our life for many years, but everybody changes. They do their work. But we've got our little Zora to take care of now. Live and let live, you know."

"Yep, the only one who bothers with them now is Ava, of all people," Steve says. It's the first time anyone has said her name. Wyatt coughs. I am very tempted to fill in the silence, but I bite my lip.

"Hey, bug, you want some ice cream?" Wyatt asks his daughter.

"Blueberry!" Zora says, erupting from her peaceful contemplation of the book at the mention of such a wonderful treat.

"I don't know if we have blueberry, sweetheart, but I bet if you ask Grandpa he'll share his Cherry Garcia with you."

"Choo chewy, choo chewy. Zo wants bluuuueberry."

"Well, let's go see what we can do," Steve says, hoisting her onto his shoulders as she giggles delightedly. I wonder, vaguely, if I was ever so easily delighted at the prospect of calories. Or whether I felt such joy bounced aloft on paternal shoulders.

. . .

I'm in bed later that night when I check my email. Wyatt and I shared a final glass of wine in front of the fire (when offered a second, I demurred, rightly guessing this would please him), chatting casually about his upbringing, his parents. I try not to straight up pump him for information about the Light, since I know this will raise his hackles, even if he is as trusting and gormless as a golden retriever. I learn that his parents used to bring him to a vaguely remembered "cabin in the woods" when he was very young, but that he has virtually no recent memories of any Light members or activities other than dropping Ava off: his parents seemed to want to keep their distance from everyone after a certain point. I change the subject, not wanting him to wonder why I'm so interested. Or, indeed, start questioning whether Ava's little research project is related to the Light, or to me.

The newest email is from my friend Topher, the one with the

start-up media company. I had a feeling he would be eager, and I'm delighted by his enthusiasm. He is laddish and "pumped," and I can tell by the ostensibly casual tone of his sign-off that he is more keen than he's even said. He wants to talk to me "like, yesterday" and thinks this has real legs. When can I record? Do I have the whole story line or is it truly unfolding in real time? He thinks that between some of my recent iffy press and the "serial-killer angle," this could be a breakout. Here we go, I think. This thing might actually happen. Now I need to find out if there's an actual fucking story here.

I return to the photo of Hannah on Insta, with the man who I now suspect is Luke and is the son of the man who founded the House of Light. As I stare at the image, trying to get any details I've missed, the paper airplane in the top right turns red. I have a message.

Flxtreehugger: I assume you're talking about HOL and that was a weird time of my life plz I'd like to just move on

I immediately respond.

I totally understand and respect that. I was just hoping that maybe I could take a few minutes of your time to talk about your experience. It would really help me out!

I'm reluctant to say anything else, even be more specific about what I want to discuss.

There's a long pause without that blinking ellipsis and I'm fretful, worried she'll just stop talking.

Ok, fine. I can meet tomorrow before work. Watkins Glen, 9 AM?

I reply:

Looking forward to it!

. . .

I hear Wyatt leave before my alarm even goes off; he's up with the dawn, wresting a living out of the ground. I'm sad not to share a cup of coffee with him, but not sad that I don't have to put on my wife-replacement skin, the diffident but lovely houseguest with whom it's all too easy to play house.

The clothes I packed for a retreat are not fully appropriate for a day spent sleuthing around a small town—my kimono and jersey knit are not ideal. But I have no options, so yet again it's leggings and a T-shirt. Poking my head onto the deck, I realize that it's nippy out. None of Ava's jackets will fit me, so as I head out, I snag a rustic Carhartt jacket that I assume must be Wyatt's from the rack by the door.

Though I called an Uber twenty minutes before I expected to leave, it's still another ten minutes before it arrives to take me just the few miles to town. I have never needed a driver's license; my father forbade me to learn after Mom's disappearance, and then I was off to the city for college. No point in driving there. In L.A. I always had a driver. But here, in the sticks, it might be problematic.

I'm only five minutes late when I arrive at the café we've agreed on. They're advertising some off-brand coffee beans, and the place is filled with rickety chairs and the smell of bacon. It will do, though.

I order a cup of green tea and, after a quick glance at the menu, a banana—none of the other food on the menu is suitable for someone who needs their body for work. When I get home, I am so doing an Organic Avenue cleanse.

Flxtreehugger is fifteen minutes late, and I'm beginning to worry that she won't show at all when she strolls in. She looks healthy, robust. Like she's outdoors a lot. She sees me immediately and comes straight over.

"Hi, I'm Liv, thanks so much for coming," I say, bounding upright to greet her.

"Hi. Um, nice to meet you. I'm Becca."

"I really appreciate you taking the time to speak with me. Do you mind if I record some of this?" I've got my phone at the ready, figuring that if I can get even some of this on file, it will add some drama to the podcast.

"Sure, I guess—who did you say recommended me? Was it the magazine?"

"They had really nice things to say about you!" I tell her. Sure, the magazine! Definitely not me internet-stalking some of your dead acquaintances and cold-messaging you!

"Look, my time at the Light was . . . really complicated. I wasn't in a great place. I don't really necessarily want to revisit it."

"Like I said, I totally respect that. I'm just working on a project right now where I'm trying to get a feel for what these insulated spiritual communities are like, and it helps me to speak with people who have lived that way. Do you mind if I ask . . . how you got into it?"

"Which part? The Light or, like, the stuff that came after?"

"Wherever you'd like to start," I say. Yet another improv scene.

"I had a friend who signed me up. That's the usual way people get involved: a member recruits them for a class or a retreat or whatever. I was looking for something in my life, and everything was just up in the air for me."

"So . . . you signed up for a retreat?"

"I enrolled in classes through the Institute at first. Just an online thing, because I was still living in Syracuse."

"The . . . Institute."

"Oikos Phaos. Pretentious name, but whatever. I really loved what I got from the workshop, and so I decided to come down here and do a retreat, and some more classes with the Institute. It was an answer, I guess. A way to give purpose to my life."

"Did you relocate here for the House of Light?" I ask.

Becca snorts. "Yeah, I guess I did. I mean, they kind of suggest you can turn it into a career, if you're good enough at recruiting, and at the time that seemed like a viable path. I moved in with a friend who was also doing the Process—"

"What was her name?" I ask, a bit too eagerly.

Becca narrows her eyes at me. "Why?"

"Just making conversation."

"It doesn't matter. She's . . . out of the picture now." Becca watches my face. I wonder if she knows Hannah is dead. "What is this project you're working on again?" she asks.

"Research for a role. I'm trying to figure out my character, and the best way to do that is to spend time with people who've lived similar lives."

"And you said you got my name from the magazine?"

"Um . . ." I stall, knowing that anything I say at this point will reveal that I've been lying. I'm considering coming clean, explaining everything, when her face changes.

"Oh shit. Look, I would never say anything to anyone. You can go back and tell them that I haven't said anything, and that I won't. I swear to God. You have my collateral, I know how this works so . . ." Becca's face is rumpled in fear, and she's falling over her words.

"I think you misunderstood—"

"Look, I get it, this is a test. My lips are sealed, seriously."

"Back up here, Becca. I'm not testing you, or whatever. I'm trying to find out what happened to some women who were involved in the House of Light. Their names were Hannah and Allison, and I think you knew—"

"Jesus, I already said I wouldn't talk! Do you think I want all that stuff I gave them out in the world? Just leave me alone!" Becca has stood up, and her hands are shaking. She nearly trips over the chair in her haste to make it to the door. I follow her, but she's already practically racing down the sidewalk.

"Becca, wait!" I call. She turns around just long enough to look me straight in the eye.

"I don't know how you're involved with them, but if I can give you any advice, just . . . don't give them the collateral. They don't fuck around. I'm living proof of that."

"Becca, hang on!"

Becca dashes across the street and clambers into a small, aging Honda. She's pulled out before I can catch her.

CHAPTER 12

The Oikos Phaos Institute, unlike the House of Light, does have a website, and a reasonably extensive one at that; from what I can see on my phone, it looks like someone quite professional set it up. Supposedly Oikos's mission is "centering the self in a decentered world by taking ownership of past trauma and future action." I have to read that sentence three times to figure out whether it actually means anything, and I decide that it doesn't, really. The Institute offers self-improvement workshops for people who "find themselves destabilized in an environment that is too often defined by upheaval." Basically, midlife crisis, please pay here. The fees are not cheap.

It takes me several minutes to remember why the name sounds familiar, but of course it does click eventually. Allison. She worked at the Institute for a few months before her death, as some kind of administrative assistant. I reflect that I really blew it with Becca—she was seriously spooked. Did she think I was part of the House of Light, sent to check up on her? Or working for someone else entirely? I send her a DM, explaining myself and repeating that I just want to find out what happened to Hannah and Allison. But I'll be surprised if she writes me back. Whatever someone is holding over her, it's very effective. Who did she give collateral to? What does that even mean?

There's not much to do in Watkins Glen, I soon surmise. It's a quaint, sleepy little town, NASCAR and wine routes and a weirdly high concentration of ice cream shops. To kill time while I wait for a car to be available, I duck into a store filled with hunting gear and waders and snowshoes and hats.

I emerge with several massive bags of country costume: flannel shirts, hiking boots, a Carhartt vest and beanie. A new wardrobe for my rural sojourn. The woman checking me out looks, unaccountably, irritated by the bulk of my purchases. I throw in a pair of wildly overpriced socks just to see her lips turn down a bit more at the corners.

After a lengthy wait, a car deposits me back at Ava's house. I should move to the hotel in town, but I'm finding Ava's life so tempting. I've taken over her project, her guest room, sitting in the living room with her husband and child. Maybe she'll never come home from the House of Light. I realize, with a jolt, that this is a possibility, given the trend of other women who have found themselves deeply involved with the group, and then I feel shitty for the thought.

I call Topher from the deck, to discuss what we'll need to get the podcast going.

"Yo, Liv! Good to hear from you, I thought I'd be talking to Jess? Normally she handles all the nitty-gritty, amirite?"

"Jess is focusing on some other stuff right now. This is kind of . . . my pet project, and since I'm on the ground . . ."

"Right, right, right, Liv, so jazzed about this, think it's going to be great, do you think you could maybe get to Ithaca? One of my investment partners has a small broadcast company there, and he's got a studio with decent enough equipment. I've got a producer who can swing by and get some shit done, we'll lay down one, maybe two episodes and see how it sounds, talk about a release ASAP. Right, we want ASAP because you're, like, breaking a case here, don't wanna get scooped, amirite?"

My participation is clearly not required for most of this conversation, and once I've promised to report to the studio this afternoon, Topher hangs up. It will be a scramble for me to put together exactly what I want to say for the first episode, and I do momentarily balk at what I'm starting, but I know that you have to just let artistic impulse rule the day; you can't second-guess it too much or you stifle it, and I just have to leap before I look if I want to do this.

The script turns out to be the easiest bit, and I have enough to get the broad strokes of a second episode. I don't have much audio aside from me talking, but I have some ideas about clips we can lift from other places: there's a YouTube video of the news report that covered Amy's death; we can get someone to read the articles about the other deaths; there are some very New Age, high-production videos from the Institute website that will sound great. I'm sure whoever the producer is, they'll be able to find some other things to add variety and tension.

The producer, I learn that afternoon, is named Naia, and she is the most focused, zero-bullshit content creator I have ever encountered. Aside from her spelling her name for me, we engage in absolutely no small talk. I assume she knows who I am, but she certainly doesn't acknowledge it. She reads my script swiftly, cuts a few paragraphs, jots in a few extra lines, and then, wordlessly, pulls out an iPad, on which she types furiously. Finally, she announces to the studio techs that we're ready to record.

I pride myself on not needing too much direction, and here, at least, Naia seems pleased with me. We get the recordings done in remarkably few takes, and the techs look a little shell-shocked themselves at all this brute efficiency. Where did Topher find her? Maybe she wants Jess's job.

I quail at the thought of Jess. She will be furious with me, possibly madder than she ever has been, even madder than after my lost weekend in Trinidad, when she was basically convinced I had drowned while scuba diving. Jesus, she had been hours away from calling a tragic press conference, and though I know she was glad I wasn't dead after all, it took a few weeks for her to say so. She's not going to like me doing this. And she's definitely not going to like that I pulled it all together without her help. Without her permission.

Too bad, Jess!

We'd been in the Caribbean after we wrapped season four, which had been especially grueling. Mina uncovers the truth about her own origins and realizes that her grandfather used her as an experiment in his quest to raise the dead, so she spends most of the season on the run or in captivity at the converted salt mine (now a high-security lab) beneath the lake. It had been physically and emotionally demanding, since I'd filmed most of my scenes alone, in front of a green screen. Her connection with Elliott severed while she is institutionalized, Mina loses her grip on reality, and becomes vulnerable to her grandfather's manipulation—basically, she goes a little nuts, and I had started to go a bit off the rails myself. Ryan and I had fought, bitterly, during the wrap party, causing a scene that involved a fully loaded craft service table, and we were subsequently spending the break in shooting apart. We were learning that this peaks-and-valleys style of being together worked better for us than constantly maintained presence and affection; we both liked space, and found ourselves almost deliberately provoking fights when we needed a break.

Jess, pragmatically, packed a bag of swimsuits and booked us into a suite in a hotel in Trinidad, decreeing a few weeks of sunshine, rum (never more than one for Jess, always more than one for me), and beach reading. No boys, no (prescription) downers, and no work. But Jess and I are happiest with each other when we're working, working toward the same goal. She identifies strongly with her Virgo self: always, always working.

For the first two weeks, it was bliss. We woke up late, loafed over plates of fruit, and staggered, sun-drunk, down to the beach to swim and float in the sea. I devoured Dennis Lehane thrillers, and Jess read all of Patricia Highsmith. Then we swapped books.

She made us appointments for massages, found the best places for fresh fish, chartered a sailboat, and we slid brainlessly from one day to the next.

But in our last week, we started to wear on each other.

"Liv, you have to wear more sunscreen. You know you can't show up on set this brown. You'll catch hell from Jane."

"I'm not sure why I couldn't find anyone less joyless to go on vacation with."

"Liv, that's your sixth piña colada of the day. Do you really think . . ."

"Can you not leave your wet bikini ON my bed?"

The sniping escalated until I couldn't be in the same room with her without gritting my teeth (which she couldn't help complaining about). I threw a caftan over my swimsuit one afternoon and trekked to the closest bar, determined to enjoy myself and let loose. The reality is that I had relaxed enough; I wanted to go back to work, was ready to refocus. It bothered me that I was like Jess in this way; I wanted to be wild and fun and stupid but I was here with someone who was none of those things, and it bugged me because that's who I'd *chosen* to be with.

So I ditched Jess and went drinking with some locals, staying out all night, eventually taking their boat to check out a nearby sandbar or island, I don't remember which. I didn't call Jess then, nor the next day, when I got a pretty bad sunburn drinking Carib and enjoying my anonymity out on the water. Even when the boat (which turned out to be part of a local snorkeling expedition's fleet) finally docked, I didn't go back to the hotel. At this point, to be perfectly honest, I simply wanted her to worry, to fret and miss me and feel my absence. Because I was needy and unsure of myself and hoping Jess would freak out and look for me. Freak out she did, so much so that by the time I eventually turned up, hungover and cocktail-shrimp-colored, members of the press (Vorchek, who else?) had already heard rumors that I'd gone missing, had been eaten by sharks, had been kidnapped, had overdosed, had run off with a louche member of the aristocracy.

When I strolled back into the hotel room, Jess was drafting a press release and was about to call my father. She had looked up when I walked in and just squinted at me. That's how I knew I'd really fucked up. She didn't even yell.

"You were right about the sunscreen," I said meekly.

"There's aloe in my toiletries."

In the bathroom, I daubed the worst swatches of peeling skin. When I emerged, sheepish, I held the bottle out to Jess, to do my back. After a long look she made me sit down on the cold stone floor so she could get my shoulders. The coolness of the floor was bliss on my toasted ass. After a long moment, and some heavenly dollops of aloe, she spoke.

"Is it that you need proof of love, Liv? Is that why you behave so badly, push people away? Because I can't figure out what else could possibly drive you to act the way you do sometimes. These meltdowns, this chaotic . . . weird shit you pull. Is it a test?"

"It could be. I don't know. Maybe I just want to see how far I can push it. You. Everyone. Before they're done with me."

"Well, spoiler alert. I'm not going to be the first one to tap out. You're playing chicken with the wrong person."

"Why don't you, though?" I asked. Jess had finished her ministrations, but I didn't turn around.

"What?"

"Tap out? Why don't you ever say 'Enough is enough' and just walk?"

"It's not how I'm built."

"Oh yeah? Or is it because you don't have anything else in your life but me?" I regretted saying this almost instantly. There was a long pause, and I didn't know whether Jess was mad or hurt or stunned.

"Wow, you actually think that, don't you?" she finally said, and it was with amusement, not fury. "But I guess that works well for both of us. You think you're my whole world, and you can pretend that I'm just . . . your helpful satellite. And I get to keep my private life the way I like it. And you know from experience that that's a real gift. I suppose it's the one thing I've got that you never will."

"Privacy is overrated," I grumbled, standing up.

"Well, let's see if that's still your position once Vorchek's pictures come out. I'm pretty sure he got a nip slip."

Jess quickly disappeared into her room, departing with the upper hand, leaving me stunned at being so thoroughly tactically routed. I knew, of course, that this was the opportunity to ask her about her life beyond me, before me. But I was scared: either to learn that she had a rich and developed world that had nothing to do with me or to learn that I was her world, that she was in love with me, as the tabloids speculated. I couldn't face either reality, so at dinner that night, our second to last on the island, I pretended all was well. And so did Jess. She can put on a pretty good performance, too.

The nip-slip pictures turned out to not be so bad. And it wasn't long after that the Director invited me out on his boat.

. . .

Naia is eager to send me on my way, and she's stern with me.

"Once we air this, we won't have much time to put together the rest of the season. I think I can get two episodes out of this, with a bit of massaging. But you need to be serious about the investigative side of things, or it's going to be a total flop. I'm good, and I can make pretty much anything sound dramatic, but if there's no story, nothing can hide the fact that it kind of sucks. Topher was pretty adamant about getting it out there, though, so here we are," she says.

"Topher does a lot of cocaine. But we go way back, he knows me. He knows if I think there's something interesting, it's worth trying."

"He knows he doesn't want you to call Pineapple Street or Wondery or Gimlet," Naia points out, and I consider whether maybe I should have done just that . . .

"I'm in between projects at the moment, so this is all I'm working on right now," I reassure her. She gives me a skeptical look, as though my promise to work really hard is maybe not entirely enough to win her confidence.

"Well, do your best. This is really promising, and I'd hate to just pad something with filler and wrap it up half-baked after a lackluster six-week run."

I feel like this is high praise, coming from her, and I resolve not to fuck this up, like I've fucked up everything else.

"Don't worry—I have some ideas and a few leads to chase down," I tell her.

"About that. I don't want to, let's say, 'nudge' your investigation in a particular direction. But I think we both know which theory plays best, in terms of audience interest," Naia says.

"Oh?"

"The serial-killer one," she says. "Obviously. I'm just saying, whatever . . . points in that direction is definitely something we want to pursue. Just so you can keep your eye peeled for that sort of lead."

"But I should, like . . . look into everything, right?"

"Just follow your instincts. We'll patch everything together in a way that makes sense with whatever you come back with. But just so we're on the same editorial page."

"Got it," I say.

"One more thing."

I cock my head, waiting.

"Have you given a thought to the title?"

"Oh, um, no. . . . We could call it . . . *Dead Girls of the House of Light*?" She just snorts at me. "Okay, what about . . . *Death on the Lake*?"

"Bit on the nose, don't you think?" Naia asks with another snort. "Is it an Agatha Christie book?"

"Isn't that the point with this genre?"

"Typically, sure. But I thought we'd go with something that . . . has a bit more self-awareness built in. A critique."

"Like what?" I ask.

"Like . . . *Vultures,*" she says with a small shrug.

I consider this. "Interesting."

"Because we're all circling the dead bodies. And the House of Light is circling the vulnerable. And the press circles you. And now, full circle, you're the press, joining in at the feast."

"Dark," I say.

"And?" Naia asks with a big smile.

"Works for me. I say go for it."

She looks relieved, and pleased with herself. "Great. I'd like to get this published in the next few days. I'll crunch the rest of the audio clips and talk about promo with Topher. We'll have to get a trailer out in the next, fuck, few hours, and talk ad budget . . ."

I can tell Naia is done with me, swiftly transitioning to the next phase. "I'll get out of your hair. Let me know what else you need from me."

"Are you available for the next couple of days, in case we need to get down some extra audio?"

"Sure thing. I've hired a driver for the week, so I should have more flexibility. Call me, anytime."

"Please update me with developments. I can use them as teasers." With this, I am dismissed, and I head down the stairs and out the door.

I'm just a block from the library, so that's where I head, on foot, texting my new driver, Fred, to take a couple hours and circle back for me later. He replies by sending me the emoji with sunglasses.

CHAPTER 13

My mother used to bring me to the library every week. She always seemed comfortable at our small library, in a way that she never did in any other public space. Restaurants, grocery stores, even cars made her nervous. But she relaxed every time we stepped inside the quiet arena of a library, and she moved sure-footed through the stacks, her long printed dresses swishing only slightly above her Converse sneakers. I would cling to the tail of the flannel shirt knotted around her waist as she zagged through new releases, nonfiction, the children's section.

Because, ultimately, we were not hugely bookish people. I always left with a small pile of more or less age-appropriate materials, and I did fall madly in love with some books. (Anything written by Tamora Pierce, basically. For years I fantasized about being cast as Alanna—and, of course, now I am too old.) But my mother liked to come to the library for two things: the magazines and the movies.

I would be dispatched to the children's section to pick out my books while my mother gathered an armful of plastic-encased magazines and sank contentedly into one of the ratty armchairs. When I returned after my distracted perusal, she would still be there, raptly flapping through the sleek pages. She can't have read any of the content: she turned the pages so quickly she barely had time to register the captions. No, she devoured the magazines, drinking in the images in a frenzied glut. I would come back and crawl into her lap or, when I got bigger, pull up a chair to watch her tear through the glossies, chewing through a *Vogue* at the same rate as a *Cosmo*. It was like she spent our days at home hungering for images, and once at the library, she could binge on what she'd craved in the drab quiet of our run-down farmhouse.

Some days I imagine her clawing through them, somewhere in the Northwest, and pausing over pictures of me. I try to guess what she might think or feel looking at my face, sixteen years older than the last time she saw it.

When she'd made it through all of her favorites (just once: she never revisited them, as far as I could tell), we would go prowl through the rows of VHS films that could be rented. The selection remained small—the library would transition to DVDs before too long, and that collection would quickly outpace the chunky cardboard wedges we fingered through. But a DVD player was an extravagance that my father insisted we couldn't afford, not while he was trying and failing to write his epic play and (as he constantly reminded us) burning through the scant allowance his modest trust fund permitted him. Either of my parents could have gotten a job—we could have then turned on the heat instead of layering on sweatshirts in the winter, or eaten something other than canned soup for lunch nearly every day—but neither parent was very suited to work. Mom was too vacant, Dad too grandiose, convinced of his own genius. As someone who has never really had a normal job, I suppose I sympathize. Maybe it's hereditary.

When I walk into the overly air-conditioned public library in Ithaca, I think immediately of Mom. Not of the version I usually conjure, of her that last week she was in my life, as I try to figure out what might have been going on behind that mask of hers; rather, I remember her flitting in and out of the library of my youth, grinning happily when she located a copy of *The Last Unicorn*, a film she'd loved when she was younger. This was one of the films we would return to again and again, even when I was far past the target age. She had other favorites, too: movies that made her feel comforted and young or, maybe, that she hoped would impart the same feelings to me. As a special treat, we would some-times go to the Blockbuster around the corner to rent a new re-lease. So much of that treasured life with my mother was about escaping reality, seeking out the more appealing versions in maga-zines, movies, make-believe.

I speed-walk through the library, trying to get a sense of the layout on my own, but eventually I relent and approach the infor-mation desk to ask where I can find local history.

"Back left, near the bathroom," I am succinctly informed.

. . .

Guys, I didn't know microfilm was still a thing. Very weird to be looking through this tiny little eyepiece at really old newspapers well into the twenty-first century. Also pretty hard to do a key-word search.

Maybe I'm just a shitty researcher—I'm probably a shitty researcher—but I couldn't find much about the House of Light in any local papers, or even in zoning records dating back to when the Light would have originally been built.

I did find a newspaper article that talks about the Light: it seemed to be a local fluff piece, dating back to the late eighties. It talked a lot about their food, their gardens, and this crazy new thing they were trying out called "yoga." Not exactly hard-hitting journalism. The weird thing is that there was a photo in the arti-cle.

Rain is in the photo and she's identified as Rain Fall (I'm as-suming that's not her real name), along with someone named Sol-stice O'Connor. The third person is identified as Dr. Samuel S. VanHorn.

I couldn't find anything online about Rain or Solstice, maybe unsurprisingly, since I doubt those are their legal names. I looked for Dr. VanHorn online as well, and found only an obituary from 2016. But since I was at the library, I decided to have a peek through some newspapers dated for that time and found some-

thing kind of weird. It's an article from just two months before he died.

Titled "Local Gynecology Practice Closes amid Allegations of Abuse and Malpractice," it went on to say this: "Dr. Samuel VanHorn of Ithaca, New York, has recently retired in the wake of a complaint regarding his private practice.

"Two patients have come forward this month with allegations that he touched them inappropriately, proposed invasive procedures, and, in one case, recommended an unnecessary hysterectomy. This second patient claims that when she sought a second and third opinion regarding her uterus, she was told such a procedure was 'outrageously unwarranted' and 'hugely irresponsible.' Both women are remaining anonymous while these claims are investigated. VanHorn, a graduate of Cornell who has worked in obstetrics since the eighties, has run his own private practice in Ithaca since 1983. VanHorn risks losing his license as a result of the current investigation into his work, a source in his office said."

Weird, right? I'll get into that in just a minute, but first a quick word from our sponsors.

Are you sick of spending way too much for everyday makeup essentials? Tired of overpaying for brand names when the ingredients are virtually the same? LuminUs uses all the same high-quality, all-natural ingredients to create simple, elegant, and effective cosmetics for women on the go. Try our concealer to cover up any flaws and blemishes, from discoloration to zits. Our bee-venom lipstick plumps up thin lips and moisturizes cracked ones. Fed up with those dark circles underneath your eyes? We have a whole range of eyeliners, shadows, and eye creams that will help make your eyes look wider, brighter, and ready for that big meeting at work. Our jade roller helps decrease puffiness and increase circulation and the glow of health. Can't decide where to start? Try our Babelicious Beauty Box, where each month, a team of beauty experts will pick out the best organic, cruelty-free anti-aging products for your beauty concerns. You can't put a price on feeling young. Don't spend one more day looking anything less than your absolute best, babe: get your LuminUs subscription today!

. . .

I wander through the streets of the small town, listening to podcasts on my phone. I'm wearing big sunglasses, so only one or two people recognize me, and I scuttle quickly by before they have a chance to take selfies in which I'll be tagged on social media: I want the podcast to drop alongside the news that I'm no longer in rehab, to give it that extra bump of drama and gossip. I won't be on the cover of anything, but maybe an insert on page two or three?

As I listen and think about the structure of an audio story, I consider my dead girls, and my responsibility toward them. I owe them this story, of course, but I wonder if my obligations stretch further. Is it good enough to find out what happened to them and to tell as many people as will listen? Is that what they would want?

But why should it matter what they want? The stories told about us are not our own. Each time someone wonders whether, after a plushy few weeks of vacation, the modest swell of my belly is a baby bump, I'm no more than a fictional character in a story that borrows my name. No one cares what the truth is, not really. Our appetite is more interested in the narrative, the stringing along of tantalizing possibility. Too often what has happened is dull, unspicy. It's not a baby, it's too many tacos and margaritas. It's not murder, it's just a sad, small life that ends, strange and lonely, with unresolved questions. My mother walked out of my life—there's no podcast for her. Because it's too easy to imagine her stultifying life of domesticity growing ever more oppressive, until finally, one day when her child is old enough to fend for herself, she can disappear into loamy pine forests a coast away, to start again.

We used to watch *Unsolved Mysteries*, my mother and I. It gave me terrible nightmares; there was a full year where I couldn't sleep in the same room as an old trunk we owned, because we had watched a segment where a woman is beaten unconscious and locked into a similar trunk, only to wake up a few hours later, trapped.

"She would have been alive for days, as many as three or four," Robert Stack intoned. "Investigators later found her bloody fingernails embedded inside the walls of the trunk, claw marks fully visible."

Remembering this, I think with unease about the missing element—the "earth" body, lying somewhere in the dirt.

Why had we watched that show? Did she want to prepare me for a life where women were locked into trunks and chucked from trucks and strangled by boyfriends? Was she preparing me for the ultimate mystery of her own disappearance? Was she preparing me for this moment, when I would go on the search for my own dead girls?

Was she setting me up to try to find her, find myself, find my light? Or did she simply want me, always, to keep looking?

. . .

Late that afternoon, I wander into the sterile lobby in what is supposedly the four-star hotel in the Glen—it resembles nothing so much as a Radisson or Holiday Inn, down to the dark and sticky bar with a dull and overpriced menu. At the front desk I'm assured that there are plenty of rooms, and, with some trepidation, I book a week on my credit card. Jess isn't sufficiently pissed at me to have canceled the thing, and the transaction goes through hitch-free.

I take the elevator up to my new digs and am pleasantly surprised by the view: the long lake glitters beneath me, a craggy finger pointing north. I try to guess where the House of Light and then Ava's house might be, but it's impossible to know for sure. I flop onto the bed, turn on the TV, flip through images on my phone. I'm terrifically bored.

Thankfully, Naia calls with a handful of small questions. She runs me through some of the audio clips she's found—she's not asking my permission to include them, merely informing me. Any notion that I might get to direct this project is dismantled: yet again, I'm just the talent. In this context, I'm not even the pretty face. Just a name, a brand, a hashtag. I sigh, disgusted, wondering why I even got into this in the first place. Naia tells me she plans to drop the episode in a day or two.

"Jesus, so soon?" I ask her.

"Well, yeah. There will be press coverage, maybe even TV spots. I want this thing out there."

"But I'm not, like, a journalist. We're not reporting on this," I clarify.

"No, even better. We're *driving* the news. We help decide what gets reported," she says, a note of glee in her voice. This does not discharge my uncomfortable sense of responsibility. Quite the opposite. But the gears are in motion, and I am merely a cog. She says goodbye, and I wonder what I'll be hearing when I check my podcast app tomorrow. I see a handful of newsletters that have gone out, pumping the series. Naia works fast.

Anxious and restless, I abandon my hotel room. My driver waits for me downstairs.

• • •

Why do we love true crime? Smarter people than I have theorized about this, and come up with much better answers. For me, though, there is a motivation that feels genuine about why I engage with these stories, why I like to consume them. Why, I guess, I'm now producing one.

All my life, I have felt the hate that is directed at my body. Every time a tabloid publishes an image of me looking "fat" or "ugly." Every time a director asks me to lose fifteen pounds, or a man ogles me in a bar or touches me without permission. Every time I'm catcalled or threatened or followed. Every time I've put on a pair of high heels, or been waxed into oblivion, or asked to conceal or augment my face until it is no longer mine. Every time a man has tried to reduce my access to healthcare. Sometimes when men I love say things about my body, or another woman's body, that turns her, me, into an object, a piece of meat. To live in a body that is perceived as female is to feel hatred, all the time.

But there is a strange corollary: should someone else do physical violence to my body, it will likely be avenged in the criminal justice system. Someone will look for and punish my killer (unlike the killers of young black men, who are the most likely to be murdered). It's a promise that all that hatred reaches a point at which it's gone too far. This obsession with young white female bodies is intertwined with the control exerted over them: we never stop looking at them, critiquing them, venerating them, dominating them. Especially when they're dead.

So when I read or hear about a story where someone has annihilated a female body—or, better yet, several female bodies, ones that maybe look like mine—I feel, in a strange way, less crazy. Less paranoid. Because I can feel the hatred, but I've been told so many times that it's in my head, that I'm exaggerating or confused. When I hear a story of a man destroying women simply because they are women, I feel vindicated for this state of vigilance I've existed in my whole life. It's unlikely that I will be targeted by a serial killer, sure. But I've been targeted by the male gaze my whole life, in all its creepy, stalking violence. I've performed to that gaze—I've made a career out of it, even when it felt exploitative. I've learned to imitate it when I look at other women. There is safety in that gaze, because if you're looking, maybe you're not being watched.

I look at these dead girls, and sometimes I think that by looking I can avoid being one.

But, of course, there is pleasure in the looking, too, right? We know we shouldn't look, but we want to look, we enjoy it. We know there is something predatory in the looking, so we feel guilt, *but it is guilty pleasure, a kind of consumption we let ourselves off the hook for. We are hungry for it. We are hungry for what we are fed.*

. . .

When Wyatt walks through the door, it smells of roast chicken—at least that's my hope. I've guessed that he'll be home not too long after sunset, and it's just gone fully dark outside when I hear the click of the door and the sound of shoes thumping to the ground. A dissatisfied squeal and the drum of small feet follows. I'm turning around when I'm struck amidships by a tiny body.

"Mama!" the little creature yelps, clinging to my calves. Wyatt enters the kitchen just in time to see my flustered expression. I crouch down to Zora's level.

"Sorry, kiddo. Not the mama. But you can help me make dinner if you want?"

Zora's face collapses in dismay, and I can see a temper tantrum brewing. "Nooo . . ." the kid begins, but Wyatt can also see what's about to happen and intercedes, swooping in and tossing her up.

"*Brrrrrmmmmm* goes the airplane. How about we fly first-class to beddy-bye?"

"No beddy-bye! Where's a sloth? Want the sloth!"

"Sloth is waiting for snuggles in your room. Let's go check on him." Wyatt gives me a brb look, and I nod: *Sure, go for it. I'm an interloper in your house, no need to look apologetic on my behalf.*

I turn back to the salad I've been assembling, and check the chicken and the potatoes roasting in its fat beneath it. Although I don't have a meat thermometer, I'd guess the chicken needs fifteen more minutes, at least. Ava's kitchen is very strangely stocked—I find six jars of capers but no mustard, a pot of fresh tarragon but no black pepper—but I'm able to toss together the basics of a simple salad dressing. Just as I'm checking the seasoning with my pinkie tip, Wyatt returns.

"Sorry about that," he begins.

"No, I'm sorry. I know I must be disrupting your routine—"

"No, don't worry about it. I wasn't sure you'd still be here but, well . . ." He looks sheepish. "Dinner sure smells good."

I laugh. "Heck, it's the least I can do for abusing your hospitality this way. Here, I opened this, I hope that's okay"—I gesture toward a bottle on the counter—"and dinner should be done in just a few minutes. Nothing fancy, just a chicken and some veggies."

"Can't think of anything better," he says gruffly, pouring a hefty glass of wine, pausing, then pouring another and sliding it toward me.

"Kiddo is in bed?" I ask.

"Yeah, she ate and had a bath at my parents'. Hopefully she'll be down for the count."

"Seems like she adapts to things pretty well."

"Well, she has to. That's just life around here."

I nod and wander over to the couch. "Can't be easy," I say. "But it looks like you're doing an incredible job."

As I hoped, he beams pinkly. What the fuck am I doing here? Wyatt sits on the couch next to me, a few respectful feet away.

"I looked you up today," he adds, after a long pause. "I thought you looked really familiar and then . . . well, I typed in your first name and you showed up pretty quick." I smile, letting him know I'm not mad, or annoyed. "We actually watched your show, you know. *Iroquois Falls*? Ava really liked it."

"Really?" I ask. I'm surprised, not least because she never said anything about it.

"She had read the book first. *The Unquiet Grave*. It was written by a local author, actually—she lives not that far from here. But what Ava was particularly interested in was the sister angle. You know, long-lost siblings, united through their dark past and their totally crazy mother. At least, I think that's what she responded to."

"Well, it can't have been the top-notch graphics, at least for the first season!" I laugh. "Our early episodes are sort of a meme for poorly executed special effects—though I do have to defend the later seasons, which improved."

"I appreciated the early seasons. It was about the story, not the CGI," Wyatt says graciously. "I guess we both connected with the whole ghost story thing, too. Speaking to the dead, all that. Ironic, I guess," he adds with a snort. I wait for him to clarify, and he finally notices my carefully arched eyebrow. "Oh, right. We watched the show with Ava's sister. And, well, now *she's* the ghost we live with."

"Ah. This is . . . the one who died . . . out back?" I clarify delicately.

"In the barn, yeah."

I wait. I need to hear the rest of this story, but if I'm too much of a ghoul, he'll clam up.

"She was . . . troubled. Ran in the wrong circles, had a lot of addiction issues of her own. Nobody knew how bad it was until . . . well, after. Otherwise we would have helped."

"She . . . died in a fire," I say tentatively.

"Yeah. Well. There was quite a bit of drama surrounding all that. A lot of questions."

"But . . . they were answered."

"Boy, were they answered. They just weren't the answers Ava wanted, I'm afraid."

"At least there's no uncertainty," I say. "That can be the hardest thing." Wyatt looks up at me. Shit, I think, he's going to tack to my mother, since he's googled me. I move on swiftly, not wanting to turn the conversation back to me. Not yet. "At least Ava doesn't have to wonder what happened to her sister. There's a kindness in that, at least."

Wyatt snorts. "Sure. She knows for sure about Zelda, so instead she goes obsessing over every other young woman who dies around here. Displaced trauma, as I think of it."

"You . . . know about her research?" I ask, surprised.

Wyatt gives a bitter chuckle. "I know she thinks I'm clueless. That I have no idea what goes on in that mind of hers. And that's fine with me, always has been. But I'm not blind, and I'm not oblivious. It just suits her to suppose that I am."

"Ah," I say.

"I poked around in her office a year or eighteen months back, just wondering what she was obsessing over. I thought she might be—" He shakes his head in sudden mirth. "You know, I thought she might be writing a memoir, of all things. Fool, I am. Anyway, I found her macabre little folder, her speculations on these dead girls. All that shit. I guess she told you all about it at the Light?"

"It came up, yeah."

"And now there's another one, I hear. So she'll have something else to fuss over for the next year while she imagines that her Shadow Man is seducing young women and murdering them—"

"Wait, what?" I interrupt. "Shadow Man?"

"Oh, she didn't spin her pet theory for you?"

"Well, she said she thought the Light was involved . . ."

"Oh, she does. She thinks there is a puppet master who controls the Light and essentially he uses Rain and Devotion to pull them into his orbit before he . . . screws them and sacrifices them to his pagan gods, I guess. Or some version of that."

"Does she have a name for this Shadow Man?"

"Well, no—that's why she has the silly moniker for him, right? She thinks if she compiles enough information on all the missing girls, she'll eventually find the link that leads her back to the Shadow Man."

"I didn't realize she . . . had such a specific hypothesis," I stutter.

"She knows it makes her sound totally insane, right? So she tends to keep that in the bag for a while."

"Wait. She *tends* to . . . Does she try to get other people on board with this project?" I ask, a shoe dropping somewhere in the cluttered closet of my mind.

"She tried to get you involved, didn't she?" Wyatt asks with a sad smile, taking a long pull from his nearly empty wineglass. "Damn. I should have suspected. You'd be just the ticket for her to get some 'attention' on the story."

"I feel like a gullible idiot," I say, shaking my head. "Damn."

"Don't feel bad. She's persuasive. Not as skilled a manipulator as her sister, but still."

"And her sister . . . I mean, you're absolutely sure she's not connected to these deaths? I mean, the date, the way she died . . ."

"The date, I can't comment on. Who knows what that's about. But her death . . . well, look through the file Ava keeps on her sister, if you want. I'll pull it up on the computer in the office, and you can read it while I set the table."

"Oh, I . . . I wouldn't want to intrude . . ." I want to intrude, very badly.

"Don't worry about it. Ava sucked you into this, so the least I can do is show you what you're dealing with. And maybe save you the time of chasing around murders that aren't murders and so on. I know what it's like to be on an Antipova wild-goose chase."

He sighs, swigs the rest of his wine, and leads me back to the office. A few keystrokes and clicks of the mouse, and he's got a letter up on the screen. Or, rather, a photo of a letter.

"Go ahead. It's dark and all, but have at it. I'll lay some plates and dress the salad." He leaves me to it.

When I try to fall asleep in the guest room later, I toss and turn, certain that Zelda isn't part of this story. Or, rather, that she's part of the story for Ava, but she isn't one of my dead girls; there is incontrovertible proof in that file, in the letter she left behind. The very premise of this investigation feels shaky now that I've gotten some glimpse into my primary informant, and a sick swoop of dread hits my innards. I'm doing something in the real world, something that will impact people's families; it's not just some teen TV show that, while occasionally exploitative, still ultimately doesn't *do* anything. Anxiety swamps me fully, akin to stage fright in its all-consuming grip, and I can't sleep. Finally, feeling shitty and weird, I skulk from the house just before dawn, unable to face Wyatt and his daughter in the light of day, knowing how I've used them both to flesh out my tale. And leaving the house, my terribly patient driver navigating along the dark navy of the lake, I think about the one thing that I might have gleaned from this: the shadow of a suspect.

CHAPTER 14

In my basic little hotel room a few days later, I awake to the sound of my phone blowing up. Several texts from Naia, alerting me that the episode is dropping, and a couple of very excited messages from Topher conveying his overall enthusiasm and hype. He's been getting lots of good vibes from people all over! Lots of buzz! This is encouraging. I open up my podcast app to listen to the whole episode.

Like most who work in the biz, I'm inured to the discomfort of hearing my own voice and the alienation that often accompanies that weird exercise in self-reflection. I take a few notes on my performance, reflecting that I need to slow down a bit. And I should probably be a bit more wry when using certain true crime clichés, lest I sound like one of those histrionic *Dateline* specials. I do not have Keith Morrison's smoky gravitas. Naia has spliced in some fucking excellent audio, and I am very pleased with her and her expertise. I text Topher that she deserves a bonus, and he sends me the cha-cha girl emoji. Cool.

I like it, I decide. It's not flawless, and I've made a lot of promises that I will now need to keep, but it's got something. Not least of which, I can't help thinking, is down to me, my rapt but slightly damaged air. My occasional breathless pauses. It's manipulative without feeling too manipulative—I can lead the audience where I like, and they'll sense that they're being led but without necessarily feeling the mechanisms taking them there. I text Naia a pleased but professional follow-up, asking her what else she needs from me.

I think I can do the next episode with what we've already recorded, she responds. They're short episodes, but I think that's better for this sort of edge-of-your-seat/seat-of-your-pants format.

I agree, and let her know that I'm available if she needs me, and that I'll be working on more details in the meantime. I sense her cautious approval.

A while later, I am strolling the streets of Watkins Glen, looking for coffee, when Jess rings me. I gird my loins.

"What the actual fuck, Liv?" she growls before I even offer my salutations.

"And good morning to you, Jess!"

"Did we not discuss this at fucking length? What in God's name do you think you're playing at?" Her voice is panicky in a way that I haven't heard for a very long time.

"Actually, I believe you expressed your opinion and promptly hung up on me."

"It wasn't opinion, Liv! Do you have any idea what you've opened yourself up to?"

"I'm not especially concerned, no. Topher's legal team vetted everything before the final edit."

"Well, I have news for you: Topher's legal team isn't your legal team. Nor, might I add, are they exactly the editors of the *Harvard Law Review*. They're shills and yes-men who are protecting Topher and Topher alone. On top of which: Topher? I mean, of all the people to involve in any kind of creative enterprise . . ."

"Look, Topher's not perfect, obviously. I trust him, but not, you know, that much."

"So you thought, Oh, cool, I'll just try out an entirely new medium, let him manage the whole thing and not even get my team to look over any contracts or paperwork? Because I'm a brilliant organizational mind?"

"Well, I thought you might say that," I reply, grinning to myself. "Which is why I insisted that we only talk contract and paperwork for the first episode. After which, I told him, you'd need to get involved with everything."

Jess is not as mollified as I thought she would be by this concession. "Oh, bloody fantastic. You knew that after the episode dropped I'd be in no position to tell you you had to back off, at which point I could just wade hip-deep into this shit and fix all the problems you've created. Lovely. Just brilliant!"

"I was thinking that it was more that you'd be able to see the potential of the project after the first episode, and that if the first one landed with enough of a splash you'd be . . . well, you'd be pleased."

"Fuck you, Liv, you do not get to have an I-told-you-so moment here! The fallout from this hasn't even started!"

"If there's big fallout, that means publicity. If not . . ." I shrug. A few people on the sidewalk have stopped to watch me conduct this conversation, and I give them a British royalty wave. They continue to observe me.

"You do realize," Jess goes on, "that you've essentially just suggested that there's a serial killer in a small American town running amok and murdering young women, right? Without any proof except that provided by an alcoholic yokel who has been famously bonkers for years? And, on top of that, you've suggested that this . . . killer is somehow related to the respectable spiritual organization you've recently been expelled from?"

"Pretty compelling storytelling, I think," I say sheepishly. I do hate to disagree with Jess, because she is so unerringly level-headed. Goddamn Virgo.

"I spent a good chunk of *my* morning on the phone with Rain, trying to smooth everything over and maybe, just maybe, get you readmitted. It would have been nice to know that you were actively sabotaging all my attempts to undo your little errors in judgment."

"I did try to be up front about all of this with you," I wheedle.

"No, you tried to steamroll me. And because you're Olivia Reed, and you're used to getting your way, you assumed you'd be able to just do as you pleased."

"C'mon, Jess. I'm interested in this project. You know that when something creatively engages me I can't help pursuing it."

"Yeah, and the last time we let you pursue your creative passions, how did it go? Swimmingly, yes?"

"*Ouch*. Meow. We just look at things from different sides of the same coin. I just feel like this is something I need to do," I say.

Jess seethes for a long moment, and I suspect she's chewing a fingernail; she'll have peeled off her whole gel manicure by lunch. It's what she does when she's stressed. Then, once she's destroyed her nails, she'll have to grumpily traipse back to the salon to have them fixed; she can't be seen as anything less than perfectly groomed.

"Well, regardless, it's done now," she finally responds. She is very evidently not happy, but the pitch of her voice is at least going down. "Liv, you just . . . you really don't know what you're fucking around with here," she continues wearily. "These people you've just pissed off, they're not going to just let you carry on with this."

"Do I smell conspiracy?" I ask. "Wait, can you repeat that while I record?"

"I can't really talk to you right now," she snaps. "I need to deal with some damage control. And you need to get me Topher's contact details immediately, so I can figure out what sort of deal with the devil you've arranged."

I forward his email from my phone as she speaks. "Done. Look, Jess, I'm sorry I've put you in this position—"

"Don't. You have no idea what position you've put me in."

I can tell from the silence that the line is dead, and that my oldest friend has just hung up on me. Again. I feel a gnawing in my stomach that I get only when she's mad at me. Which, I realize, is rare. It's always me and her against the world, and I don't like this new oppositional dynamic. Sure, she's always fussing at me to (a) straighten up, (b) fly right, and (c) grow the fuck up, but usually that fretting has the quality of a mother hen's. She doesn't shut me out, ever.

"Do you think we could do a selfie with you really quick?" The mother who'd been standing there with her tween daughter, observing me, swoops in the minute it's clear I'm no longer on the phone. "I just loved watching your show back in college."

I'm nearly back to my hotel when I realize I've forgotten to get a coffee, so I have to double back for it, my head in a bit of a fuzz. It occurs to me that I've made quite a mess of things here and that, indeed, following my artistic impulse was maybe not the most sensible thing I've done. But as I wait in line, and then for the barista to prepare an iced coffee, I check my email and my breath catches.

Because in there, amid the usual bullshit, is a different sort of email.

The subject line is:

THEY TRIED TO BURY MY FRIEND ALIVE

...

I'd forgotten that Naia had set up a website for the podcast, of course, and that she would forward anything of potential interest for me to follow up on. Naturally, the starfucker factor was a concern, and Naia had wanted to insulate me from the creeps and the crazies. The subject line I was reading now was a bit, er, stagy. But the body of the email piqued my interest.

I've been keeping my eye on these people for eighteen months and then this podcast drops, stating a lot of the things I've suspected for years! No Im not a conspiracy theorist and no im not crazy, but I think House of Light is much stranger than they seem and I've been trying to get to the bottom of it for years. Last year my friend did a retreat with them and came back totally weird and changed and was trying to get me all involved in it saying it would change my life and everything and I'll admit I was curious. I did a retreat with them and it wasn't so bad but then it just started to feel really creepy, especially when they kept asking me to bring my cousin and then I could do a special advance level workshop with them. And I said pyramid scheme much? And then they like freaked out and asked me to leave, but my friend stayed with them until last year when she showed up at my house in the middle of the night and she was totally filthy (like dirt in her nose and ears filthy) and she wouldn't say what happened just that she was done with the Light and she needed to get away. Then when I heard your podcast and you asked that question I was like, woah hang on. Do you think they tried to bury my friend alive? I'd be totally willing to be interviewed or whatever, I just want these sickos brought to justice.

xoxo Andy

I have no idea how to read this email. Genuine lead? Deranged attention seeker?

Naia texts me immediately, following up.

You have to go talk to this girl!!!

It's the only time her tone has been anything other than entirely neutral. So I guess I'll go find her, batshit or not.

• • •

A few emails later and I am in possession of an address just about an hour from where I am now, near somewhere called Penn Yan, at the top of yet another lake. My solid, sort-of-bald driver shrugs when I tell him the address, then grins broadly in the rearview mirror, as though conveying that he's up for anything. I spend the car ride making notes on my phone and glancing somewhat ner-

vously at the Google Street View results of the address. It's gritty.
I regret the blazer and tall boots I'm wearing, not least because of
the warm day, so I untuck my white T-shirt from my jodhpur leggings and put my hair up in a messy bun.

The woman's name is Andy, and she seemed lucid-ish in our
email exchange, but I still feel some apprehension and doubt.
Naia, though, was encouraged by the initial download numbers
and kept talking about "momentum"; her enthusiasm hasn't been
dampened in the slightest, and she is, after all, the professional. I
had promised to follow her lead, so I relented. It's not as though
the idea of a day gazing out at the placid lake and thinking about
my choices from the barren span of a hotel room held much ap-
peal. It's also not lost on me that Jess is the only person in my life,
really, and that, having alienated her, I'm terrifically alone. That
thought made me consider Wyatt and his cozy house and how
easily I could slide into it, and that made me slide into the smooth
leather seats of my hired car to get the fuck out of town and out
of my head, even if just for a little while.

We drive up the other side of the lake, past some large vineyards, barns in both good repair and disrepair, some grubby gas
stations, farmhouses, and double-wides. I quickly stop counting
cows because, Jesus. I do a preinterview over the phone, just to
get some basic information before Andy and I sit down.

When we pull up at the advertised address, I check my face in
my phone before uncertainly approaching the door.

Andy has been waiting for me, though, and she spills through
the screen before I can finish knocking.

"Holy shit, it's actually you. I kinda thought it would be, like,
some kind of prank."

"I guess it still could be," I say with a shrug and a winning
smile, and she guffaws.

"Fuck me, this is cool. No one is gonna believe me. Actually,
can we do a selfie?"

I relent. I can't imagine that her social media following can be super influential, so there's probably no plus or minus to exposure here at her house. She invites me inside.

The grim little trailer is dark, and the decor does nothing to brighten the place. A lot of brown dominates the overall interior scheme: brown carpets, brown curtains, a dark fake-wood cabinet arrangement that lurks heavily across the brow of the kitchen. No natural light, and an exposed bulb in the center of the living room ceiling. It's messy.

A spot is cleared for me on the graying couch, which, I note with some alarm, feels ever so slightly damp.

"Beer?" Andy calls from the kitchen, and I agree. She tosses me a can of Miller High Life. "Sorry, I don't have nothing fancier," she apologizes, though with a slight tone suggesting that she's not all that sorry.

"I don't mind," I answer with a good-natured shrug. "If it's okay, I'm going to record this . . . ?" She nods enthusiastically as I take out the recorder Naia has provided.

"Right, so," I say, adopting my beat-reporter cock of the head and slightly squinted eyes. I miss my jacket, suddenly. "Let's jump right in. Your name is Andy Crispin and you've . . . had some dealings with the Light." As I say this, I look around, perhaps a bit unsubtly, thinking that she's not the usual clientele. Andy appears to be a not-terrible reader of faces, even though I'm pretty sure she smoked a bowl before I got here, because she catches my look and laughs.

"I know, I'm not the usual granola-munching sort to go paying for some fancy retreat. This was a few years ago, though. I'd had to go to rehab for a little problem, and after I got out, I was in this halfway house that was sort of decent. And I met a more . . . I guess you could say 'spiritual' type. They were all about meditation and mindfulness and working in the fucking garden and all that, and I, well, got sorta into it. After you get outta rehab your brain isn't, like, totally firing on all cylinders, if you know what I mean. It's weird, it can sorta be like being high. You do shit you wouldn't normally do."

"So you . . . ended up involved with the Light."

"Well, I tried. I went to a few classes, and did a couple of weekend retreats. 'Yogurt and Yoga for Better Self-Discipline,' or some shit. I needed something in my life, and hey, 'probiotics' seemed a little less, um, destructive than some other things I've tried. But, shit, that place is expensive!"

"It sounds like you did some work exchange, though," I prompt.

"Yeah, they'll let you pay for part of the workshop with manual labor, basically. Scrubbing shit, digging shit, that sorta thing. The community, well, they're weird, but I liked it. I needed to have sober people around me, at the time, and I didn't exactly have many of those, you know, in my regular life."

"Did you feel safe at the House of Light?" I ask.

"Mostly, yeah, I did. They were kooky, and the food was wack, but they seemed like they wanted good things for us. I mean, I got the impression they definitely wanted our money, but they were, like, hoping we were okay, too."

"So what changed for you?"

"Well, after a few workshops, they started basically pressuring me to do more. To come for longer ones, do the advanced level. And then they wanted me to bring people."

"To recruit?"

"Basically, yeah. The problem was, I just wasn't the right sort of client for them." Taking a long swill of beer, Andy looks around her house, then laughs again. "They were pretty quick to cut me loose when they realized I was a dead end."

"Okay, so tell me about your friend. The one who first brought you to the Light."

"Yeah. Iris. She was great."

"Did she have a last name?"

"Well, probably, but she didn't mention it. I met her through the halfway house where I was staying. She was a counselor, but she did what she called 'bodywork.' Acupressure and shit. After a few sessions she told me I had some blockages or whatever, and I should check out the Light. So that's how I started coming. We'd drive together to do workshops, and I signed up for a few with her. She was trying to get a certification with them or something, so she was taking hella classes, like it was college or something. But she swore by it, and it kept me out of trouble, so I figured it was about as good as anything else."

"But you felt like Iris started to change?" I say.

"Oh yeah. She was this really chill girl when I met her, but she just started to get more and more stressed out. And, like, more . . . quiet? She'd tell me just about anything when we first met, but she started to shut down. She was getting really thin, and every time I asked her she said it was this new birth control thing she was trying and just shrugged it off. But all the time, she was just going to more and more workshops. Like her life kinda depended on it, if you know what I mean.

"And then one day, she just stopped showing up for her sessions at the halfway. She'd always been really fucking reliable, so it was a surprise. I texted and called her for a few days straight, but I didn't hear jack shit for a good week. I was real worried for her, but I'm, like, not her family or anything. I didn't feel it was my place to start freaking out."

"So you never called the police?" I press.

"Me and Five-O aren't, like, tight." Andy snickers. "I waddn't about to go calling them and having 'em show up in my doorway some night, you know. Besides, I figured she had people."

"But she did get back in touch?"

"Well, as it happened, *she* was the one who showed up on my doorway one night!" Andy laughs. She drains her beer and cracks open the one she has, with great forethought, placed next to her plaid chair. "I hear this knock on the door pretty late some night, and my first thought is *Fuuuccckkk*. I've been pretty good since rehab, but I'm no angel, and I'm on probation here, and I know I've got weed just sitting there in the living room. So I'm freaking out, trying to think of all the shit I've got here that might get me in trouble when I hear Iris say through the door, Andy, hey it's me, can you just let me in? And I fucking died with relief.

"So in she comes and my first thought is Fuck, girl, who buried you alive? Because Iris is just filthy. Like, covered in dirt—it's stuck in her hair, all over her face, her clothes are disgusting. She's managed to brush a lot of it off, but she seems a little out of it, she's not talking much, and she is looking around everywhere, like someone's gonna pop out of a cupboard in my kitchen. Finally, I hold on to her wrists like she's done with me in some of her sessions and I get her to calm down.

"I get her to change out of her clothes, and I put her in my shower, and we get her into some fresh shit. I make up the couch for her, and she's barely talking this whole time, and I don't want to give her too much shit. Like, my sister used to let her husband beat on her, and she'd have that same look when she came over sometimes. I just didn't want to freak her out. But before we go to bed, I ask her, like, Hey, girl, what the hell happened to you? Were you down at the Light?

"And she says, I don't think I can ever go back there. And then she looks right at me and says: I don't think you should, either.

"And I kind of left it at that. I figured in the morning we'd go to the diner and she'd be a little less shook, we could talk it through and figure out just what happened," Andy says, staring down at her filthy coffee table.

"But you never got the chance," I say.

"Nope. Because when I woke up, she was gone. Left a note, saying she'd send my clothes back to me and not to worry and thanks. And that was it."

"Have you spoken to her since?"

"No, ma'am. And I tell you what, she didn't ever send my

clothes back, neither. If you find her, tell her Andy wants her fucking favorite flannel shirt back."

. . .

Has staying up all night listening to true crime podcasts given you the feeling that your safety might be at risk? Do you sometimes find yourself triple-checking the dead bolts, only to wonder if someone could have crept into your house before you locked the door and is now lurking behind you in the dark of your kitchen? Does the creaking on the staircase at night sometimes make you clutch your phone with 911 already dialed as you wait breathlessly for a shadow in the light beneath the door?

If you can relate to any of these feelings—and boy, I sure can!—then you might want to check out our home security system, Vigilance. With Vigilance you can monitor the entrances of your home and driveway, manage motion-activated lights across your property, and instantly trigger a Mayday alert if you feel you are in danger. You can manage all the add-on features, like cameras, lights, and alarms, through our revolutionary interface, the Vigilance app, which allows you to keep track of all your security features, even when you're not at home. If you're pulling up your driveway late at night and get that skin-crawling feeling, you can review all the footage of your home for the previous eight hours and turn on every light between you and your bedroom. You can even message a security adviser to place them on standby until you have safely entered your home. Don't spend anymore time paralyzed with fear: go to www.vigilancesecurity.com today. Remember, you can't put a price on your own safety.

. . .

I loop Naia in as I'm driven back south, and she seems pleased with my report. We arrange to meet up and record some monologue to go along with the interview, start polishing the next episode to drop.

"In the meantime, Liv, you may want to check the message boards. I'm sending you a link to the most promising posts, and you can start to weed through them. It might take a little longer for people to really crawl out of the woodwork, but let's see how it goes."

"Okay, sounds good. Anything else you want me to be doing?"

"Well, I'm guessing you probably can't get back over to that Center? Start recording some responses?"

"I doubt it. They're not going to want to talk to me, probably ever."

"Okay, okay, we'll come up with a plan to deal with that. We want to let the suspense build, anyway. No point in defusing the tension by airing someone saying reasonable things. It'll take the oomph right out of the story."

"I hear you, but . . . aren't we trying to figure out what happened here?"

"Sure," says Naia casually. "But the more important thing is for it to be a good yarn. Of course it needs to seem like we want to solve the damn case—that's our whole justification for doing this. And that's everyone's justification for listening."

"Otherwise we're all just a bunch of ghouls," I clarify.

"The bloodthirsty mob and the gladiator ring," Naia says, and I can hear the smile in her voice. "So basically, we want to telegraph our good, ethical intentions. Getting justice and all that. But our goal, as storytellers, always has to be about the entertainment factor. Whether the story hooks you, whether you feel like you're getting closer, whether you think it can be solved. That's where the art comes in."

"I wouldn't want to muddy the art with too much reality," I say.

"See, I knew we would work well together. Okay, darling, good work. I'll probably talk to you later, after you send me the interview. Stay focused!" We sign off, and I watch the same scenery from earlier this afternoon unfurl before me in reverse.

I've never felt too much compunction about the fragile boundary between reality and fiction—as an actor, it's a gossamer distinction that becomes unhelpful for me to parse. My job is usually to lose the reality (of my body, my own self) in the fiction I'm playing. With this project, I'm almost being asked to do the reverse—to use my self, the reality of my identity, to create a fiction, out of real people and real events. It feels very strange, and my neck has already begun tensing. I know from experience that if I don't figure out how and why I'm feeling the things I do, my neck will gradually tighten until I can barely turn my head, until I'm locked, eyes straight forward. This makes me very worried: my neck started tensing in rehearsals for *Play*. It was a precursor that I ignored, to my detriment.

I sigh, wondering at the likelihood of finding a decent chiropractor here, then realize, with some irony, that my best chance for treatment is probably back at the Light. That was the last time someone touched me with understanding.

After I've arrived back at my room, Naia sends me a text with a link to the message boards that have started proliferating.

> Just so you can get an idea of what the chatter on Websleuths is. Haven't had a chance to vet any of this yet, but we'll get someone on it.

I open up my laptop and click on her link.

PrayersForSally: hey loving this new podcast y'all just wanted to sum up some of what I've been thinking theory-wise. It sounds like we're supposed to think they're some weird cult that's like sacrificing virgins and whatall, but I think there's a tie-in with a serial-killer case I've been following in the Blue Ridge mountains. Same dates (solstice/equinox) and most of the girls have been strangled and left outside, sometimes with their bodies arranged in weird ways. What if he's moved to new territory and is using this cult as a way to shield his activities. He could even be involved with the Light in some way (groundskeeper or something). Just thinking aloud, here's the link to the thread: Pagan Mountain Killer.

> **volleyballmom:** This is so nuts. I wonder if anyone has contacted law enforcement down there about this/asked them if they see any connections.

> **PrayersForSally:** nah fuck the police.

I read that thread, too, and yes, there's a serial killer who does (maybe) seem to kill on the solstice somewhere down in Virginia. The thread is fairly sure that this man is also the Zodiac Killer, and the whole conversation veers off in that direction, with some impressive commitment to detail.

> **WhereWeGo1:** I think it's really obvious that there's a connection here to what we've been seeing all over the country atm. Like just go ahead and google the first names of these dead girls and see what comes up. A link to the MOTHERFUCKING ANTHROPOLOGIE WEDDING WEBSITE. Does anyone think that's a coincidence? There's a wedding dress named after each of these girls, and they cost, like, thousands of dollars. Anyone can obviously put the pieces together.

>> **notparanoidiftheyrewatching:** HOLY SHIT. Like, you can legit buy these women as brides, like, right there on the internet.

>> **SherriG:** I can't believe how transparent their being!!! I hope they burn inhell

>> **BoogalooBaby:** Like what are the chances of these names showing upindependently of each other? Theia???

>> **WhereWeGo1:** Yeah, when a Tadashi or a Catherine shows up, we'll have our answer, right?

Genuinely baffled by this exchange, I go down into the abyss
and learn a number of really wild things about furniture companies and online sex trafficking. But I do go to the Anthropologie
website and confirm that, indeed, three of the four women who
have died have wedding dresses named after them. Or, at least,
happen to bear names that someone in a marketing department
thought might sell wedding dresses. Hmmm. Not sure what to
make of that.

It's the last thread that causes a hitching in my throat.

LIV REED'S FAMILY (thread):

Cristoff307: So, I've been thinking a lot about how Liv's mom
abandoned her when she was little and has been totally absent
from her life, but now theres this organization that has taken her
in and all. Has it occurred to anybody that this might be her
mother trying to get back in touch without revealing her identity?
Like, say she went into hiding and found the HOL and now wants
to reconnect with her daughter—maybe this is the only safe way
to do it?

> *volleyballmom:* yeah there's not much online about her mom's
> case because it happened a while ago and was not real high
> profile at the time but from what I could find her home life
> was not great. Let's say the mom wanted out and thought the
> dad might kill her, she goes into hiding just a couple states
> away with this organization and then later finds a way to
> convince her daughter to come there.

> *deathtohipsters:* wait, are we saying the mom murdered
> people so Liv would show up?? Don't buy it.

> *Cristoff307:* No, but maybe she figured out a way to
> make it seem like the girls were being murdered to draw
> Liv in.

deathtohipsters: Umm why not just send Liv and email or something like I'm ur longlost mom?

Cristoff307: Because that whole family are starfuckers and they just want to be famous.

RememberLoren: I think her dad killed her mom, and now he's killing these girls. He's like a classic stage parent, just wants to be famous himself. What a perfect opportunity to become notorious, and to boost his kid's career.

volleyballmom: Do we think he's a member of HOL? Maybe he joined back in the day?

RememberLoren: Totally possible.

volleyballmom: here's a theory. What if Mom disappears, finds her way to the Light somehow and stays in hiding there for a while. Then these girls start dying. She's afraid, she's in danger, she has no connections, . . . except her super famous daughter. So she figures out a way to get her to come to the Light and uncover the murders and she's just waiting until she's safe to reveal herself to Liv.

The thread ends there, though I suspect it will keep unfolding. I shut my laptop with a queasy feeling. I try to let go of the unease that the various theories have sown somewhere deep in my belly, and try to massage the knot in my neck.

I can't rule out any of these whack-a-mole hypotheses, but I do have some actual information to work off. Iris, whoever she is.

In the preinterview I recorded with Andy, I've got the name of her halfway house, and I ring them up. I get the runaround while they figure out whom to foist me off on, but finally, an office manager for the larger organization that operates Simple Transitions is on the other line, informing me that she's not comfortable releasing information about any former patients.

"Oh, well, that's okay, because I'm actually looking for a former employee," I explain. "Someone who worked at Simple Transitions in the winter of 2018. Her name was Iris."

"And who did you say you were?"

"I'm actually a former patient. I worked with Iris, and she was really important to my recovery. I'm having some physical pain at the moment, and she worked with me to help deal with it—it's been one of my triggers." The lie comes very easily as I nod my head from side to side, my neck flaring. The woman on the phone seems to be considering.

"So you were in one of her bodywork clinics?" she asks.

"Yeah, they were kind of the game changer for me. I'd done a couple other rehabs that never really stuck, but she helped me with a lot of physical symptoms that really changed my relationship to substances."

"Well, that's very good to hear. It's always nice to hear a success story."

"I'd love the chance to work with her again, maybe hire her as a private contractor. I just, you know, really don't want to go back down that road, and I think she might be able to help. I just need her phone or address or something. I'm pretty sure she'll remember me."

"Look, I'm not comfortable giving out Ms. Reebuck's contact details, even to a former patient. We do have a list of practitioners who are currently working with Transitions on our website, and they'd certainly consider taking on an outpatient—"

"Okay, tell you what. I respect that you look out for your employees' privacy. Honestly, it makes me feel good about your overall confidentiality. How about this: I'll give you my new number, and maybe you could just pass it along to Iris? Text it to her, or send an email. Then if she feels comfortable, she could go ahead and get in touch with me?"

The woman on the line falls silent for a little while, considering. "That seems reasonable. I can do that, but I can't make any guarantees that she'll be back in touch."

"Oh, I totally understand, I'm so grateful. It really would mean the world to me," I gush, and I give her my "updated" number.

"And I hope you'll consider looking at the website. The parent organization of Transitions offers a number of supplemental services, and you'll be able to book sessions with some of our consultants directly through the organization. The rates are very reasonable, and most insurance providers cover them."

"Neat! Do you have a link? Is it easy to find through your website?"

"You betcha—just google us and it should pop right up. You can book into our other facilities or get in touch with our network of practitioners."

"Yeah, I will definitely do that in the meantime. You can't really put a price on health or sobriety, right?"

"We say that all the time!" she replies, delighted. "Also, would you be willing to fill out a survey about your success in the Transitions program? We've been putting together some new promotional material and I'd just love to include your story."

. . .

I'm sure that the survey will arrive in Andy's in-box within moments, and I'd love to read her responses—though what I really care about is that the helpful office lady sends a message to Iris with my phone number, asking her to get in touch with me, masquerading as Andy. There's a slender possibility that she might, though the fact that she hasn't been in contact with Andy for all this time suggests that she doesn't want to stay in close touch. But it's not impossible. And if she hears the podcast, it might nudge her into reaching out. Or the opposite, I suppose.

I have a look at the Simple Transitions website, hoping to recognize a name on the list of approved practitioners. The website links to several other facilities in the region, all owned by a parent company, Lux. Lux also has a nutritional line, and you can, apparently, become a direct seller of this life-changing product! Take control of your health and your career!

But I have something more urgent to look for. Now I have Iris's last name.

She doesn't have much of a social or Google presence. (Did you mean: *Reebok*?) No helpful Insta photos to sort through. I realize that I'm not going to be able to open all these doors on my own. We're going to need someone who knows what the fuck they're doing, and who has access to things like DMV records, police databases, arrest warrants, all the official hoopla that has just barely stayed off the larger internet.

I sigh, realizing who I'm probably going to have to call.

CHAPTER 15

My father is the sort of person Americans often assume has some kind of title squirreled away in his lengthy list of names: William Bartholomew Regis Sumner-Reed. I have always suspected that some of these names were willfully tacked on after my dad came to the States and realized the effect his plummy accent and polished manners had on the Yanks. The reality is that his family did actually start off upper-crust, but everyone had mostly squandered their fortunes by the time Dad skipped across the pond; all that remained of the family inheritance was the aforementioned accent and manners, along with a fondness for expensive brandy and a very aristocratic collection of debts (horses, back taxes, hotel bills, that sort of thing).

Though more or less impoverished (and by many people's standards, Dad was less), Bart had no intention of working for a living when he arrived stateside. His credit cards carried him far, and after that, he lived as a professional hanger-on, the full-time companion of the rich that only those who have grown up in immense privilege manage to be.

Rich people don't like to hang out with those who balk at ordering the "good" champagne or staying at the nice hotel. At a certain point, the ability to actually pay for things is less important than the overall assumption that it is necessarily right and good to purchase the better things in life; therefore, a holiday with an impecunious but firmly approving companion who reads the finance section is preferable to a nouveau riche bourgeois who flinches in disapprobation each time you upgrade to a suite or the luxury rental car. The pleasure of flaunting your cash is substantially diminished by those who remind you that it's simply not normal to have so much of it. So my father became the obvious choice of companion for many lonely men and women of his social set; he was always glad to spend a week at the country home or to tag along for a day at the races, on any continent. It was accepted that he didn't have much money, but he was always excellent fun, and the perfect gentleman.

But eventually, even his paltry walking-around cash (which still amounted to more than most people make in a couple of years) was insufficient to sustain his occasional round, or delivered bouquets, or dry-cleaning bill, and my father realized that he was probably out of the game, at least for a while.

I always wondered why he didn't marry rich. Maybe he tried— I don't know. But he did pursue another type of currency, one that is rarer and more fleeting than what you can put in the bank. He invested in beauty.

Because while my mother wasn't wealthy, she was stunning. Rose-petal skin and willowy limbs, exquisite. People say that I look like her, and her genes have no doubt paved the way for my career, but I am certainly less obviously beautiful than she was. She had grace, whereas I can only simulate it for a role.

My parents met at a benefit (for what, I've never really been sure; Dad tends to change his story around) where he was attending as a chaperone for a friend with a drinking problem, and she was someone else's date. So they were both, as Dad likes to say, *parvenus* of their own sort. He was smitten, she was shy, he pursued, she relented, and it sounds like it all happened very quickly. The small farmhouse she had inherited was nothing fancy, but it suited Dad's notion of romance well enough. I came along soon after.

A more cynical person might wonder if I was not part of my

father's plan to restore his standing in the world all along. Marry the beautiful but shrinking violet, reproduce with her, and mold your progeny into your ticket to wealth and fame. I don't know if that was his plan, but after Mom's disappearance, it certainly became his purpose.

After she disappeared, Bart played his role brilliantly. He was distraught, frantic, and composed as the circumstance required— I might have Mom's looks, but certainly some of my talent comes from Dad. During the investigation, he chummed up with reporters, concerned neighbors, and the cops. When one of those cops retired, he hired him independently, as a private investigator, to help him continue looking for my mother. I don't know how much they managed to learn about her disappearance, but they did smoke a lot of cigars in our garden over the years, concocting scenarios for where she might have ended up.

I don't have the man's details—indeed, I spoke to him only on official business. He was Dad's contact and, eventually, his confidant and friend. I was treated deferentially, cautiously even. I was a pretty teenage girl, and this guy wasn't an idiot. He knew well enough to steer clear.

Let's hope that the years have eroded his good sense.

· · ·

"I wondered when you'd come to your senses," my father drawls slowly. I assume he's back in L.A., where he's been sponging off my career since the start of *Iroquois Falls,* in various roles and capacities. But he could be in London, or even New York, for all I know. We haven't spoken for nearly a year.

"Always contrite, hey, Bart?" I say.

"I see, this isn't any sort of apology. No, no, I'm not trying to bait you, darling. I'll apologize, if you like. I'm sorry for kicking up such a fuss over your little play."

I grit my teeth. It doesn't help that he turned out to be right about my "little play": it *was* a bad call, and I really *wasn't* up to it, and I *would* have been better off auditioning for the new doctor drama on network, which has actually taken off. But that script had been so grim, so vapid. I had wanted a challenge, to stretch.

"Well, in retrospect you might have had something of a point," I concede. I can feel my accent sliding toward his upper-crust diction. I'd had a small role in a costume drama five years ago and had been very proud that I didn't need a dialogue coach to nail the accent. "The play is, as you can guess, on hold for the moment."

"I think that's likely for the best, given . . . well, everything taken into consideration. How are you, darling?"

"I'm sure you're aware that I've been better," I retort. "They still get *Us Weekly* out there in L.A., don't they?"

My father laughs good-naturedly. "Well, my girl, I'd be lying if I said it wasn't nice to actually *see* you in one of the glossies. Rather notorious than forgotten."

"I'm not sure I'd agree."

"Rehab didn't stick, then?"

"It wasn't rehab!"

"Ah, yes, Jessica did try and explain the distinction. Though I'll confess I find that she still does run on a bit—makes it hard for one to focus entirely."

"You've been speaking with Jess?" I ask sharply.

There's a pause in his breathing.

"Mmm, yes, well, she thought it best to check in with me, wanted to double-check some medical history things—"

"Bart, we both know that Jess has dealt with all of my medical appointments for years. She has every piece of paper she could possibly need."

"Yes, well. I believe she wanted to double-check something on your mother's side . . ." He's not even bothering to lie convincingly.

"It was about money, wasn't it? You called her."

"I merely reached out to let her know that I'd been contacted by someone who wanted a comment about 'mental health' problems in the family. Someone who was hoping to write that your mother was likely a nutter, and lo, here you were, checking in to the loony bin. I debunked the man, of course, disabused him of any such notion—"

"After Jess paid you a good ten percent more than whatever whoever was offering, I'm sure. There's some paternal loyalty." If I wasn't so used to this, I'd be tempted to hang up on him in disgust. But honestly, I can only muster relief that he bothered to shake us down, rather than selling a comment to a tabloid. Especially given my current project.

"Now, Olivia, I don't think I need to remind you that your career has come at a cost for everyone, and that expecting us all to grovel thankfully for your scraps whenever you deign to distribute—"

"You don't have to rehash your usual complaint, Dad. It's fine, I'm not upset." A little upset with Jess, maybe. But then, this is her job: to put out the fire before I even smell any smoke.

"So were you calling to just check in, darling? How are you doing, in the wake of your, ehm, recent spiritual voyage?"

"I'm surprised you don't know about my new project yet," I say. I know he has a Google Alert for me, and I'm sure he follows my hashtag on Twitter. There are bound to be people mentioning the podcast, even if I haven't been actively posting about it.

"Well, I heard something about a radio show, but it's not really in your wheelhouse, is it?" he says dismissively. "I assumed it was for charity, or fun or something. I can't say I looked deeply into it."

"You mean you quickly determined that it wasn't likely to be a lucrative venture for you and went back to the pool and cocktail hour."

He laughs. "It's just not the sort of media I'm typically interested in, that's all, darling. I'm sure you'll do a wonderful job with your radio play. You know I think you're brilliant, whatever you're doing."

"As long as it's not theater. Or 'radio,' as you call it."

He's quiet for another moment.

"I just think you dazzle on the screen, my dear. Not everyone does, but you do, and it's a shame to waste it."

I sigh. I don't have the energy to walk through these old arguments again. "Bart, did you happen to glean what my little radio play is about?" I ask tiredly.

"I got the impression it was a spoof on, what, something like noir? A wry, millennial whodunit?"

"Not exactly." I explain the show, then start polishing my pitch as I walk him through the basics. Bart's a shitheel a lot of the time, but he has a nose for how to make things seem appealing.

"All of which brings me to my current situation," I say. "I'm actually starting to get some leads, but I've hit a wall. I think I need to bring in a professional."

"Ah," Bart says. "Which leads us to the crux. The real reason you rang up your old dad."

"Well, I don't have contact details for anyone who does that sort of work. I could contract with a private investigator or something, but . . ."

"But you thought the personal angle might help the story. Working with the ex-cop who tried to find your mummy," he says coolly.

"I don't think you have any right to judge anyone about cannibalizing family history for personal gain, Dad."

He's silent for a long beat.

"Olivia, I need to know one thing before I even continue this conversation." He takes a breath. "You're not going to start looking for your mother again, are you?"

His question takes me aback. Of course, over the years, I've done some casual poking around online, looking for any hint of her. But I've never really tried, have never really considered it.

"Umm, no, that wasn't on the docket, no. I figured that waiting fifteen years would hardly make locating her easier. If she's still alive, she doesn't want to be found," I answer.

"Because I can't—I won't—get back into all of that again. Olivia, we've moved on."

"I know, Dad. I honestly didn't even consider starting to look for her again. I really am just thinking about this case, and I thought, well, as you said, the personal angle would be a good hook."

"I can see, narratively, why you'd find that route compelling," he muses. "It makes sense."

"So you'll get me Burke's information?"

"I think I can lay my hands on his phone number, maybe even an email address. But I'd like to talk for a minute about my involvement in the project going further."

"Of course you would," I say with a sigh. "Let's just talk numbers." I dearly wish Jess was taking my calls so she could handle this negotiation with my father.

I shoot former detective Burke an email the minute I hang up with Dad. Dad has warned me that he was never a great digital correspondent, but times have changed. He still lives not too far from the county I grew up in, in Massachusetts, which could, conceivably, be driven to from where I am right now.

. . .

While eating a Caesar salad in the hotel restaurant, I go back down the Reddit rabbit hole. It's not huge, but there are certainly some people commenting and conspiracy theorizing. Not much is promising, but I am nevertheless encouraged by these legions of digital gumshoes, sucked into the mystery of faraway dead bodies.

I avoid the thread dealing with my family as long as I can, but ultimately I relent, reading through the newest comments.

> **Cristoff307:** been looking into this as much as I can manage, tho its def a cold case disappearance, not a lot breaking these days. Still, managed to find a picture of the missing mom from fifteen years ago and have been comparing it to any of the social posts I can find from the Light. Take a look at these two photos side by side and tell me I'm crazy:

There are two images linked, and I do my best to pull them up next to each other. Instead of the official photo for my mom's disappearance, I'm surprised to see a slightly younger image of her; I was in that photo, just to the right, but have been cropped out. She's smiling, blond, and her graceful figure is unmistakable in the very-nineties tank-top dress she's wearing.

The next picture seems to be lifted from a former version of the Light's website, accessed through the Wayback Machine, a resource I'd entirely forgotten about. There's a group photo of a handful of Light members in front of a construction site—it looks to be from when they were completing the Center. I don't know what I'm looking for, and simply scan for faces I might know. The quality isn't fantastic, though I can tell which one is Rain (her bare feet) and Devotion (heavy brow and cranky scowl). I look for Dora and Steve but don't find them.

I stop scanning when I find what Cristoff307 has meant us to see: the willowy woman with a pixie cut standing just off to the side. She's shielding her face with her hand, but the set of her shoulders, the slight ballerina turnout of her hips look familiar. It *could* be her.

> **Cristoff307:** It could be her, right? I know there's absolutely no way to draw anything conclusive yet, but I'm going to keep looking through the "archive" online to see if I can't make a

positive ID. In the meantime, I wonder if there are other Light members who might be able to confirm or deny?

　　volleyballmom: woah I think it's uncanny

They're grasping. I know they're grasping, and yet. It's too easy to see connections, to hear a resonance in every little thing. No wonder QAnon is playing *The Da Vinci Code* with the universe. There's too much text, too much information—the digital dartboard is simply too big. I shake it off, move on, think of what I need to do next. I text Naia. She calls back immediately.

"Topher's really pleased with the audience numbers so far. A really promising start, and I'm pretty sure if we can drop a few episodes quickly, the momentum will carry us. What do you think about pushing another episode in the next few days?"

"I mean, do you really have enough material for that? Won't it be . . . a bit light?" I fret.

"I've been up all night pulling audio clips, digging around for things we can layer in. That Institute has some really wacky recordings out in the ether. Chants and weird prayers and the like, inspirational videos. I've pulled a few, and we just have to pray that we get some more concrete stuff. But I think we can use most of your interview, and you just have to go find this Iris—"

"About that," I say, and explain about Burke.

"Fucking fantastic," she says when I'm done.

"Oh good—I was a little worried you'd be upset over me going rogue."

"No way, this is great. I don't want to lean too heavily on your mom's disappearance, but it will add some great depth to the story."

"Yeah, I don't want it to, like, be about my mother. I don't think I'm game for reopening that book." I don't bring up the online threads I've just read. Neither does she.

"I don't blame you. But it will give your motives another layer, and listeners will connect with you as the victim."

"I wouldn't say I'm a victim."

"Sure, sure, but you know what I'm saying. It can only help. So, your priority right now is to find this Iris girl, see if you can get her to talk, figure out what her connection is. There are a couple of other threads we want to follow up on, too."

"Do you want to, like, give me a rundown on things I should be looking for?"

"We're working on getting some more from the House of Light people. Any audio we can use, or comments are great, but I doubt they'll even return so much as an email from you, so . . . maybe just let me worry about it. Iris is your first priority, though it might not be the worst idea to see if you can't track down some other former members of the Light. People who'd be able to speak about its history or any strange experiences they've had with them."

"Right. Okay, I actually do have one or two ideas on that front. I don't know if they'll pan out, but it's worth a try."

"Fabulous. I have an assistant working the internet side of things—you know, the 'audience participation' angle."

"You mean, like Websleuths and all that?" I ask casually.

"Yeah, she's keeping a close eye on the thread, watching Reddit, that sort of thing. Most of it is pretty bonkers, as you might suspect, but there's always a chance we hit gold. I'd say the email account has already paid off."

"True story. Assuming, of course, that it is a true story," I point out.

Naia snorts. "Sure, to some extent. Though also, to another extent . . . it doesn't matter all that much."

I draw a deep breath. "Naia, I don't mean to sound, um, prudish or anything. But how do you feel about this, like, ethically? You have a degree in journalism, don't you?"

"Media studies. Look, I hear what you're saying. But the reality is that the story is going to get told. Our responsibility is to tell it in such a way that it brings as much light to bear on these dead women as we possibly can. Does that mean we sensationalize it a bit? Sure, yeah, maybe. But ultimately what we want is visibility, for people to pay attention to this." She sounds sincere, though the answer shines of polish.

"That does, however, happen to coincide with our own personal interests. High visibility, I mean."

"That just means we're more motivated to do our job well," she says. I can hear the shrug. "There's a demand for this. Someone is going to supply it, and I'd rather it be me, a woman, a person of color, someone who thinks about these things, rather than some white middle-aged bro who will end up getting a fucking movie deal because of how 'sensitively' he treated the material while he was jerking off to naked autopsy photos."

"Wow. That's . . . quite the image."

"People are obsessed with this shit. Sometimes it's David Lynch, sometimes it's *America's Most Wanted,* but there's no saturation point. Possibly because there's no end to violence. Since someone is going to turn it into tabloid fodder, it may as well be us."

"It's just that as someone who has been tabloid fodder . . ." I say.

"Okay, sure. I give you that. But in the end, we're just trying to solve a crime here."

"And sell ad space."

"Maybe we can't do one without the other," she says. "Look, I have to get back to editing. I want to publish again soon, so it's all a bit of a shit show over here. Talk later?"

"You bet," I answer. I push the wilted romaine around my plate, but I've lost my appetite.

Dear Miss Reed,

It's very good to hear from you after all these years. You have been in my thoughts much since I first met you (under those tragic circumstances) and I will admit that your mother's case continues to puzzle and trouble me, after all this time.

Which is why I guess I was surprised that you were reaching out not to talk about that case, in fact, but to discuss another. No judgment from this corner, though: I've seen firsthand what happens when you can't let go of a case, and in many ways I'm relieved that you don't wish to collaborate on your mother's disappearance. I, for one, am happy to have put it behind me, at least for the most part.

As to your questions about this case, the "suspicious" deaths occurring in upstate New York . . . I will confess that it seems a bit thin. Having peeked at the reports I was able to access, I believe that the evidence corroborates the official story. I see the temptation to sensationalize, of course, and I won't state that it's an impossibility, but I also wouldn't be comfortable stating outright that your case has legs.

That being said. I looked into the woman whose secondhand story you're interested in (Iris Reebuck) and, troublingly, learned that she has been missing from roughly that time. A sister filed a missing person report which, unfortunately, was not taken very seriously due to the fact that it was the third such report filed on Ms. Reebuck. There hasn't been much follow-up, and from what I understand, she's still unaccounted for. I don't know whether this lends credence to your overall theory, but it does seem to be worth the effort to locate her, if only because she is, simply, a missing person. I'd be willing to undertake this project as a private commission—I believe your father furnished you with my rates?

If you're comfortable with this arrangement, I'll forward my contract and move ahead with my investigation. I understood from your email that there is some urgency—as a client, you are of course entitled to make clear your priorities, but I need you to understand that I cannot rush work just to accommodate publicity needs.

Of course, not being naive, I recognize the potential value in public interest, particularly with cold cases, so I would be amenable to discussing participating in your project. Discussing, not committing to, mind you.

In any case, it was very nice to hear from you. I remember when you were just a little sprog.

Sincerely,

Former Det. Elton Burke

• • •

Burke's email reminds me why he and my father got on so splendidly: he's not your taciturn noir cop; nor is he full of brash, macho bluster. He is careful, considered, weighing all sides of everything, articulate. I remember him carrying books when he was investigating my mother's disappearance: a thick tome on the history of nautical exploration, the letters of some Victorian poet. I like him instantly, trust him instantly, instantly want him on my side. I type back furiously, spelling out my own reservations, justifications, self-interest, hoping to lure him in with candor and logic, his own values. I'm desperate to get him on the phone.

He answers my second call, explaining that he was outside in his garden. He is businesslike but not unfriendly, and his cool competence is reassuring, just as it was when I was a teenager. That, of course, didn't change the outcome of the case, though.

"If you're amenable, I can drive over there tomorrow," he says when I ask if he'll be working remotely or on the ground. "I prefer to do interviewing in person, obviously, and I wouldn't mind seeing some of the sites of these, well, incidents. I will, of course, need accommodations."

"No problem," I answer quickly. "You'll have your own vehicle, though?"

"Never go anywhere without my trusty steed," he says. "But I do want to be clear: you're not my backup, and we work separately. I'm just providing what information I uncover. I won't be party to interfering with any local law enforcement, and I won't be breaking any laws. I'll offer some statements for your podcast, but I'm not an official spokesperson, and if I get uncomfortable, I walk away."

"Understood," I agree. "All very reasonable." I'm about to hang up, but after a pause, I don't. "Can I just ask, though, why you agreed to do this? I can tell that you feel some, er, compunction about the whole thing . . ."

"That's true. Well, I'll be totally honest. I can use the money. My husband, Dave, needs some in-home care, and it's been out of reach, financially speaking. There aren't so many contract jobs that I can afford to turn up my nose at a good one. But the money alone wouldn't be enough to motivate me." He sighs. "I guess I feel a sense . . . of responsibility. Toward you. I never found your mother, and it seems that I still feel there is an outstanding debt between us."

"Oh," I say, surprised. "You never promised to find my mother, or anything like that. It wasn't, I mean, your responsibility."

"Who else's?" he says simply. "And if that's all, I need to go about getting Dave settled here before I head out tomorrow. I'll call you from the road." He hangs up before I have time to assent.

I change my clothes up in my room, preparing myself to do something I'm not entirely excited for.

CHAPTER 16

After Fred has driven me around vineyards and fields for the better part of an hour, I finally spot Wyatt's truck parked, partly hidden, down a steeply sloping road.

"Not a good idea to drive down there, miss," Fred informs me cheerfully. "The car does not have four-wheel drive."

"That's okay, you can just drop me here. I'll text when I'm finished if I need a ride back—maybe twenty minutes?"

"If you're sure, you know I'm happy to do whatever. I'll find a pull-off."

I hop out of the car and stride off into the dust, sporting some of my newly purchased country gear. It's cooler now, as sunset nears, and I'm glad I've got my flannel shirt. Wyatt is at the far edge of a field, and I stroll through the lanes of grapevines, sniffing the deep scents of dirt and leaves and the not-so-far-off notes of the lake. There are maybe two other people in sight, but they're a ways off and probably haven't even noticed me. I glance around instinctively, as I do everywhere, looking for cameras.

Wyatt has seen me, though he doesn't stop working as I approach him. I sidle up to a post near where he's working and kick my leg up on it.

"Howdy," he finally says. "Nice to see you again."

"Is it really?" I ask, with an apologetic scrunch of my face.

"Sure," he says with a shrug, sliding the clippers into a belt loop and looking at me. "I was a little worried when you were just gone, of course. Thought maybe you went out for an early run. Then I started to worry you fell in the lake."

"Shit, I'm sorry—I didn't even think you would worry," I say.

"Well, then I caught your podcast and figured you were probably alive and well. Which I was glad to hear. Maybe a little less glad about the contents."

"I should have told you what I was working on."

He takes a long, deep breath. "No, I should have figured. You said Ava had approached you, so I should have assumed she had you convinced. Dragged you into it, the way she does."

"I still feel like I lied, even by omission," I say, wishing he would look directly at me. But he's gone back to inspecting grapes.

"I've put up with bigger untruths," he replies with a grim smirk.

"Well, I apologize. And I also apologize for just disappearing from the house. That was a dick move, too."

"Got an Airbnb?" he asks.

"Hotel in town. I wanted to get out of your hair. I would have called, but I realized I don't have your number."

"Don't worry about it." He waves his hand, and I realize he's preparing to dismiss me.

"How's Zora?" I ask, wanting to prolong the conversation, looking for my angle.

"She's spending the night with my parents. Ava's going to be back in a week or so, and she'll want her at home."

"Ah. And Ava . . . is doing fine?"

"Well, she doesn't have any media time until the day after tomorrow, so I can only guess." He lapses into silence. I poke the toe of my boot into the dirt.

"Would you . . . would you show me what you're doing?" I ask. "I've never actually seen anyone work on a vineyard before. And you never know—I could end up in a role where I need to, er, clip grapes?"

Wyatt laughs, and I'm relieved. A crack in the armor.

"Sure, come over here, I'll show you how. I'm trying to make a call when we want to get this Riesling harvested—it's been a warm, dry season, so we'll go a little early this year . . ."

After he's spent a few minutes explaining the principles of what's he's doing and why, and after I've evaluated the undersides of some cloudy grapes, Wyatt looks up at the sky.

"Light's just about gone. Probably going to have to quit for the day." He glances over at me. "How in hell did you even get out here? Don't tell me you walked?"

"No." I laugh. "Well, I walked from the road. I hired a driver. He'll be nearby somewhere—I'll just text him to come get me."

"Don't be silly. I'll give you a lift wherever you need to go," he says gruffly, as I hoped he would. After a pause, he adds: "You had dinner yet?"

"Nope. Can you recommend somewhere good?"

He just smiles broadly at me and gestures toward his truck.

We end up at a café that looks out on the water, on a deck perched high on a hill that slopes down to the lake. Wyatt is a bit grimy, but in spite of the prices on the menu, no one seems concerned with his grubby boots and sweaty tang. I personally think it smells spicy and masculine and don't mind it, either. We make small talk over glasses of wine, and though I don't feel especially hungry, I nibble at my catfish and coleslaw. He asks about my childhood, tactfully avoiding any mention of my mother. I ask him about his life, tactfully avoiding any mention of his wife. Though it's occasionally awkward, we're both having a good time.

I insist on paying the bill, and it's completely dark and quite chilly as we bundle into the truck.

"Do you want—I mean, where should I take you?" he says, as we realize the reality of this strange date we're on. I don't know how to ask for what I want.

"I'm not sure," I answer slowly. He's quiet, just drives down the road, headed both back to Watkins Glen and toward his house.

He slows as his vineyard appears on the right, and he glances over at me. I look back and give him a look that is not quite a smile, but conveys a sense of vulnerability. It's dark in the cab of the truck, but I think he can see it. The blinker flicks on and we pull down the drive toward his house.

Inside, he bustles through the familiar choreography of homecoming, turning on lights and lowering windows, protecting the last of the day's heat inside the house. The night is perfectly clear, and the warmth from the sun has vanished; I wonder if there will be frost. Wordlessly, and as though I live there and this is my routine, I fetch a bottle of wine and two glasses from the counter and sit down on the couch. Wyatt lights the fire that has already been laid in the hearth, and I wonder for a moment if he expected to be entertaining me here tonight. A second thought makes me wonder if he maybe wasn't planning to entertain someone else. Either way, I'm the one who pulls a cozy blanket onto my lap and watches his broad shoulders as he deftly gets the fire going.

The routine has disrupted the awkwardness of the unspoken invitation, and he stretches back on the couch, yawning massively.

"Long day?" I ask.

"This time of year, they all are."

"You're obviously physically suited for manual labor," I say with a coy glance at the tight curve of belly I can see where his shirt has lifted up. "But you speak like someone who spends a lot of time reading." It might be the firelight, or he might have glowed a little.

"Well, I did go to an Ivy League school," he says. "And just because I spend all day with farmers doesn't mean I didn't grow up with plenty of book learning."

"Do you mean Ava?"

"Sure. That girl always kept me on my toes. Her sister, too. But my parents are scholars of a sort themselves. They'd read to me out of the Bhagavad Gita before bed."

"Really?" I ask, delighted. "That's pretty special."

"I mean, we read *Frog and Toad,* too. But they . . . cared about my spiritual development and all that."

"Ah," I say. I realize that he has pegged me. He knows I'm here fishing for information, and he's willing to dish out some. But he wants me to know he knows he's being manipulated. I realize how much I like him. "You mean . . . the House of Light."

"More or less. Like we said, it was different back then. Not so uptight, doctrinal. My parents cared more about the meditation, the communing with nature, all that. I think they kept me from the weirdest elements."

"But you don't remember spending a lot of time at the Center?"

"Well, the Center wasn't much back when I was a kid. It got remodeled maybe fifteen years ago? And no, we mostly spent our time outdoors. It was all about the seasons."

"Did you ever . . . I don't know, see something weird there?" I ask.

"I mean, yeah, of course. You'll have to be more specific."

"Erm . . . okay, did you ever watch people sit in a circle and watch someone get really sick? Like, puking sick." Wyatt raises his eyebrows. "And then they maybe . . . did something with the, um, leftovers?"

"With the puke?" His face conveys the idea that no, this doesn't ring any bells.

"Yeah, I know. It was just a thought. Figured I'd ask."

"I think I would have remembered that." He smiles at me, swigs his wine. "Look, I know you're hoping to hear something crazy, sensationalist about what growing up there was like. But there were no animal sacrifices."

"No virgin sacrifices?" I ask, grinning.

"Again, I think that would have stuck in my memory. It was mostly just a bunch of hippies being 'spiritual' out in the woods."

"But your parents left," I point out. "They must have had a reason."

Wyatt takes a deep sigh. "You want to talk to them again," he finally says. I bite my lip. "If I agree, do you think we can not talk about the Light for a bit?"

"That seems eminently fair."

He looks at me from over the rim of his glass, his eyes meeting mine, unblinking. He sighs again and shrugs.

"Whatever. You're welcome to it. Ava has been trying to get information out of them for years, so I doubt that you'll learn much. She's a little more devious than you are, too."

"People respond well to frankness," I say with a shrug of my own. "Sometimes it's best to just ask."

"Well, in all fairness, you didn't *just* ask. You buttered me up, bought me dinner. And, I should say, flirted shamelessly."

"Me, a flirt?" I laugh. I can tell my cheeks are pink, and I raise my hands to cup them.

"Are you too warm? Do you want to stand on the deck for a bit? It's a perfect night."

I assent, and we let ourselves out onto the deck. He's right.

"So all this is yours," I say, leaning out over the railing like it's a ship.

"It's ours. For now, at least."

"What do you mean?"

"It's pretty heavily mortgaged, and I won't lie, it's been a struggle to turn a profit these last few years. We'll just have to wait and see how it goes."

"That must be nerve-racking. Especially with a kid."

"Hey, life doesn't come with guarantees," he says, setting down his empty wineglass and turning toward me. "I feel like that's something you have to really know about, right? I can't imagine an acting career always feels like it's on totally firm footing."

I snort. "Yeah, you're completely right. Not exactly a nine-to-five gig."

"What's it like?" he asks.

"Acting?"

"Being someone else. Whenever you want to."

"It's more like being someone else whether you want to or not. And then wondering which of them might actually be you."

"Surely there's an element of freedom to that?"

"Sometimes. But then, I guess, sometimes . . . it's lonely as hell."

"Even when you have . . . a person?" he says softly, and I can tell he's not just talking about me.

"Maybe especially then. My last relationship . . . didn't go all that smoothly."

"Oh yeah?"

"Really, you're saying you're one of the few people in America who didn't feel the need to watch that whole train wreck? And then write about it on Twitter?"

"Don't have Twitter," he says with a shrug. "And there's not much use for the tabloids out in the boonies here. What happened?"

"I was in love. I thought he loved me. We worked together on *Iroquois Falls*—he was my love interest on the show, you know, Elliott, the ghost I was in love with—and we were together most of the time that we filmed it. I needed him, his stability, to play that part. He *was* my other side, on-screen and off, and I think we fed off that. He had a darkness to him, I guess, that I was drawn to, and that I needed to understand Mina, and myself. We'd been on-again, off-againing for years, but got back together about a year ago, and it felt like it might stick. But I . . . I fucked things up."

"What does that mean?"

"It's all rather complicated, and not that interesting."

"I beg to differ," Wyatt says with a grin.

I punch his shoulder playfully. "Yeah, well, you can read about it in the glossy magazines soon enough. There will be plenty of gossip and speculation. And photos." I flinch, realizing I haven't bothered to look up what new images Vorchek might have published of my mostly naked ass dangling off a fire escape since the first one came out and I fled here.

"Why on earth does everyone care so damn much?" he asks.

"Fuck if I know! My life has been a spectator sport for as long as I can remember, though. There's always someone . . . circling around the edges of it."

"Like who?"

"The paparazzi. And, by extension, the 'fans.' My manager. Any director I've ever worked with. My father, I guess, most of all."

"Your father?"

"A stage parent. He basically nudged me into this life and has been feeding off my career ever since."

"And of course, your mom . . ."

"Right. Out of the picture."

"Shit, Liv, you almost make Ava's family look functional!" He laughs, and I'm jolted out of my self-pity enough to join him.

"I know, poor me. I've had a really rough life."

"Damn, I didn't mean it that way," he says, reaching for my arm. "Really."

"It's okay, I know you didn't." I shiver, and goosebumps rise on my skin, beneath his palm.

"Ack, now you're cold—let's get you back to the fire." He rubs my shoulders briskly with his big hands and angles me back inside. I think I like that he's trying to manage my body temperature with such solicitous concern. We sit back on the couch, and I ask him questions about his childhood, and he asks me questions about his job. It is companionable, cozy, intimate without being sexy. Or almost: at some point I stretch out my legs, cramped from sitting cross-legged, and he takes my foot and rubs it, my heel pressed into the rock-solid meat of his thigh. Neither of us acknowledges it, but I do make my other foot accessible, and he holds them both in his lap. My head lolls to one side, and the heat of the fire makes me groggy, and then drowsy. I don't recall the moment I fall asleep, but I'm fairly sure Wyatt is still there on the couch with me, the blanket covering both of us.

. . .

I'm on my own in the morning, though, with the blanket pulled up around my shoulders and an extra pillow beneath my head. The embers are still burning in the fireplace, so I imagine Wyatt must have fed the fire during the night, while I slept. I sit up, stiff, and peer through the big window, where the sun is just coming up. From outside on the deck, I can see that it hasn't frosted, but there is mist rising from the grass and, below, the lake. It looks other-worldly.

Creeping through this house that belongs to another woman, I find my boots at the door. I want to go for a walk, but I don't want Wyatt to think that I've run off again, left without comment. So I put on a pot of coffee as silently as I can and leave a note on the kitchen table: *Out for a stroll, back soon* ☺.

As I walk through the fields that stretch below the house, I work on a script in my head.

Wyatt is up when I get back to the house, sitting on the deck in a sweatshirt. He beckons me outside and hands me a cup of coffee and a sweatshirt of my own.

"I'd give you one of Ava's, but it would never fit," he says, smiling.

"Thanks, it was a chilly walk." We sit in our strange intimacy, watching the sunrise. Finally, Wyatt stands.

"I reckon it's time to go get Zo. You still want to tag along?" he asks.

I pause, biting my lip. I do want to tag along, but I also don't want to hurt this man. "If it's still okay with you?"

"It's up to you. Like I said, I can't promise they'll say much, but I'm happy to drive you over there, invite you in. I can't stick around, though—Zora's got a doctor's appointment in town."

"No, of course, I can definitely text my driver. I told him I might need him this morning, so he's on call. He can come and get me."

"Yeah, okay, let's leave in ten." There's a coolness in his voice this morning that wounds me, but I know this is the price of my manipulations.

"Ready when you are," I say.

. . .

DORA: I guess I feel a little strange talking about the Light in this context, that's all.

LIV: Why do you say that?

DORA: Well, they were a really big part of our lives for many years. I mean, our son was practically raised by some of the members, and just because we're no longer . . . part of that scene, I just don't, well—

STEVE: It seems like a betrayal. Gossip-mongering.

LIV: I don't want to ask you guys to do anything that makes you uncomfortable. I'm just trying to get a sense of the culture surrounding the Light. What it was like to be a member and, um, I guess, how things changed over the years.

DORA: Well, I mean, it was just a very easygoing, healthy place—

STEVE: Back to the land and all that.

DORA: Right. We were building the house we live in now, which is just a few miles from the Light, but spending a lot of time over there. We actually spent a whole summer in one of the cabins before we got the roof on this place—

STEVE: The Light pitched in for all that—all the members helped us do basically a barn raising to get this house livable.

DORA: Right. I learned a lot of my gardening and cooking from them—

STEVE: And making beer! (Hiss of a bottle being opened.)

DORA: And just so many things. It was a real community, and we were on a spiritual voyage together—it was very, very special. (Silence.)

LIV: So, if you don't mind my asking, what changed?

STEVE: Well, ultimately, the leadership changed. We went from having really no particular leader—we had a . . . I guess you could say a spiritual guide, but the internal politics of the group kind of fell apart when he got sick and was no longer at the center of everything. You know how it gets: all of a sudden there were all these people who suddenly felt they should be in charge of the Center, and we should expand our following and we should do this and we should do that—

DORA: Building the new Center happened around then; some people were pushing for all these renovations.

LIV: Do you remember who was pushing for these renovations? (Pause.)

DORA: Well, everyone wanted something different. But if I remember correctly, Rain was in favor of making things more "accessible" to the wider world.

LIV: (aside) Rain, as you probably remember, is the apparent leader of the current iteration of the House of Light.

STEVE: A couple people wanted to go the alternate direction, you know, like basically devolution, let the band break up. Rudy left, and then I think Robby effectively left and started the yoga practice—

DORA: And Betsy, right? She wanted to expand the Center to include a midwife practice, I think, and that was really contentious for a while.

STEVE: Once Luke left to go on his vision quest or whatever, it was kind of down to Rain, and she took everything in hand, finished the renovations. She got the website going. She filed LLC paperwork, and all of a sudden there was the retreat center, and the classes, and I think they released a couple of books from their own little press—

DORA: All of a sudden it was this lifestyle and wellness brand and it looked nothing like our airy-fairy co-op. We just didn't recognize it—

STEVE: Didn't recognize ourselves.

DORA: Right. And we haven't really been back for, oh, gosh, can it really be twenty years now? That's crazy to think. Wyatt was just a little guy the last time we went for a weekend retreat— remember, he stayed with my mother? But, yeah, we really have no idea how things have been since around the millennium, I'd guess.

LIV: Can you tell me a little more about Luke and Rain's relationship? Or about Luke himself? He doesn't really appear in any of the online material, and I never saw him at the Light. (At this point, Dora and Steve exchanged a look that was pure marital shorthand.)

DORA: Rain . . . well, she sort of thinks of Luke as the second coming, if I'm being totally honest. She's had a lot of loss in her life, and when we lost our teacher, she was heartbroken. Luke was just a young man, but he's always been . . . very unusual.

STEVE: He's a weirdo, is what my wife is saying.

LIV: In what sense?

STEVE: Look, the kid grew up in a pretty unusual community, and was told he was special from the minute he could talk. Think of someone who's been homeschooled and then add a messiah complex.

LIV: Has he ever been . . . violent, for example?

DORA: (in a rush) We left when he was still just a teenager. He's an odd boy, but he's not, well, violent. Honestly, it was more Rain's . . . preoccupation with him that made things strange. We were just uncomfortable with the new direction of the Light, is all.

STEVE: Who knows what their little "dynamic" is like these days.

LIV: I'm actually trying to track down some former members of the Light to talk to them about their experiences, to get a sense of these changes. There's someone in particular from more recent years who I'm especially interested in speaking to. She would have been there after your time, but did you know a young woman named Iris Reebuck?

STEVE: No, her name was Lara Reebuck—

DORA: No, my love, Sara Reebuck, remember? Because she pronounced it with that long *a*. And now, come to think of it, she had kids, didn't she? Little girls?

STEVE: Oh, right, she was screwing that dude Buttercup or Pansy—

DORA: Don't be rude. His name was Bloom, and we don't know if he was the father—free love was very much the order of the day— but I can't remember the girls' names.

LIV: Do you think one of them could have been Iris? (Pause.)

DORA: Of course it's possible. For some reason I want to say their names were . . . Lilac and . . .

STEVE: Lily and Iris, maybe? Definitely flowers.

DORA: Hmm, yes, it could have been. They would have been around Wyatt's age, I guess, so they probably played naked in the yard during a Beltane festival!

LIV: The girls were named Lily and Iris and their dad was named . . . Bloom? (DORA titters.) What's the deal with the names at the House of Light?

DORA: Well, we were encouraged to take new names that better suited our relationship to, I guess, the natural world, to our nature selves.

STEVE: You tried calling yourself Summer, my love. Don't be coy.

DORA: Yes, well. (Sounds embarrassed.) That's true, but it never felt . . . right. And then when we left, I obviously moved on from that. . . . But it was part of a way to show that you were committed to the Light. Later, they wanted to formalize the name change, make it this whole symbolic rite-of-passage thing. That's when it just felt too . . . odd.

LIV: Got it. And do you remember when you last spoke to Sara Reebuck?

DORA: Oh, God, we hadn't been close in a long time. . . . Sara was involved in expanding the Light—she wanted to turn it into the next Esalen, you know. She was very close to Rain during all this, and I think she was instrumental in getting the Institute started.

LIV: I don't suppose you happen to have any contact details for her?

STEVE: (laughs) Well, she was living without running water or electricity the last time we spoke, so I'd be very surprised if she's got the latest iPhone. But she's probably still living in that shack of hers. It's not too far from here.

I don't record the part of the conversation where I pull out a photo of my mother and ask them if they recognize her.

"Sorry, sweetheart," Dora tells me. "She doesn't look familiar. But then, like I said, we haven't been around in nearly twenty years."

CHAPTER 17

As Fred navigates his way down the dirt track that is only a potholed interpretation of a driveway, I have a quiver of qualms and second-guessing. I have no training for this, no training for much other than improv and movement exercises and cold reads and taking direction and tap dancing. The house in the woods is a simple, A-frame cabin, with a swarm of solar panels perched on its roof. It's dark back here, and I wonder whether there's ever enough energy to run a household—but even from the outside, one gets the sense that this is not your typical household, and that inside Alexa won't be switching on the climate control and tuning to your favorite Spotify station.

"You gonna be okay on your own?" my beefy driver asks, eyes squinting at me in the rearview mirror. "I could come inside with you."

I won't lie: I'm tempted to take him up on it. "I'll be fine. I'm looking for a sixty-five-year-old woman," I explain.

"If you're sure. Just a bit creepy back here," Fred says. I concur.

Without being able to call ahead, I'm walking into this without knowing anything more than what Dora and Steve could tell me, which wasn't much: just that Sara has been out in this place for decades, raised her two girls out here, and may or may not still be involved with the Light. Detective Burke has managed to send me a JPEG of Iris's image and her missing person report, to confirm her identity, but everything else I've got is rumor and secondhand.

I knock on the door, twice, three times. I'm wondering whether to leave when I hear something get knocked over inside. Someone is home.

"Hello?" I call out. "Is someone there? I'm looking for Sara Reebuck!"

"Mmmm," says a human voice behind the door. I can hear footsteps. I glance behind me at the safety of the town car. Fred gives me a thumbs-up. The handle jiggles, and the door falls open.

A shriveled old woman stands before me: she looks closer to eighty than the sixtyish Dora and Steve mentioned. Her hair is stringy, and she wears a shapeless linen dress with huge pockets. A cane clearly supports her weight; she's listing dangerously.

"Um, hi. My name is Liv. Are you . . . Sara?"

"Mmhmmm," the woman moans.

"Dora and Steve Darling gave me your address—I hope . . . that's okay. I was actually hoping to talk to you about your daughter."

The woman gurgles at me, and her eyes flick behind me.

"You want to talk to me?" someone says behind me.

I whirl around, startled. A much younger woman is standing on the deck just a few feet away, holding a dead chicken in her arms. She cradles it almost like a child.

"Are you Iris?" I ask.

A wary look crosses her face at the name. "No, I'm Lily. Iris is my sister. Sorry about Mom—she had a stroke. She's in there, she's just slowed down a bit. I'm here to look after her."

"Ah. I'm sorry to hear that. Do you think it would be okay if I spoke to you both? About Iris? I'm trying to find her."

"You with the police?" Lily's eyes narrow suspiciously.

"I am very much not. I'm . . . doing a story. About young women in the area, and their involvement with the House of Light."

Sara gurgles again. She's hard to interpret.

"I see." Lily stands, motionless, appraising me. Her arm lowers, and the chicken drops to her side. I notice that it is headless. She notices me noticing. "Um, yeah. Was about to start prepping for dinner. Fine, if you want to talk, we can talk. Come around back, though—I've gotta get this thing plucked."

I nod. "Can I help . . . Sara, can I help you to a seat?"

"Don't worry about her," Lily says brusquely. "She's independent—she'll make it around back in her own time. It keeps her from deteriorating."

I glance at Sara, who fixes me with a milky eyeball. I break her gaze and follow Lily around the side of the cabin, glancing back at Sara just once, to see her hobbling carefully, slowly, behind us. I text Fred to tell him he can pick me up back at the road when I ring him.

Behind the cabin there is a sort of outdoor kitchen arrayed on some flat stones: a fire, an old pot hanging over it, a table, a collection of tools. Lily busies herself topping the pot off with water, organizing her mise en place. Sara, I can see, has just barely reached the corner of the house. I fight the urge to go help her.

"So, you're looking for Iris," Lily prompts.

"I am, yeah. I should explain—I'm putting together a piece about some young women who have recently died and their connections to a local organization—"

"House of Light. You said. I know who they are."

"I understand you grew up there?"

"In a manner of speaking, sure. Mother's been involved with them for as long as I can remember. Though not so much these days," she acknowledges with a nod in Sara's direction.

"Shoot, sorry—do you mind if I record?"

"I don't care. You can probably guess we don't get newspaper delivery out here. Or internet."

I don't bother to correct her assumption about the format of my story. Like I said, no real training in the ethics of journalism.

"What was growing up there like?" I ask.

"What do you think?" Lily snorts. "Fairly fucking weird. Doesn't exactly prepare you for the real world."

"Well, killing and cooking a chicken requires some specialized knowledge," I say, pointing to the chicken she's preparing to lower into the boiling water.

"I suppose. But being homeschooled for most of your life doesn't make switching to the outside world all that simple. Getting a job, stuff like that—helps if you know something more useful than phases of the moon and how to play the drums."

"When *did* you leave? You and your sister?"

Lily snorts again. "Iris never really left. She had a boyfriend, moved away from the Center for a little bit, but she'd always circle back. She took her acupuncture and reflexology classes at the Light, and paid through the nose for them. You'd think there would be a lifelong-member discount or something, but that's not how they roll over there."

"But you left?"

"Well, I tried. Made it for a few years, living in Buffalo. Worked in an assisted living facility. It wasn't great, but in a lot of ways it was better than the Light. No fasting, no moon-blood days."

"Moon-blood days?" I echo.

Lily laughs. "When you're menstruating, you're supposed to go sit in this circle of rocks they've built up on a hill. Consolidates the power of the goddess in you. It's a much bigger deal when you're a teenager, of course. The closer you get to menopause, the less interested everyone is. The closer to a Sun Day it is, the more powerful the ceremony."

"Sun Day?"

"You know, the solstices, equinoxes, Beltane, all that."

"So . . . you would menstruate on a stone on pagan holidays?" I ask.

"Yep. It was supposed to be a measure of your sacred feminine power. The Light is . . . pretty invested in everyone's reproductive health."

"Sounds . . . kind of weird," I offer, hoping to strike the right note of judgment with Lily.

"Yeah, and I never even went to one of the ordinations. Those sounded genuinely fucking strange."

"What's an ordination?"

"Well, like I said, I never went. But there was an inner circle at the Light, and they would meet at night for these weird rituals, usually around the Sun Days. I know Iris went to at least one not too long before she . . . dropped off the grid. She was really excited about it."

"Did she say anything about what would happen, what it would be like?"

"She'd get all secretive. Like she wanted to tell me but I just wasn't . . . qualified to be let in on it."

"And this was around the time she disappeared?"

"I guess. Like late April, early May. It was still pretty cold out."

"How did you figure out she was . . . gone?" I ask.

"Even after I left, we stayed in pretty close touch—we'd talk just about every week. Mom's health wasn't great, and Iris'd give me updates. She was seeing a guy, she was starting to teach not just at the Light but all over the lakes. 'Finding fellow seekers' and all. She seemed okay, but then she . . . just stopped calling one week. When I couldn't reach her, I booked it back over here and found Mom sitting in a pile of her own piss, hadn't eaten in a few days. And couldn't find Iris anywhere."

Lily has since pulled the chicken from the pot and is now tugging the slippery feathers from the chicken's fleshy hide. Sara has shuffled into the outdoor kitchen and she's swaying a bit from side to side, staring at the flames and then at me.

"Was all her stuff still here? Do you think she packed up and left?" I ask.

"If she did, I couldn't really tell. There was no note, nothing to say where she'd gone. I filed a missing person report, but as far as I know, no one really gave a shit. I lost my job because I kept missing shifts, trying to look after Mom. So I just went from wiping strangers' assholes to wiping my mother's. Less money in this, though." She flings wet feathers to the ground with a splat.

"Do you have any theories about where she might have gone? Or what might have happened to her?" I ask.

Lily glances up at me shrewdly. "You mean, do I think the Light had something to do with it?"

I shrug.

"Well, sometimes I think they maybe did. But then, sometimes, I look around me and I think, Who the fuck wouldn't run away from this if they had someone else to step in and deal with it?"

"You haven't," I point out.

"There's nobody left."

"Not your dad? Bloom?"

Lily scoffs. "I haven't seen that fruitcake in fifteen years. Last time I did—well, let's just say we didn't part on the best terms. There's no chance he'd come back here, not to look after her." Lily sighs, flipping the chicken over. She's marvelously efficient. "Nope, I honestly don't know where Iris could have gone to. I wouldn't have thought she'd leave the Light, though. It was all she knew, and she really thought she was helping people, you know. Her work, she was always going on about her work, how she was changing lives, changing the world. Hard to imagine she'd give it up, but then . . . who knows, maybe another cult came along."

"What's the last thing you remember talking about with her?" I ask.

"Shit, probably what to do with Sara. What the, um, long-term plan might be." Lily glances over at her mother, and though it's a tough look, it's not without love. I figure Lily must love her, to stay here. It's not a life I can imagine. "We'd talk about whether we could keep her safe and healthy out here. What happens with the next stroke, all that. But Mom built this house herself, with her own hands. It's not much, but it means a lot to her. And I guess even to me," Lily acknowledges with a wry snort. "It's the house I grew up in. Hard work, but it's where I was raised. So we always said we'd keep her here as long as we were physically able. That's what we were talking about, the last time she called."

I nod, unable to tear my eyes away from the chicken plucking.

"I guess she did mention that she was going to be doing more at the Light. She was usually saying something like that—'I'm going to be more integral in how we do things there, I'm really deeply involved in the organization these days.' She'd say that all the time. But the last time, she said she was doing something totally new, a new branch of the organization."

"The Institute? Oikos Phaos?" I leap in eagerly, all ears.

"Nah, she'd done stuff with the Institute for ages. That's where she got her acupuncture accreditation, and she'd already started teaching classes there. She was a regular instructor, on the website and everything." Lily seems proud of this; she squares her shoulders ever so slightly, mentioning this accomplishment of her sister's. "Nope, I have no idea what she was talking about, and, honestly, I didn't ask. All the politics at the Light, everybody trying to climb the ranks, 'change things,' I was never interested in it. All that fucking drama, and over what?"

Sara gurgles again. I move a step closer to her, trying to discern whether there's meaning behind her sound. She doesn't make eye contact, though, and I notice some drool dribbling from the corner of her flaccid lips.

"That's all she said? 'A new branch'?"

"Something like that, yeah. I was more interested in whether she was making enough money to buy diapers and all that. Overhead is low here, sure, but we still need basics, and I always sent home some of my paycheck to cover some stuff. Mostly that's what we talked about."

I linger around the fire, asking Lily questions about the cabin, about her childhood, occasionally throwing in a question or two about Iris, but after a while she seems to grow bored with me. By the time she's started breaking down the chicken with a massive cleaver, I'm trying to excuse myself.

"Thank you, Sara," I say, reaching out for a gnarled claw in farewell. The drool on her face is reaching unignorable proportions, and I glance awkwardly at Lily, who is covered with chicken blood. "Shall I just . . . ?" I say politely, and lift Sara's sleeve to her face to rub the drool with the fabric that covers her wrist, mimicking the movement she might make if she were more capable. She makes another noise at me, though this one seems to have a consonant at the end. "I didn't catch that, Sara," I say. "What did you say?"

"Loooooooook," she repeats. "Looooooook."

"Ah," I respond. "Yes. I am. I will. I'll keep looking." I smile tightly at her, then walk briskly away, anxious to get the hell out of these woods and back to open skies and sunlight. Striding off, I hear Sara calling behind me:

"Loooooooooook!"

• • •

At the hotel, I'm forced to deal with the practicalities of having again failed to plan ahead. Apparently this weekend is nearly peak leaf-peeping season—who knew—so the tourists have descended. There are no more rooms at the inn and I've agreed to put a roof over the good detective's head, so I begrudgingly relinquish my own. I'll figure out where to sleep later. I pack everything into my new camo hunting bag (could almost be Dolce & Gabbana!), not bothering to fold anything.

Thus having completely exhausted my planning and practical skills, I prepare to meet the former detective in the hotel restaurant for lunch, like we agreed. I haven't seen him since I was a teenager, and I wonder if he will at all resemble the memories I have of him; the world is so distorted when you're seventeen that impressions of people and experiences seem completely unrecognizable with the passage of time. I wonder if he has qualms about seeing me, given my high visibility.

As I'm heading into the restaurant, my phone rings. Jess! I scramble to answer, not caring if it's good or bad.

"Olivia, you've gotten us into a real fucking pickle, you know that?" she begins, without any salutation. I'm so pleased she said "us" that I break into a big red-carpet grin.

"What did I do now?"

"Well, in addition to the overall shitty optics your behavior has generated, we now have some legal troubles to boot."

"Oh . . . that doesn't sound encouraging."

"No shit, Liv. Couldn't listen to me, just had to go ahead and follow your artistic impulses or whatever the hell this is. We've been served with a cease and desist order by the House of Light."

"Goodness, that sounds serious," I say.

"You know what, it actually fucking is, so it would be nice if you could treat it that way. Topher is being a brat and won't respond, but I'll need to speak with their legal, too, and we need to look over that bullshit temporary contract you cooked up. I have to say, your utter disregard for professionalism is really fucking us over here, Liv."

"That's why I wanted you to be involved," I say, affecting meekness.

"Nope, don't even try pinning blame on me here. You don't get to play cowboy and then complain that you got, whatever, shot in a shootout."

"I'm not sure what kind of a scene you're trying to paint, Jess—"

"You know exactly what I mean. You made this mess, and you knew perfectly well you were creating it, and you just didn't fucking care. Next up is probably a lawsuit, so maybe let's tread carefully now."

"Jess, don't you find it very interesting, though?" I ask slowly.

"Interesting?"

"That the Light is responding this way. It's sort of how someone might react if they had a lot of skeletons to hide. Er, so to speak."

"It's also how someone who is perfectly innocent would react to being accused of, oh, I don't know, serial murder. In a very public setting. By someone famous. So there's that."

"I just find their defensiveness . . . intriguing."

"Olivia, you do not seem to be hearing me. This needs to stop. I'm really sorry, but I said it from the beginning, and I'm saying it now. Shut it down. Or, better yet, let me shut it down. I'm begging you."

"I hear what you're saying, Jess. I do. And I know getting sued isn't going to make me look fantastic. But won't it make them look worse? And, for that matter, won't flaking on the project make me look worse? Not to mention financially liable to Topher, if I remember a specific clause in the contract."

Jess groans. "I actually don't think you're hearing me. These people . . . they're not going to just toss a little injunction at you. They have deep fucking pockets, Liv."

"What do you mean, Jess? What do you know about it?" I ask.

Jess takes a long, deep breath. "While you've been running all over the damn lake, I made some calls to people. Do you know who their lawyer is? The name Mark d'Agnello probably doesn't mean much to you, but guess what. He's not the guy you want suing you. He got his training working for the law firm that represents Scientology, and he doesn't play nice. One of his tactics is to dredge up every embarrassing thing you've ever done and publicize it. And as you may remember, you have a couple of things we're trying to keep under wraps at the moment."

"Why does a small retreat center in the middle of nowhere need a big-shot lawyer who has experience protecting cults, Jess?" I ask. "Doesn't that seem really bizarre for a handful of barefoot, granola-munching spiritual seekers?"

"Liv, I don't know. Maybe they're just conscious of the fact that we live in a very litigious society and they want to protect themselves as best they can. Who knows? Additionally, who cares? The reality is that you're the one who is going to suffer, and you need to pull your head out of your ass and start thinking about how to protect it."

"It just seems very suspicious to me."

"Well, given your current state of mind, that doesn't fully surprise me. You haven't been exactly firing on all cylinders, Olivia. Maybe it's time to let someone else do the problem-solving?"

"Meow," I say, trying not to let her hear that she's actually scratched me. "Incidentally, I'm doing just that. I've gotten a professional involved."

"Wait, what?" Jess shrieks, sounding panicked. "You are supposed to be defusing this, not ramping up!"

"A former detective is willing to help me do some of the legwork, bring his professional expertise to bear on the case. I'm actually late to go see him right now, so I'd better hop off the phone. Thanks for the update!"

"Olivia, this is really serious, I need you to—"

"Also, do you think you can maybe send me some clothes? And Richard? I'll text a list in a little while. Thanks, Jess!" I say brightly, and hang up on her before she can tear me to shreds.

From the bench outside the restaurant, I stare out at the bright water, and a sailboat whose sails snap jauntily in the wind, and a little girl in a blue dress racing along the pier, and I think that Jess is probably not going to be falling over herself to send me my belongings. I think I may have to make a quick trip to the city.

• • •

Burke is already sitting at a table looking out at the water when I saunter inside. Someone points at me and immediately pulls out her phone, and I try not to get ruffled when the hostess recognizes me. I miss L.A., where I'm scarcely remarkable, and where everyone is too wrapped up in themselves to remark on my celebrity.

"Hi," I say, sliding into the seat across from Burke, and he makes a gesture to stand, so old-fashioned I barely register it. "No, no, don't get up. It's good to see you again, Detective."

"Well, I'm not a detective any longer, so you may want to dispense with the nomenclature."

"Mr. Burke, then?"

"Or even just Elton, if you like." He smiles that same warm smile that made me feel listened to, years ago. He looks mostly the same, though he wears glasses and is grayer, of course. The predictable ravages of time; no plot twists here.

"I feel like you'll always be Detective Burke to me, but I'll try to remember. Have you ordered anything?"

"Not very hungry," he says. "Ate on my way over here. Though I probably won't say no to a beer."

"It's wine country, but I'm sure that can be arranged." I smile winningly. "You mentioned something about your partner? Dave? You manage to get him settled in before you left?"

"We have part-time in-home care, and this was a good opportunity to see what full-time would feel like. And cost," he answers.

"I'm happy to talk about contracts—" I start to say, but he interrupts.

"There'll be plenty of time for that, don't worry. We'll figure out what seems fair. I owe you a debt, in any case, so let's just make sure there's something I can contribute to this situation before we start horse-trading."

"I like that." The server appears and we order drinks: a lager for him and a Riesling for me. Wyatt has told me which ones to try and which to avoid, and I'm pleasantly surprised with the results when the wine arrives with my side salad and soup.

"How about you lay everything out for me, in order, and then we'll see what needs to happen next," Burke prompts, and I launch into the summary of my "case." I find myself adopting the poise of a stalwart FBI agent, determined to solve this case even as her career teeters on the edge of scandal and she risks losing her badge. The role is not a stretch.

I get the impression that none of this is news to Burke, that he's listening for things I'm not saying, or places where I'm maybe trying to bolster the story though the facts are thin. It's sort of like being interviewed by a cheetah, and his watchful stillness—head cocked slightly, ears pricked—is hard to get used to. I swill my Riesling, though, and settle into my role, and by the end of my monologue, I feel like he's at least hooked, if not fully convinced.

"Tell me about your podcast," he says succinctly when I've finished, and I roll out a description. I conclude with the cease and desist, and one gray eyebrow rises dramatically.

"Interesting" is all he offers.

"I thought so, too. Seems fishy to me, quite honestly. I'm not inclined to take it too seriously for now, but my manager is probably in a huddle with my lawyer as we speak, so . . . I guess we'll see."

"But you plan to go ahead with the podcast."

"I mean, I expect the next episode to drop . . . any minute, really. We were on our way to having it pretty well tidied up, and I just sent along the audio I got from Iris's family to round it out. Actually, I'd be surprised if Naia isn't already working on the next episode while the techs or whatever polish up. I'm not super involved in the production side of things. I'm just the talent," I add with a shrug.

"Somehow I doubt that," Burke says, not cruelly, but not exactly kindly. "You found a way to stay at the center of your mother's case."

"That's . . . not how I remember that, honestly. I felt sort of checked out, not sure what was going on that whole time. Very much on the sidelines."

"Hmm, well, I certainly wasn't the one who called *Dateline* and *Unsolved Mysteries*. It occurred to me your father might have, but . . . to tell you the truth, I wasn't convinced he had the vision."

"Oh, right. That." I blush. "I do feel rather silly about that. I was sixteen, I was frustrated, it just seemed . . . I don't remember exactly what I was thinking. Just that I wanted answers, and those were also people who went looking for missing people."

"I think *Dateline* didn't air the segment, but the other one, they did, right?"

"And nothing came of it, of course. You gave me a copy of *My Dark Places,* if you remember, right afterward."

"Ah, yes, I do. It was mine and Dave's copy, but it seemed like you needed it badly at the moment."

"I suppose I did, though I resented it at the time. I felt nothing like Ellroy, with his rage and his incestuous jerking off and breaking and entering. If anything, it seemed cruel of you, to give me a window into . . . well, that version of masculinity. The scary kind, the kind that steals and murders and kidnaps. But the later versions of Ellroy . . . that helped, I think."

"I'd hoped to draw your attention in particular to his engagement with the media," Burke says drily.

"Or perhaps you were prefiguring our eventual meeting? The adult survivor rekindling the investigative fire with the case's original detective?" I say with a head tilt of my own.

Burke laughs, sincerely, his catlike poise dissipating. "Very good point. One I seem to have missed, in all my elderly wisdom. I'm surprised Dave didn't point it out to me as I was leaving. He certainly had some other insights he was all too happy to share."

"Oh yeah?"

"Mainly he seemed to be jealous of your father, and very interested to know if he would be involved in this . . . leg of the investigation." Burke doesn't ask, but it's clear that he's asking.

"Not as far as I know. My father doesn't see any . . . further personal benefit in pursuing my mother. I think at this point, he rather prefers the mystery it confers upon him." I realize I'm mimicking Burke's style of talking, trying to be the same kind of detective. I wonder if he notices; most people don't.

"Ah. Well, that's all for the best then," Burke says, though he seems a trifle disappointed. I wonder if he and Dad ever had something going on. "Okay, I'm caught up. Now I think it best if we outline our plan of action for the next few days. And I suppose this is a good time to talk expectations."

I lean back, ready to receive the disclaimer. He gave me a similar one when I was a teenager, and it turned out to be true.

"We're looking for a young woman who has been missing for several months. We have virtually nothing to go on vis-à-vis her whereabouts, but her state of mind before her disappearance seems to have been erratic. I'm willing to assist in looking for Ms. Reebuck, but I am very uncomfortable participating in an attempt to portray what appears to be a spate of unfortunate suicides as a serial-murder plot perpetrated by a local business, particularly when this hypothesis directly contradicts local law enforcement's conclusions. It should be relatively clear why I feel that way. I'd like to state that for your benefit, but I also think you should record it and include it in your podcast, for accuracy."

"I appreciate your not mincing words," I say, meaning it.

"I've been accused of mincing, but not words." He smiles, softening. "I respect your attempt to make sense out of these deaths. I really do, and I get the temptation. I've fallen prey to it myself. Which is precisely why I don't want any part in spinning tales, tweaking facts, or pulling theories out of the air. Or the ground, if you prefer," he adds with a self-consciously ghoulish smirk. "Turning death into story time is a very human practice, but I've seen it done for too long, and with too many negative consequences. It's a bad idea to glamorize murder, or suicide. Humans will do just about anything for the right story, and I respect *that*, above anything, at this point in my life. If you can live with my personal recalcitrance, then you've got my help. But only so far, Olivia. I owe you enough to be straightforward on that score."

"I appreciate your frankness. And your help, which I accept very gratefully," I say, and clink my glass against his.

After a long minute, I clear my throat. "I . . . I do have a totally crazy thought. I feel absurd even bringing it up."

"I've seen more absurdity than you can comprehend, Olivia."

"Right. So, I've been treating the, um, online participation with some skepticism. But there's a theory. That my mom might be somehow involved in the Light."

Burke's eyebrows shoot up just a teeny bit.

"It's tenuous, and crazy, and there's no evidence, but . . ." I show him the two photos of her, which I have glanced at periodically over the course of yesterday and today, willing them to confirm each other. He squints, then looks back up at me.

"Obviously it's pure conjecture," he says slowly. "Though I do understand the temptation."

"It's just . . . she could have easily ended up at the Light and no one would ever know. They have off-grid facilities, she would have changed her name to, I don't know, Sunflower or some shit. It's conceivable."

Burke shrugs, giving nothing away.

"Good investigators don't rule things out simply because they're improbable," he finally says.

"But you think it's delusional."

"I think it's unlikely. Not that this wouldn't be exactly the sort of community your mother would have sought out or been able to disappear into. But that you would stumble across it by chance all these years later."

"What if it isn't chance, though? What if she wanted me here and . . . I don't know, managed to get the House of Light on Jess's radar somehow?"

"And it's completely unrelated to the deaths and disappearances?" Burke presses.

"What if she's . . . some kind of whistleblower? And wants the whole thing to come to light? Er, so to speak," I add.

Burke looks at me levelly. "Nothing you're proposing is impossible. But there's a lot more wish fulfillment in there than fact. As long as you're aware of that."

"Oh, believe me," I acknowledge with a snort. "I'm aware."

"That's all I ask," he says.

"There's one more thing, I guess."

"Let's hear it."

"I saw . . . an ordination rite while I was there, at the House of Light. And I've just learned that Iris Reebuck participated in one before she went missing. I'm a little concerned about one girl in particular, who seemed to be part of the rite. I feel like she might be in danger."

Burke is making notes in his pad. "Got a name?"

"Just a first name. Robin. And it could well be an alias. You know, her hippie pseudonym or whatever." I'm about to tell him about Luke, and maybe some of Ava's suspicions, but something makes me pause and keep it to myself.

"Not much to go on, but we'll have a look." Burke looks back at me with that watchful gaze, and I feel too visible and wonder: Why am I tingling with something akin to guilt?

· · ·

After meeting with Burke, I want fresh air, a hike. I'm concerned about the trails being thronged with people who might recognize me, photograph me, hassle me, but when Fred pulls into the parking area, I'm pleasantly surprised to find it empty. Fred agrees to meet me at the other end of the trailhead, and I tighten up my boots in anticipation of a decent sweat and some time alone, not being observed.

The water runs along on my left as I climb up the gorge, the carved stone steps zagging along the banks of the creek. The sound of the water is a static backdrop to my busy thoughts, and I try to lose myself in the *thock* of my heartbeat as I pick up the pace. I miss Barry's Bootcamp, the sound of all those initiates running nowhere to get what they want, to reach who they really are. The smooth grace of a barre class, where you can lose yourself thinking about a pointed toe for long moments. Perching on a Peloton, pedaling your way to self-improvement. All of L.A., steadfastly committed to this program or that one, everyone on their path.

I haven't been hiking for long when I figure out why no one else is on the trail: a slight drizzle picks up, and soon my hair and clothes are wet. It's not properly raining yet, but it's headed that way, and the slate walkway suddenly becomes slick and precarious. I peer at the drop off the side, into the rushing water of the gorge. My shoes feel steady, but I choose my steps carefully, even as I try to maintain my cardio-bruising pace.

When I pause at the top of a staircase to catch my breath, I notice a flash of clothing on the trail behind me. For a second I assume, with relief, that it's another hiker—confirmation that this isn't a dumb and dangerous thing to be attempting in this weather. But whoever was there is gone when I turn to look.

I continue upward, warily now. Twice I think I hear footsteps, the crackle of a broken branch behind me, and I spin around, trying to locate my fellow hiker. But each nervous whirl reveals me to be alone in the woods, with no one but the silent chipmunks for company.

The third time I whirl around, I know I'm no longer by myself: I glimpse a swatch of cream-and-oatmeal fabric disappearing behind a bend.

"Hello?" I cry out. "Is anyone else there?"

Nothing answers. I bite my lip. Should I go back down, around that curve, to confirm that it's just some other foolish hiker, traipsing around in the rain? But, like a scared kid, I think: But what if it isn't?

"Hello?" I try again, somewhat more feebly. I face the stairs again and head up, quickly, as quickly as I feel I can safely manage. I'm not running, but I'm moving my ass. I wonder how far it is to the trailhead above me. Whenever I hear the slap of a foot from behind, I don't turn my head to look, but push on, faster.

The rain picks up, and even in my new boots I start to slip, particularly when I go around curves. My legs skate out from under me when I take a turn too fast, and I almost go down. I don't stop moving, but my heart starts to drill. The sound of my breath is loud, almost louder than the rain—but I can still hear something behind me, doggedly coming up the trail. I risk a glance back and see someone dressed in flowing off-white clothes plodding up the trail behind me. They're not bothering to hide themselves any longer, and in a panic, I lurch up the stairs, losing my footing several times.

Then I start to run, recklessly, along a part of the trail where only a low barrier separates me and the chasm feeding into the gorge, which is churning with water. Tripping now would probably be fatal, I realize, and I try to choose my steps as carefully as if they were a choreographed action sequence. But I'm quickly losing any thought other than blind panic. Whoever is behind me is more sure-footed and is gaining on me.

I come around a bend and gasp. A narrow bridge stretches across the rushing water, and it looks slick and perilous. A bit of yellow tape cordons off the entrance, and I can see why: the stone railing on one side of the bridge has partially crumbled. A stone face prevents me from continuing up the gorge: cross or go back. I duck under the tape and skid along the surface, not looking down at the water below. I hear the tape tear just behind me. My feet shoot out from under me, and my hip slams into the stone.

I twist around.

"What the fuck do you want?" I scream, panting heavily. It's

Devotion, facing me on the bridge, her colorless linen clothes dripping. Unlike me, she doesn't seem remotely winded, or rattled at all. Her dour composure is intact. "What the fuck, Devotion?! What do you want?"

Her mouth quirks, and my stomach sinks as I realize she is attempting a smile. That cruel burn makes one side of her face unmoving, and the effect is disturbing. She takes a few steps toward me. I'm clinging to the rails on one side, but Devotion seems unconcerned about the missing protection. She approaches me, then crouches down in a squat. Her grin widens as she looks into my eyes.

"Your shadow self. Is catching up with you," she rasps in a low voice. She reaches out and chucks me softly under the chin, playful and sinister at once. "Olivia. You have made so many mistakes. With every opportunity you are given, you run in exactly the wrong direction. Do you have any idea how lucky you are, what a chance you've been offered?"

"I'm not . . . can't say I do," I mumble vaguely. I shift to more of a crouch, to be less supine. My heart feels like it's trying to lurch out of my Lululemon.

"You were invited onto shamanic land, to work with someone who comprehends shadow and light. And all they wanted was to show you, to bring out your gift. And you? You throw it away?"

"Who's Luke?"

Devotion looks surprised; her face twitches quickly before resuming its customary scowl. "You would have met him if you'd stayed the course. If you had earned the privilege to be in the presence of a true teacher. He doesn't show himself to just anyone who walks in the door. But I know he wanted to meet you. Very much. The information he has is too powerful, too dangerous for just anyone. But he wanted to share his gift with you." She shakes her head, clucking her tongue.

"What keeps happening to women who join the Light, Devotion? That doesn't seem like such a gift to me."

"That's where you're wrong. Instead of waiting to learn, to receive instruction, you left. I couldn't believe how wrong Rain was about you. They both were. They're so rarely wrong. And yet . . . here we are. And now I have to undo the damage."

"Is this what happened to Hannah? Did you have to 'undo the damage' with her?"

Devotion laughs, a quick, humorless bark. "Hannah earned her ending. *You* have not."

"Is that what Luke calls it? Earning your ending?"

Devotion tilts her head and just looks at me, like a bird who has encountered an unusual insect.

"I have to say, I'm feeling a little threatened here," I add nervously. I look around at the slick bridge, the rushing water. Never have I felt less like fearless Mina. Devotion leans closer to me.

"*You're* the biggest threat to yourself, Olivia. Didn't you see that that's what she was trying to show you? You will be the one to unmake your life, your own soul. You will be the one to crumble into dissolution and ambition. Do you know the Sabian symbol that guides your life? It is collapse. It is waste. Rain chose to see the other sides, the exalted sides, but that is because even she can be blind."

"I genuinely have no idea what you're talking about."

"Because you cannot be taught. You refuse your gift. And you will undo all the good work we have done. Leave the lake, stop looking for answers to questions that are beyond your grasp. Go home, Olivia."

"Again, is that a threat?"

"It's a recommendation. From those who have seen further into your future than you have bothered to look."

Then she turns around and heads back down the trail, the rain spattering harder on the slate.

I remain on the ground for a minute, panting, before I drag myself upright, and then up the next staircase, and the next, until I make it to the safety of the town car in the parking lot.

CHAPTER 18

Yesterday I was followed by a member of the Light while hiking alone in a gorge. While no explicit threats were articulated, I was definitely made to feel intimidated. It was unsettling, and I will admit that I did reconsider this investigative report, or at least my role in it. If that's how the Light can make me feel, how easy must it be to manipulate women who are lost, confused, alone? That thought is what made me continue.

Our investigation into the House of Light suicides has, at least for the moment, become a missing person case. Right now, our priority is to find Iris Reebuck, a young woman who was closely affiliated with the Light and who has subsequently gone missing. Now that we've spoken to her family and friends, it seems increasingly clear that she was troubled at the time of her disappearance, and there is some evidence that she might have been buried alive. Or, at least, it looks like someone might have tried to bury her. Whether or not they eventually succeeded is what we're trying to determine.

I'm also hoping to track down the whereabouts of a young woman who was at the House of Light with me. I saw her participate in an activity that I've since learned is part of an "ordination," one that Iris Reebuck may have participated in just days before her disappearance. For obvious reasons, I'm concerned about her welfare. Unfortunately, I know only her first name, which is Robin, although that may be an assumed name. Without more information about her, there's not much we can do to locate

her. In any case, the next solstice is a couple months away, so I'm
hoping that time is on our side.

I've enlisted some professional assistance to help move the case
forward, particularly in finding Iris Reebuck. This man was the
detective working my mother's disappearance, and I'm engaging
his services to help me track down Iris and find out where she is
now, or whether something has happened to her. He was able to
locate the missing person report filed when Iris disappeared. Her
sister, after several days with no contact from Iris, filed the report
on May fourth of this year. Iris's friend Andy, who came forward
with the information about her attempted burial, reckons that
Iris had shown up at her house on May first or May second. That's
the last that anyone has seen or heard of Iris Reebuck.

· · ·

I spend a few days tinkering with scripts, talking to Naia, and
dealing with dull promo crap; there is little intrepid reporting to
do. But after the episode drops early, several mornings later, I turn
off my phone for an hour or two, such is the volume of the calls
and texts. Nearly all of them are from Jess or Naia, but there's
also one each from Burke and Wyatt. It's the latter call that makes
me switch the phone off in a flustered panic. I should have warned
him, should have told him that his parents agreed to an interview,
should have given him a heads-up about what they said, which
was now downloadable by his neighbors. I'm suddenly exhausted
with the whole business, and just want space from the whole
damn project. This is a lot harder than making a film; I'd rather
simply be memorizing lines and showing up for fittings, instead
of trying to cobble together this ludicrous story, taking flak from
all sides. Bart always used to talk about the "incredible vulnerability of the creative calling," how much of yourself you expose
when you undertake such an endeavor. He'd always spoken as
though he knew something about it, though of course all he'd

ever done was surround himself with others who did that fraught labor.

I stroll out onto the pier, considering my options. The weather has turned cooler, and I wrap a scarf around myself like a shawl, over the chunky cable sweater that is currently my warmest outer layer. Regardless of what I choose to do, I need a wardrobe change. The lake rises up in choppy peaks as I make my way out onto the stone walkway, watching a sailboat tilt perilously, almost parallel to the surface of the water, as it executes a turn.

I can't abandon the story. It has become as simple as that. As much as I'd like to abdicate responsibility, creep home to my apartment and apologize to Jess, and just start over, I can't. I breathe easier after realizing this. I've pissed some people off, but it can't be helped. I've got to find some sort of ending to this story. I'm still nurturing that little glimmer of Mina, doggedly pursuing the truth down the dirt roads of her spooky hometown; she's been a part of me for so long, and some of her moxie is still with me. I remember that her birthday was November 2, the Day of the Dead.

As I stroll back toward town, I check my email. There's one from Naia, from just a few minutes ago. The subject is: WE'RE VIRAL, BITCH. I open the message and skim it, gleaning the important information. The podcast is hitting near the top of the charts, we're getting millions of downloads, it's on track to be a bit of a sensation, check your Twitter hashtags. It's what we wanted, the thing I hoped for, and yet the realization that I am back on the map makes my stomach churn. I know only too well what being a sensation involves; yet why do I seek it out, keep working toward this conspicuousness? Still, I keep refreshing, wanting to see the number of downloads keep ticking upward.

The hotel where Burke is staying is a few hundred feet away, and I consider ringing myself up to his room. I've been staying in a grim motel up the road. Maybe he will have heard the new episode, maybe not, but he's got a level head, and he, at least, probably won't scream at me.

"Congratulations—seems like it's a big deal," a voice says behind me, and I startle. Wyatt is sitting on a bench outside the hotel, leaning back with his thick arms crossed behind his head.

"Oh, hi," I say, at a loss for words. "I didn't . . . we didn't plan to meet, did we?" I know for a fact we did not, because I basically ghosted him again. What do I owe this man, though?

"Nope. But I saw there was a new episode this morning, and I thought I'd take a listen while I got started at work. I shouldn't have been surprised to hear some familiar voices on there, but I guess I was. That's some fast work."

"I'm sorry, I should have mentioned it. . . . My producer is . . . I don't know, she's maybe superhuman. I assume she doesn't sleep. She thinks things are going to break quickly with the case, and she's very committed to this whole real-time thing."

"I read an article about it while I was waiting for you to come downstairs. Someone was saying it's an entirely new podcast experience, this live-action whodunit format. They're saying it could be a game changer."

"I'm just trying to tell the story," I say wearily.

"I noticed you didn't come down from the hotel, though. Just taking a walk, or do you have some other . . . acquaintances to crash with?" Wyatt asks. I can't decide whether he's pissed off or entertained, and it sounds like he can't, either. "I was sort of surprised you didn't come back to the house after speaking with my parents. Thought maybe they'd said something that had you mad at me."

"No," I chuckle. "Just wanted to give you a little space. I'm staying at the motel just down that way. I . . . Never mind. It's not very interesting to hear why." Exhausted, I sit down on the bench next to him.

"I'm sorry I involved you in this," I say.

"Honestly, I sort of feel like I should apologize to you."

"Why? What on earth for?"

"Well, Ava's the one who got *you* involved in all this. With her crazy pet theories. Now you've got quite a lot of eyes on you, and I feel bad for you."

"Why's that?"

"Because her pet theories are, in fact, crazy. Losing her sister made her a bit nuts, and she was not the most even-keeled person before. This whole thing is just another way that she doesn't have to say goodbye to Zelda. Another way they can communicate from either side of the grave."

"But . . . we know Zelda isn't part of this. She wasn't involved with the Light."

"But Ava will believe that her sister is the one who pointed her in the direction of all these women. Even if her death isn't directly related, Zelda is telling her something, even now. Like I said, she's somewhat unhinged. And now . . . well, you're going to have to make sense of all that, while everyone watches."

"Quite the pep talk," I say.

He grins. "You seem pretty competent. I believe in you." He gives my shoulder a friendly punch. "Also, I listened to the podcast, and it's actually pretty damn good. You're pulling some good stuff out of the woodwork. Even that interview with my parents . . ." He whistles. "It's all pretty compelling. I can see why people are getting into it."

I smile back at him, pleased. Beyond his shoulder, though, at the corner of the building, I can see the glimmer of a telephoto lens, pointed in our direction. I straighten, and Wyatt whips his head around. "What is it?"

"I think we're being photographed," I say. I squint as nonchalantly as I can, trying to figure out if I recognize the figure lurking near a bush. At this distance it's impossible to say for sure, but his slim build and slick gray jacket look disturbingly familiar. "It's fucking Vorchek."

"Who?"

"My personal paparazzo. He turns up everywhere. He's the one who . . . contributed to my departure from New York. Little creep follows me everywhere."

"Why don't I go over and talk to him?" Wyatt says calmly, already striding off.

"I don't think—" I start to say, but then stop. Fuck him up, Wyatt.

Wyatt moves so quickly he's nearly on top of the bush before Vorchek cottons on that he is now the prey. Wyatt looks fully capable of ripping the camera from his hands, and Vorchek promptly takes off, sprinting down the block, narrowly evading Wyatt's outstretched arms. Wyatt chases him a few dozen feet, then stops, like a mastiff content to get an intruder out of the yard.

"Can't say the paparazzi have been a feature of my small life so far," he drawls.

"I envy you. Look, I better get off the street. If there really is buzz, and that guy already found me, I'm probably going to spend the day being well documented. I don't want you to get caught in the crosshairs. Well, any more than you already have," I add apologetically.

"Actually, there is one more thing." He reaches up and tugs at the collar of his shirt, and it's the first time I've seen him less than totally confident.

"Oh?"

"Can you . . . can you keep it out of the podcast? It's . . . well, it's about Ava."

"Yeah, of course. What's up?"

"She . . . she's left the Light. Ended her stint there a bit early and came back home last night. She says it's sort of chaotic there, Rain has been AWOL . . . and she says she has to go looking for someone."

"Oh?"

"She said she was worried about a girl who was at the Light

with you both. Ava thinks her name is Robin, but she's not sure. I think you mentioned her in the last episode?"

"I did, yeah," I agree.

"Apparently Ava thinks she's in trouble, too, and she wants to get to her before Samhain." Wyatt runs his hands through his hair, clearly uncomfortable.

"And who is that?" I ask.

"Oh. Not who, when. Another pagan holiday. Halloween."

I'm an idiot. How could I not have realized a Sun Day was just a couple weeks away?

"Fuck," I say. "I was worried about her, too, but I thought we had plenty of time to figure out where she was before something happened to her. Shit."

"Oh?" Wyatt seems surprised. "Well, I assumed Ava was probably just being paranoid. Actually, no, I thought she was lying. Trying to come up with an excuse for taking off again."

"She's not still at home, then," I say, mildly crestfallen. I had already been thinking about racing over to her house to interview her, fill in so many of the blanks. Her, her past, why she sold me out to Rain . . .

"No. She left this morning, ostensibly to go looking for this Robin girl. She thinks she has an idea where she could be, and she said she has to go alone." He shrugs and ruffles his hair again. "I don't know if she wanted me to tell you or not. She was excited about the podcast—I think it gave her a lot of ideas."

"Well, I'm glad you told me. I won't talk about it on the air. At least the Ava bit. As for Robin . . . I don't have enough to go on right now. Don't even have a last name. So, I can't really pursue it."

"If Ava turns back up, I'll let you know," Wyatt offers. He's embarrassed, I can tell.

"Thank you. For everything. I appreciate it."

"I better get back to my vines."

"I'm sorry, too," I say. "For everything."

"No need. For what it's worth, I am, too. But, you know, don't be a stranger. Swing by if you like. Stop in for a drink."

"You sure?"

"You bet," he says, and leans in as though to hug me. Instinctually, I flinch and look around, scanning for other photographers who would be only too delighted to capture us in a posture that could be suggestive of God knows what. Wyatt doesn't complete the gesture, just pats his thighs. "Right. Good luck, Liv. And my door's open, if you need it."

I wave as he strides back up the sidewalk, and I swallow, wishing, for that instant, that I was nobody except his petite wife, happily heading home to spend the day making jam or pickles, with no one watching us except our sweet baby girl.

Instead I turn and head into the hotel, alone, to make sense of the thing I've created.

. . .

Burke is nonplussed to see me at his door, but when I explain about the photographer, he lets me inside with a taciturn nod.

"I've got to shower. Make yourself tea or coffee while I get ready for the day," he says.

The room is a suite, so I'm able to sit at the breakfast nook without feeling too invasive, and I listen to my voicemails. Jess, pissed. Jess, pissed and now pissed at my silence. Jess, menacingly calm. Naia, with the good news, Naia with a question, Naia hoping I can meet up for some voice cuts later. A few texts from my father, excited and pleased about the attention *Vultures* is getting; he's actually meeting with some studio people later in the week, maybe it would be worth talking film options with them? I assume Jess is getting the media requests, if there are any.

As I'm scrolling down, a series of texts from Naia come through.

The online forums are blowing up

It's still dross at the moment, but I'd be surprised if we don't get a few solid things to check out by the end of tomorrow.

The scavenger hunt is on! Let the internet do its work.

Have tasked an extra assistant to deal with the hotline and email address. Am anticipating high traffic!

And though I don't expect it to garner a response, I send Ava a quick email:

Wondering where you've gotten to and what's going on with Robin . . . I was starting to worry about her too. If you come across anything, reach out. We can talk on or off the record.

I don't allude to the fact that I'm mad at her for getting me kicked out of the Light, that I suspect she's incapable of objectivity on this case, that she's been misleading me for her own purposes. Maybe because I feel guilty in my own way: I have claimed her project, made it very publicly my own, and I'm making headway with it. I have spent the night in her house, with her husband and her baby daughter. Her investigation is now mine, and the world knows it.

By the time I've sorted through all this, Burke has emerged from the bathroom, freshly shaved and smelling sudsy. He wears a suit, and I tell him he looks the part.

"So," I say. "Things have been happening quickly."

"Mmm. Do you think you could get me a schedule for when you're planning to publish these episodes? Some heads-up would be helpful." He's irritated with me.

"I hardly know myself, but I've got to set up a time with Naia for today, so I'll ask her. She's obsessed with momentum."

"Right." He goes quiet.

"Also, I think I'm going to need to head to New York for a minute or two. Just to take care of some basic things there. I shouldn't be more than twenty-four hours, but I thought this might be a good window in which to dash down." I bite my lip; I can tell I'm confirming his anxieties that I'm just a flaky actress who's now about to disappear after having dragged him into a mess and directed the spotlight right at him. But then he actually seems to brighten.

"That isn't a terrible idea. You're . . . well, high-profile, so it might help me to have a day or two on my own. Maybe even get to some people who haven't heard the podcast yet."

"I should have explicitly told Naia to wait, at least until you got your footing."

Burke sighs. "Barn door, horse. A media shit show was inevitable. I was just anticipating . . . a few more days before the storm." I give him my best flinch face, and he cracks. "I'll manage, though. But keep your phone on, in case I have questions."

"Deal," I say. "And I'll talk to Naia about airing your . . . disclaimer."

"It's more important that *you* understand it. But thanks, all the same."

"Listen, there's something else that's got me worried," I begin. I fill him in on Robin, and my concern over the fact that Samhain is right around the corner, just two weeks away. I've been trying to figure all this out for three weeks now, and have made depressingly little headway. Burke shakes his head in frustration over how little we know about Robin.

"If I thought we had a chance at probable cause, I'd go to the local police," he says. "But we don't."

I breathe a sigh of relief. Though I know Burke is uncomfortable not working alongside law enforcement, it's one of my requirements, so he's tolerating it. Still, he's said more than once that if he thinks anyone has been harmed or is in imminent danger of being harmed and he has any proof at all, the cops are getting a phone call.

We chat politely for a bit, sketching out a plan for moving forward, but I can tell Burke wants me out of his hair, wants to get on with his job without the burden of my presence, the scrutiny that follows me. I can't help watching the way he turns slightly away from me, how his eyes drop to the coffee cup rather than looking straight at me, the way he did over drinks the other day. My hypersensitivity to this language is what makes me talented, but it's sometimes just a fucking drag. I let myself out of my former hotel room feeling a roil of emotions, most of them shitty, and call Fred to let him know that we're headed home.

CHAPTER 19

I approach the door to my flat in SoHo almost as though I'm a stranger to the place. The last time I was here, packing and having a temper tantrum, feels like another life. Part of me almost wonders whether Jess has changed the locks or ended my lease or moved all my things into storage; she certainly could if she wanted to. It's probably not healthy for one person to have so much control over another's life. It's certainly not healthy that I like it.

But everything is as I left it. Indeed, moments after stepping through the door and smelling the slight must of the central air of abandonment, I hear the clatter of little claws on the poured cement, and Richard comes scampering from my bedroom.

"Oh, buddy, oh my God, haaiiii," I coo, bending down to scoop his solid little body into my arms. He wriggles manically and drools on my cheek as he attempts kisses, wheezing ever so slightly through his bulldoggy nose. He makes his little Richard grunts as he treats me to my first facial in weeks. "Oh, little dude, hey. I'm so happy to see you. But why aren't you at Jess's?" I hold him away and look at his face, as though he can somehow answer me. He just squirms his tush and pants at me. I give him a kiss between the ears and set him down on the ground, and he sprints off to attempt to drink water, splashing it into a puddle around his bowl.

"Liv, is that you?" Jess emerges smoothly from my bedroom, holding her phone and looking surprised.

"I still live here, right?"

"Well, last I heard you were ruining both our lives somewhere upstate. But hey, nice of you to drop in."

"You're still mad at me," I say.

"Still? Oh, you mean from a few hours ago, when you did the thing that I explicitly asked you not to do? Still? From when what was a stupid, misguided project blew up into pure internet gold and everybody started talking about you online? Yeah, Liv, still mad."

"Is it that bad?" I say, moving to the couch. I pat the seat next to me, hoping she'll join me. Richard immediately bounds up and plonks himself where I've patted. Jess stands by the couch.

"I'm in the middle of a conversa— You know what, let me just sign off with them." She stabs a button on the phone and gives me a murderous glance before she turns around. "Yeah, she actually just walked in the door. Yeah, in New York. I hope it means she's done chasing wild geese upstate, but . . . yeah, I'll keep you posted. Let me just deal with her now." She hangs up and turns around.

"Legal?" I guess.

"They're delighted. They're going to get to bill us a fortune this week. Not to mention start a very expensive exchange of papers with Mark d'Agnello. A hotshot entertainment lawyer's dream." I contort my face to look both pained and apologetic; it would work on most people, but Jess is entirely unmoved. "Does this mean you're giving up the project, at least?" she asks. "You can hardly keep at it from here."

"I just wanted to pick up some things. Especially you," I say to Richard, pulling him into my lap.

"Right. Okay. In that case, I think I'm just going to go." Jess strides toward the door and grabs her purse from the counter.

"Wait, Jess!" I jump up to race after her. "Hey, I know you're mad, and I know how frustrating this is for you. But we're a team. We work best when we're working toward the same thing, not opposing each other. I hate this. I hate feeling like you don't have my back. Our back."

"No, Liv. Ultimately, there is no *our* back. There's you, and your career, and everything you've made of your life, for better and worse. And then there's me. Scheduling meetings and packing your suitcase and making sure you make call time. We're not equals, and we never have been."

"Jess, I could never have done any of this without you! I *can't* do any of it without you. You're the one who keeps this all afloat. Please don't leave here angry. Talk to me about the next episode of the podcast. Tell me how to be smart about it. I want to get this one thing right, and I'm worried it will be a disaster without you."

She appears to soften; I can see her sharp, busy brain calculating her options, how best to get the right response, the right performance out of me. She takes a deep sigh.

"I just don't think I can, Liv. Not this time. Your Beckett play was one thing, but this . . . this is going to end badly. I can't get on board."

"Think about it," I beg. I don't want to grovel, but I am willing to, if that's what it takes. "This is the first thing I've done in so long that feels like it's . . . mine."

"Livvy, don't you get it? Nothing is yours. Not *Iroquois Falls,* not your own body, your image. And certainly not 'this.'" She shakes her head and looks at me with sad eyes, then reaches out to stroke my hair, like she's done so many times, but she stops short. As though she's too disappointed in me to reach all the way there.

"Your suitcase is mostly packed," she says, gesturing to my closet. "I hadn't quite finished, but it's mostly done. Richard's things are ready to go, next to his bag."

"Jess," I say flatly as she weaves around me and releases the dead bolt of my door. "Jess. Who told you about the House of Light?"

Her hand rests on the doorknob, but she doesn't turn it. "What do you mean?"

"How did you find it? Were you just googling, or did someone send you the information?"

"Jesus, Liv. I get half a dozen promotional pitches a day. I can't remember who sent me something about the retreat at the Light. It was probably some slick PR dude."

"Do you think you could check for me? It's important. I need to know. . . . I think there's a possibility that someone wanted me there."

Jess stares at me blankly for a long moment. "You're coming unhinged—you know that, right?"

"Please. Just check your email. I know you vetted a bunch of different places for me, I just need to know who nudged you toward the Light. I think it's . . . I think it might be about my mother."

Jess's forehead scrunches upward; the only time you can detect surprise through her (subtle but regular) Botox is if you've genuinely startled her.

"Ah. I see." She rolls her tongue around her mouth, considering. She's going to cave, I know her. Finally, she answers: "I don't have to look it up. I was talking to your dad about . . . what we were going to do with you. He called me, furious, after the first images came out after your . . . episode. He was actually throwing around the word 'conservatorship,' just so you know. But he mentioned one or two places that he knew of where you could go to clear your head. Said he could vouch for them, personally. So I added both of them to the list of places to call and check availability. The Light was the best option, and the only one that could take you right away. Especially at the price point we were shooting for. The other one was full and, frankly, way over budget." She shrugs.

"How could you not tell me that? Especially after all this started to happen?"

"Because your family makes you crazy, Liv. I get that, and I get why. I just didn't think we needed any extra interference. Any more excuses. You need to get some help, and I don't know how to make you." She holds her palms up, her manicured nails flashing. Then she turns and leaves. I hear her heels click once or twice in the hallway before the thick door bangs shut.

...

There are a million things to do, and I enjoy getting swept up in the mania of dealing with all of it for a few hours. Phone calls to Naia and Burke, letting them know where I am and setting up meetings and times to talk further. Unpacking and repacking my suitcase, walking the dog, thinking of anything I might need as the season gives way, stops hovering between summer and autumn. It occurs to me that I've been bored; with Jess doing everything, I've been cut off from the constant distractions of organizing a life. But maybe it's the organization of a life that makes it feel full and worth living. Maybe I've driven myself a bit mad by abdicating any sense of ownership over this life, its small nuts and bolts, its dreary quotidian managements. Maybe what I needed all along was to answer my own fucking phone calls and go shopping at the bodega. I should start a retreat center where people just have to deal with their own daily minutiae.

Pleasantly fatigued from the drive and all the tedium of arranging things, I don't have the energy to call Fred at his hotel room and tell him we're going to turn around and go back. It's probably against his union policy for him to drive me back tonight, anyway.

Pacing around my flat, I think about whether there's anyone in town I'd like to see. It's a depressing train of thought. My "friends" tend to be people I'm working on a project with: costars, sometimes assistant directors or even the director. There is, of course, the Director, who I can't risk seeing. I text Ryan, pointlessly, silently begging him to text back but knowing he won't, aware that he might never. Jess isn't speaking to me, Naia is a workaholic I barely know. I text Topher, not sure whether he's in New York or not; he's bicoastal, and swings back and forth with little predictability. Jess probably wouldn't like me speaking with him, but we could talk about the show. If nothing else, he would make me feel excited about *Vultures,* like I'm doing the right thing.

I fetch a Perrier from the fridge and a kimono from my bedroom and flop on my massive pink velvet sectional before tugging my laptop onto my legs. I have to dislodge Richard's nose somewhat to make space.

Naia has sent links to a handful of websites that are chattering about the podcast already, and I'm immediately sucked into this world of both strange precision and wild speculation. I tinker around, flipping through threads, watch as a moderator removes a comment about a local man who lived near the Light and was rumored to be responsible for the death of his wife; the moderator gently scolds those posting, reminding them not to share unfounded speculation. Lots of links are posted: to the Institute's website, to Facebook pages, to a local news site. I realize with some unease that a local online paper has written about the story; really, the reporters have written about the podcast, but they have also included some basic details about the deaths.

I open the thread that deals with my family, unable not to.

Cristoff307: look what I found on youtube!!: <u>Unsolved Mysteries Season 3 episode 3</u>

> *volleyballmom:* omg she was so young look at that baby!

> *Cristoff307:* right??

> *volleyballmom:* the mom just totally disappears tho . . . haven't been able to find a single mention of her name, and I've combed through every social media site I can find looking for her

> *Cristoff307:* Yes I've tracked her ssn haven't found a trace, honestly I'm starting to think she's dead otherwise there's no way she'd be this invisible

volleyballmom: its always hard with these older cold cases of course

PictureCurator: Have you all seen this photo of Liv? Doesn't she look just like her mom?

I look at the photo; it's recent, taken in the past few days. I'm alone, walking on the pier in the Glen, and the photographer zoomed in on my face. I look upset, unsure. But PictureCurator is right . . . I do look like my mother. Right before she disappeared.

Cristoff307: Also, has anybody else looked at an age progression of the mom's pics? She looks like she's getting sick. My aunt looked exactly that way when she got cancer.

PictureCurator: I see what you mean. Let's say she's sick, doesn't have insurance, is looking at a few hundred k of medical bills or slow painful death. Sure sets the scene for her to off herself, right?

Cristoff307: Or for the dad to kill her . . .

WhereWeGo1: Or get someone else to do it?

They're very quick to throw their theories around, aren't they? The whole thing makes me feel suddenly queasy, and I shut my laptop, wanting to not think about it. To not reflect on what I might be doing.

I'm pouring myself a drink in the kitchen, wishing I had a benzo to quiet my unease, when my phone rings. It's my father. I consider not answering, but in the end, I pick up. I need to speak to him, after all.

"Darling, hullo! Jess tells me you're actually in the city right now? I had to practically tear it out of her. She's not in a fantastic mood."

"Um . . . yeah, probably just for tonight."

"Well, then, it's wonderful that I caught you. I'm also just passing through New York for the moment, headed to London in a few days and stopping over for a minute here. Listen, why don't we meet for a nightcap? I'd love to catch up."

"Oh, I mean, I was just thinking of going to bed," I say. But then I glance around at my empty apartment, at the sad glass of gin I've just poured for myself. I remember the craving for a pill, and how quickly that can get hairy. "But okay, yeah, I could go for a drink. Where are you staying?" I know better than to ask him to come to me.

He's not staying far, as it turns out, and I arrange to meet him in the Rose Bar at the Gramercy. I've always liked that place, and I'm glad to have an excuse to put on a dress and some makeup. I've enjoyed my sojourn in flannel and boots, but I can't help wanting to feel something of my old self, walking the twenty or thirty blocks to the hotel in the low heat of the last few warm days, just a blazer tossed over my shoulder in case it gets chilly, which it most likely will not, heels clacking familiarly on the sidewalk. I feel like myself in my Agnès B. baby-doll dress.

My father is already down at the bar, and we give each other the requisite cheek kisses before I settle in and order a flute of champagne.

"You look very nice, Livvy. One could never tell you've been drying out in the woods for the past few weeks."

"And one could hardly tell that you've been running around like a debauched lout for the past few decades. Perhaps it's genetic."

Bart laughs good-humoredly. "Perhaps it is, at that. Not a bad trait to pass on." He pats my knee and finishes his martini, orders another. "It seems like your little radio project is going well."

I narrow my eyes. Surely he didn't fly all the way across the country to talk about my new project? But then, of course, it's entirely possible that he did. If he heard the buzz.

"Oh, it's making some waves, I guess. It's just a podcast, though. Not a lot of money in it."

Bart eyes me up with a shrewd glance of his own. "Well, the publicity can't be a bad thing, regardless. It's not bad for you to be visible."

"I just want to tell a good story!" I say, brightly, with a toss of my head and a sip from my glass.

"I wonder if you've given any more thought to a film adaptation. You know, I was speaking to one of my contacts in L.A., and he was saying that they're definitely keeping an eye on the podcast charts for potential development."

I begin to piece together what's happened: Bart started asking around and realized that people do actually care about podcasts, and now he wants to make sure he's not going to get cut out of the project if it actually turns into something. So he's here in New York to be supportive and interested and paternal. And, I'm guessing, to pitch something.

"I think we should just see how it goes. After all, I don't even know if there's an ending!"

"Really? That seems a bit risky, doesn't it, Liv? What if the whole thing just . . . fizzles out?"

"It may do," I answer lightly, concealing that I am very much concerned about precisely that. "But I guess anytime you start with a story, you have to just have faith. That you'll get there eventually. There are—"

"—no guarantees in art," we both finish simultaneously, and he grins at me.

"Indeed. Well, nevertheless, it's a very bold and interesting project you've taken on. I was actually wondering, did you ever get in touch with that detective? The one who was searching for your mother?"

"I sure did. He's actually working on the case. Well," I amend, "he's agreed to help me look for the missing woman, the one who has disappeared and was involved with the House of Light right up until she vanished. He's reluctant to get involved in investigating the other deaths, but he's helping look for Iris, at least."

"Oh, that's lovely news. I quite liked the fellow, for all that it was a very traumatic and strange time when we met. Seemed serious. Thoughtful."

"He is," I agree. I've nearly finished my champagne. The pitch will be coming now.

"I was thinking," Bart says after a pause. "I'd be happy to go on your little show, if you want. To speak about your mother and her . . . disappearance. That particular cloud has been hanging over us for such a long time now, and I think speaking publicly about it would, well, help. Obviously it's not a huge part of the case you're currently working on, but I can only imagine people will be interested in your past. You've never really spoken about it, either."

"It was something I always wanted to keep private."

"You've clearly changed your mind. Not that I pass any judgment on that," he hurries to add. "In fact, I think it will do you good. I admire it. Maybe that's why I'm offering to do the same—you've shown me how." He gives me a diffident smile. Father, you were the one who was made for the stage.

"Um, well, yeah, let me think about it. I have to talk to Naia—she's putting together the script for the next few episodes—so let me discuss it with her, see where it fits in."

"Not that I want to insert myself into your little project," he says. If he calls it my "little project" one more time, I may crack. "I just wanted to make myself available in the eventuality that you wanted . . . my help." Actually, he's being strangely casual about *Vultures*. He has to know that it's turning into a big deal. And who doesn't know what a podcast is?

"Very thoughtful of you," I say slowly. "Can I ask you something else, though?"

"Of course, darling."

"Had you ever heard of the House of Light before? I mean, before all this?"

"Hmmm . . . well, I have a lot of friends who do the whole rehab circuit somewhat regularly, as you know. But, no, this one's not exactly Passages or Crossroads or the like. I can't say it rings any bells."

"Nothing to do with Mom, maybe?"

"Your mother? Good Lord no, she never even drank."

I push him a little: "Nothing to do with her disappearance, either?"

"Darling, you don't think . . . I mean, you're not formulating some theory that she's one of your missing or dead girls, are you?" He looks genuinely concerned.

"I just wondered. There are people online who think she might have ended up there, at the Light, after she disappeared. I was just curious."

His brow furrows, and he shakes his head.

"So, there's no way it could have come up in conversation with Jess a few weeks ago, right? You wouldn't have mentioned it to her, suggested it as a place I could maybe lie low while I recovered?" I ask.

My father looks puzzled. "Jess and I have had virtually no communication since you asked me to take a step back, out of your life. I'm the last person she'd consult with on where to send you for your recovery. And I certainly wouldn't have mentioned the Light, as you call it. Never heard of it."

I nod. I'm not even remotely surprised that he's denying it. But I don't particularly like it.

"Well, I should probably get going . . ." I slide off the chair.

"You won't stay for another? You're more than welcome."

"Oh, thanks, but I have to hit the road early tomorrow, so I should get home."

"You'll think about what I've said?" Bart asks.

"Of course." I don't offer to pay the bill.

As I'm about to leave the dark bar, I turn back to him. "Do you think . . . do you think she's listening to it? The podcast?" I ask.

He bites his lip, then takes a long breath. "My love, I wish I could tell you. I think we'll probably never know."

I nod again and give him a small wave. Outside, I expertly wipe the corner of my eyes so that my eyeliner will sweep up in a cat-eye, rather than running down my face. I head back to my empty apartment.

. . .

By the time I get back to my building, I'm composed. That changes swiftly when I open the door. The Director is lounging in my lobby. I'm struck by how scruffy he looks, with his paunch and his gray, unkempt whiskers, his blazer that fits his once-squared shoulders but is loose around his chicken arms.

"What are you doing here?" I ask slowly, looking around. The sight of him and me in my lobby would be quite a scoop. I'm relieved that Vorchek thinks I'm still in the Finger Lakes; I even posted to Instagram earlier to make it seem like I was at a vineyard.

"I wanted to talk to you. Thought it was best in person."

"A phone call probably would have worked. You're lucky you caught me. I'm only in town for a few hours."

"Call it a sixth sense," he drawls unctuously. I glance over at the doorman, who, I trust, has yet to sell me out. But.

"Come up and we can talk through the contracts," I say loudly, fooling no one. "You shouldn't fucking be here," I hiss in the elevator as he sidles closer to me.

"I wanted to see you."

"I told you that wasn't going to happen!" I stride into my loft, ushering him inside. "I can't really have this in my life right now."

"I thought sneaking around was sort of your thing." The Director reaches for me, and I swat him away. Richard has hopped off the couch and is considering whether to growl.

"What did you need to talk about?" I ask. With a sickening swoop of my stomach, I fear that he'll tell me it's about his wife: she's found out, or he's left her, or she's left him, or some similarly wretched turn of events. As it turns out, it's worse.

"Someone else knows about us," he says casually, unperturbed by my rebuff.

"Who?" I can feel myself turn pale.

"I'm not precisely sure, but someone from the fourth estate, I believe. Someone wanted a quote, said they were fact-checking. I didn't tell them anything, of course. But I figured I'm probably more motivated to stay quiet than, say, certain ex-boyfriends of yours. You are exes, yes? With young Ryan?" He looks at me with those director eyes, the ones that undress you, that know what the curve of your ass looks like without your ever having shown him. Though, of course, I have.

"I haven't heard from him since . . . he found out. But yes, I imagine so."

"Do you think he might be inclined to comment to the press, if asked?" The flirtation is dropping, and I realize that the Director is not as relaxed as he seems. He's worried about this coming out, too.

"Honestly, I don't know. He was mad." I squeeze my eyes shut. "Was it *TMZ*? Or *Us Weekly*?"

"They didn't say. It was all sort of cloak-and-dagger, actually. The tabloids aren't usually interested in an old bag like me—I'm not as picturesque in a bathing suit. They said they had documentation of our relationship and that you had the power to squash the story—"

"Wait, they said what? What words, exactly, did they use?"

"Um, well, those ones: 'Ms. Reed has the power to squash the story, and she could prevent it from ever going to print, but she has chosen to . . . ' I think they said 'go ahead with the story' or something? I got the impression that they wanted me to think that you were leaking the whole thing, or at least not denying it. Which seemed fishy to me. I know how badly you want it kept secret, after all." He looks around my loft, toward the couch. "I notice you haven't really invited me in."

I'm thinking too quickly to even register his last comment. Journalists, even tabloid journalists, will say who they're working for when they're trying to get a comment. And I knew that I for damn sure wasn't leaking the story about the disgraceful shambles of my life.

"They called you? When? Can I see the number?" I ask.

The Director shrugs and pulls out his phone, handing it over. I see the call record. It's a 607 area code.

"This is an upstate number."

He shrugs again. "Oh? Can't say I noticed. Seriously, Olivia. Let's have a drink, catch up. It sounds like you've had a rather dramatic few weeks," he adds drily. He reaches out and catches hold of my wrist, stroking it with his long fingers. His eyes slowly rise to meet mine. I hand him back his phone and look at him. What was I thinking with this man? What possessed me? I feel shame, and a hollow fear that it will be revealed for everyone to see, to gawk at.

"It's been a really long day," I say, distracted, not even bothering to try for a real excuse, to make him feel less dismissed. "Thanks for the heads-up—I'll call you soon." I usher him out the door with a few more vague assurances. He gives me a hurt and puzzled look before I slide the door shut in his face.

I immediately dial the number. It goes to voicemail.

"You have reached the House of Light. Please leave your name, number . . ."

They know, they know, they know. Of course they do: I told Rain everything. I unwittingly provided her with all the collateral she needed. How long until they confirm it? How long until they release it to the press? I bury my head in my couch and give in to self-pity, for just a few minutes.

• • •

Richard and I doze through the return upstate, stretched out in the backseat. We started early, after a sleepless night, and I'm content to nap until we've turned off 81, at the exit toward the Finger Lakes. I screw around on my phone; the number of subscribers grows and grows, and it is a comfort to my bitter, hollow heart. It's the only thing that can comfort me at the moment. The success of the podcast, the hope for a redeeming movie project, salvaging my life. *Vultures* is all I have.

When I look at the photo that was posted of me on one of the message boards, I notice that it doesn't seem to have been pulled from any of the tabloid websites, or to be a screenshot from one of the glossies. In fact, I can't find it published anywhere. Is PictureCurator a paparazzo? I text Jess, not addressing the fact that she's as furious with me as she's ever been.

> Have I been in any of the tabloids in the last few days? Found a weird picture online and trying to figure out where it came from.

She replies almost immediately:

> A little blip in People last week (see email). But that's all I've seen. Could it be that little worm Vorchek? He's always hanging around, the bloodsucking leech.

I get a surge of pleasure at her condemnation of Vorchek, her casual defense of me. This would be so different if I had her on my side, instead of trying to shut it down. I wonder if she wasn't completely right all along, and a flutter of anxiety that has been gradually building makes me reach for a pill that isn't there. *Jess, Jess, Jess,* I chant with my eyes closed, forehead against the cold glass. *I need you.*

We pause in Ithaca, long enough for me to swing by the recording studio for a quick huddle with Naia. She asks me to record a few ads, then read from a script she's drafted, and we talk over the possibility of including anything further about my mother.

"Honestly, your celebrity is part of the pull for this thing," she says, "so listeners will probably be thrilled to hear about your painful past and all that. If you're game, I don't mind working it in at all, as long as the pacing stays tight. Can you get this Burke fellow over here or . . . ?"

"He says he wants to clarify a couple of things for the record anyway, so I'm sure he'd be willing. Also, I wanted to see if you've got a schedule for releasing episodes—that was another of his requests."

Naia and I walk through some practical stuff (including, apparently, a bonus for her for hitting a million downloads) and she is all business, trotting me efficiently through my paces. She is vibrating with excitement over her success, *our* success, and even though there is a nervous feeling in the pit in my stomach, I still give in to the thrall. We are making it, people like it, it is a hit! This is why, this is worth it.

As Fred and I leave the city and drive toward Seneca Lake, Burke texts to say he has news.

> Promising lead on Iris's current whereabouts. Meet in lobby?

I agree, and Fred grins silently and capably at me in the rearview mirror as we cruise along, slowing down when we pass a waterfall coming into the Glen.

Burke is pacing in the lobby when I arrive, looking pleased

with himself. I've already decided not to mention any of the things happening with my dad, my suspicions about him; I'm hardly ready to put it in the podcast, after all.

"That was pretty quick," I say, gliding over to meet him. I've brought all my rustic country gear back with me, but I'm dressed similarly to him, in wide-legged trousers and a blazer. Playing the part of gumshoe. But while Burke sports nice leather shoes and a button-down, I'm wearing dainty white sneakers and a thin white T-shirt.

"Well, let's not go counting chickens just yet. It might be nothing."

"Still, tell me, tell me!"

"I'll fill you in while we drive." He's itching to get going, already heading for the door.

"My car or yours?" I ask. He doesn't answer me, merely heads toward his own vehicle. "Take the afternoon, Fred!" I call to my driver as I rush past where he's been waiting in front of the hotel.

Burke drives fast and smoothly, his little sports car elegant and tidy, just like him.

"This thing is gorgeous," I say, stroking the leather interior.

"Dave restores them. This one was a special project," he explains. I wait for him to go on, but he doesn't add anything about his private life.

"Okay, so what's the tip?" I finally press.

"It actually came in via your hotline. Someone who's been on the true crime blogs or whatever and has been following a thread. Apparently there's someone on there who has a knack for following social media trails."

"But Iris stopped using all her social ages ago, I thought."

"She did. But—and this is some impressive obsession with detail—there's a picture of her on someone else's."

"Connected with the House of Light?" I ask, eagerly.

"Perhaps even better, at least for tracking her down now. It was at a work benefit for a residential center in Canandaigua. Go

ahead, my phone's unlocked—I saved the image in my photos."
He tosses me his phone, and I grab it eagerly.

The photo isn't terribly high quality, and there are ten people
in it. It takes a minute, but I spot Iris's face, smiling but not altogether relaxed. She's at the farthest right of a group of people all
wearing matching blue shirts that read NEW DAY RESIDENCE. The
poster, someone named Sheryl Redmond, has gone a bit heavy on
the capitals in her caption.

> AMAZING day raising money for the AWESOME
> work we do here at NEW DAY. TRULY INSPIRING
> guys, I can't believe we met our goal!!! RAH RAH
> RAH!!!!!!

"It's another halfway house, though I guess they do have a
small outpatient clientele," Burke explains. "I'm assuming she
was, at least until recently, employed there. Look at the date on
that thing."

I squint at it: September 5, just over a month and a half ago.

"Well, now, that is encouraging. How on earth did they find
her in this photo? She's not even tagged."

"These people are next-level. I mean, this woman who emailed
must have been scouring the Web nonstop. Basically, she combed
through everything on Iris's and her sister's social sites, and Iris
had liked a post these guys made more than six months ago. Then
she went through and looked at every photo the organization has
posted since then."

"She must have a good eye. What's her name?"

"She wouldn't give me her name," Burke says with a grin. "She
said her handle is CatDetective. She mostly works on animal-
cruelty cases, tracking down people who abuse animals in online
videos. But thankfully for us, she sometimes dabbles in missing
women. I guess the online community is very intrigued with your

case." Burke lets out a low whistle. "Sort of makes me feel like my skills are quite modest and *quite* out of date. I never would have found this, not if I looked for years."

"God bless the internet," I say, meaning it. I can't help but wonder about the tip. My mother loved cats. "So, I guess we'll just go to Canandaigua and . . . hope she's working?"

"I'll flash my PI credentials, see if that gets us any traction to look at an employee file. My fear is that she's going under a different name, but at least we've got the photo. There's likely to be someone who's willing to talk to us. I'm glad you've dressed the part today; you look very official."

"Well, let's hope they don't recognize me. Might blow my cover," I point out.

Burke snorts appreciatively. "Indeed. Does that happen often? You getting recognized?"

"Not as much as it used to. But yes, it's definitely a feature of my life. It tends to be generational; my show had a sort of niche audience of millennials, and I can't say my work has garnered vast interest in the general population since then."

Burke is quiet for a moment. "I watched your show, you know," he finally says. "Not right when it came out, but a bit later." He seems to be searching for the right words.

"I wouldn't have thought you were the key demographic," I say lightly.

"Well, I guess not, but I was still . . . intrigued by it. You took on the role very well. It was dark without being too melodramatic, and I liked the characters rather a lot. A girl who is quite literally haunted by a death, who struggles with her mother's absence . . . I could see why it resonated with you."

"It wasn't a perfect show, but those were good years. I was proud to work on it."

"You acquitted yourself admirably," Burke says somewhat stiffly. I feel like he wants to pat my hand, but he doesn't.

The drive is only about an hour, the lake sprawling to our right, looking vast and dazzling. A handful of sailboats skate across it, their captains clutching at the last few days of fair weather. As we drive, I see a sign in a front yard that reads WHERE WE GO ONE, WE GO ALL. I pause, trying to place it, then remember it from my rabbit-hole dive into online conspiracies. The sight of it makes me feel strange, uneasy about all the digital speculation I had written off. Now some of it seems less crazy.

Burke is mostly quiet, but he starts to coach me as we draw nearer, reminding me to let him do the introductions and ask the questions.

"I'd like to record, if at all possible," I insist.

"Once we've got the preliminaries out of the way, we'll see about that. It's going to be about feel, whether or not we think we can get anything useful, whether the information is trustworthy. You'll have to trust my instincts."

"Yes sir," I say, but he doesn't seem to like that. He takes the job very seriously, I reflect. While he's not a humorless man, this business is deadly real to him, and I don't think he does anything lightly, without considering its impact and consequences. That gravitas is what always made me feel safe around him, as a teenager. He deals in life and death, and this is not a lark or a diversion for him. I square my jaw and shoulders to match him, and reflect that I could learn something from this man. I am a dilettante in this arena.

"By the way, have you found out anything about Robin?" I ask.

"I'm afraid not. We don't even have a photo of her or know if that's even her name. For now, I'm afraid we just have to hang on. Hope maybe Iris knows something about her."

I nod. This is what I expected, but the days until Samhain are ticking down swiftly. We have less than two weeks to find her.

We park in front of a slightly ramshackle house with a chipped but cheerful sign that advertises New Day Residency. A fading rising sun is etched and painted into the sign, a predictable but inoffensive logo. There's a handicap ramp and a wraparound porch. All in all, the place looks like a vaguely institutional bed-and-breakfast.

Inside, it's cool and musty, and there's a reception desk just through the entryway. It seems to be temporarily unmanned, so Burke takes the opportunity to peer around some corners into the sunroom and what looks like a library. Compared to the House of Light, this is distinctly down-at-heel, but I imagine there are worse places to wrap up your second twenty-eight days. I almost shudder with gratitude.

"Can I help you?" a young, round woman with springy curls asks us as she bustles up to her post behind the desk.

Burke turns to face her, a pleasant, trustworthy smile on his face, badge in his hand. "Hello there, my name is Detective Elton Burke. What's your name?"

"Um, Susan. Masters," she answers. "Hi."

"I'm an investigator looking into a missing person case, and I was wondering if I could speak to some of the employees or residents here in connection with a young woman we're trying to track down. Would you mind if I asked a couple of questions?"

"Um, I guess," Susan says, looking wary but willing.

"I was hoping to locate Iris Reebuck—I believe she's an employee here?"

The woman's forehead crinkles. "Hmm, nope, I don't think we've got anyone working here by that name. You're sure she's an employee and not a client, though? I don't have all their names memorized, and, of course, there is some turnover."

Burke pulls his phone out and leans over the counter to show her the photo. "We think she's actually in this photo, taken a few weeks ago. Right here, on the end?" He points to our girl, and Susan leans in to squint.

"Oh, you mean Hannah! Yeah, she's been with us a few months

now. She mostly keeps to herself, but she seems like a really sweet girl. She's not in yet, but she will be at . . . I think her first session is at four—I can double-check."

Burke glances over at me. *Hannah?* I mouth while Susan clicks at her laptop. Burke raises an eyebrow.

"Yep, she's got an appointment in the acupuncture and massage room at four. I'm sure it wouldn't be a problem if you wanted to wait outside on the porch for her."

"Can you tell me what her last name is?" I ask before Burke turns away.

"Giordino. But we mostly go by first names around here!" Susan says. Maybe she wrote the saccharine caption for that Facebook post, I reflect. Or maybe that's just the corporate dialect of this place.

"Thanks, we'll just wait outside on the deck," Burke says.

"One more thing," I ask. "Can you tell me . . . is New Day at all associated with Simple Transitions?"

"In Penn Yan? Well, I think we do belong to the same affiliated group of outpatient residencies. We share accreditation, I believe."

"Who runs that group?"

"Oh gosh, it's something quite generic, if I remember. Luck Group? Lux Group? Yeah, I think that's it."

"Lux?" I repeat.

"You mean, like the word 'light' in Latin?" Burke clarifies.

"Yepper-doodles, let me just . . . here you go, here's a flyer about their facilities. They go as far as Pennsylvania and Ohio, I think."

"Thanks," I say, accepting the brochure. "Is this . . . is this a good place to work?" I add. "I mean, do you like it?"

"Oh, sure," Susan says. "Facilities like this can be a little grim, but this place is actually really nice! I mean, the holistic treatments are a great addition, I think. But yeah, it's pretty good."

"Thanks, we'll just wait outside," Burke says again, steering me toward the door.

On the porch, we settle into a couple of Adirondack chairs that place us disconcertingly at rest, leaned back into the deep scoop of the seat.

"Have some theories you'd like to float?" Burke asks with a wry smile.

"It does seem weird, right? The Lux thing, the Light thing? The research institute with the Greek name that means light. I looked at their website when we tracked down Simple Transitions; they own a bunch of self-help companies, a direct-sales type deal. For skin care or nutrition or something."

"Certainly something worth keeping our eyes on, you bet," Burke agrees. "But I'm more interested in hard connections." He pauses. "Wait, what did you say about a direct-sales company?"

"One of the companies owned by Lux. It's called . . . hang on, let me look it up . . . Illuminate." I show him the website, and he frowns, looking concerned. "What is it?" I press.

"Probably nothing. I just . . . had the beginnings of a thought. But right now, I'm trying to focus on the task at hand. Finding Iris."

"What about her assumed name? Isn't that sort of weird?"

"Hannah?"

"Yeah, since it's the name of the woman who died while I was staying at the Light. But also Giordino," I say.

"That was the last name of another one of the girls who died, right? The one who jumped off a waterfall."

"Exactly, and who was working at the Institute when she died. Why on earth would Iris take their names?"

"More interesting would be what name is on her pay stub, and what Social Security number she's using for her paychecks here," Burke muses. "I'm assuming this place probably doesn't pay in cash. And there will be Medicare and other insurance companies generating even more paperwork."

We bandy these ideas about while we wait for Iris/Hannah to arrive. After a while I'm yawning furiously, tired from the day's driving. I could probably nod off in the chair, but Burke's voice makes me stir.

"Hannah? Hannah Giordino?" With his nimble Astaire feet, he's already crossed most of the porch to intercept the young woman coming up the stairs. She's recently dyed her hair, but I can recognize her easily. She stops warily, her foot on one step. "I was hoping to ask you a couple of questions—" Burke begins, but she looks like she's about to bolt like a tweaked-out rabbit. She's got that stillness that comes before incredible movement.

"We're doing a story on holistic healing practices in treating addiction," I say, coming up behind Burke, hoping my female presence (and my lie) will put her at ease. "We'd love to talk to you for a second or two—we've just heard great things about your practice."

Iris/Hannah glances at the door of New Day, but some of the frantic spring has left her, and she's taken a breath. She glances down at her phone, and her thumb moves delicately over the screen.

. . .

Folks, when we finally found Iris Reebuck, she did not seem very happy to be found. For that reason, we don't have a recording of her voice. And for the same reason, I won't share any details about where we finally tracked her down. Or, rather, I won't give any specific details. But I will say this: we found her working for an organization that is linked to another organization, one called Lux. Lux, of course, comes from the Latin word for . . . "light." Make of that whatever you will. Lux seems to be an umbrella for several other self-help organizations.

Some of what Iris had to say seemed eerily familiar, but mostly, locating her just kicked up way more questions than it answered.

. . .

"I'm sorry to ambush you like this," I say after a long pause. We are seated, but Iris/Hannah is perched on the arm of an Adirondack chair—I can tell she doesn't trust us. "But we're not here to talk about acupuncture." Iris/Hannah blinks and stays perfectly still.

"They found me," she says finally, squeezing her eyes shut ever so briefly.

"Who found you?" Burke presses.

"The Light, of course. I knew you would, eventually. I just wanted . . . well, a little more time here. I liked this place."

"We're not with the Light," I interject. "On the contrary, I'm trying to figure out what's going on with those crazy people."

"With all due respect, how dumb do you think I am? You think they didn't prepare us for exactly this type of thing? You think that I trust you, in any way?"

"You *can* trust us," I insist. "We're trying to expose the Light, and what's happened to other young women involved with them."

"Rain sent you, right? Trying to keep the whole Committee quiet. I guess she hoped it would take care of itself, but . . . I guess not."

"Did Rain do something to hurt you?" I ask. "Did she try to bury you? I mean literally?"

Iris laughs. "Oh my God, you guys are good. Look, I know the only reason my collateral hasn't been released is because I kept quiet. Honestly, I was hoping Rain would just think I was dead after that night in the woods. For all I know, she assumed I was. I guess you guys being here means she's checking up on loose ends, though. But I'm not going to say anything. You promise her that." She leans back and glances behind us at the road, as though looking for someone else observing us.

"Can I just clarify that you are in fact Iris Reebuck, going by a false name with your employer?" Burke cuts in.

Iris laughs again. "Sure, for what it's worth. But I won't be Iris ever again, and I probably won't be Hannah Giordino, either. Tell Rain that this time, she won't find me. Go ahead and release my collateral if you want, because I'm staying gone this time." Iris stands up and stretches her back, casually.

She has sprinted off the porch before either of us realizes that she's making a run for it.

CHAPTER 20

Burke stands in the middle of the road, swearing and stamping his feet, his typical composure full-on cracked. I can't tell who he's most angry with, but I suspect I'll find out very shortly.

"Didn't even get the goddamn plate number," he growls, bending over his knees. "Goddamn it to hell. She must have sent a text to someone and was just stalling for time."

"Who did she think we were? Who did she think sent us?" I ask, bewildered.

"Well, it very much sounds like she thinks the Light is still looking for her and is planning to exact some kind of retribution for her desertion."

"Her 'collateral,'" I clarify.

"Most likely. It's a standard tactic used by cults to control members and prevent them from defecting. Incriminating photos, affidavits about close family members, legal documents. Sometimes it's just access to bank accounts or holding liens on property or possessions," Burke explains, a little more calmly.

"One of the other women I interviewed said something like that," I add. "Becca, one of the former members. She got scared, too, and ran off when she thought I was somehow involved with the Light. She mentioned collateral."

"Right. We really needed to interview Iris properly—she's clearly holding a lot of answers we need. Which, I believe, is why I suggested that you let me handle the interview." Burke scowls in my direction, remembering to be disgusted with me.

"I just didn't want her to take off before we even got to speak to her," I say weakly. "It looked like she was about to book it before we even got to ask her a thing. I thought she might trust us more—"

"Yes, clearly we had a real rapport going there. Jesus, we got basically nothing! Damn!" Burke paces along the side of the road. Then he turns and heads straight back toward New Day. I follow along behind.

"What are we doing now?" I ask.

"We're going in there to get her damn employee file so I can figure out where she was living. We're going to go find her."

. . .

On the car ride home, Burke mostly ignores me. He's mad, and I know that some of that is directed at me, but he seems more frustrated at his own professional failure. His jaw is stiff, and once or twice I hear him grinding his teeth. I consider apologizing, only I suspect just giving him some time to unwind and get his panties untwisted will be the most effective tactic.

At the very least, we don't walk away from New Day empty-handed. Our affable Susan handed over "Hannah's" personnel file without balking; by this time, Burke had reassumed his winning calm, and she seemed to respect the badge without asking questions about whether he actually had any legal authority. We left with a photocopy of Hannah's application and the one employee review she'd gotten since beginning at the halfway house a few months ago.

The phone number she'd provided was useless; it went straight to voicemail with a generic message. But she'd listed an out-of-town address as her permanent residence. I'm itching to go there; it isn't far. But Burke is cagey in the car and won't commit to anything. When we pull into the hotel parking lot, I ask him what his deal is.

"You asked me to help you find a young woman. I helped you find the young woman, who is alive, if not entirely well."

"Yes, job well done," I say, impatient.

"I think that's where I need to leave it."

"What? Leave it? You mean . . . leave me? You're done?"

"Olivia. I don't know if I'm meant to be involved in chasing down rumors and infiltrating cults and churning up mud for however many thousands will listen to your rollicking good tale. My obligation is to justice, however pale and flimsy and occasionally evanescent it may be."

"Finding the truth *is* justice," I say—a nice little sound bite.

"That's not your primary concern here, and you know it, Olivia," Burke says brusquely. "I'm not saying I'm completely done helping. But . . . I do need to take some time to consider my own responsibilities. And my own motivations."

"We're . . . protecting people," I argue, weakly. I know that this isn't what's had me chipping away at this. He knows it, too.

"I'm sorry. I just don't think I want to be part of this . . . media-driven . . . rubbernecking."

"I see. Well."

"I wish you the best of luck, Liv. You turned out well." He stretches out a hand to me and, eventually, I take it. I get it, I do.

. . .

I call Naia with an update; she sounds chipper and unbothered.

"Boomers are deadweight anyway. He added a little flavor, but we don't need him. Solo intrepid investigator is better optics anyway."

"Well, we got an address at least, even if the interview with Iris was a total bust."

"Fuck, that's excellent! You should have led with that. Why aren't you already there? Go see if there's anything there!"

"I gave my driver the rest of the day off. So it'll have to keep until tomorrow."

"Nope, no way. I'll be there in forty-five."

She's off the phone before I can tell her that I'm sick of the car, sick of the chase, sick of myself. I want a bubble bath and a glass of wine in a nice hotel room. But Naia arrives forty-two minutes later.

"It's actually better this way. The audio will be better. Not that I'm throwing shade on your perfectly adequate skills," she adds with an eyeroll.

"I mean, she's not actually going to be there," I muse as we drive. "Even if that's where she was staying before we found her, she was pretty clear that she was going to disappear again."

"No, she didn't strike me as a total ninny. But maybe she has a roommate. Or there's some mail lying around."

"Or the door will be left open with a trail of blood leading down the pathway!"

"Oh, you're kidding," she says flatly. "Because . . ."

A little while later, just a mile or two outside Montour Falls, Naia keeps looking in the rearview mirror.

"If I didn't know better, I'd say we're being followed," she mutters. I don't say anything, but my neck starts to seize up as I stare fixedly in the side mirror, my eyes glued on a car that does stick pretty close.

Our destination is a leafy suburban street not far from downtown, and the neighborhood seems decidedly upmarket. We pull up in front of a tidy, well-kept house that looks to my unschooled eye to be old, maybe mid-nineteenth century. It is painted a deep yellow with blue and red trim, and out front, the last flowers of the season are still bright and robust. The car following us drives past, then out of sight. I take a deep breath.

I rap on the screen door, and within moments, a woman appears in the hall, which is visible through the warped mesh of the screen.

"Hello?" she says. She looks like she's in her fifties or early sixties, gray hair tidily bobbed, no makeup, a crisp button-up floral shirt that looks like it might even have starch in it.

"Hi there, I'm Olivia Reed. I'm looking for Iris?"

"You're not . . . you're not with the Light?" She doesn't open the door, just sizes us up.

"No, not at all. I'm actually . . . well, I'm trying to figure out what exactly is going on at the House of Light. Do you think we could come in?"

The woman nods, mutely, and nudges the door open. She turns to walk down the hall, into her living room, and we follow. The house is all dark wood and well-made furniture, most of which looks antique. Fresh flowers sit on a buffet in the hall, and the walls are lined with photos. Naia sits on an ottoman, and I perch in a rocking chair, keeping my barre-strengthened core taut to stay still.

"Can I ask what your name is?" Naia prompts.

"I'm Bea. Beatrice Giordino."

"Are you . . . related to Allison Giordino?" I ask, surprised.

"I'm her mother," Bea answers.

"Oh. I'm so sorry to intrude . . . Um. How do you know Iris Reebuck?"

"Oh, my. I don't know what I would call our relationship. A friend, maybe? Someone who cares? I've known her, oh, less than a year I suppose. She . . . reached out and said she was very sorry for our loss and she wanted to meet us. She's been in our life ever since. Is she . . . has something happened to her?" Bea Giordino looks as though she fully expects the worst.

"She's okay," I say.

"Oh, thank God," Bea gasps, her shoulders dropping from their high-alert position.

"We spoke to her earlier today, but she had to leave. Sort of abruptly. This is the address listed as her home. Does she live here?" I ask, wishing I had prepared a script.

"No, she's never lived here. But I told her she could always use this address, if she needed. I don't think she's been using her real name ever since . . . well, everything that happened to her earlier this year."

"Can you talk to us about why she's going under an assumed name? What happened earlier this year?" Naia asks.

Bea looks at her, full in the face. "Maybe I can. But first, I need you to tell me exactly who you people are."

• • •

Buckle up, folks, because this is one of the weirder interviews I've conducted yet. Do you remember Allison Giordino? She was the young woman who jumped off a waterfall back in 2015, the first of the people who committed suicide on the mysterious dates we identified. Well, Beatrice Giordino is her mother, and apparently is also involved with Iris Reebuck, the young woman we've been searching for. When we finally tracked Bea down, she didn't really want to talk to us; like so many people we've encountered, she seemed to be deeply concerned that we ourselves were involved with the House of Light. When we reassured her that we weren't, that we were, in fact, working on this story that would help get to the bottom of what happens within that organization, she agreed to an interview. We caught up with her in her home, where she spoke to us about her daughter, about Iris, and about what she knows about the House of Light.

LIV: Thanks again for speaking with us.

BEA: Of course. I just want to spare another mother the pain of losing a child the way I have. If there's anything I can share that helps someone get their daughter or son back, I want to do it.

LIV: Your daughter died in 2015, of suicide. Can you speak a little about that?

BEA: Yes, Allison . . . jumped to her death on March twentieth of 2015. She'd . . . well, she was a troubled teen and had experienced a lot of difficulty in those last couple years. She'd been involved in a statutory rape case as a teenager, and it really, really disrupted her life. To the point where I was pretty sure we were going to lose her. She seemed to be rudderless. But a friend brought her to a workshop series at this organization, the House of Light, and she just . . . she loved it. She came home seeming so much better than she had in years. College was not exactly in the cards for her at that point—she'd barely managed to scrape through high school, and we were just so worried for her future. And then she said she got a job working at the Institute.

LIV: This is the Oikos Phaos Institute, right? Which is part of the House of Light?

BEA: Correct. Allison said she was doing outreach, which I took to mean recruitment of some kind. The Institute is mainly online. She was spending all her time at the Light, but my husband and I . . . well, we supported her because it seemed like she might finally get her footing. So her death was . . . well, really quite the shock.

LIV: I can't even imagine.

BEA: I guess all parents who have lost a child that way say that it was a shock. If you'd had any suspicion, you would have done something, right?

LIV: I am so very sorry for your loss.

BEA: Thank you, sweetheart.

LIV: (At this point in the interview, Bea leaned over and actually patted my hand, as though she was comforting me. Interviewing grieving family members has been the hardest thing about this whole process, and Bea was so consummately lovely and compassionate, it felt like an intrusion to continue the interview. But I know there are other people out there who want Iris back, and I know there are other families whose children are involved with the Light. So I kept going.) Can you talk a little bit about how Iris came into your life?

BEA: Iris tracked me down through some friends of Allison's, I think, maybe less than a year ago. She knew about what had happened to Allison, and she . . . well, she wanted to speak to me. She had been a member of the Light for her whole life and was starting to, I guess, have some . . . misgivings about certain practices. She wanted to know about Allison's experience, but I got the feeling that she, well, she wanted someone to look after her. So many of the people at the Light seem to be lost, or at least at moments in their lives where they need guidance, and Iris just seemed to want support. She'd found it at the Light, but things were changing there and she came to me to talk.

LIV: How were things changing? Or, rather, what was making her feel so uncomfortable at the Light?

BEA: (laughs nervously) I almost feel ridiculous repeating some of the things she said once she started to open up to me. It seemed . . . well, implausible. I thought she might be making it up to elicit pity or . . . who knows, something else from me. My husband thought she might be a scam artist, even. I was worried that she was mentally ill. But looking back, I can't see what angle she could have possibly been working. (Long pause.) Iris said that the Light had been a safe haven for her while she recentered her life, but it had gotten to the point where the Light was her whole life. She worked at the Light, she lived there, all her friends were there. She'd gotten to the point where there wasn't a piece of her existence that wasn't wrapped up in something over there. Which is why she said that when they asked her to join the Committee, she said yes, of course.

LIV: The Committee?

BEA: I really don't know all that much about it. I wasn't there, of course. But I got the impression that it was really an elite group within the Light, a special membership for those who were fully committed to the organization. Iris told me that Allison had been on the Committee, too, and that was when she'd learned about her.

LIV: Are there special membership requirements for the Committee?

BEA: (long pause) Again, I don't know for sure. I only know what Iris told me. But there seemed to be a very specific preoccupation with . . . well, with human reproduction.

LIV: Meaning . . . sex? Or meaning procreation, pregnancy?

BEA: I got the impression that it was largely about *limiting* procreation . . . that one of the main functions of the Committee was to monitor its members and restrict their ability to have children. Iris said . . . well, she said some of the women had had hysterectomies, and that she was being pressured to do the same. Or to have her tubes tied, though I got the impression that the hysterectomy was preferable.

LIV: That seems to be a pretty extreme way to provide birth control.

BEA: Everyone at the Light is required to practice normal birth control, but the Committee wants its members to do something permanent, something that indicates their complete commitment to the Light.

LIV: Do you have any idea why they would want people to offer up this particular proof of loyalty? Why birth control, why hysterectomies?

BEA: Honestly, I have no idea. Iris at one point compared it to being branded, but on the inside, internally. She said it also had to do with the Light's belief that humans were destroying the planet, and that the most ethical thing they could do as seekers was to limit procreation. This was . . . a permanent way to ensure that, I suppose.

LIV: Do you think she might have gone through with it? The sterilization?

BEA: (takes deep breath) I don't think so. I don't know. But I do know she was frightened, and a few months ago, she said she was trying to cut ties with the House of Light. She seemed scared.

LIV: Do you know if anything specific happened to scare her?

BEA: She said she was being followed. And surveilled. That people were taking her photo and tracking all of her movements, nearly all the time. She said something about threats, about having private information released. At the time, I thought she was being paranoid, but now... I suppose I believe it. She said she was going to stop using her own name and was going to move, try to get some distance from everything here. And she asked if she could use Allison's Social Security number.

LIV: So you gave it to her?

BEA: I did. I just wanted her to be safe.

LIV: I want to ask you something, but I know it might be painful...

BEA: This is all painful. Go ahead.

LIV: Do you know... do you know if your daughter was also forced to undergo some kind of procedure before her death?

BEA: (breaks down) I'm sorry, I don't think I can talk about this anymore.

CHAPTER 21

Turns out I should have left Richard in the city. Well, turns out I should have done a number of things differently, probably starting with not alienating my manager and best friend. Spoiler: I am not good at keeping track of my shit. I spend several exhausted, frustrated hours looking for a place to lay my head while my ridiculous little dog snores from his bag, but the only options nearby are booked up.

Feeling adrift and wanting comfort, a specific kind of comfort, I know where I want to end up. I want to kick my feet up on Wyatt's lap and talk about normal things, not hysterectomies and suicide. I don't want to be alone in a hotel room, and I don't want to be anywhere Vorchek can find me, and I don't want to have to be me for a little while.

When Fred drops me off, I smell barbecue and figure Wyatt's around back. I find him in snug jeans and a plaid shirt, and he's nothing like any of the men I've been with, not Ryan and certainly not the Director. I have a bad feeling about why I've really come here.

"Hey, you," I say, and he whirls around as if he was hoping for someone else, for Ava—I can see it in the quick flash of his eyes. He's out on the lawn, the gas grill pulled out from beneath the deck.

"Well, hello."

"You did say not to be a stranger," I point out, trying not to sound defensive.

"That I did. And guess what, perfect timing. Now I won't have to eat dinner on my own."

"Ava's still not back?"

"No word from her. I'm sort of hoping she's just found a little cabin to drink in for a few days; she's done that before."

I nod. "And the kiddo? She with Grandma and Grandpa?"

"In bed," he says, nodding toward the baby monitor propped up on the grill. "You like steak?"

"Only if it's rare," I say, and he beams. Richard emerges from his bag only briefly, and Wyatt is cutely enamored of him as he romps in the grass for a full four minutes before he starts wheezing and huffing because he can't breathe, the poor horribly designed critter. We take our food to the picnic table that looks out on the lake, and the screech of knives on plates is companionable. Is it just me or is this wine getting better? He tells me about his work and going to Cornell and I tell him about Jess and L.A.; we steer clear of anything to do with the House of Light or his wife.

Wyatt takes a deep quaff of his drink and looks at me. I've seen that look before. My hair is loose and so are my morals, and instead of looking away, I meet his eyes.

"Things are . . . complicated between us," he finally says, an explanation for what he hasn't said, hasn't mentioned.

"I feel like I got that," I say with a smile.

"I don't imagine . . . Never mind," he says. "Not important."

" 'Not important . . .' "

"Well, there are big things and there are small things, right? Important ones, less important ones?"

"And your . . . things. They're less important?"

In answer, he smiles at me and raises his glass in a "cheers" motion before tossing it back.

"How long do you plan to keep that up? Being less important?" I ask.

"Until Zora is eighteen?"

"At which point it will . . . magically not matter anymore? Whether you love her mother, what you're doing here—?"

"I love her mother!" Wyatt interrupts. "Jesus, if you had any idea . . ." His hands go through his hair, and am I insane to want him more because of his desperate love for another woman? "That's not . . . Christ, that's not the problem."

"Oh no?" I meet his eyes, deliberately, and he looks at me. We're only a few feet apart. "What is?"

He doesn't speak for a long moment. "How could you ever understand?" he asks. "Look at you." When he says those words, I am unhinged, completely thrown, and I can't keep pretending I don't want him, want something from him. Want to be just a little less lonely for one day.

"*Don't* fucking look at me," I snap, and I stand up, walk away from the picnic table in a huff. It's nearly dark and the lake is there beneath us and he's standing behind me. "Don't you dare look at me." And when I find his mouth, his eyes are, obligingly, closed, and when my hips find his, he isn't looking at me; he has listened and I can feel in every one of his ribs something like surrender. In that instant I know he wants me, that there are few things he's ever wanted more, and he knows he shouldn't but part of him also knows it doesn't matter. I want to tell him that she doesn't love him and that she can't and that he deserves to be happy, but even if all that is true, which I'm not sure it is, it makes no difference—that is not the important thing here. Because even as I feel his ribs want to give way to mine, to enmesh mine and lock into place and never unhitch, there's a piece of him that doesn't belong to me, and maybe it's his sternum and maybe it's his hip bones, but I can feel it there between us. So I let my mouth find his and I wrap my fingers in his hair and I know our time is limited and I try to enjoy just that minute, when I know he wants me, and that is all that matters for that one minute, and that's why I came here after all.

"Liv, I can't" is what he says when he pulls away. I've been waiting for it and it's no surprise but it still hurts, like a sucker punch but somewhere deeper. Of course this Good Man doesn't want me, of course he is thinking about his wife and his baby daughter. And I don't mind, I don't take it personally, not really, but it is still something I suspect I will carry around with me for a long time, buried in a secret cupboard of personal hurts. And maybe he will, too, I don't know. Maybe he feels something different right now, maybe he is just wretched and wants to be done with me, and that's it, that's what makes existing with other people so insanely terrifying, unknowable. Or maybe he feels something similar right now but probably he will barely even remember that I was here, and later if we were to compare notes this would be nothing to him, he wouldn't remember my name, that I was even here.

Of course he would remember my name. I'm Olivia fucking Reed.

But he loves his wife and he doesn't love me and it's entirely possible that no one has ever loved me and that's not good but also I HAVE A GIFT and he does not and you know what, I don't want his stupid kid and his debt and his small little life because look at me. LOOK AT ME. I am something else entirely. I am different, I am special. And so, when I lean over and give him a brief kiss and pull back, I'm not mad. I'm not hurt.

"I know you can't," I say. "And I'm glad for you."

That's when Ava walks in on us. Or in on us outside, as it were.

"Well, hey there," she says. She doesn't sound mad, or even surprised, but I don't know how long she's been standing there. "Didn't reckon I'd see you here, Liv Reed."

"Well, I wasn't exactly planning on it," I answer, trying to play it cool.

"I like the work you've been doing. You've made way more headway than I have. I'm impressed." She crosses over to the picnic table, where we had been eating, and takes a good old swig from a wineglass—it doesn't matter which one. "And you've been helping out, too, Wyatt! It's nice to see you getting involved."

Wyatt clears his throat. Nothing really happened but we all know that's not exactly true and, boy, is this uncomfortable.

"Did you find Robin? I've been worried about her," I ask.

"Best I can tell, she's back at the Light. But she's been through the ordination, which means she's now on the Committee. And very possibly next."

"And Samhain is getting close," I add.

"Yep. Glad to hear you picked up on all that. Like I said, I'm very impressed."

"But you've . . . been off looking for her?" I ask to clarify.

"Among other things," she says with a shrug. The monitor crackles, and we can all hear the sound of a toddler working up into true fury at the world. I'm the first one to break.

"I should go. Leave you to . . . it."

"Stay if you like," Ava says breezily, and it's entirely possible that she means it. But I can't remember why I'm here anymore anyway, and it's time I hightailed it and got out of this bizarre scene, and why am I cosplaying at being an unhappy alcoholic wife and mom in the sticks anyway? As I pop the collar on my leather jacket, I've got to hand it to Ava: her confidence isn't rattled by no less than a movie star trying to sweep her husband off his feet. And I suppose I've got to hand it to Wyatt, too, for those ridiculously solid legs that stayed so firmly planted. I doff them a mental chapeau and stride up toward the road with my dog bag slung over my shoulder, hoping Fred hasn't gone too far, because that will be just so awkward.

"Thanks for dinner!" I call.

Sometimes I think I'm the loneliest person in the world.

I can't get ahold of Fred and an Uber will apparently take close to an hour, so I look on my phone and there's a motel less than two miles from where I am. They have an opening. I stroll there in the dark, going deep into the shoulder every time a car passes. A hit-and-run accident would be all too plausible an end on this road. Am I being paranoid? Sure. But so are the folks who believe the lizard people are controlling the deep state and look at how things are turning out for them.

When I check in, I don't tell them about Richard and they don't recognize me and it occurs to me that for the first time in a long while no one actually knows where I am. I like the cozy anonymity. No one would know if I disappeared.

This feeling evaporates when I enter my room, which is floral polyester and scratchy curtains and dark rings in the tub and sink. But fuck it, there's cable and I'm in time to catch *Entertainment Tonight* and Lili Reinhart is having a fucking moment, so I watch *Kardashians* instead and I manage to kill two days in the motel room this way. My favorite part of each day is getting updates from Naia about the intense popularity the show is garnering (might be as big a hit as *To Live and Die in L.A.*!). I tweet about it, and I post a few pictures to my stories on Instagram, like she suggests, though I try to keep it generic so that no one can triangulate my location. But on day three, I'm restocking on Diet Coke from the vending machines (that and pretzels have been my primary nutrition, and I'm thinking I should call Gwyneth and the Goop people because I might have invented a new cleanse) when housekeeping comes into my room uninvited. It's not like Richard exactly bites anyone, but he does make a little scene and startles the young woman. Apparently dogs aren't allowed in the motel, which was clearly in the document I signed, so I am asked to leave. Which is fair, so I decide not to trash the place on Yelp. Which I don't know how to do, in any case.

Fred is relieved to hear from me (he'd been worried, and he's there within minutes). I can't think of anywhere to go except a vineyard, so I ask him to take me to one Wyatt had recommended.

I just sit in the car, checking motels on my phone while he goes in to buy a bottle of wine for me. I can't face being seen or photo-graphed, tagged in any selfies, even though Naia is at this very moment trying to get me to post some images of myself. She doesn't like the generic pictures, she'd like me to be ME, visibly gumshoeing around Seneca Lake, but the thought fills me with despair. And I don't have my makeup—it's still in the trunk. When my phone rings, I answer the unfamiliar number.

"Darling, I'm so glad you picked up!" my father says affably. After a radio silence of so many months, now I'm getting multi-ple calls from him within days—I really should check the ratings of the most recent episode; they must be stellar.

"Hi. Wasn't expecting your call," I answer.

"Well, I wasn't expecting to call, as a matter of fact! But do you know, I've had an extraordinary change of plans, and I thought I'd let you know."

"I take it you're not in London."

"As a matter of fact, my trip was postponed. But just before my plans changed, you'll never believe what happened."

"Are you going to make me guess?" I ask snippily.

"Of course not, and I don't think you'd manage regardless. As it turns out, your little project is garnering quite a lot of interest, and not just in the millennial set. I wouldn't have known, but a number of my own crowd are positively rabid for true crime. One of my very dear friends out in L.A. was actually listening to your show and not only recognized your name but recognized the or-ganization you're looking into!"

"Wait, what?" I ask, sitting up straight. I had been expecting him to offer to come on as a producer or to reintroduce his sug-gestion that I interview him on the podcast. "Which friend? How do they know about the Light?"

"I don't know if you remember Xavier, my friend from Corsica with whom I spent the summer of 2010, at his family's home? He's tall, quite swarthy—"

"And Corsican," I interrupt. "How does he know about the Light?"

"Well, Xavier is very fond of spiritual retreats and has done one in practically every state in the Lower Forty-eight. And Hawaii, I believe. He attended a workshop at the Light several years ago and absolutely raves about his time there. He's quite a fan, and was really quite troubled to hear about all these missing women. Anyway, he wanted me to know he was available for an interview."

Fred gets back in the front seat and shows me the label on the bottle of Riesling he's just bought. I flash him a grateful smile and a thumbs-up.

"Is he in L.A. these days? Or . . . in France?"

"Well, darling, that's the best news. He was in New York when he called me, and I was still in New York, and when we realized that, we decided it would really be the most sensible thing if we were to come visit you. To make it more convenient for you, of course! We've rented an entire house here on this bloody huge lake—Seneca, is it? And I thought if you had a moment of downtime, you might like to come pop in."

I pause, but not for long. This is too convenient for coincidence. He has an angle, and this might be my best shot at figuring out what he's been up to. He said he'd never heard about the Light, and now here's one of his closest friends who has actually attended a Light retreat? And wants to discuss it with me?

"Where is it? And, um, how many bedrooms does it have?"

• • •

The house is on the lake's west side and is gaudily opulent, in my father's characteristic taste. A large manicured lawn stretches around it, and the view down to the water is broken only by some vineyards and trees. My father is already waving at me from the porch when we pull in.

"Hey, Fred, do you want me to see if there's a room for you?" I ask.

"I'm okay. I actually live in Geneva, so I'll just head home," he explains. I'm relieved; I'd feel guilty trying to look after him. I already feel guilty about hiring him, about needing a driver, about my whole parasitic lifestyle. But not guilty enough to get a driver's license, so.

"Text you in the morning!" I call as I dash out of the car and toward the house, carrying only Richard in his bag. Fred follows with my suitcases, which have been in the trunk for days, and leaves wordlessly after dropping them on the porch. I've already changed out of my old clothes and into something fresh, a floaty Natalie Martin dress in autumnal colors that feels relatable enough to wear around here, with a chunky Irish fishing sweater and a shawl.

"Darling! What a treat!" Bart calls to me, and we give each other two cheek kisses when we collide. I'm more kindly disposed to him now that he's brought me something useful (two somethings: information and a roof), so I play along cheerfully with his good spirits. "Come in, I'll show you around and introduce you to Xavier. I see you've brought some of the local sauce?" He plays the part of chipper host, ushering me around and pointing out nice little details of the house he's rented. I'm too anxious to get started, though, and my itchiness shows.

"Well, let's just get to it, before you crawl out of your skin," Bart says, and leads me out back to a spacious field where Xavier sits, dozing in a sun chair. He leaps up when he hears Bart's voice.

"'Ello, very nice to meet you," he says in an accent that feels somewhere between French and Spanish, with maybe something else chucked in. Like many of my father's friends, I'm sure that he grew up transnationally.

"What good luck this is!" I say enthusiastically, giving him cheek kisses. "Really, I'm so pleased."

"She's anxious to get down to brass tacks, Xavy—go on, show her what you brought," Bart prompts.

"Of course, of course." Xavier springs into action, and from his colorful beach bag, he produces a book. I take possession eagerly.

"So, you got this at the House of Light?" I ask, flipping it open. It's called *Light Heart,* and the author is Luke Trask. Inside, I recognize the logo; beneath it are printed the words "Oikos Phaos Press."

"It was our, how do you say, workbook, while I was doing the workshop. I find it to be very helpful, even now. A clever man, this Luke."

"Did you meet him? While you were at the Light?"

"But of course! He ran the workshop. This is his book, and he teaches the class. I would not have attended for someone else, but a friend recommended this one, special."

"Was a woman there, with a shaved head and bare feet? Sort of tall?"

"Emmm, it is possible—there were several women who could be described such. But this group was for men seeking to connect with each other, so the women were elsewhere during the workshop. We did not speak to them."

"They were silent?" I press.

"At least when I was there."

"Okay, okay, can you take a look at some pictures? I'd love to see if you recognize anyone." I whip out my phone and pull up the saved and zoomed-in images I have of each of the girls.

To my disappointment, Xavier shakes his head at each of them. I grit my teeth in frustration. But when I show him the Instagram photos I have that feature other Light people, he bobs his head in recognition.

"Yes, that woman you were asking about, with the bare feet, she was there," he says, pointing to Rain. "She was in charge of the women's group, totally separate. And him"—he points to the man with the very blue eyes—"he was our leader. The man who wrote this book."

"Luke Trask. The guru's son," I say. "Have you . . . have you had any contact with him since then?"

"I still get some promotional emails. Invitations to come back for workshops, when they publish a new book, that type of thing."

"Could you—would it be terribly intrusive if I could ask you to send me anything you've received from either the Light or Oikos Phaos? Registration material, promotional emails, any personal correspondence?" I ask hopefully. I'm expecting Xavier to balk, but he merely shrugs and pulls out his phone.

"But of course. Very simple. What I really want to know"—he looks up at me with a dangerous grin—"is when you will put me on your show."

. . .

I creep up to my room as soon as I can manage to without being explicitly rude, and I plunk down with Richard on my bed to swipe my way through nearly a decade of newsletters from a self-help organization. Though they've been more restrained than, say, Wayfair, there are still dozens of emails to go through, and all written with the same mind-glazing jargon I remember from group sessions at the Light. The terms are like so many others I've heard over years of group work and mindfulness retreats and therapy, but I know that this particular constellation of words and recommendations and ritualized repetitions will mean very particular things to the people who accord them the power of spiritual truth. Though I see only a word salad, I know that Allison, and Iris, and Hannah, and Theia, and Amy all saw in these words something like salvation from the limitations of their lives, of their own bodies. How many dozens have gotten an email like one of these and seen not just a Mad Lib of self-help terminology but real potential for change, for a journey into light? And have I, maybe, missed out on something real?

I open Luke's book and start to read.

· · ·

Hello there, fellow Vultures! Have I got a book club recommendation for you. I've recently gotten my hands on a fascinating text that connects directly back to the House of Light, and it has been (cough, cough) illuminating. Some backstory for you.

So, as you might remember, Allison, Dead Girl Number One, worked for an affiliate of the Light, an institute that mostly offered online seminars and "leadership exercises." They were not cheap, but everything we found online seemed no more nefarious than your average meditation group. The Oikos Phaos Institute seemed like a fairly harmless moneymaker, and it also served to help identify clients who might be interested in a more in-depth experience—like a House of Light intensive retreat, for example.

I've recently just gotten my hands on an old publication produced by . . . Oikos Phaos Press. It's essentially a textbook for one of those retreats at the Light. And it was written by a Luke Trask, who also led the workshop in question.

A few sharp listeners have remembered Luke; I saw on both the Websleuths message board and our website comment section that some of you were working to track down the blue-eyed man who was photographed with both Hannah and Allison. This man, Luke, is also rumored to be the original guru's son. In our interview with former members Steve and Dora, it was implied that Rain has a special affection for Luke, and that institutional decisions are made by Luke or at his suggestion. You might remember from interviews that former members of the Light started to defect when Luke began assuming more of a leadership role; not all the members were happy with the direction the Light was taking, though no one has seemed able to say exactly why. Or to provide a last name for our mysterious blue-eyed boy.

He has been effectively deleted from any House of Light mate-rials, and his name is never mentioned. In fact, there seems to be an overall effort to protect him, to shield him from public scrutiny at every turn. But he did leave at least one footprint.

I believe that Luke is Luke Trask, and that he wrote this bi-zarre book that I just read. Light Heart is, like many self-help books, filled with pages of indecipherable exhortations to "con-nect deeper" and "confront your shadow self" and "allow light-ness to penetrate your inner darkness" and other such meaningless clichés. There's lots of chatter about "finding your path" and "achieving stillness." But there are a couple of things that make this book a little stranger than your average Eckhart Tolle.

The first is that the book offers a programmatic plan for you to achieve this level of enlightenment, what is called "the Process of Return," or just "the Process." It's not that unusual for self-help programs to offer step-by-step instructions, but this book goes into real detail. It tells you what to eat, how to exercise, even offers a sleep schedule. Much of the advice is tied to the natural world: phases of the moon, seasons, and, most interest-ing to me, the solstices and equinoxes. For example, one entry reads: "The spring equinox holds the potential for fantastic growth and expansion. On that day, allow all the energy that you have been accumulating during your season of hibernation to burgeon. Eat any of the foods from the Growth menu (oats, sprouts, and base foods). There will be a strong temptation to sow seeds of your own at this moment of pure potential; if you resist, and channel that sexual energy, you will find that those raw reserves enable you to go deeper into your practice than you ever have before." The autumn equinox is the one time a year followers of this program are encouraged to eat meat: "As the season turns away from the harvest toward death, mark the movement into the next phase of development with, appropri-ately, blood. Sacrifice is the nature of all improvement, and you may honor yours and others on this date by recognizing the death of another being, as you yourself will one day be recognized." Anyone's skin crawling yet?

There's plenty more advice on how to deal with your own physical body, but honestly, most of it wouldn't alarm anyone who's been to an especially pushy Reiki practitioner. It's weird, and it's specific, and it's trademarked, but hey, so are most of the diets I've been put on by personal trainers over the years. No one's had me drink the blood of a young deer under the full moon yet, but I have eaten cactus paste while sitting naked on a rock in the desert, so I'm not gonna cry "human sacrificial cult" just on that count.

Things grow a little weirder when Luke gets into ways you can bring the "message of the Light" to others. Practitioners are expected, at some point, to introduce someone else to this system, and to help them begin their own journey away from the darkness. Those who resist are "clinging to their shadow shelves" and are perceived as "in gloom" until they take steps to bring themselves out of it. A final step of the program is to bring someone to a workshop and help them find the Light.

Again, anyone who's had a conversation with an especially gifted Amway or Nutralife salesperson is accustomed to both this logic and this pressure, and I feel pretty comfortable at this point saying that there's a lot to suggest that the House of Light and Oikos Phaos are at least multilevel marketing–adjacent. But honestly, it feels more like Bikram yoga than Avon.

No, the thing that gets really fucking weird is this.

The man who gave me this book was attending a workshop that was just for men. It's not unusual to create safe spaces that exclude other genders—women's-only retreats are de rigueur in many places, and there are increasingly lots more opportunities for men to spend time trying to work on toxic masculinity in an all-male space. Nor is it unusual to market a book to one gender rather than another. And, I'll tell you, Light Heart is definitely intended for men. There are entire pages dedicated to ejaculation and birth control and abstention from sex and conquering male need and lots of things that are frankly very obviously not about me, not about my body.

We've heard from other former members of the Light that there is a specific preoccupation with birth control and limiting procreation. This book explores that in some depth, suggesting that the energy harnessed by sexual abstention can expand your spiritual practice. But there are several indications that part of the philosophy of the author is an ethics of what he calls nonexistence, a refusal to bring new life into a world that has already been damaged beyond repair by human interference. He links this directly back to the spiritual practitioner's relationship to nature; only by protecting nature and existing in cooperation with it can the seeker find his true spiritual self. And it is only through the refusal to create new life, Luke Trask feels, that the seeker is truly working in and toward nature.

This all-male workshop is still held periodically, according to the Oikos Phaos website. And it does still seem to be led, at least some of the time, by the elusive Luke Trask himself; this is apparently one of the only instances of him publicly participating in the House of Light. But the thing that kind of weirds me out is this: I'm pretty sure there's a corresponding women's workshop, and possibly a women's textbook. The man who gave me this book and attended that all-male workshop said the women were doing their own retreat simultaneously. He recognized the woman who leads those retreats, and she is the same woman who is the current director of the House of Light, Rain. But that retreat has never, as far as I can tell, been advertised online. And I can't find a single woman who has attended it, and lived.

· · ·

I'm pacing the house restlessly as the sun comes up and my father pads downstairs in the early light. I've waited to put on coffee so as not to wake anyone, but he does it with his quiet, smooth grace.

I watch him, his waist thickened somewhat by age, but still straight and trim, like an older Cary Grant; his vanity won't let him run soft. He notices me noticing and sends me off to the porch in vague irritation; he's never been a morning person. I watch the sunrise through the wildflower field behind the house, obnoxiously stunning in its late-summer beauty. It almost makes me wish myself back in the city, which demands vigilance and a strong stomach and not this constant sensitivity to beauty.

On the back deck, Bart slides me a cup of coffee and we sip quietly for a few minutes while we collect ourselves for the day.

"I heard you recording in the night," he finally says, not crankily.

"Shit, did I wake you?"

"I was up anyway. I have to use the facilities much more often at my age," he tells me ruefully. He mentions this often, as though I might not have otherwise noticed him aging. As though calling attention to it himself prevents me from observing it on my own. I think he's more sensitive to aging than I am. But I can still pass for twenty-five, so.

"Well, I just had a lot of ideas, I wanted to get them down before I forgot. I sent some things off to my producer before getting up."

"Sounds like you're terribly productive these days. Figuring things out. I'm happy for you. You know what I always used to say: find your light. And maybe you have."

"Who would have predicted it would be off camera. In the dark, so to speak," I quip.

Bart waves me off. "We both know this is temporary. You'll be back in the limelight soon enough."

"We'll see," I reply.

"I must say, though, you've recovered from your little slump quite easily. Almost miraculously."

"It wasn't a slump, actually."

"Oh no?"

"No, it wasn't. You don't remember what date it was, huh?" I ask casually, biting off as much sarcasm as I can.

Bart wrinkles his forehead, trying to think. "It wasn't . . . I mean, your mother did disappear in early autumn, if I recall?"

"She did. September fifteenth, actually."

"What are you saying, Olivia? That you . . . acted out because it was the anniversary of your mother's disappearance?"

"I wasn't acting out, actually. I was at my house, drinking alone. I may have taken a few pills to mellow out. And then I went to go speak to someone and buy cigarettes. It was late, and yeah, I was a bit fucked-up. And then there was a photographer. Taking pictures of me swaying in front of the bodega, mascara halfway down my face. Like he wanted to scoop up my sadness and feed it to anyone who would pay a few bucks for it. So, yeah, I may have . . . snapped."

"You urinated in the street, Olivia. And then assaulted the man. 'Drug-Fueled Rage' was one of the headlines I saw, I believe."

"It doesn't matter what I did, or why I did it. He didn't care, and certainly no one who read the headlines did, either. What they wanted was puffy eyes, my torn dress, my mess. They wanted the wreck of my body. Ideally, I would have died on the sidewalk and they could have had everything they wanted, complete possession. What I was doing, why I was upset . . . that's the last thing that's important." I shrug, wondering why I'm telling him this. My father is the last person who ever wanted truth or reality from me—he is the one who taught me about spectacle.

"Don't you think that's rather . . . gratuitous of you, darling? I mean, after all these years? She's been gone for a decade and a half. You can't—"

"But I don't know if she's gone or not," I interrupt. "I know I haven't seen her. But she could be twenty minutes away. Jesus, she could be a member of the House of Light, luring me in so that I can be part of her little cult. She could be reaching out to me."

"Christ, Olivia, listen to yourself. Do you really believe that?" He looks alarmed.

"I don't know, maybe? Sometimes I sort of do. And does it matter if it's true or not? Do you know there are people who think that she's been at the House of Light all this time? They've even dredged up photos to prove it." I thrust my phone at him, showing him the saved image, the tenuous thread that barely links my mother to the Light.

"Livvy, this could be anyone," he says slowly, peering at my face.

"Sure. It could be. But I have one very real question: How'd they get ahold of that photo? The one of her in the dress, the picture you took that day we picnicked in the yard before she disappeared?"

"Well, I'm assuming online, darling," Bart says drily.

"That's what's weird, though. This photo didn't exist online until just over a week ago, when an Italian tabloid published it. They must have just recently acquired it; otherwise it would have been printed sooner. Who sold it to them, do you think?"

"You think I did?" Bart asks, full of outrage. "You think I'm so hard up for funds I'm still selling pictures of your dead mother to Eurotrash tabloids? Please, Olivia. Listen to yourself."

"How do you know for sure she's dead, Dad? Do you know because you killed her?" My voice rises. "Dad, was Mom sick when she disappeared? Like, cancer sick?"

Bart blanches, and before he can shut it down, I see something there.

"She was, wasn't she?"

"Nonsense. She was barely forty years old."

"Did we have health insurance, Bart? If she had gotten sick, could we have paid for it?"

He stares at me. Is he going to lie, or is he going to brush it off?

"Olivia, this is pathological. I'm worried about you, darling. I think you need to check yourself back in to an inpatient facility."

"I'm sure you'd like that. Nothing like the 'damaged starlet' story to get everyone all juiced up. Or prime the judge to award you a conservatorship."

"You're not a starlet anymore, darling," he snaps. "Everyone forgave Judy Garland's escapades when she was young and pretty, but there's a fine line between youthful folly and aging tragedy. And much like old Judy, you haven't much of an estate to be conserved."

"Yes, I'm a tragic figure, for sure," I say. "Poor little famous girl, has it all but all she wants is her mommy."

"You drove your mother off with your endless preening, so I'll thank you to stop the pity party," Bart spits out.

I'm speechless.

"Didn't know you felt that way, Bartholomew," I finally say, standing. "Thanks for last night, and for your help with my 'little project.' I've got a big day, though, so I'd better get to it. Ta."

I'm already through the door and climbing the stairs when he calls after me.

"Does your precious Detective Burke have access to that photo of your mother? I hear he's the one who's in need of some extra cash these days."

Leaving, I know I should feel more hurt, or shaken by his betrayal. But I find that I'm mainly relieved that I don't have to include any of that conversation in the podcast.

· · ·

Hello, listeners. Just a quick update in between episodes here for you all. You all, in fact, are responsible for this quick update. The message board and several other online sites have been absolutely on fire these past few days, and people are really generating a lot of information—and a lot more questions.

A particularly sharp citizen detective, going by the handle ArmchairSherlock, has turned up something that we think is almost certainly relevant to everything that's been going on. We

*mentioned the Lux Group in the previous podcast, and said that
Iris Reebuck had been working for an organization that is tied to
Lux. Since Lux means "light," in Latin, we thought it was interesting, but there wasn't anything concrete for us to really follow
up on, besides a quick Google search.*

*But you folks out there are more persistent, and a Reddit sub-
thread dedicated to Lux popped up almost the minute the episode
aired. Within a day or two, we got a message including attach-
ments with some really, really interesting information.*

*The Lux Group is an LLC that is, apparently, the parent com-
pany for not only the organization that had employed Iris Reebuck, Simple Transitions, but also the Oikos Phaos Institute, the
Oikos Phaos Press, and . . . the House of Light, as well as two or
three organizations that we had never heard of and are now investigating. Though there is limited information about the Lux
Group, we know from looking at its subsidiary businesses that
they are all, in some way, self-help-oriented, providing services to
"people seeking to improve themselves." As far as we can tell (or,
rather, as far as you all were able to find out), Lux files its taxes
offshore, in the Caribbean.*

The CEO of the Lux Group is Luke Trask.

• • •

What I don't mention in the podcast is the name of one of the
other companies Lux owns. Illuminate. I don't mention this because Burke has sent me an email and I can't really think.

> I'm reluctant to bring this up, but I've thought about it since leav-
> ing and I'd be remiss in not mentioning it to you. You have likely
> forgotten, but shortly before your mother disappeared, she was
> trying her hand at a direct-sales organization: Illuminate. They
> sold nutrition systems designed to help you lose weight, look
> younger. Supplements and smoothies, that sort of thing. I've just
> searched through my notes, and I can confirm that she purchased

an Amethyst Package six months before she disappeared. We
spoke to her up-line back then and could glean nothing relevant,
but your father mentioned that she'd been increasingly concerned
about her health around that time. It sounds like he was trying to
encourage her to seek treatment. Your internet sleuths will likely
make a connection to the Lux Group at some point, so I thought
you should know.

Unsure of where to go, I ask Fred to take me back to town. I
call my original hotel and they tell me yes, they do finally have a
room for this evening, but I can't check in until later. I agree read-
ily, and tell Fred to take the day off after dropping my things at the
desk, with the caveat that he take Richard with him. Then I spend
the day wandering the streets, buying more thick socks, making
audio recordings of the lake, the seagulls. I go to a matinee in the
strange little cinema downtown, a double feature, and it's nearly
dusk by the time I emerge. I stroll along, watching American flags
flap in the breeze. It's getting cooler.

I'm walking down to the pier, planning to watch the sun set,
maybe get a drink somewhere, when I get a text from Ryan. Frantic to read it, I nearly drop my phone into the lake, then scramble
to open it.

> How the fuck does the press know, Liv?? They say
> they're going to run the story tomorrow unless
> they hear from you.

Fuck. The Light has found him, tracked down a way to contact
him personally. It won't be long now before my collateral is released and my embarrassing escapade turns into a full-blown
scandal. "Slutty Starlet Breaks Up Marriage, Betrays Longtime
Boyfriend." "Washed-Up, Unhinged Actress Self-Destructs, Takes
Down Two Relationships with Her."

As I'm trying to decide whether there is anything I can plausibly do about this, a flash alerts me to a camera, not far away. A scramble near a tree betrays the presence of someone documenting me. Vorchek has probably been lurking around the village for days, waiting near the hotel. I'm disoriented: first the text from Ryan, then the appearance of paparazzi. Another flash captures what I assume is my panicked expression, stupid baby deer in the headlights. They will have found out where I'm staying, and I'll have to pass through a gauntlet of them before I can be alone. I'm desperate to disappear, to not have to face up to them, to not have my face on display.

The man running the boat-rental place is packing up, and I race toward him.

"Is it too late to rent a kayak for a quick sunset paddle?" I ask, with my best winning smile.

"Last rentals were nearly an hour ago," he says apologetically.

"Okay, what if . . . I buy the kayak? I've got plenty of cash." My lips quirk up, and my nose rumples adorably. "This has been on my bucket list for such a long time—my friend said I absolutely had to do a sunset kayak, and I'm leaving tomorrow . . ."

The man considers, relents, takes my money.

"You've got forty-five minutes before sunset. And if the harbor patrol bumps into you after that, you are on your own."

"Deal!" I grin. Within minutes I'm afloat and paddling out into the lake, away from photographers, from podcasts, from everyone circling around me.

The sky turns the most incredible shade of pink, and I paddle hard, facing into the sunset until the light starts to fade. When I turn around, it's with reluctance—I wish I could stay out here all evening. I should have rented a yacht for the night. For this whole damn undertaking. Two boats motor by in the center of the lake, their running lights on, heading back to the harbor, still a ways off. I've headed toward the western shore of the lake, and now I'm in the shadow of the ridge above me.

It's getting hard to see in the dark, so I almost don't spot the canoe bobbing nearby. At first it's so still I think it's empty, or even a trick of the failing light. I'm coasting up toward it when a flashlight switches on and shines in my face. Raising my hand up to my eyes, I try to squint beyond it. Then someone hisses to someone else: "Are you sure it's her?"

At these barely heard words, I start to paddle. As hard as I can. The light goes off abruptly, and as I swish by the canoe, I can see the off-white clothes of two people as they scramble for paddles. I hear their commotion as I speed by, my whole upper torso straining in a burst of power to pull me boat lengths beyond them. Fleeing doesn't obey rational thought—I don't have time to determine whether it's paparazzi or the Light, or even just some random outdoor enthusiasts who maybe recognized me.

I try to gauge the distance to the harbor, but I suspect I won't make it that far, not at a sprint. I angle instead toward the western shore. Maybe I can lie low in a cove or even make it up the beach, to someone's house.

The swift dip of paddles sounds not far behind me, closing the distance. I can't see much other than movement; the light is nearly gone. I point my boat in a straight line and feel the burn of my shoulders as they rotate again, again. The water slaps against the plastic hull of my kayak, and I can make out the different sound of the water against the aluminum of the canoe behind me, closing. The rhythm of their paddles is different, too: two almost simultaneous dips, then a pause. I think I can hear the paddlers' breaths in between, ragged huffs with the splash of water on either end. My own breathing is becoming more labored.

I pull ahead, then zag slightly to the right, hoping they won't be able to see me in the gloaming. I let my kayak coast for a few beats, willing myself to be small, invisible. At least I'm wearing dark colors. My boat is closer to the water, too, and I imagine them not being able to glimpse me in my stillness, my silence. Maybe it works: the sound of their paddles and the water sliding beneath the canoe fades, and I dip my paddles as delicately as I can. They've continued in a straight line, directly toward the southern shore, while I'm now traveling somewhat perpendicular to it. The distance between us isn't massive, maybe fifty yards, but it's growing. I hold my breath, willing them to keep going until they run aground.

I carefully angle toward the western shore of the lake, though I'm now far enough away that I can't really hear the canoe. I glide, breathless, straining my ears for any sound that might tell me where they are. I don't hear the canoe, but I do notice the sound of water slapping up against something else, something bigger. Out of the dark, I suddenly make out the shape of a large dock, and I've bumped into it before I can reverse the kayak. I freeze at the sound—surely they've heard? Listening for their return, I reach out and grab the dock, then pull my kayak all the way underneath, steadying it with my arms braced on either side of the dock. If a wave comes, my boat will smack into the wood and make an unmissable noise.

From under the dock, I hear the splash of paddles. They're trying to be quiet, but in my current state, I feel like my hearing is ratcheted up several notches. From my hiding place I can see even less than I could if I were out on the dark of the lake; I can only listen. They haven't turned their flashlight back on—hoping, I assume, to ambush me. I close my eyes, waiting for the wave that will come, slamming me into the pilings with a large crack. My pursuers come closer.

The prow of the canoe becomes visible, angling in toward the shore between the dock I'm hiding under and the neighbor's. It splices through the water, slowing, its occupants silent except for the sound of their breath. I hear the crunch of the canoe as it draws into the shallow water, the prow gently beached on the stony bottom. For a moment I'm sure they've seen me, are just waiting for me to burst out of my hiding spot before they intercept me. I can see only their white garments as they step out of the canoe and pull it nearly soundlessly up onto the shore. In the dark, it looks like they don't have heads or hands.

"She's on land," I hear one of them whisper as they confer. "I saw the kayak two beaches up, on the shore. I'll go along the water—you go up and make sure she hasn't made it to the road."

They must have seen someone else's kayak and mistaken it for mine. I watch as one of them—I think it's a man, but I can't be sure—hops out of the canoe and cuts across the beach, heading north. The canoe reverses back out into the lake, less graceful now with just one oarsman, and heads parallel to the beach, alongside its pedestrian accomplice.

It nearly kills me to wait the five minutes that I do, clinging to the dock. When I release, I wonder if my shoulders have enough left in them to get me home. The harbor isn't that far down the lake, though, and while I move briskly, I'm no longer sprinting. I stop every few seconds to listen for the sound of a boat behind me. When I reach the lights of the town, I beach the kayak clumsily, barely bothering to drag it out of the water. Shaking with relief and fatigue, I jog toward the safety of the pier, the restaurants, and my hotel room. At the first sign of people, I start to feel better. But I'm still glancing around, looking for anyone in the Light's pale garb. Looking out for photographers. Any photo of me right now would show my hunted look, the way I hunch into my sweatshirt. With dry land under my feet, I can wonder whether I was overreacting, whether I'm being paranoid. But my hammering pulse won't be talked down.

Upstairs in my room, the first thing I do is draw the curtains. Then I order room service. I'm not really hungry, even though I've scarcely eaten all day. What appetite I might have mustered disappears when I lift the lid of the tray covering my French fries. A note is tucked under the ketchup ramekin.

Your secret comes out with the next episode.

A photo of the Director and me in the lobby of my building is folded inside, blurry with a sheen of grease. I put the uneaten fries out in the hall and double-lock my door.

Then I strip off my damp clothes and fall onto the bed.

. . .

A knock at the door late that night sends me scrambling off the bed where I have been unable to sleep. I glance around, but of course, there's nowhere to go—I'm on the fourth floor of the hotel. I wrap my kimono tighter, creep to the door, and peer through the peephole. It's one of them.

I take a deep breath.

"Hi, Liv," Dawn greets me. He's not wearing his pinkish flaxen robes today.

I don't say anything, just stand in the doorway, looking at him.

"Do you mind if we talk for a little bit?" he asks. "There are a few things I'd like to discuss. With you."

After a long pause, I let him inside. I gather up my bags and clear off the table where I dumped them, gesturing for him to sit. I leave the recorder on the edge of the table.

"I assume you're here to warn me about what I'm doing? Threaten me into staying silent?"

"What?" Dawn jerks his head back. "Christ, have they threatened you? Seriously, Liv, have they threatened to hurt you?"

"What, you're saying you don't know about that? I haven't been threatened with physical harm—though they have scared the shit out of me, at least twice. But yep, there are threats, all right."

"Liv, you have to believe me: I have nothing to do with that."

"Why should I believe you, Dawn? You're one of them. I assume you're here to do reconnaissance and to play good cop. Offer me the potential for my own salvation."

"I wish I had the power to do that. But I don't. Liv, I've left the Light," Dawn says slowly, looking me in the eyes.

"Really? For . . . good?" I ask, surprised.

Dawn buries his head in his hands. "I don't know. I think yeah, maybe. For good." He doesn't raise his head for a long moment, and when he does it's with a deep breath. "I've been listening to your show." I raise an eyebrow. "I didn't know about all these things that were going on. I mean, I knew about some of it. But—" He stops and looks down at my recorder, the live mic on my recording app, which I switched on before I answered the door. "Could you maybe turn that off while we talk? I'll give you an interview later, if you still want, I just . . . I need to talk to you. Not as podcast host, but as a person."

I'm trying to read him, but all I can feel from him is distress, frustration. I switch off the recorder, keeping my face as impenetrable as I can.

"Are you okay?" is the first thing he asks me.

I nod. "I've been better. But I'm keeping it together."

"Good. This whole thing . . . has gotten out of control."

"You think."

"Liv, please, you can't think I would want to be involved with hurting anyone. I've been trying to find Iris and Robin, too. Using any Light contacts I can, asking as many questions as I could."

"And? Have you found either of them?" I ask eagerly.

"If I knew where they were, I'd tell you. I think they're both safe, but I don't know for sure." He is visibly concerned, but I still don't feel fully sympathetic toward him.

"Fuck," he swears sincerely, and presses the heels of his hands to his eyes. "This is so unreal. I can't believe I got sucked into this. I feel like such a simpleton."

I don't leap in to correct him, but I pause, long enough to reflect that if he is telling the truth, then he must be heartbroken. And ashamed. And quite possibly scared.

"Do they have collateral on you?" I ask gently.

He lets out a shaky huff. "Yes. They do. It's pretty bad."

"Tell me about it," I snort.

"Mine is worse than yours," he says without a smile.

"You . . . know about mine?"

"It's sort of what nudged me over the edge. I overheard someone talking about it in Rain's office, found out they were preparing to release it. It was . . . I guess the last push that I needed. I grabbed my stuff and left. Left my home of seven years, without telling a soul." He stands up. "Don't suppose you've got a minibar here, have you?"

"I thought you were sober," I say.

He snorts bitterly. "Never have I been more aware of it. But of course you're right. If there's one thing that will make this worse, it's that." Dawn paces over to the window and pulls aside the curtain, stares out at the lights in the harbor through the blinds. "How did you know? How did you figure out so quickly that there was something wrong?"

"I wish I could say it's my spectacular intuition, but I got a tip," I confess with a shrug. "And then the more information I gathered, the weirder things seemed. If it's any consolation, without that hint, I'd probably still be there, floating around in the sensory deprivation tank and vomiting up my darkest secrets to Rain."

"Rain hasn't been there for days. I've no idea where she's gone. She just . . . left us."

"Oh." I'm quiet for a moment. "Dawn? What do you know about the single-sex workshops? The ones just for men or women?"

"You mean Luke's modules," he says.

"I think I do, yeah."

"They're one of the first ways of fully committing to the Light. It's a two-week intensive, and he runs you through his program. The Process. Or, at least, he does with the men's group. Rain runs the women's group. Honestly, it's weird, but it always seemed . . . mostly benign."

"You deal with . . . your sexuality."

Dawn turns around and faces me. "Yeah. That's one of the main things. How to control your sex drive. How to not let it control you. How to enjoy sex without . . . completing it, if you like." His cheekbones shade a bit pink, but he doesn't drop his eyes.

"And the women's group? What do they discuss?" I ask.

"I honestly don't know. We aren't allowed to see their curriculum, and we're not meant to talk about it. Heterosexual couples are . . . discouraged, so there aren't so many moments of intimacy between us. The men and the women."

"What is the deal with this Luke guy? Who the hell is he?"

Dawn takes a deep sigh. "He's . . . well, he's a pretty strange bloke, honestly. Very intense, extremely fucking smart. He has a way of just . . . watching you, as though he's waiting for you to reveal yourself. Aloof, sort of unknowable. He's sharp, and he can talk philosophical circles around pretty much anyone."

"Especially Rain?" I press.

"They're . . . I guess you could say 'spiritually attuned.' It's been the two of them for such a long time."

"It's not, like, sexual, is it?"

Dawn guffaws. "God, no. More like mother and son. Or maybe brother and sister. Rain . . . well, she's always felt that he was a gift that was sent to the Light. That he was the actual physical embodiment of Light. She thought he was, well . . . an angel."

"Like, wings-and-a-halo angel?" I ask.

"Not exactly. That would be a Christian angel. Luke was more of a spiritual entity sent to help us move closer to Light. More of a metaphorical angel. God knows he isn't exactly like other people."

"Do you think he's a killer?"

"I don't think so, no. But he doesn't play by the same rules as everyone else. He doesn't believe in a traditional morality the way most people do. He's created his own."

I try again: "So he could be capable of it?"

Dawn again drags his hands through his hair. "Look, nothing

I've seen leads me to believe that. But the intuitive acumen I prided myself on is clearly a load of bollocks." He shrugs, helplessly.

"Why can't I find Luke anywhere? Why aren't there videos of him?"

"Luke . . . well, he vibrates at another level. On the quantum level. If you're not sufficiently elevated to spend time with him, it can be destructive. It's dangerous to expose yourself to that much energy, that much Light. And being around him can sort of be like looking directly into the sun."

"They say that he can be destructive? Dangerous?" I ask, and Dawn flinches. "Dawn, do you know what happened to the four dead women who attended that workshop?"

Dawn shakes his head, looking like he might cry. He crosses to the bed and sits on the foot of it.

"Liv, if I've participated in the deaths of these women . . . I'll never get over it. You couldn't know, but the collateral I gave to the Light—"

"Shh," I say to stop him, and cross over to sit next to him. "I don't want to know. Don't tell me."

Dawn takes a deep breath. "Okay."

"You can tell me something else, though."

"Okay."

"What's your real name?"

His face splits into that grin, the wholehearted, wide-open one I remember from our first meeting.

"It's Jake," he says. I lean over and take his lower lip very softly between mine. His breath changes, but he doesn't pull away. I tug at his lip with my teeth very gently, and he makes a noise like a growl. He still doesn't move closer. I reach out, and he catches my hand.

"I don't know what will happen if you touch me," he says, not pulling away from me or opening his eyes. Deliberately, I take my hand away and place it on his chest, dragging it slowly downward, brushing the nub of a hard nipple beneath his T-shirt.

This is when he reaches for me, and my kimono slides off, and it has been a long time since anyone really touched me, and I tug him farther up onto the bed, pulling off his T-shirt in the process.

"Dear God, look at you," he mumbles, thick in his throat, and I want him to, so I take off my bra and square my shoulders before I lower my head to his neck. I reach down for his jeans, but instead he flips me onto my back and tugs my underwear down my legs smoothly, efficiently, and kisses the spot in between each pair of ribs as he lowers his head. I cannot remember the last time this happened, and my thighs are around his shoulders for a long couple of minutes before I move them under his arms and try to lift him toward me.

"Come here," I say. Normally I don't have to ask twice, but he gazes up at me over the slope of my belly with this sad look that suddenly makes me freeze. "Why won't you come here?" I ask.

He bites his lip and glances down, then back up, meeting my eyes. "I can't," he says.

"Why?"

"Can't you guess, Liv?"

"But you . . . you left the Light. This . . . abstinence thing . . . it's no longer relevant."

"It isn't that simple, love. It never will be." He raises himself up between my legs, and I am so torn between wanting to fuck him and wanting to tear his face off that I am speechless. He gathers his T-shirt and wisely departs before I can find my words. What the fuck is it with men in this town.

• • •

Stressed out and unsatisfied and feeling like my room itself is exposed after Dawn's visit, I can't sleep or settle down. After a few hours of fretting, I sit up in bed. I miss my pills. It will be morning soon, and I decide I want to watch the sun rise over the lake while I take a run. Suited up and eager for the exercise, I prance down the stairs and outside, turning to exit the hotel's grounds and follow the path that runs along the waterfront in town. I nearly jump out of my skin when she speaks.

"Liv. I thought you might be an early riser today."

Rain is sitting on a bench, a shawl wrapped around her shoulders. She smiles and gestures me over.

Seeing her here, so soon after I spoke with Dawn, I again wonder if he had lied or had an additional motive in coming to see me. I take my phone from my pocket and open an app. "I'm recording, just so you know," I say.

Rain shrugs. "If that feels important to you." She pats the seat next to her. "Luke asked me to speak with you."

I look around, wary of goons in flax, of the flash of a camera. But she appears to be alone. I sink down next to her.

"Why didn't he come and speak to me himself?" I ask.

"He's aware of the great responsibility he bears. Too often, when a man finds himself in the role of teacher and leader, the emphasis is about ego, how he is perceived. Luke has withdrawn from the world, to ensure that the focus is never on him."

"So, he's holed up in a monastery somewhere?" I ask, and Rain grins, that disarming glee coming over her face.

"In a manner of speaking," she says.

"What does he want me to hear? I've received the various threats loud and clear, so I think I've gotten the message."

"Ah, Liv. We were just hoping to influence you . . . in the right direction. We've found that there is often a lot of spiritual resistance to change, to finding the Light. People sometimes need help, and that's why collateral is useful. It is the ego's way of destroying itself."

"Thanks—I'm just not interested in being destroyed," I say.

"And yet you maintain the same path that brought you to us." Rain's eyebrows tilt upward.

"That's the thing about this circular cult logic. You say I have to do what you say to save my soul, I say no, you say 'That's just your inner darkness talking,' I say 'Don't think so,' you say '*That's your inner darkness talking.*' Until I agree with you."

Rain smiles again, more softly this time. "Ah, Liv. You rely on your head when you should trust your intuition. Your gut." She reaches out and places her palm on my belly.

"So, you came here to . . . keep trying to recruit me?" I ask, shaking my head in surprise. "Surely you know that that ship has sailed."

"Luke is an optimist. He trusts that, eventually, your inner Light will bring you where you're fated to be. If that means you need to complete your crusade—" She shrugs. "Then that is part of your journey."

"Even if my 'crusade' destroys your organization?"

"A podcast can't undo the work we have done, what we will continue doing. Luke isn't interested in the press, or in the perception. He understands that change is painful, and that most people resist it with their entire being."

"So why bother trying to get me to stop?" I ask. "If he doesn't care?"

"Just because he's immune to public criticism doesn't mean I am," Rain says. "Unfortunately, I *am* attached to how the Light is seen. The work I've done at the Center all these years . . . I'm not sure I can bear to see it undone. It is my journey, the work of a lifetime. And with this much public pressure, the Center is in jeopardy. Luke understands this, and said that I should come and talk to you. Bare my soul, so to speak," she adds with a wiggle of her head and a smile.

"Rain, I . . . this isn't personal. I was excited to come to the Light, and I would have stayed. *You* asked *me* to leave."

"Perhaps an error in judgment on my part. The Committee felt . . . unnerved by what was happening with you. The questions you were asking. I let them convince me that your presence was making things worse."

"They felt they had something to hide," I counter. "And that I was going to find it if I stuck around."

"There is a reason we don't show everyone what the Light has to offer immediately. The journey is a spiral upward, with many levels and moments of insight. No one can start at the end. You were learning things right away that we like to introduce people to slowly, so that they can process."

"I guess that's why hysterectomies don't feature in the promo materials."

"I see you understand," she says with a laugh. "I didn't have faith in you, Liv. That's why I asked you to leave. It was a great hope of mine that you would come to the Light, and perhaps when I saw that failing, I reacted emotionally. Wrongly. I came to ask you to forgive me."

I say nothing for a while, taken aback. I fully expected further threats, not this. Finally, I answer: "I can forgive you for kicking me out, Rain. But I can't forgive you for Hannah. For Allison. For Theia. For Amy. Where is Iris? Where is Robin?" I ask.

Rain takes a deep breath. "I see." She pauses. "So I have failed you. And that failure may cost me my life's work. So be it."

"Wait, that's it?" I say.

"This is an expensive lesson, for me. But that is my path. The best I can hope is that I learn this lesson well, so I don't have to relearn it later. Sometimes you slide down the spiral before going back up."

"You're not going to answer any of my questions? Luke doesn't have . . . a comment for the record?" I press, frustrated. "How can you not want to defend yourself? And the Light?"

"That's not for me to do," she says, with a sad smile. "That's not why I asked you here."

"Can I . . . at least have a conversation with Luke? Maybe it would . . . help me understand."

Rain looks me full in the face, really looking into my eyes. Seeing me, it feels like. She just shakes her head.

"So, wait—does this mean . . . my collateral won't be released? That you'll back off with the threats? The lawsuit?"

"Ah." Rain tilts her head. "I'm afraid that just because I personally wish you no ill will, that's not the, er, overall policy of the Light. When we are attacked, we respond, regardless of who it is. I wanted to speak to you for myself, as someone who regrets their choices."

"So basically you'll still fuck up my life if I carry on with the podcast," I say.

"I'm afraid all that has already been set in motion. By you." She shrugs apologetically. She stands. The sun is coming up over the right side of the lake. She reaches her hand out to cup my cheek.

"Be well, Liv."

CHAPTER 22

All I do for the next few days is pace around my hotel room and watch crap TV and read the message boards. I don't want to do any more interviews, or even leave my room. I'm sick of the whole thing. But Naia keeps calling, and calling. The only people I've interacted with have been those responsible for room service, and I'm leery even of them, half-expecting to find messages spelled out in pepper every time I order a salad. But I finally answer the phone.

"You won't believe who I've got on the line," Naia whispers breathlessly, as though she's worried that speaking too loudly will scare them.

"Oh yeah?" I ask. I'm trying to muster the enthusiasm to reinvest in work, but it's not coming. Since my surreal close call out on the lake, my interest in investigative journalism has taken something of a hit. I know I should brave the scandal that releasing the podcast will unleash; that's the courageous, right thing to do. But I don't feel brave. I feel worn-out, tentative.

Burke's departure, too, has furled my sails. I don't blame him in the slightest; the media circus has chewed me up, too, and it's still gnashing its teeth. I've been following the online speculation a bit, but the wild carousel of theories and unsubstantiated finger-pointing gave me an anxiety attack, and since then I've stayed in my room ordering Caesar salads and watching anything other than true crime on the not-smart TV in my room. Everything I turn to has a dead white girl, though, and I end up watching *Dr. Phil* and reality courtroom dramas. These are true crime–adjacent, too, I realize at some point, and they certainly capitalize on the suffering of strangers for the purpose of entertainment. But after that panicked evening spent peering out the curtains, looking for pale-garbed pursuers, and Dawn's visit, I don't trust my own judgment, so that's where I've left the channel changer.

I haven't heard from Jess once. I'm pretty sure this is the longest we've gone without speaking. I'm honestly too afraid to call her.

Naia has been trying to get me back out to interview people, but I've been deep in a funk, and she hasn't been able to find a chink in my self-imposed media blackout. I haven't told her about the threat because I'm too ashamed, preferring to bury my head in the sand (or in heaps of romaine lettuce). I suspect she's been out interviewing on her own, and splicing my voice into certain clips. I'm fine with this, as long as I don't need to be outside, risking being photographed or followed. I venture out in the evenings to walk along the pier, thinking of all the movies and shows where a troubled woman takes a walk near the water and is found in it the next day. I'm saturated with all of it.

"Your girl Iris wants to go on the record," Naia informs me smugly, and my hazy brain almost isn't sure what she's talking about.

"You found Iris?" I ask.

"She found me. I guess she's listened through your whole podcast and checked out everything online and she's decided we're legit. She says it's time to come forward, to save other women."

"What on earth? I mean, she was practically putting herself in witness protection the last time we spoke. And now she wants to be interviewed on the record?"

"Well, I may have pointed a few things out to her in our initial conversation. That the truth is almost certainly going to come out on its own. That she has the choice between protecting the Light or being the brave whistleblower who helps uncover what's been going on. That you're famous and have a few million Instagram followers, and that the podcast is number two on Apple Podcasts right now—"

"Wait, it is?" I interrupt.

"If you'd answered your phone or checked your email, you would have known that, sweetheart. It sure is. But the cherry on top for our girl Iris was when I pointed out that there was almost certainly going to be a documentary or movie about this down the line, and that she was perfectly poised to get a killer book deal. I told her to think about it, and she called me back later that day."

"What about her collateral?" I ask.

"She wants to get out ahead of it. She'll talk about it in the interview, refute the claims before they're made, that sort of thing. She's the key to all this, Liv. This could maybe even wrap it up with a pretty little bow. I'm smelling film options, I'm thinking *Dirty John*–levels, I'm thinking our little media company is now a challenger for the top slots in podcasting. I'm thinking the Wondery people are pretty fucking upset this week."

"Does it have to be me?"

"What?" Naia practically shrieks. "Yeah, it fucking has to be you. I hope you're kidding. And in case you're not, you have a contract, so . . . snap out of it and go put on your big-girl boots. You have an interview to do."

"Naia, I'm just the talent. The pretty face that gets everyone to turn their head. Someone else, someone better qualified, they should do the interview."

"Girl, that's some bullshit, and I hope you know it. You're not just a pretty face, you're running this show. Get to it. I'm not going to ask again."

I consider disappearing. I consider jumping into the lake. I know the trade-off for doing this interview, for releasing another episode: my reputation. But I can't not finish it.

There's no such thing as bad press, right?

For a long moment, I stare out the window at the lake, pretending to be anyone other than me.

. . .

In earlier episodes, you will remember, I was trying to track down Iris Reebuck, a former member of the House of Light who had vanished under mysterious circumstances. After a close friend of hers suggested that someone had tried to kill her—had, indeed, tried to bury her alive—we were especially interested in locating her. When we finally did, she was living under an assumed name—and using the Social Security number of one of our other dead girls. When we caught up with her, she seemed to think we were members of the House of Light, and she fled in a car before we were able to get any answers from her.

Since last week, when that episode aired, we've had a lot of interest in this case, and a lot of people have gotten in touch with tips, stories, rumors, and, frankly, some truly crazy shit. Our team has been sorting through all of it, identifying which things we should take seriously. It's so heartening to see everyone's response to this story—thank you to everyone who has written or called or tweeted with information. Thanks to you, we're close to finding out what happened to Allison, Theia, Amy, and Hannah.

Because of the attention this story has been receiving, Iris Reebuck contacted us and said she was ready to speak about what happened to her at the House of Light. And if what she says is true, a much clearer—and more disturbing—picture of that place is emerging.

LIV: Iris, I'm so glad you decided to reach out and speak to me after all.

IRIS: Yeah, I'm sorry I booked it the first time you tried to talk to me. But you have to understand, I've been running from these people for months, and I was just really scared that they'd caught up to me. After we spoke, I was able to go back and listen to the other episodes of your podcast and look at everything that was happening online. After all that, I figured I needed to speak to you. You know, so that no one else gets hurt.

LIV: I know you're scared, and I know how much courage it takes for you to come forward now, given the risk that the House of Light will release damaging information about you.

IRIS: Yeah, well. Like I said, it's time to tell the story about that place.

LIV: Can you? I mean, can you tell me a little about what drew you into the Light, and what your time with them was like?

IRIS: (deep breath) Well. Yeah, there's not really a part of my life I can remember before the Light. They were always there, since I was a kid. My mom joined when she was in her twenties, and she met my dad there, and my sister and I were born there.

LIV: Like, on the property there?

IRIS: Yeah, there was a midwife back in those days, and a handful of kids were born in the cabins there. We lived on-site at the Light until I was five or six, and then my mom bought a piece of land a couple miles away and built our little homestead. We were home-schooled, and we mostly ran wild at the Light. There was a lot of communal childcare.

LIV: Was it a happy childhood?

IRIS: Honestly, it wasn't too bad! (Laughs.) We helped make the food, and we were always outside, and our classes were, like, for-aging and making a fire. I'm surprised we managed to learn to read. I actually loved it. My sister, Lily, wasn't crazy about it, especially as we got older, but it really worked for me. After I got my GED, I kept training at the Institute—you know what the Institute is?

LIV: Yeah, I think we do. (As loyal listeners will remember, the Oikos Phaos Institute is the public-facing part of the House of

Light—the Institute has an online presence that serves as a conduit to accessing more intense House of Light experiences, and brings in income through online programs that benefit the House of Light. The Institute makes the Light more accessible to people all over the country—or even the world—by getting them involved online before drawing them into in-person workshops.)

IRIS: I did some vocational training and got an acupuncture accreditation, and started holding clinics and the occasional workshop there. The culture of the Light was changing around that time, so we were getting a lot of new members, and a few of the older members left—

LIV: That's around the time that your original teacher died, right? The man who started the Light?

IRIS: Yeah, he died, so there was some in-fighting over what to do with his teachings, who would take over. The obvious choice was his son, Luke, but around that time he went off to, I guess, find himself for a couple years. We heard that he was walking alone through the desert or in Tibet meditating at an ashram—no one knew for sure, I think, except maybe Rain. They said he was psychic, that he would change the world, that he was a genius, raised in Light, all that. He was definitely different; you could tell that much. She ran things while he was gone, and she definitely helped, I guess, mythologize Luke. She thought he was basically the chosen one, but he needed to go and become a man before he could take over the Light. While he was gone, she started to do things her own way, and not everyone loved it.

LIV: People like your sister, for example.

IRIS: Right, she'd always been on the fence, but Rain just did things differently, and she left. She was almost a little bitter about it, and it made me really sad. But I was a believer, I guess. I'd never known anything else, and this was my whole life. These people raised me.

LIV: But then, Luke came back?

IRIS: Yeah, he came back and he was . . . well, he was pretty intense. He'd studied with some other people while he was off finding God or whatever, and he had a lot of ideas for how he wanted to run the organization. That was when the Light became an *organization,* a company even, and Luke wanted to expand, to bring our message to other people.

LIV: Is that when he founded the Institute?

IRIS: Yep, it was a great tool for reaching people remotely, and if they liked the online stuff, they could visit the campus. Plus, it made a lot of money. The Institute is mostly harmless, though. It's expensive, but I've seen people really get something out of the publications and the classes, so who knows. But that's when Luke started the Guidance Committee.

LIV: And what was that, exactly?

IRIS: Well, it was sort of like an inner circle. Or a board of directors, I guess. It was a by-invitation-only group of people who followed stricter rules and who were deeply committed to the Light. Most of us lived at the Light, worked at the Light, dedicated all of our time to maintaining the garden and the property and the website. We were really tight-knit. Luke wasn't really interacting with members of the public at that point. He didn't want the message to be all about him, and he said it could be dangerous or disruptive for people to just be exposed to him. So we were his inner circle.

LIV: How many people were on the Committee?

IRIS: Luke said there needed to be twelve at all times. Whenever someone . . . left . . . a new member would be found.

LIV: Was there anything . . . unusual about this group?

IRIS: (laughs) Pretty much everything at the Light was a bit unusual. Not that I knew it then, but I do now. But yeah. The Committee was all women.

LIV: Except for Luke?

IRIS: He actually wasn't technically a member of the Committee. He was the head of the Light, and he was involved in some of the Committee meetings, but he told us that it was important for there to be a matriarchal power structure at the heart of the Light. Again, this goes back to the ego thing: he said he didn't want everything to revolve around him. He tries to stay out of the limelight. So Rain called most of the shots. And Devotion, too, back when she still spoke.

LIV: And I guess we're getting down to it. What was the purpose of the Committee?

IRIS: Well, at first we just talked about how to grow the organization, how to allocate resources, ten-year plans, that sort of thing. But our focus began to shift toward controlling members' decisions, keeping track of what they ate, who they slept with, that sort of thing. And the agenda was increasingly focusing on how to minimize our impact on the planet as much as possible. We started to get obsessed with low-impact farming, sustainable architecture, reducing waste, education programs.

LIV: Doesn't seem all that nefarious to me . . .

IRIS: It didn't start that way, but things took a bit of a turn about six or seven years ago. Around the time Allison joined us—I'd say that was a turning point.

LIV: And we've reached a turning point here, folks—we've got to take a quick break to hear from our sponsors.

We all know how hard it can be to land the perfect job. Many of us spend years working in an industry or a position we don't love just to make ends meet or to climb the corporate ladder. As a working creative, I know particularly well how hard the gig economy can be to navigate, and how finding your true path can feel

*next to impossible. With DreamJob, you can connect with a net-
work of like-minded people working in your field. The subscription rates are so reasonable, you'll wonder why it's taken you so
long to invest in your future. Don't spend another day just paying
the bills: start working toward your real self with DreamJob. For
a two-hundred-dollar discount on your first year, use promo code
"vultures." Offer details apply.*

LIV: So, Iris and I were just discussing her past with the House of
Light, and we'd gotten to the point where, Iris says, everything started
to change. Can you tell us exactly what you mean by that, Iris?

IRIS: (chuckles nervously) I can try. But even now, it's sort of hard
to believe I got caught up in all this, that I . . . believed in it. Anyway,
sometime in, like, 2013, 2014, Rain came to us and said that we
needed to commit fully to the Light, and to our roles on the Guidance Committee, or GC, as we sometimes called it. We all needed
to know that everyone was totally in, and that none of us would, I
guess, defect and leave the others unprotected. So that's when we
were all encouraged to contribute collateral.

LIV: And what's that, exactly?

IRIS: Everyone had different collateral. Some people signed over
property deeds, so that they would be held jointly by the Light, or
even, in some cases, by Luke. Some people contributed naked
photos of themselves, with the understanding they would be released if they ever left GC.

LIV: I can sympathize with what a powerful hold that can be. Anyone who's ever sent someone naked photos knows how difficult it
is to break up with them or disagree with them, knowing the lever-
age they have over you. As many listeners are aware, I've personally had naked photos of myself released to the public, against my
consent. It's a brutal violation.

IRIS: Exactly. Everyone contributed something that was related
to their particular "weakness." So much of what we were doing in

our GC workshops was self-introspection, self-diagnosis of problems, so we all knew what each other's hang-ups were. People who were weird about money or possessions had to sign over a bank account. Women who were weird about their bodies did the naked pics, that sort of thing. I remember Allison— (Cuts herself off.)

LIV: You were going to say something about Allison?

IRIS: I don't know if it would be a betrayal to reveal her collateral. But I guess she's dead, so . . . (Takes a deep breath.) Allison had been involved with another group of people before she came to us and, apparently, had been raped. Because she'd been a minor, the records were sealed, and pretty much only her parents knew about it. She turned over copies of the police report, and photographs of the man who did it. She always maintained that it had been consensual but that everyone had freaked out because she was seventeen and the guy was in his thirties, and she didn't want to damage him. She was pretty unstable, though, you could tell. Something had happened to her, and she was never totally right afterward. That's probably why she was the first one.

LIV: The first one to . . . the first one to die?

IRIS: The first one to give herself to the Light. That's what we called it. For a couple years, we'd been having these increasingly tricky philosophical debates about our ethical responsibilities. To the planet, sure, like I was saying before and like you talked about with Allison's mom—shout-out to Bea!—but also about how human suffering is an absolute bad that is amplified through every human that comes into contact with it, and how we could isolate that, limit it, and live as closely to our principles as possible.

You know, we wanted to save the world. It became a pretty basic tenet: that according to our philosophy, we were ethically bound not to procreate. At first it was just birth control, and monitoring who was having sex and when. But pretty soon, a lot of us started to feel that this wasn't enough, that we weren't being serious enough. People started to talk about vasectomies and tubal ligation. Permanent solutions, you know. And one of the women, Theia, ended up having a hysterectomy. I think she was diagnosed with endometriosis, but I also think the main reason was our commitment to this new thing, this decision to not create any more people who would go on to suffer and cause suffering and destroy the earth, which would cause even more suffering.

LIV: Forgive me if this sounds a bit callous but . . . it seems pretty clear that a big piece of the Light's mission was to expand. Surely one of the best ways to do that would be to basically . . . create new members by giving birth to them, right?

IRIS: You're totally right. Luke and Rain cared about growing the organization. But, as Luke liked to say, there were seven billion sufferers on the planet and counting. There was no shortage of souls we could bring into the Light. There was a shortage of drinkable water and breathable air, though. And it wasn't really about the numbers. It didn't matter how big a difference we made, it was more about *how* we made that difference. Darkness gets amplified, but so does the Light. The symbols and our example for the world mattered. As for finding new members, Luke started a new course through the Institute that targeted families with young kids, because that seemed like a reliable way to get, um, young blood in. But we had all decided together that we weren't going to have children ourselves. There was some talk about working with adoption agencies, down the line . . .

LIV: Was there any pushback to this idea? What about among the men at the Light? I know there are some there.

IRIS: Honestly, everyone was pretty much on board. Dissent doesn't work very well in this type of environment, and if you didn't agree with something . . . well, it's sort of like being the only person at Thanksgiving dinner who votes the opposite party. You learn to sit down and shut up or you end up outside crying and smoking a cigarette while everyone else eats pumpkin pie. Besides, you had to be ordained into the Light's inner circle, the Committee, even to be part of the conversation.

LIV: Did you undergo an actual ordination, a ceremony or something, before joining the Committee?

IRIS: "My tubes are tied, my lips are sealed." (Laughs.) Not much of a joke, but yeah, that was something we'd say, sometimes.

LIV: Right. So, after ordination to the Committee... you might be encouraged to enter the Light?

IRIS: If you were called to, yes.

LIV: Okay, I feel like we're inching up to it, with the dates, and the discussion of the elements, the ordinations. I guess this is the moment where I ask you if you know how any of these women died.

IRIS: (long pause) I feel like I should talk to a lawyer before I incriminate myself.

LIV: Okay, hang on, let me just turn off the recorder.

. . .

I fumble to switch off the device that has been recording our conversation so far. Everything Iris has said has left me reeling, but being this close to the answer I've been looking for, I'm desperate to keep her talking. I can't stop here; I feel like it would kill me.

"I understand you might not want to talk on the record," I say, looking into her eyes and giving her my very best empathy. "You've already helped so much. But I just . . . I owe it to these women to find out what happened to them. Even if we don't include it as part of your interview . . . do you think you could tell me? Please?"

I can see her considering, torn between her desire to give me what I want, to get this off her chest, and her need to protect herself. If she was there when those girls died, she could be held accountable for their deaths, and I can tell she knows it.

"I could go to jail," she finally says softly.

"Did you help kill them?"

"Jesus, no! No." She looks down at her lap. "Not exactly. I'm not sure. But I was with them while they died."

"Iris. Look at me. This wasn't your fault." I reach out to take her hand, and she lets me. "These people had you in their web before you even knew what the world was. You were totally caught up in this. You can't be held liable for what they did."

"Are you sure?" Iris finally looks up. "You don't know what I did. How I participated. Did you know that I recruited Hannah? She would never have been there without me. She would never have died if I hadn't found her."

"You don't know that."

"One of the things being involved in a cult teaches you is belief. I know what I know. I'm hardwired for certainty. And I know that at least one person is dead because of me."

I can tell she believes this, that it is one of the reasons she came forward. Not just for a book deal, though I'm sure the promise of that helped. After a long, deep breath, examining my own needs, I exhale.

"Okay. I have another question," I say. She nods apprehensively while I pull out a picture. "Do you know this woman? Have you seen her anywhere at the Light? Or at Simple Transitions or . . . anywhere?" I slide over the pictures of my mother, both an old photo and the picture that could be her, could be anyone.

Iris studies them for a while, then slowly shakes her head. I let out my breath.

"I don't recognize her, no. Who is she?"

"It doesn't matter. I keep thinking she might appear but . . . she never does." I shake my head, shake off my hope. "I don't suppose you know a girl named Robin, either? She underwent an ordination just before disappearing."

"Ah," says Iris. "You're worried about Samhain. You think she might be the next person called to the Light."

"Is that something . . . that might have been decided for her?" I press. "Something she would do against her will?"

Iris looks at me, bites her lip. "Look, I . . . think I need to get some legal advice. I'm happy to be a whistleblower and all, but I don't want to go to jail. I'll tell you whatever I can, and I wanted to get this off my chest, but . . . the rest of the story is complicated."

"No, I understand. Let me get on the phone with my producer. I'll talk to her about getting you a lawyer. We should probably take this to the police at this stage anyway. It's irresponsible of me to keep going without bringing some of this information to the official channels."

"I'm . . . Don't call your producer. At least not on my behalf. I already have a lawyer. Actually used to be involved in the Light. And I think it's time for me to go speak to her. Now that I've come out against them, there's no point in hiding."

"You do? I mean, that's great, are you sure . . ." I delicately don't ask whether this lawyer is up to snuff for dealing with a case that is, in all likelihood, going to be an extremely public shit show.

"She's great, and I trust her. I should have told her everything before all this, but . . . I was hoping that I wouldn't have to. I was honestly hoping it might just go away. But once I heard your podcast . . ." I flinch. "It's not your fault, either, Liv. You've brought some more attention to it, but . . . that's probably for the best. I'm glad it's going to come out. Even if it means my collateral gets released."

"Do you mind if I ask what it is? Your collateral? We could even mention it on the show, get ahead of it. I know a little something about managing bad press," I add weakly.

"Sure, you can deny it on your show. I don't know if it will matter. My collateral is that I told them that my dad, Bloom, sexually molested me and my sister when we were nine and ten."

"Oh, fuck," I say.

"It's not actually true. But they made me sign an affidavit. I'm not sure the truth will matter too much to my dad—he works with children now, so his career will pretty much be finished if there are even allegations. The irony is that Luke wanted to have something to hold over him because Bloom left under . . . shitty circumstances. Bloom always preferred Luke's father, and he didn't like the new Light. So even my collateral wasn't really about me."

I sit silently for a long minute, needing to ask my next question but feeling like an asshole. I tell myself that I really must remember this feeling for the next time I play a journalist; it feels like shit.

"Did they try to kill you? Bury you alive, I mean?"

"That's not exactly what happened. Honestly, I don't remember everything that happened that night. There were some drugs involved. But I agreed to everything, I went into it knowing what would happen. I guess I just changed my mind when I woke up in the ground. It was like something else in me had to die so that I could dig my way out of that hole and leave."

"You . . . agreed to be buried alive?"

"You'll agree to anything when the right person asks it of you and gives you a good enough reason. And they had a way of making it seem better than the alternative."

"Death was . . . better?"

"Death is the path into Light, the way out of darkness. The true suffering is right here. I still know that's true; I just lost my courage."

. . .

"This is fucking bananas," Naia says breathlessly. "I mean, are you sure that you believe her?"

"She didn't look like she was lying. And I feel like this is a pretty elaborate story to just . . . fabricate, no?"

"Not if what she's after is publicity and a book deal," Naia points out.

"Still, fact-checking and all that," I say.

"You wouldn't believe the shit people get away with. Fuck,

well, regardless, that means it's time to involve the officials. Sitting on this is obstruction, so I better get on the phone, at least try for official statements and all that rigmarole. Ugh."

"Better you than me," I say heartily.

"Well, you've got a job to do, too. And it might be a little tense. I can hold off for two days before I do my due diligence and give you time to get your interview done."

"Seriously? Another interview?"

"You didn't think we were just going to leave the story there, did you? Jesus, Olivia, where's your sense of closure? Nope, it's time for the golden goose interview." Naia is excited, and that gives me an unsettled feeling.

"You don't mean . . ." I trail off.

"I emailed the Light right after I listened. Sent them a few clips, so they knew I wasn't bluffing."

"Shit, Naia, they'll know that Iris came forward!" I protest.

"Um, pretty sure they were going to notice when we published this for a few million people to hear in a few days. Relax, this is a great way to get them on the back foot. I'd rather you speak to them now than after the cops have had a chance to grill them. The lawyers are probably already involved, but hey, at least they've agreed to talk on the record. We'll see. They might just give you a statement and send you on your way."

"Here's hoping," I mumble.

"While you're there, can you use the good recorder to get some of the ambient sounds? Wind, waves, whatever? Chanting would be ideal."

I sigh.

• • •

Naia calls me a few hours later, sounding uncomfortable. Because this is so unlike her usual brass-tacks no-bullshit self, I find that I'm uncomfortable, too. I decide to let her talk before I tell her that I'm considering pulling the podcast. After beating around the bush for a while, she finally knuckles down and says why she's called.

"I feel a bit weird about bringing this up," she says.

"Well, I feel a bit weird about this whole thing, so . . ."

"Okay, well, we've gotten . . . some information that pertains to your personal life."

"Fuck. Is it—?" I don't finish my sentence, too afraid. I've been petrified of opening up any social media, waiting every second for the news of my disgrace.

"It's about your mom." Naia pauses, and I'm thrown. "We've gotten a few so-called tips about her, but most of them were just too bogus to take seriously. This one . . . well, there was some documentation attached."

My hands are shaking, and my neck is suddenly stiff. I pop my earphones in so I won't have to crane my neck to speak into the lowered phone.

"She's dead, isn't she?" I ask.

Naia takes a long breath. "I think so."

"Was she at the Light? Did they kill her?"

"What? No." Naia is genuinely surprised. "That's not what it looks like at all. The email comes from someone who worked in a homeless shelter in Portland. She says she thinks the woman she knew as 'Rebecca' is your mother. She looked up a photo online, and I guess she watched the old *Unsolved Mysteries* episode you mentioned in the podcast after she heard it, and . . . she recognized her."

"My mom was in a homeless shelter?"

"Well, it sounds like she stayed there for a month or so after she arrived in the city, but then she started volunteering, and eventually working there. Look, do you want the contact details of this woman who wrote? Her name is Nancy, she seems fairly legit and doesn't have any particular agenda that I can figure out. I spoke to her on the phone, and she, well, she seemed genuine," Naia explains.

I stare mutely out at the lake for a long moment. "How about you just give me the CliffsNotes and I'll get in touch later," I finally say. "I'm not sure I'm up for another interview right now."

"Right. Um. Well, it sounds like she worked at the homeless shelter for a while, and eventually got a job helping people transition into city housing. Nancy said she lived really simply, and seemed to just want to help people."

"Did she ever mention . . . me?"

Naia doesn't say anything.

"Never mind, it doesn't matter. What happened to her?"

"It sounds like she got sick not long after arriving in Portland. Or was maybe already sick when she got there. She battled cancer for several years. Nancy said she always talked about 'just having to get better so she could go back' and would never say anything else about it. Never said where 'back' was. And, well, she never got better. Nancy sent an obituary that she wrote back in 2010. She died there, of breast cancer."

"Can you . . . I'd like to see it, if you don't mind."

"Already sent it to you, along with Nancy's contact details. She said she would love to speak with you, would love a visit, anything. It sounds like she really loved your mom—or at least, this Rebecca lady. It's impossible to be absolutely certain without more research, but there is a photo in the obituary."

I close my eyes. "Okay, thanks, Naia. I appreciate . . . that you sent this along."

"For what it's worth, I don't think she's full of shit," Naia adds, just before she's about to hang up. "You've been famous a long time, and I'm sure you've come across the occasional scammer. Nancy just turns out to be a true crime enthusiast and . . . well, recognized something in the story."

"I'll bear that in mind," I say.

"That said, she could be wrong. The photo could just be . . . an eerie coincidence. It's not, you know, definitive."

"Thanks again, Naia," I say, and hang up.

I open the email attachment and scan the obit.

Rebecca Morse died in hospice last Monday, June 21, 2010, after a long battle with breast cancer. A selfless caretaker for those around her, she left this world with a gentle smile on her face. Though she has no family, she leaves behind friends, coworkers, and countless people she has helped through her work. We all hope she has found peace wherever she is.

The photo is of my mother. I curl up on my bed and cry softly for several minutes. I no longer have an appetite for answers.

• • •

Fred pulls down the driveway of the House of Light, and I remember, just a few weeks ago, rolling across this gravel in the dark. Richard sits on my lap this time, too, and again, I will leave him behind in the car—although this time I expect to reemerge in just a few minutes. While I'm nervous, I don't genuinely feel at risk; they would have to be nuts to try to hurt me, regardless of whether they've hurt the other women whose deaths I'm interested in. My celebrity protects me.

I've put on a white pantsuit, and my hair is bouncy and clean—today I'm not the humbled actor prepared to dry out, nor the scrappy investigator, nor the fledgling reporter. Now I am, I suppose, just me. Whatever that is.

The Light is as still and quiet as the first time I came here, and Devotion meets me at the door. Her face is stony and unreadable, and I follow her. We don't go to Rain's office, which is what I had expected; instead she takes me to a small conference room I hadn't yet seen. Like the Group Work room, it looks out on the water, a few taller pine trees breaking the otherwise unobstructed view.

Devotion points to a seat, then bustles away. I arrange my things and lean back in the chair, making sure my posture communicates ease and confidence. I'm listening for the sound of Rain's bare feet when I hear the door close behind me. I know only one person who can move that soundlessly.

"Oh, Liv. I really did ask you to stop," Jess says behind me.

CHAPTER 23

I don't know my lines. I haven't prepped this scene. But Jess is, after all, one of my oldest improv partners.

"Well, your advice hasn't been spot-on lately, has it? Pretty sure this ole place was your recommendation, too," I say.

"This place was exactly what you needed. You just responded in completely the wrong way."

"What the fuck are you talking about, Jessica? Should I assume that you haven't heard the most recent interview I did? You thought I needed to come spend some time with a . . . pagan cult that will try to sterilize me?"

"Such a drama queen, honestly. You needed time and a supportive community to help you recenter. Most of all, you needed a space where you could get to know yourself. The Light is the sort of place where you could have done that. You could have taken all these tools and come back to L.A. a totally changed person. Instead, you attack the people who are trying to help you."

"These people do not want to help me! They want to control me, to own me, and then probably to use whatever benefit my modest fame can give them to make more fucking money. Jesus, Jessica, where did you find these people? Was it Bart all along? Has he been . . . angling to get me here?"

"Bart has nothing to do with any of this," Jess says, irritated. "As usual, he's just an opportunist. And, as usual, you give him credit for making things happen when I've been working for years to set it up." She takes a long sigh and shakes her head at me.

"Years, eh? I didn't realize the waiting list for rehab here was *that* long. I knew you pulled some strings, but—"

"Liv, you have no idea. You think this was all just some coincidence? That you accidentally ended up at this place? The only coincidence was the fact that you wound up in the room next to that fruitcake conspiracy theorist—a coincidence that might destroy everything we've worked toward all this time. I'm not sure whose error in judgment that was, but when I find out, they're out of the Light. Not that *that* matters now, I guess." Jess has abandoned the seething irritation and near panic with which she's addressed me during these last few weeks. Now she seems simply tired. But calm.

"When you say '*we've* worked toward all this time' you don't mean me and you, do you," I say slowly.

"No." Jess glances down, then back up at me, defiantly meeting my eyes. "Or at least, not primarily. I suspect *our* work together is probably over, too, but no, that's not what I was talking about."

"You're a member of the Light."

"Ding ding ding! For more than a decade and a half. Since before I met you, in fact. Did you honestly never pause to think where I came from or who my family was?"

"You . . . said you were estranged from your parents."

"And you thought, Meh, there's probably no story behind that. I'll just let it be for fifteen years."

"You never wanted to tell me!" I say.

"You never asked! I found the Light after I ran away. And it's lucky I did, too, or I might have ended up on the street. That Leadership Seminar we did was a Light initiative, an early version of some our executive workshops. The first one for teenagers, actually. Rain suggested I join it after she met me at a halfway house in Cooperstown. She knew I had the potential to cultivate talent. She called me a 'facilitator.'"

"They sent you to target me?" I ask, startled.

"Jesus, Liv, you really are the most narcissistic person I've ever met. You were just another pretty teenager when we met. What on earth was there to target? I *made* you into someone worth targeting. It was my idea, my project. And I did it with everything I learned here at the Light."

"You were looking for someone," I say softly. "When we met. Someone like me."

"You were looking for someone like me, too," she points out with a shrug. "We found each other."

"Why didn't you ever tell me? About this place, about . . ." I'm unsure how to finish that.

"Liv," Jess says softly, tilting her chin down so she can look me straight in the eyes, the way she does when she's serious. "Why didn't you ever *ask* me? About where I came from, what I wanted from life, who my people were?"

"I . . . I thought I did. I thought we were both following our dream, that you wanted to be, I don't know, a power broker in Hollywood. Run a talent company someday. That's what we always discussed."

"Yeah, well. That's a version of it, I guess." Jess leans back in her seat, taking another long breath. "But that was earlier. When your—our—career was trending upward. The idea was to wait until we were both at the top of our game. Then I would tell you about this place, bring you home to the Light. And we would . . . bring more people with us."

"So . . . I would just be a recruitment tool? A way to make the Light seem more appealing?" I ask.

Jess shrugs pragmatically. "In a manner of speaking. You'd legitimize the Light, and make it higher profile. In retrospect, I should have brought you here earlier. Before, well . . ."

"Before I ruined things."

"Before I let you ruin them. Part of my job, my gift, is to facilitate your talent, *your* gift. I failed you, at some point. But I thought . . . someday, bringing you to the Light, that will make up for it." She rubs her eyes in exhaustion. "Luke kept asking if you were ready, but you seemed . . . lost, still. Unfocused. Uncommitted."

"So you planned to tell me only after I won my Academy Awards?" I ask.

Jess snorts. "Yeah, something like that. I would have told you that you already were in the Light, and had been, all this time. But you just kept sort of spiraling instead, and I thought maybe Luke had been right, and you just needed to come home to the Light to get well. You could have recovered, gotten the Manson role we'd been talking about, relaunched your career. . . . It could have worked out, so easily. I had a vision. It just didn't . . ." She stares out at the lake, clearly seeing our lost future.

"Jess, do you think maybe you were . . . trying to protect me? By not bringing me here earlier?" I ask.

After a pause, she looks at me. She needs to touch up her roots; her usually immaculate hair is scraggly.

"I've wondered that, yeah. You always seemed so malleable. I was worried that if you came here you'd lose that last little piece of yourself. I wanted you to . . . bake a little longer in the oven, I guess."

"And maybe you didn't want anyone else screwing with your project? That was your job. What you were so good at," I say.

Jess narrows her eyes, but then smiles in recognition. "See, you know me, too, after all this time. It was just us. We were doing it together."

There is so much in the look we share, of so many years working in careful concert, of mindlessly reaching for the other and always finding her where we expected. She doesn't quaver, but I see her sadness.

"And, of course," I point out, "there's the fact that once I was the poster girl for the Light, you'd be decidedly less important. Just one of my handlers, not my right hand anymore."

Jess nods. "True. I dreaded that, you're right. I suppose there was something of our life that sometimes superseded the Light. I got caught up in the glamor of it, sometimes lost sight of what was important, sure. And yeah, maybe I didn't trust Luke to handle you right."

"We could have taken over Hollywood, you and me. Given those Scientologists a run for their money," I joke.

"We don't really like comparisons to Scientology," she says with a wry wince.

"No way. There was that whole sending people to follow me and chase me in a canoe, though," I point out. "That's straight out of their playbook."

"Ah. Yeah, I learned about that after the fact. I thought the whole thing was a bit, er, theatrical, but I guess you were meant to feel exposed out there on the water. I told them an anonymous email would have been just as effective, but . . ." Jess shrugs. "The writing was on the wall, things were falling apart, people were making bad decisions. I'm not surprised it didn't work. At that stage I knew you were out of pocket, that even the possibility of having the details of your affair leaked wouldn't stop you."

"You're more certain of my tenacity than I was."

"I've known you an awfully long time," Jess says.

We look at each other and laugh together, and I feel a pang of such surreal loss I almost gulp back a sob.

"What now?" I finally manage.

"Well, now we face the music, I guess. Cleaning up the mess is my job, after all."

"Wait . . . you're not . . . taking the fall for them? Where's Rain? Where's Luke? I thought I would be speaking to one of them today."

"You seriously thought Luke stuck around for even a day after all this started? Rain followed not long after you left the Light," she says, shaking her head as though she can't believe my naïveté.

"So the Light is . . . over."

"The Light is wherever we are. This spot will always be important to us, but the Light can be on a beach in Mexico or a private island in Polynesia. It doesn't matter, Liv. You can't touch us."

"I'm reasonably sure the federal government can, when they figure out that you're responsible for the murder of four women. And God knows what kind of financial fraud," I add.

"Oh, Livvy. You think we killed them." She tilts her head in bemusement.

"Umm . . . yeah, that's pretty much what every piece of information we've found so far has suggested."

"Poor sweet Liv. As long as I've known you, you've been absolutely sure that your mother was abducted. That there are bad people out to sabotage you. That things happen to people, against their will. The paparazzi are persecuting you, and all that. Pretty soon you'll be thinking about how *I* did all this to *you*. But the one thing you've never understood is that people make choices. We didn't kill those women. Because we didn't have to."

· · ·

I'd like to back up for just a second. When we last spoke, I was interviewing Iris Reebuck, a former member of the House of Light who'd been involved in the deaths we've been investigating. She, too, had come close to dying because of her involvement with the Light. On the advice of legal counsel, she has declined to speak with us any further, to comment on either her own near-death experience or her participation in the deaths of the four women. Unsurprising, really, though frustrating.

After her interview, we contacted the House of Light, asking them for a statement and giving them the opportunity to clarify. We were granted an interview, and I assumed I would be speaking with Rain or, possibly, even Luke Trask.

When I arrived at the House of Light, I found myself speaking with neither of them but, rather, with someone I've known for many years, someone who turns out to have been a longtime member of the House of Light. I've chosen to not release their name, not least because of legal proceedings currently underway. Suffice it to say I was shocked to learn that someone I've worked with for years has been effectively trying to recruit me to this organization as long as I've known them. And no, that person is not my father, just to put to bed some of the online speculation. In an off-the-record interview with this person, I learned a number of things that, again, legally, I've been discouraged from disclosing; I'm hoping to share all of it with you in a later episode. But I've pieced together some other details in the meantime.

Bear with me for just a second while I walk you through some contemporary philosophy. I know that sounds dry, but I promise it's relevant.

Anti-natalism is the philosophical belief that assigns a negative value to birth. Its proponents believe that, philosophically speaking, it is better to have never been born. Life is suffering; suffering is bad; therefore, existence itself should be avoided.

Luke Trask was introduced to these concepts while he was off on his spiritual pilgrimage, sometime in the early 2000s. He brought many of the ideas he learned back to the House of Light, and modified them to suit his own needs and preferences. One member in particular found profound comfort in this new philosophy. Rain, previously known as Tina Tritter, had given birth to a child who died at the age of three. When she came to the House of Light and encountered this philosophy, and in particular the message that procreating was not only undesirable but was, in fact, a sort of evil, she found a way to live with her personal loss.

So it went from radical birth control and sex avoidance to tubal ligation and hysterectomies, all in a few years. Ultimately, Trask was no longer simply content to limit reproduction. If it was unethical to create new life, maybe it was also unethical to continue life, because remember: life is suffering; suffering is bad; therefore, suicide should be encouraged. So he began to encour-

age the women on his Guidance Committee, the inner circle of Light leadership and the people he trusted the most because he had the most control over them, to consider removing themselves from the population, and "entering the Light." All of which is a euphemism for committing suicide, often in ritualized, collective settings. The so-called Sun Days, the solstices, equinoxes, and other pagan holidays, were often used as a—pardon the pun— deadline to a way of marking spiritual progress. Only those who had spiritually developed enough in their shadow work and in the Process of Return would enter the Light.

Those who decided to sacrifice themselves were told that they were making the best decision they could ever make. That their souls were exalted by their choice to die. That they had been chosen, destined to help save the world. That the light of their soul would help bring others to the Light. They believed they were fulfilling the highest function available to a member of the Light. A sacrifice.

Those who died were vulnerable young women, most of whom had suffered from mental illness in the past, most of whom had very little external support outside of the House of Light.

As of right now, and due in small part to this podcast but in large part to the massive media and public response it has received, there is a criminal case pending against Luke Trask and Tina Tritter. Though they apparently left the country when they realized that public interest in the case was intensifying, there are extradition orders being processed. Trask and Tritter are currently believed to be in Belize.

My former associate has agreed to cooperate with the prosecution for a brief prison sentence and a lengthier probation. Because they were not present during any of the deaths, and because they were very young when they became involved in the Light, they have been charged only as an accessory. The charges against Trask and Tritter have not been formally stated, but we can only hope that they will be prosecuted to the full extent of the law for their involvement in the deaths of at least four women. Since the release of this podcast, it has, ahem, come to light that there are also two former members of the Light, one male and one female, who are not accounted for. One, named Robin, we've been attempting to locate for weeks; the other hasn't been heard from since last year. Their whereabouts are now being investigated. We're praying for their safe return to their families.

As for my own family: I know there has been a lot of interest in my past, and in how my family has intersected with the House of Light. I'd like to clear a few things up.

My mother never was, and never has been, a part of the House of Light. She was, however, part of a direct-sales organization that was owned by the Lux Group. As you may remember, Lux owns a number of companies all across the East Coast. One of them was Illuminate, which sold a nutrition system that was intended to "heal the body and cure the soul." Before she disappeared, my mother had been diagnosed with cancer, and was, apparently, hoping that a radical change in her diet would help with her symptoms. She didn't have health insurance at the time, and I believe that one of the reasons for her leaving her family and disappearing was to avoid saddling us with the extensive healthcare costs associated with her treatment; she kept her illness secret, hoping to cure it on her own, though I think my father suspected she wasn't well. Illuminate was one of the most profitable nutritional systems sold in the Northeast in 2014, and remains a central source of income to the Lux Group. The rehab facilities and self-help press are also crucial cash cows for the organization. But the House of the Light and the Oikos Phaos Institute remain the largest feather in Lux's cap.

So while my mother was never directly involved in the Light, she did have contact with the Lux Group. As, it turns out, I did as well. I met the person who would eventually enroll me in the retreat at the Light at a youth leadership program in our small town. Lux had a strong presence there, and in several other counties throughout a wide swath of Massachusetts, New York, Connecticut, Pennsylvania, and Ohio. They had their very profitable direct-sales company, Illuminate, which grew to have an extensive online presence, but they also had wellness centers, rehab facilities, and yoga studios. There's a good chance that if you've been in that part of the world, you've come in contact with a Lux Group subsidiary. We're still figuring out the extent of their reach. And so is the IRS.

As many of you tech-savvy listeners have pointed out, the internet has played a big role in the rise of the House of Light, and other organizations like them. One of the most disturbing things we've learned about this is that the Oikos Phaos Institute was specifically targeting vulnerable people with search-engine optimization. Odds are, if you googled about suicidal ideation, you would eventually have found your way to the Institute's YouTube page, where you would have been invited to participate in a workshop. Likewise, the rehab facilities and halfway houses were places where people who were necessarily going through periods of transition and disruption might be targeted. All of this increased the likelihood that people who were already struggling with their mental health might be drawn into destabilizing philosophies, and might ultimately be more likely to be swayed or controlled by a strong personality with a radical vision.

If you or anyone else you know is involved in a cult, there are a lot of resources available out there. One of the most effective ways to help is through exit counseling, facilitated by a trained professional. There are lots of memoirs by people who have successfully left cults, and by their family members. I suggest you check them out. A bibliography on the podcast home page is a great place to start, if you need suggestions.

Finally. As is the case with many true crime stories, the women at the heart of this story, those who lost their lives, have gotten somewhat lost in the telling. The mysteries that surround their deaths overtake their lives. I'd like to recognize them, just for a moment, as young women who will never get married, will never run marathons, have children, write code, grow gardens, have knee-replacement surgery.

Allison liked to draw, and she made portraits of everyone in her family. They're still hanging on the walls in her childhood home. Hannah used to make cinnamon scones for her roommates every Saturday during the autumn. Amy won a triathlon competition when she was just fifteen years old, and she was training for an ultramarathon when she died. Theia once went backpacking alone through Southeast Asia for three months.

I don't want the realities of their individual lives to be entirely overshadowed by the way they died, so I like to think of them sharing a macrobiotic meal together, proud of what they've accomplished and happy to have found one another.

We wouldn't have been able to get to the bottom of this case without all of you. I thank you all—it's been a privilege to work with you. I'm Olivia Reed, and this has been Vultures.

· · ·

I'm standing in line at the DMV when I get a phone call from Naia.

"They have pictures of them at a beach house outside of Punta Gorda," she says with no preliminaries.

"I guess the paparazzi are being useful, for once," I respond. "And? Will they be deported?"

"It sounds like we're a ways off from anything official. There's been some jurisdictional leg-raising, yada yada, it's unclear which charges will actually be extraditable. My money is on the tax evasion, if we're being totally honest. The feds will want their money."

"Is anyone filing a civil suit? That could help add pressure."

"You remember Beatrice Giordino? Well, turns out she's Iris's lawyer, and she's talking about putting together a class action. It will all be really slow, of course, so Rain and Luke will probably have a pretty decent tan before they see their day in court," Naia says with a snort.

"Maybe they'll take their own advice and walk into the Caribbean."

"Somehow, I doubt it. Maybe Rain will, but this Luke dude . . . he's a true crusader. He thinks his ethical duty is to stay alive and preach the word. You know, the word he came up with and sells for twenty-six ninety-five a pop."

"Is the Institute at least shut down for future workshops?" I ask.

"Technically, yes. But there's nothing to stop them from using their mailing list to start up a whole new organization and recruit from Belize. So."

"How very encouraging," I say. "Such a happy ending."

"Buck up, kiddo. I'm still optimistic. And the happy ending is that the podcast is a fucking HIT. I'm sure your people—" Naia stops short. "Um."

"It's okay. You can mention Jess. In the end, it was actually sort of amicable. She's a scrapper. She's agreed to testify, and she might go to jail for a bit, but I think she'll be okay. She'll probably start a self-help group in prison. I guarantee she'll have a book deal by this time next year. She'll land on her feet."

"But you don't . . . you're not still"—Naia's voice goes up a little, making it almost a question—"working together?"

"No, that would be a little codependent, even for me. It's weird: we were completely reliant on each other, but so much of our relationship was based on mutual contempt. I thought she was joyless and brittle; she thought I was directionless and undisciplined. In a way, the thing that makes me saddest is having spent such a long time with someone I didn't really like, and who didn't like me."

"Working relationships can be like that," Naia says wryly, and

I imagine she's thinking of Topher, who has been giddy and obnoxious.

"My agency set me up with a new manager—she seems nice. I was actually . . . I've been thinking about it. I don't suppose you'd consider taking the job?" I ask, tentative.

"Oh wow. Um." Naia pauses, genuinely surprised. "Honestly, I had never considered that. Do you think I could think about it for a few days? I'm not sure it's my wheelhouse."

"Of course—I didn't mean to spring it on you. If you wanted to do an interim thing, or a trial period or whatever, I'd be open to that. It's just with the HBO deal coming down the pike, I thought you might be the perfect person to handle some of that. Maybe bring you on as a producer or something." I bite my lip and inch forward in the line, which is, admittedly, very tame here at the almost empty Ithaca DMV. I can tell that the two people in front of me are eavesdropping, but they're doing so very politely. I wonder if they're listeners.

"Okay, let me think about it. I appreciate the offer, though. And I've really liked working with you. But I have to consider some things, not to mention look at my contract with Topher."

"Let me know if you want me to harass him," I offer with a laugh. "I think he owes me."

"That he does."

An awkward silence falls.

"Look, I'm waiting in line to get my learner's permit for a driver's license, and I'm next up," I explain. "Catch up later?"

"Of course—I'll call you tomorrow or the day after." She stops to take a breath. "There's one more thing, though."

"What is it?"

"Ummmm . . . that Ava girl. She wrote. She was actually . . . well, she wanted you to come for dinner. This evening, if you're available, though she's flexible. She says you know where she lives."

I laugh. "Sure, it's not like I have anything else going on today. It can be my first drive."

• • •

Fred gives me gentle instructions as I guide the town car over the winding hills along the lake, patiently correcting me when my instincts are wrong.

"I'm just glad we're not driving a stick," he says as we pull down the bumpy drive at Ava and Wyatt's house. "Here in one piece, though. Good job."

"Thanks, Fred. And for helping me learn."

He nods gruffly and agrees to come back for me later, when I call.

I pause in front of the door, trying to collect myself, but it is yanked open before I have a chance. Ava stands in front of me, Zora propped on her hip.

"You know where everything is—come make yourself at home," she says with a wicked glint, and like that, so much of the awkwardness and dread has lifted. If she was put out by the weird boundary crossing we all engaged in, she's not bothered by it now. Zora is squirmy, and Ava sets her down in exasperation. "Go with Liv, kiddo. Take her to see Daddy." She heads off to the kitchen, her bangles jangling. "There's wine out there!" she calls after me.

Wyatt is on the deck, and he hands me a glass of something red with a shy smile.

After a long, uncomfortable pause, he says, "It's a syrah."

"Lovely," I say. The intimacy we shared is still, surprisingly, here, but neither of us knows what to do with it. I settle for squatting down to engage in some "conversation" with Zora, who is showing me either a butterfly or some kind of sign language.

"Means flubber-by," she informs me.

"Wow," I say. I straighten back up as Ava emerges.

"So, this is weird," she finally says. She's got a bottle of white wine in one hand, and she pours herself a glass. "But I did want to catch you before you headed off to New York or L.A. or wherever you're jetting to next."

"Portland, actually. There's a lady there who's got a story to tell me. But I wanted to see you, too," I say, and I mean it. "I wanted to . . . thank you. For . . . I don't know. For choosing me."

"Kismet," Ava says with a shrug. "I guess I wanted to say thanks, too. For believing me, for not bungling it entirely. You did good."

"I didn't always believe you, though," I admit. "For a while, I thought you were probably crazy. Rain didn't exactly portray you as a bedrock of perfect sanity," I add. Ava snorts. I don't mention any of the things Wyatt said.

"Of course. She was hoping you would drop the story if I seemed nuts. Good thing it didn't work."

"It almost did," I answer with a small laugh. "Especially when I learned you'd sold me out and tattled on me. Kind of a dick move, but I guess it got my ass in gear."

"Tattled? I didn't . . . what are you talking about?"

"Rain knew what I was up to. What we were up to. Rain said you told her, and I guess I believed her, especially since you'd literally just had a meeting with her," I explain, sipping the wine.

"Is there any chance you told your assistant about all that?" Ava asks drily.

"Oh Jesus, I'm so stupid!" I say, squeezing my eyes shut. "Christ, even now, it's hard for me to credit Jess with such . . . sneakiness."

"Yeah, I recommend you don't start thinking about all the choices that led you to the Light and which of those she might have orchestrated," Ava suggests with a dark smile. "Being manipulated by someone who knows you that well is a very . . . disturbing experience. Brings out a pretty cynical side of you."

I shake my head and look out at the glimmer of the lake. It's cold now, and I'm wearing a leather jacket with a thick scarf, but the evening is otherwise perfect. The leaves are peaking, the chaos of dying chlorophyll putting on quite a show.

We chat over the baguette I've brought, Wyatt and I sipping at the red, Ava her white, talking about the podcast, about its aftermath, about the harvest, about the future. We discuss Robin. No one has found her, but likewise no bodies have turned up yet.

"Not that one would yet, given the date," Wyatt says. We have all been uncomfortably aware that it's the last day of October.

"But the Light is disbanded, people are in jail. The lights are out at the House of Light—nobody's there," I say. I feel like I failed Robin, so I'm anxious to believe that we put an end to things in time.

"Very true. But it's not like we'd know if her body showed up in Belize," Ava points out a bit callously as she heads inside to the kitchen. She has a point. We hear her swearing at the stove, then clattering some dishes. When I make an attempt to get up and help, Wyatt waves me off.

"She's a control freak, and she likes to be a martyr. Just make a big deal out of whatever she puts on the table," he says, and I chuckle.

"Even without maternal guidance, I probably could have managed that." I'm tempted to tell him about my mother; I haven't divulged the whole story to anyone yet. Without Jess, I feel that everything is entirely my own. It's a new sensation.

I hear a motorcycle puttering loudly nearby, and Zora and I both tilt our heads.

"Don!" Zora squeals, scampering toward the front door through the living room.

"Is someone else coming for dinner?" I ask Wyatt.

"Ah. She didn't tell you." He looks away from me. "Um. Yeah. Do you remember Dawn? From the Light? We go back a ways. Ava wanted him to swing by . . ."

"Wow, okay. Um. Huh." I shake my head, suddenly feeling

buzzed. "That's a surprise. I'm just going to go tidy up for a second before dinner. Hang on." I stand up and bustle to the bathroom, feeling weird and blindsided. Ava has to know how
uncomfortable I'd be to see Dawn. But she wouldn't know about
our almost-hookup, surely? If they're friends, she must know he's
left the Light, but there's still something going on with him that I
can't figure out. I can't help but think: bonus episode.

I splash some water on my face in the bathroom and tidy my
hair, which has been blowing around while I've been out on the
deck. I look in the mirror, at the uncanny reflection of my face,
the face that is me but also so many other people, before heading
back toward the kitchen. I pause in front of a photo of Ava and
Zelda perched on a bookshelf, each girl an eerie echo of the other.

I'm about to move on when a book next to the photo catches
my eye. I slide it off the shelf.

It's midnight-blue and has familiar gold lettering. I don't have
to flip open to the imprint page, but I do, to see the Oikos Phaos
logo. *Light Womb,* by Luke Trask.

"What the hell is this?" I ask Ava as she pulls a pot off the
stove, brandishing the book in my hand. Dawn has entered the
house, and he stops in the process of removing his shoes.

"Hi," he says, not as sheepishly as I would like.

"Ava? This book? What is it?" I demand.

"That old thing? It . . . actually belonged to my sister. I found
it the other day and set it out for you, thought you might get a
kick out of it. You remember Dawn? He's an old friend of my
sister's, too. When I asked him for dinner, he said it would be
great to catch up with you," she says casually. I stand, tongue-
tied, in her living room. Wyatt has come inside. "Would you all be
dears and get the silverware and the napkins?" Ava asks. "I made
a very seasonally appropriate dinner, just in time for Samhain."
She winks at me as she begins to set the table.

THE NEW YORK CARIB NEWS, DECEMBER 22, 2020

The body of an American woman was found on a beach outside Punta Gorda earlier this morning by local fishermen, a government official has said in a press release. Her body became entangled in fishing nets as the workers were returning to shore, and law enforcement was called to the scene. Though an official cause of death has not yet been released, drowning appears to be the most likely.

Though they have not made an official statement, the American embassy has asked for "time while we reach out to the young woman's family before identifying her publicly in the media." When asked for comment, local law enforcement said that the case was "open and ongoing." They clarified that the death will receive as many resources as if the young American were a citizen of the country, and they resolved to determine what led to her death.

No foul play is suspected at this time.

HOLLYWOOD REPORTER, JANUARY 2, 2021

Actress turned podcast media mogul was spotted starting off the New Year right, shopping for various dusts at Moon Juice in Venice. Clearly, the star has been taking care of herself in the wake of her massively successful podcast earlier this season: she was long-legged and toned in leggings and a cropped shirt, looking like she'd come straight from yoga, her face fresh and makeup-free. Is it the new beau or the new TV show that has her glowing?

After several years of personal and professional

knocks, it looks like Reed has finally found her stride. Following the leak of private texts and emails, alongside intimate photographs that revealed an extramarital affair she had been conducting with the director of a recent project, her career seemed in jeopardy. But the publicity only seemed to bolster her image as a maverick and risk-taker. The director in question has issued several apologies and has effectively been canceled, but Reed's frankness regarding the relationship has won her fans. She said that "I was courting a reasonably high level of self-destruction for a little while. I was so drawn to people who would allow me to give up my power that I was putting myself at risk. It took a pretty radical set of circumstances to jolt me out of that. Telling that story and seeing it resonate has been so special and so healing."

And it seems like her gamble to step out of her comfort zone and try out an entirely new medium has paid off in spades. In recent weeks, she's been seen holding hands with acclaimed screenwriter Dan Frederichs, who is rumored to be writing the script for the upcoming series based on Reed's hit podcast, *Vultures*. The podcast, which has gotten nearly twenty million downloads at this point, is being adapted into a prestige drama at HBO Max, though it's been released that they will change the title of the show to *Dark Circles*. This will be Reed's directorial debut. But if those photos of Frederichs carrying her tray of fresh juices is any indication, it looks like Reed is fully in control of the situation.

ACKNOWLEDGMENTS

The first thanks always goes to my agent, Molly Atlas, for being with this book from when it was still just a vague notion all the way through to finished object. Thanks to Kara Cesare, whose faith in me lets me take chances and experiment and ultimately find my way to the right places. Thanks to Jesse Shuman for insights at every step, and to the whole Random House and Ballantine family: Allyson Lord, Allison Schuster, Cara DuBois, Jennifer Hershey, Kim Hovey, Kara Welsh, Bonnie Thompson, and dozens of others, all of whom are essential and accomplish more than I could ever have imagined to get a book out into the world.

Thanks to my mom, Peggy, for many talks about weird retreats, and for tearing through an early version of the manuscript. To my dad, Mike, who (unlike certain fictional fathers in this book) has never tried to profit off my professional life and who remains amused at and proud of my vocation. To my sister, Emily, who obsessively talked through the book with me at every stage, and who insisted I add one of the better passages toward the end. To my Steyn family, Elbert and Marinda, who are always early, thorough readers and tell me what's working and what isn't. Thanks to Chris Honey, for excellent feedback, and especially for pointing out some general things about toddlers. Thanks to Katy Schoedel, who always has a totally unique insight into the characters and always just Gets It. Thanks to Legs, for taking a walk with me every day while I listened to true crime podcasts.

And always, always, the most gratitude goes to Jan Steyn, who spends countless hours talking through basically every element of the book, who comes up with the best solutions to stupid problems I create myself, who encouraged me to quit my day job and write a damn book more than six years ago and never doubted it would work out.

About the Author

CAITE DOLAN-LEACH is the author of *Dead Letters* and *We Went to the Woods* and is a literary translator. She was born in the Finger Lakes region and is a graduate of Trinity College Dublin and the American University in Paris.

Facebook.com/caitedolanleachauthor
Instagram: @caitedolanleach